All things in a single book bound by love.

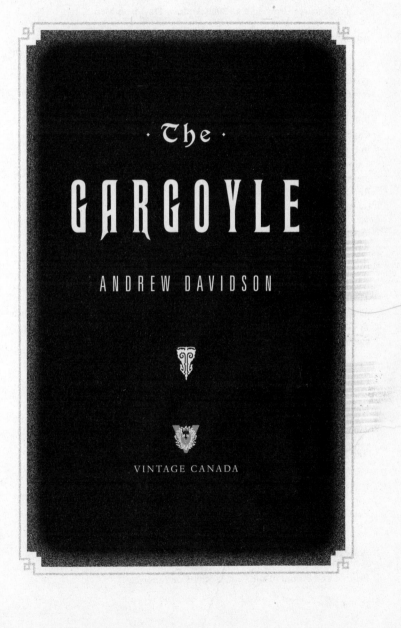

·The·

GARGOYLE

ANDREW DAVIDSON

VINTAGE CANADA

VINTAGE CANADA EDITION, 2009

Published in Canada by Vintage Canada, a division of Random House of
Canada Limited, Toronto, in 2009. Originally published in 2008 in hardcover
in Canada by Random House Canada, a division of Random House of
Canada Limited, and simultaneously in the United States by Doubleday,
an imprint of The Doubleday Broadway Publishing Group, a division of
Random House, Inc., New York. Distributed in Canada
by Random House of Canada Limited.

Library and Archives Canada Cataloguing in Publication

Davidson, Andrew (Andrew F.)
    The gargoyle / Andrew Davidson.

ISBN 978-0-307-35678-9

    1. Dante Alighieri, 1265–1321—Translations into German—Fiction.
I. Title.

PS8607.A785G37 2009   C813'.6   C2008-906548-4

Book design by Amanda Dewey

Printed and bound in the United States of America

10 9 8 7 6 5

"Die Liebe ist stark wie der Tod, hart wie die Hölle."
Der Tod scheidet die Seele vom Leibe,
die Liebe aber scheidet alle Dinge von der Seele...

MEISTER ECKHART, deutscher Mystiker

Predigt: "Êwige Gerburt"

♦ ♦ ♦

"Love is as strong as death, as hard as Hell."
Death separates the soul from the body,
but love separates all things from the soul.

MEISTER ECKHART, German mystic

Sermon: "Eternal Birth"

· The ·
GARGOYLE

I.

ccidents ambush the unsuspecting, often violently, just like love.
It was Good Friday and the stars were just starting to dissolve into the dawn. As I drove, I stroked the scar on my chest, by habit. My eyes were heavy and my vision unfocused, not surprising given that I'd spent the night hunched over a mirror snorting away the bars of white powder that kept my face trapped in the glass. I believed I was keening my reflexes. I was wrong.

To one side of the curving road was a sharp drop down the mountain's slope, and on the other was a dark wood. I tried to keep my eyes fixed ahead but I had the overwhelming feeling that something was waiting to ambush me from behind the trees, perhaps a troop of mercenaries. That's how drug paranoia works, of course. My heart hammered as I gripped the steering wheel more tightly, sweat collecting at the base of my neck.

Between my legs I had wedged a bottle of bourbon, which I tried to pull out for another mouthful. I lost my grip on the bottle and it tumbled into my lap, spilling everywhere, before falling to the floorboard. I bent down to grab it before the remaining alcohol leaked out, and when my eyes were lifted I was greeted by the vision, the ridiculous vision, that set everything into motion. I saw a volley of burning arrows swarming out of the woods, directly at my car. Instinct took over and I jerked the steering wheel away from the forest that held my invisible attackers. This was not a good idea, because it threw my car up against the fencepost wires that separated me from the drop. There was the howl of metal on metal, the passenger door scraping against taut cables, and a dozen thuds as I bounced off the wood posts, each bang like electricity through a defibrillator.

I overcompensated and spun out into the oncoming lane, just missing a pickup truck. I pulled back too hard on the wheel, which sent me once again towards the guardrail. The cables snapped and flew everywhere at once, like the thrashing tentacles of a harpooned octopus. One cracked the windshield and I remember thinking how glad I was that it hadn't hit me as the car fell through the arms of the convulsing brute.

There was a brief moment of weightlessness: a balancing point between air and earth, dirt and heaven. *How strange,* I thought, *how like the moment between sleeping and falling when everything is beautifully surreal and nothing is corporeal. How like floating towards completion.* But as often happens in that time between existing in the world and fading into dreams, this moment over the edge ended with the ruthless jerk back to awareness.

A car crash seems to take forever, and there is always a moment in which you believe that you can correct the error. *Yes,* you think, *it's true that I'm plummeting down the side of a mountain in a car that weighs about three thousand pounds. It's true that it's a hundred feet to the bottom of the gully. But I'm sure that if only I twist the steering wheel very hard to one side, everything will be okay.*

Once you've spun that steering wheel around and found it doesn't make any difference, you have this one clear, pure thought: *Oh, shit.* For a glorious moment, you achieve the empty bliss that Eastern philosophers spend their lives pursuing. But following this transcendence, your mind becomes a supercomputer capable of calculating the gyrations of your car, multiplying that by the speed of the fall over the angle of descent, factoring in Newton's laws of motion and, in a split second, coming to the panicked conclusion that *this is gonna hurt like hell.*

Your car gathers speed down the embankment, bouncing. Your hypothesis is quickly proven correct: it is, indeed, quite painful. Your brain catalogues the different sensations. There is the flipping end over end, the swirling disorientation, and the shrieks of the car as it practices its unholy yoga. There's the crush of metal, pressing against your ribs. There's the smell of the devil's mischievousness, a pitchfork in your ass and sulfur in your mouth. The Bastard's there, all right, don't doubt it.

I remember the hot silver flash as the floorboard severed all my toes from my left foot. I remember the steering column sailing over my shoulder. I remember the eruption of glass that seemed to be everywhere around me. When the car finally came to a stop, I hung upside down, seatbelted. I could hear the hiss of various gases escaping the engine and the tires still spinning outside, above, and there was the creak of metal settling as the car stopped rocking, a pathetic turtle on its back.

Just as I was beginning my drift into unconsciousness, there was the explosion. Not a movie explosion but a small real-life explosion, like the ignition of an unhappy gas oven that holds a grudge against its owner. A flash of blue flame skittered across the roof of the car, which was at a slanted angle underneath my dangling body. Out of my nose crawled a drop of blood, which jumped expectantly into the happy young flames springing to life beneath me. I could feel my hair catch fire; then I could smell it. My flesh began to singe as if I were a scrap of meat newly thrown onto the barbecue, and then I could hear the bubbling of my skin as the flames kissed it. I could not reach my head to extinguish my flaming hair. My arms would not respond to my commands.

I imagine, dear reader, that you've had some experience with heat. Perhaps you've tipped a boiling kettle at the wrong angle and the steam crept up your sleeve; or, in a youthful dare, you held a match between your fingers for as long as you could. Hasn't everyone, at least once, filled the bathtub with overly hot water and forgot to dip in a toe before committing the whole foot? If you've only had these kinds of minor incidents, I want you to imagine something new. Imagine turning on one of the elements of your stove—let's say it's the electric kind with black coils on top. Don't put a pot of water on the element, because the water only absorbs the heat and uses it to boil. Maybe some tiny tendrils of smoke curl up from a previous spill on the burner. A slight violet tinge will appear, nestled there in the black rings, and then the element assumes some reddish-purple tones, like unripe blackberries. It moves towards orange and finally—finally!—an intense glowing red. Kind of beautiful, isn't it? Now, lower your head so that your eyes are even with the top of the stove and you can peer through the shimmering waves rising up. Think of those old movies where the hero finds himself looking across the desert at an unexpected oasis. I want you to trace the fingertips of your left hand gently across your right palm, noting the way your skin registers even the lightest touch. If someone else were doing it, you might even be turned on. Now, slam that sensitive, responsive hand directly onto that glowing element.

And hold it there. Hold it there as the element scorches Dante's nine rings right into your palm, allowing you to grasp Hell in your hand forever. Let the heat engrave the skin, the muscles, the tendons; let it smolder down to the bone. Wait for the burn to embed itself so far into you that you don't know if you'll ever be able to let go of that coil. It won't be long until the stench of your own burning flesh wafts up, grabbing your nose hairs and refusing to let go, and you smell your body burn.

I want you to keep that hand pressed down, for a slow count of sixty. No cheating. *One Mis-sis-sip-pi, two Mis-sis-sip-pi, three Mis-sis-sip-pi* . . . At *sixty Mis-sis-sip-pi,* your hand will have melted so that it now surrounds the element, becoming fused with it. Now rip your flesh free.

I have another task for you: lean down, turn your head to one side, and slap your cheek on the same element. I'll let you choose which side of your face. Again sixty Mississippis; no cheating. The convenient thing is that your ear is right there to capture the snap, crackle, and pop of your flesh.

Now you might have some idea of what it was like for me to be pinned inside that car, unable to escape the flames, conscious enough to catalogue the experience until I went into shock. There were a few short and merciful moments in which I could hear and smell and think, still documenting everything but feeling nothing. *Why does this no longer hurt?* I remember closing my eyes and wishing for complete, beautiful blackness. I remember thinking that I should have lived my life as a vegetarian.

Then the car shifted once more, tipping over into the creek upon whose edge it had been teetering. Like the turtle had regained its feet and scurried into the nearest water source.

This occurrence—the car falling into the creek—saved my life by extinguishing the flames and cooling my newly broiled flesh.

◆ ◆ ◆

Accidents ambush the unsuspecting, often violently, just like love.

I have no idea whether beginning with my accident was the best decision, as I've never written a book before. Truth be told, I started with the crash because I wanted to catch your interest and drag you into the story. You're still reading, so it seems to have worked.

The most difficult thing about writing, I'm discovering, is not the act of constructing the sentences themselves. It's deciding what to put in, and where, and what to leave out. I'm constantly second-guessing myself. I chose the accident, but I could just as easily have started with any point during my thirty-five years of life before that. Why not start with: "I was born in the year 19——, in the city of———"?

Then again, why should I even confine the beginning to the time frame of my life? Perhaps I should start in Nürnberg in the early thirteenth century, where a woman with the most unfortunate name of Adelheit Rotter retreated from a life that she thought was sinful to become a Beguine—women who, though not officially associated with the Church, were inspired to live an impoverished life in imitation of Christ. Over time Rotter attracted a legion of followers and, in 1240, they moved to a dairy farm at Engelschalksdorf near Swinach, where a benefactor named Ulrich II von Königstein allowed them to live provided they did chores. They erected a building in 1243 and, the following year, established it as a monastery with the election of their first prioress.

When Ulrich died without a male heir, he bequeathed his entire estate to the Beguines. In return he requested that the monastery provide burial places for his relations and that they pray, in perpetuity, for the Königstein family. In a show of good sense he directed that the place be named Engelthal, or "Valley of the Angels," rather than Swinach—"Place of the Pigs." But it was Ulrich's final provision that would have the greatest impact on my life: he mandated that the monastery establish a scriptorium.

• • •

Eyes open on a red and blue spin of lightning. A blitzkrieg of voices, noises. A metal rod pierces the side of the car, jaws it apart. Uniforms. Christ, I'm in Hell and they wear uniforms. One man shouts. Another says in a soothing voice: "We'll get you out. Don't worry." He wears a badge. "You're gonna be all right," he promises through his mustache. "What's your name?" Can't remember. Another paramedic yells to someone I can't see. He recoils at the sight of me. Are they supposed to do that? Blackness.

Eyes open. I'm strapped to a spine board. A voice, "Three, two, one, lift." The sky rushes towards me and then away from me. "In," says the voice. A metallic clack as the stretcher snaps into place. Cof-

fin, why no lid? *Too antiseptic for Hell, and could the roof of Heaven re-*
ally be made of gray metal? Blackness.

Eyes open. Weightless again. Charon wears a blue polyester-
cotton blend. An ambulance siren bounces off a concrete Acheron.
An IV has been inserted into my body—everywhere? I'm covered
with a gel blanket. Wet, wet. Blackness.

Eyes open. The thud of wheels like a shopping cart on concrete.
The damn voice says "Go!" The sky mocks me, passes me by, then a
plaster-white ceiling. Double doors slither open. "OR Four!" Blackness.

. . .

Eyes open. Gaping maw of a snake, lunging at me, laughing,
speaking: `I AM COMING . . .` The serpent tries to engulf my
head. No, not a snake, an oxygen mask. `. . . AND THERE IS`
`NOTHING YOU CAN DO ABOUT IT.` I'm falling backwards
gas mask blackness.

Eyes unveil. Burning hands, burning feet, fire everywhere, but I
am in the middle of a blizzard. A German forest, and a river is near.
A woman on a ridge with a crossbow. My chest feels as if it's been hit.
I hear the hiss as my heart gives out. I try to speak but croak instead,
and a nurse tells me to rest, that everything will be okay, everything
will be okay. Blackness.

A voice floats above me. "Sleep. Just sleep."

. . .

Following my accident, I plumped up like a freshly roasted wiener,
my skin cracking to accommodate the expanding meat. The doctors,

with their hungry scalpels, hastened the process with a few quick slices. The procedure is called an escharotomy, and it gives the swelling tissue the freedom to expand. It's rather like the uprising of your secret inner being, finally given license to claw through the surface. The doctors thought they had sliced me open to commence my healing but, in fact, they only released the monster—a thing of engorged flesh, suffused with juice.

While a small burn results in a blister filled with plasma, burns such as mine result in the loss of enormous quantities of liquid. In my first twenty-four hospital hours, the doctors pumped six gallons of isotonic liquid into me to counteract the loss of body fluids. I bathed in the liquid as it flowed out of my scorched body as fast as it was pumped in, and I was something akin to the desert during a flash flood.

This too-quick exchange of fluid resulted in an imbalance in my blood chemistry, and my immune system staggered under the strain, a problem that would become ever more dangerous in the following weeks when the primary threat of death was from sepsis. Even for a burn victim who seems to be doing well long after his accident, infection can pull him out of the game at a moment's notice. The body's defenses are just barely functioning, exactly when they are needed most.

My razed outer layers were glazed with a bloody residue of charred tissue called eschar, the Hiroshima of the body. Just as you cannot call a pile of cracked concrete blocks a "building" after the bomb has detonated, neither could you have called my outer layer "skin" after the accident. I was an emergency state unto myself, silver ion and sulfadiazine creams spread over the remains of me. Over that, bandages were laid to rest upon the devastation.

I was aware of none of this, and only learned it later from the doctors. At the time, I lay comatose, with a machine clicking off the sluggish metronome of my heart. Fluids and electrolytes and antibiotics and morphine were administered through a series of tubes (IV tube, jejunostomy tube, endotracheal tube, nasogastric tube, urinary tube, truly a tube for every occasion!). A heat shield kept my body warm enough to survive, a ventilator did my breathing, and I collected enough blood transfusions to shame Keith Richards.

The doctors removed my wasteland exterior by débriding me, scraping away the charred flesh. They brought in tanks of liquid nitrogen containing skin recently harvested from corpses. The sheets were thawed in pans of water, then neatly arranged on my back and stapled into place. Just like that, as if they were laying strips of sod over the problem areas behind their summer cabins, they wrapped me in the skin of the dead. My body was cleaned constantly but I rejected these sheets of necro-flesh anyway; I've never played well with others. So over and over again, I was sheeted with cadaver skin.

There I lay, wearing dead people as armor against death.

. . .

The first six years of my life.

My father was gone before I was born. He was evidently a most captivating good-time Charlie, quick with his dick and quicker to split. My mother, abandoned by this nameless lothario, died in childbirth as I surfed into this world on a torrent of her blood. The nurse who was grasping my greasy newborn body slipped in a puddle of it as she attempted to leave the delivery room, or so I was told. My grandmother first viewed me as I was whisked past her in the arms of a red-on-white Rorschach test of a nurse.

The delivery went wrong for me, as well. I was never told exactly what happened but somehow my body was cut from stomach to chest, leaving behind a long scar—maybe it was an errant scalpel as they tried to save my mother. I simply don't know. As I grew, the scar remained the same size until eventually it was only a few inches long, centered on the left side of my chest where a romantic might draw the heart.

I lived with my grandmother until I was six. Her bitterness towards me, as the cause of her daughter's death, was obvious. I think she was not a bad person but rather someone who never expected to be predeceased by her own daughter, nor to be charged, so late in life, with the care of another infant.

My grandmother didn't beat me; she fed me well; she arranged all the necessary vaccinations. She just didn't like me. She died on one of the rare days that we were having fun, while she was pushing me on a playground swing. I went up into the air and stretched my legs towards the sun. I came back towards the earth expecting her hands to catch me. Instead, I sailed past her doubled-over body. As I swung by her again on the forward trajectory, she'd collapsed onto her elbows. Then she sprawled facedown in the playground mud. I ran to a nearby house to alert the adults, and then sat on the monkey bars as the ambulance came too late. As the paramedics lifted her, my grandmother's corpulent arms swung like bat wings with the life squeezed out of them.

. . .

From the moment I arrived at the hospital, I stopped being a person and became an actuarial chart. After weighing me, the doctors pulled out the calculators to punch up the extent of my burn and calculate the odds of my survival. Not good.

How did they do all this? As in any proper fairy tale, there's a majick formula, in this case called the Rule of Nines. The percentage of burn is determined and marked on a chart not unlike a voodoo map of the human body, divided into sections based upon multiples of nine. The arms are "worth" 9 percent of the total body surface; the head is worth 9 percent; each whole leg is worth 18 percent; and the torso, front and back, is worth 36 percent. Hence: the Rule of Nines.

Of course, there are other considerations in rating a burn. Age, for example. The very old and the very young are less likely to survive, but if the young do survive, they have a much greater capacity to regenerate. So, they've got that going for them. Which is nice. One must also consider the type of burn: scalds from boiling liquids;

electrical burns from live wires; or chemical burns, be they acid or alkali. I ordered up only thermal burns from the menu, those strictly from flames.

What, you may wonder, actually happens to living flesh in a fire? Cells consist mostly of liquid, which can boil and cause the cell walls to explode. This is not good. In a second scenario, the cell's protein cooks up just like an egg in a frying pan, changing from a thin liquid into something gooey and white. If this happens, all metabolic activity of the cell ceases. So even though the heat was not sufficient to kill the cell outright, the loss of ability to deliver oxygen ensures the tissue will die soon enough. The difference is slow capitulation rather than immediate immolation.

· · ·

With Grandma gone, I went to live with Debi and Dwayne Michael Grace—an aunt and uncle, the quintessence of trash, who were annoyed with me from the moment I arrived. They did, however, like the government checks sent for my upkeep. It made scoring dope considerably easier.

In my time with the graceless Graces, I relocated from one trailer park to another until my guardians found an all-night party that grew into a three-year methamphetamine festival. They were well ahead of their time: crystal meth was not nearly as popular in those days as it is now. If there was no pipe available with which to smoke it, a hollowed-out lightbulb was used, and sometimes the run on bulbs was such that we lived entirely in the dark. The drugs never seemed to run out, though. The Graces, flashing smiles like smashed keyboards, would hand over their every penny to the dealer.

One of our neighbors traded the use of her daughter, a few years younger than me, for the equivalent in drugs. In case you're wondering, the street value of an eight-year-old is $35, or at least it was when I was a kid. When the mother became savage-eyed and withdrawn, the young girl would come to cry fearfully in my tiny room, anticipating an impending sale. Last I heard, her mother had cleaned up, lost addiction, and found God. Last I heard, the girl (now adult) was a pregnant heroin addict.

For the most part my childhood was not agreeable, but I was never sexually auctioned so my guardians might crank up. Still, a man should be able to say better things about his youth than that.

The only way I was able to survive that shitty world was to imagine better ones, so I read everything I could get my hands on. By my early teens, I was spending so many hours in the library that the librarians brought extra sandwiches for me. I have such fond memories of these women, who would recommend books and then talk to me for hours about what I had learned.

Long before I discovered the desire for drugs that would occupy my adulthood, my basic nature had already been established as compulsive. My first, and most lasting, addiction has always been to the obsessive study of any matter that took hold of my curiosity.

Although I was never much for school, this was not because I believed education an inferior pursuit. Far from it: my problem was always that school interfered with matters more fascinating. The courses were designed to teach practical information but, because I understood the core concepts so quickly, they could not hold my interest. I was always distracted by the esoterica that might appear in a textbook's footnote or a teacher's offhand remark. For example: if my geometry teacher mentioned something about Galileo giving lectures on the physical structure of Hell, it became impossible for me to refocus my interest when he returned to talking about the sides of a parallelogram. I would skip the next three classes to visit the library, reading everything I could on Galileo, and when I returned to the school I would fail the next math test because it did not include any questions about the Inquisition.

This passion for self-directed learning has remained, which should already be apparent in my depiction of burn treatment. The subject has such personal relevance it would be impossible for me not to learn as much as I could about it. My studies do not stop there:

research on Engelthal monastery, for reasons that will become apparent, has also commanded a great many hours of my time.

While it is true that outside the library I have lived a life of wickedness, inside it I've always been as devoted to knowledge as a saint to his Bible.

• • •

Burns, I learned, are also rated according to how many layers of skin are damaged. Superficial (first-degree) burns involve only the epidermis, the top layer. Partial thickness (second-degree) burns involve the epidermis and the second layer, the corium. Deep partial thickness burns are very severe second-degree burns. And then there are full thickness (third-degree) burns, which involve all skin layers and result in permanent scarring.

Severe cases—such as mine—usually feature a combination of burn thicknesses, because no one is turning the spit to ensure even roasting. For example, my right hand is completely undamaged. It experienced superficial burns and the only treatment was a common hand lotion.

My partial thickness burns are primarily located on my lower legs beneath the knees and around my buttocks. The skin curled up like the pages of a burning manuscript, and took a few months to heal. Today the skin's not perfect, but hell, it ain't so bad. I can still feel my ass when I sit.

Full thickness burns are like the steak your old man forgot on the barbecue when he got drunk. These burns destroy; this tissue will not heal. The scar is white, or black, or red; it's a hard dry wound, hairless forever because the follicles have been cooked out. Strangely enough, third-degree burns are in one way better than second-degree ones: they don't hurt at all, because the nerve endings have been cooked dumb.

Burns to the hands, head, neck, chest, ears, face, feet, and perineal region command special attention. These areas rate the highest scores in the Rule of Nines; an inch of burnt head trumps an inch of burnt back. Unfortunately, these are the areas where my full thickness burns are concentrated, so I came up snake eyes on that one.

There is some debate in the medical community over whether there is actually such a thing as a fourth-degree burn, but this is simply a bunch of healthy doctors sitting in a conference hall arguing semantics. These fourth-degree burns, if you accept the nomenclature, tunnel themselves right down into the bones and tendons. I had such burns as well; as if it weren't enough that a floorboard severed all the toes from my left foot, these so-called fourth-degree burns took three toes from my right foot, and a finger and a half from my left hand. And, alas, one more body part.

You will recall that I spilled bourbon onto my pants moments before the accident, and the timing could not have been worse. In effect, my lap was soaked with an accelerant that caused the area to burn with increased intensity. My penis was like a candle sticking out of my body and burned accordingly, leaving me with a seared wick where the shaft once had been. Unsalvageable, it was removed shortly after my admission in a procedure known as a penectomy.

When I asked what had been done with the remains of my manhood, the nurse informed me that they had been disposed of as medical waste. As if it would somehow make me feel better, she went on to explain that the doctors left my scrotum and testicles attached. Too much to take everything, one supposes, kit and caboodle.

· · ·

The Graces died in a meth lab explosion, nine years after I first arrived in their trailer. It was not surprising: is there a worse idea than addicts cooking their drug in a confined space, with ingredients that include lantern fuel, paint thinner, and rubbing alcohol?

I was not particularly disheartened. On the day of their funeral, I went to talk with the librarians about the biography of Galileo Galilei that I'd been reading—because, in fact, my geometry teacher *had* piqued my interest in the scientist.

While any schoolboy can tell you about Galileo's persecution at the hands of the Inquisition, the truth of his life was more complicated than that. It was never his intention to be a "bad" Catholic, and when ordered not to teach the idea of a heliocentric universe, Galileo complied for many years. His daughter Virginia entered a convent under the lovely name of Sister Maria Celeste, while his daughter Livia took the habit under the equally extraterrestrial moniker of Sister Arcangela. There is something poetically fitting in this because—even though his name is now used as conversational shorthand to signify science oppressed by religion—Galileo's life twinned religion *and* science. It is said that when Tommaso Caccini, a young Dominican priest, became the first to publicly denounce Galileo's support of the Copernican theory, he ended his sermon with a verse from the Acts of the Apostles: *Ye men of Galilee, why stand ye gazing up into heaven?* What Caccini did not suspect, however, was that if Galileo was gazing up at the sky, he was just as likely to be praying as to be charting astronomical movement.

At the age of twenty-four, Galileo auditioned for a university teaching position by delivering two lectures on the physics of Dante's *Inferno*. Most modern thinkers would consider this wonderfully whimsical, but in Galileo's day the study of Dantean cosmography was a hot topic. (Not coincidentally, the lectures were at the Florentine Academy, in the poet's hometown.) The presentations were a great success and helped Galileo to secure his position as a professor of mathematics at the University of Pisa.

It was not until later that Galileo came to realize the position he'd argued in the lectures was incorrect and his contention that the cone-shaped structure of Hell was scale-invariant, meaning it could increase in size without a loss of integrity or strength, was not true. If Hell actually existed in the Earth's interior, the immensity of the cavity would cause the roof (the earth's mantle) to collapse unless the walls of Hell were much thicker than he had originally argued. So Galileo set to work on the nature of scaling laws and, late in life, published his discoveries in *Two New Sciences,* whose principles helped establish modern physics—a science that now exists in part because Galileo realized he made a mistake in his application of natural laws to a supernatural location.

But if Hell were a real place, there is little doubt that Debi and Dwayne Michael Grace would be there now.

◆ ◆ ◆

I was unconscious for almost seven weeks, wrapped in my deadflesh body bag. My coma was first caused by shock but then the doctors decided to keep me in it, medically immobilized, while the healing commenced.

I didn't have to consciously deal with the collapse of my circulation system, nor did I have to consider my kidney damage. I was oblivious to the shutdown of my bowels. I knew nothing about the ulcers that made me vomit blood or of how the nurses had to scramble to make sure I didn't asphyxiate when this occurred. I didn't have to fret about the infections that might set in after each emergency surgery or skin graft. I was not notified that my hair follicles had been incinerated or that my sweat glands had been destroyed. I wasn't awake when they suctioned the soot from my lungs—a treatment which, by the way, is called pulmonary toilet.

My vocal cords had sustained extensive damage from smoke inhalation, and a tracheotomy was performed so my larynx could start to heal without the irritation of a tube pressing against it. Nothing more could be done. Another part of my body that received little attention in the earliest stages was my right leg, which was severely broken. The doctors had to wait for my condition to stabilize before they could begin the operations to rebuild my shattered femur and busted knee. Keeping me alive took precedence over retaining a pretty voice or limp-free walk.

During the coma, atrophy of the muscles couldn't be avoided. There was my lack of movement and the fact that with large portions of my skin eradicated, my body was eating itself. It consumed the protein within, spending a tremendous amount of energy just trying to maintain a constant temperature. The heat shield was not enough, so my body ceased delivering blood to the extremities. The body's concern is for the center, the outskirts be damned, and I stopped producing urine and became toxic. As my body contracted, my heart expanded: not from love, but from stress.

I was covered with maggots, a treatment used more frequently in the past but which has recently come back into medical vogue. The bugs ate away at the necrotic flesh, becoming fat on my decay, while leaving the living flesh intact. The doctors sewed my eyelids shut to protect my eyes and all that I required was for someone to cover them with coins. Then, I would have been complete.

• • •

I have one happy memory from my time with the Graces: happy, yet marked with a most curious occurrence.

The air show was on a hot day in mid-August at a nearby airfield. The planes did not excite me—but the skydivers, with their parachutes open to the heavens and the colored streams of smoke that trailed behind them! The falling from sky to earth, a Hephaestian plummet slowed only by fluttering swells of silk, seemed like a miracle. The skydivers operated their magic levers, circling large white bull's-eyes stenciled on the ground, invariably hitting their marks, dead center. It was the most amazing thing I'd ever seen.

At one point, an Asian woman moved behind me. I felt her before I saw her; it was as if my skin jumped just from her presence. When I turned around, there she was, standing with a tiny smile. I was young and I had no idea whether she was Chinese or Japanese or Vietnamese; she just had Asian skin color and eyes and she was barely as tall as I, although I was only ten years old. She wore a dark robe of a simple material that made me think that she must belong to some sort of religious order. Her attire was completely out of the ordinary but no one in the crowd seemed to notice, and she was completely bald.

I wanted to give my attention back to the skydivers, but I couldn't. Not with her behind me. A few moments passed, with me trying not to look at her again, before I could no longer stop myself. All the other people had their faces turned up into the sky but she was looking directly at me.

"What do you want?" My voice was steady; I simply wanted an answer. She said nothing but continued to smile.

"Can't you speak?" I asked. She shook her head, then held out a note. I hesitated before taking it.

It read: *Haven't you ever wondered where your scar really came from?*

When I looked back up, she was gone. All I saw was the crowd of upturned faces.

I read the note again, not believing she could know of my imperfection. It was on my chest, hidden under my shirt, and I was certain I'd never seen this woman before. But even if I had somehow improbably forgotten a previous encounter with a tiny bald Asian woman in a robe, there was no chance I would have shown her my scar.

I started to weave through the crowd, looking for any trace of her—a robe slipping through the masses; the back of her head—but there was nothing.

I put the note into my pocket, taking it out a few more times during the day to assure myself that it was real. Dwayne Michael Grace must have been feeling unusually generous, because he bought me cotton candy from the concession stand. Then Debi hugged me, and it was almost like we were a family. After the show, we attended an exhibition of lit paper lanterns floating down a nearby river, a display that was quite beautiful and unlike anything I had ever seen before.

When we got home late that evening, the note had disappeared from my pocket even though I had been extra careful.

• • •

I dreamt incessantly in my coma. Images reeled into each other, competing for the center ring of the circus.

I dreamt of a farmwoman heating bathwater. I dreamt of the blood from my mother's womb. I dreamt of the flabby arms of my dying grandmother, pushing me up into the blue blue sky. I dreamt about Buddhist temples near cool rushing rivers. I dreamt of the little girl who was sold by her mother for meth. I dreamt of the twisted furnace of my car. I dreamt of a Viking warship. I dreamt of an ironworker's anvil. I dreamt of a sculptor's hands working furious chisels on stone. I dreamt of flaming arrows bursting out of the sky, I dreamt of raining fire. I dreamt of glass exploding everywhere. I dreamt of a delirious angel frozen in water.

But most of all, I dreamt of the gargoyles waiting to be born.

• • •

It was after the incident at the airfield that stroking the birth scar on my chest became a habitual action. I never noticed I was doing it, but others did. Dwayne hated it, slapping my hand away from my chest while telling me to "quit playing with yourself." Then he'd smoke more drugs, making it difficult to take his criticism seriously.

When Dwayne and Debi died, I lost my only remaining relatives—from my mother's side, anyway; my father's side was nothing more than a question mark. I was placed in a group home called Second Chance House, which only made me wonder when I had had my first chance. It was while in Second Chance that I obtained most of my government-sponsored instruction. I went to high school classes fairly regularly, even though I found them boring, and acquired the basics in math and the sciences. All my hours in the library were not wasted. Long before anyone tried to teach me anything, I had already taught myself how to learn.

With the help of the other kids at Second Chance, I soon discovered a variety of drugs with which to experiment. Although disgusted by crystal meth, I was intrigued by marijuana and hashish. In fact, I'd received early encouragement towards these substances from my aunt and uncle who, not realizing that people could actually survive without chemical assistance, were trying to protect me from anything harder.

I also discovered a third hobby to go with libraries and narcotics: the miracle of making the sheets sing. It began by trading exploratory blowjobs with my new best friend, Eddie. This is the sort of thing that teenage boys do: they dare the other to kiss it and then call him a fag when he does. The next night, the same thing. I liked sex but homosexuality was not my flavor, so I soon progressed to some of the young female occupants—in particular, one girl named Chastity who was blissfully unaware of her name's meaning. She was, in fact, unaware of a great many things. The first time that Chastity heard the phrase "oral sex" she thought it somehow involved the ear. Aural sex, one supposes.

By seventeen, I'd moved on to indulging my sexual curiosity with one of the counselors. Being a ward of the government was not without its advantages. Sarah was a troubled adult if ever there was one: an alcoholic in her mid-thirties with a cheating husband and an early midlife crisis. I provided her with consolation and excitement, and she provided me with sex. It did not hurt that my handsomeness, which hitherto had been little more than chubby-faced cuteness, had bloomed. My cheeks had acquired striking angles, my hair had curled pleasantly, and my body had made the transition to graceful muscularity.

When it came time for my discharge at eighteen, I had two talents. One was smoking drugs, the other was fucking my counselor, and I needed to convert one of these abilities into food and shelter. It did not seem that consuming drugs would be a well-paid occupation, but it was easy to find some work posing nude for $50, as the world is not short of middle-aged men who will pay boys to stand naked in their living rooms. I had no moral judgment about it; I was too busy calculating how many hamburgers fifty bucks could buy. From there it was a short jump to $150 for photos involving sexual activity and—since you're already posing for stills, anyway—it makes a lot of sense to double or triple your income by acting in videos. Besides, who doesn't want to be a movie star? Each shoot took, at most, a couple of days; more often, simply a few hours. That's good money for an eighteen-year-old with no skills and, as simple as that, my career in pornography had started.

II.

L ight spread across the insides of my eyelids and I awoke to the snake slowly swimming up my spinal cord, swallowing it with her disjointed jaw. There was the flick flick flick of her tongue as she hissed, `I AM COMING AND THERE IS NOTHING YOU CAN DO ABOUT IT`. The voice was feminine—this is how I knew it was a she—and her tongue tickled each vertebra as she searched her way towards the top of my spine. When she reached it, she licked at the undersocket of my skull, and then twisted a few times to let me know that she'd nestled in. Her scales chafed my internal organs and my liver was bruised by her casually wandering tail.

I was lying upon an air flotation bed that reduced friction and facilitated healing; my bandages lightly fluttered in the upward draft. On each side of the bed was a railing, painted white like bleached bones, so that I could not fall, or force myself, out. I soon named this bed the skeleton's belly and I lay in the wind that rushed through its rib cage, while its very bones prevented me from wandering off to find a new graveyard.

I was off the ventilator but there were still enough tubes sticking out of me that I looked like a pincushion doll. The tubes twisted in circles around, around, around, and I thought of Minos presiding at the entrance to Hell, directing sinners to their final destinations by curling his tail around their bodies. For every coil of the tail, that's one ring deeper into Hell. So I counted my lovely tubes, in simple curiosity: how deep was the grim sorter of the dark and the foul going to send me?

• • •

The nurse seemed happy to find me awake. "Dr. Edwards modified your drugs to bring you out of your coma. I'll get her now."

I tried to speak, but it felt as though someone had inserted a Coke bottle in my throat and stomped; I had crushed glass where my vocal cords had been. The nurse shushed me and answered the questions that she knew I'd be asking if I were able. I was in a hospital, a burn unit, she said. There had been an accident. I was very lucky. The doctors had worked hard. Et cetera, et cetera, et cetera. I was finally able to rasp, "How—long?"

"Almost two months." She granted me a pity smile and turned on her heel to get the doctor.

I examined the skeleton's ribs. There were a few places where the shiny white paint had been peeled back by restless fingers. These patches had been painted over, of course, but the minor excavations were still visible. Down through the layers of paint, my thoughts wandered. *How often do they paint these beds? For every patient? For every six, every dozen? How many before me have lain here?*

I wanted to cry but my tear ducts had been burned shut.

• • •

There was not much to do but drift in and out of consciousness. The morphine dripped and the snake inhabited each inch of my spine, continuing to flick at the base of my skull with her wicked tongue. Lick and kiss, drip drip drip dropped the drugs, hiss hiss hiss spoke the snake. The sibilant sermons of the snake as she discoursed upon the disposition of my sinner's soul seemed ceaseless. There was clack and clatter of footfalls in the hall, a thousand people coming to pay their respects to the dying. Rooms reverberated with the drone of soap operas. Anxious families whispered about worst-case scenarios.

I couldn't quite grasp the enormity of my situation and wondered about things like when I might be able to get back to my film work, or how much this little trip to the hospital would cost me. I hadn't yet grasped that I might never return to work, and that this trip would cost me everything. It was only over the following weeks, as the doctors explained the grisly particulars of what had happened to my body, and what would continue to happen, that I came to understand.

My body's swelling had decreased and my head had shrunk to almost human proportions. My face felt vile under the fingertips of my unburned hand. My legs were raised and taped to supports, and I was swaddled in thick dressings that restricted movement so that I would not tear at my grafts. I looked at my wrecked right leg and saw an amazing set of pins stabbing into my flesh. Burn victims cannot have casts made of fiberglass—too irritating by far—so mechanical spiders were growing out of me.

There were three primary nurses in the burn ward: Connie, Maddy, and Beth. They provided not only physical ministrations but also keep-your-chin-up speeches, telling me that they believed in me, so I had to believe in myself too. I'm sure that Connie believed the rubbish that was exiting her mouth, but I sensed that Maddy and Beth were closer to grocery clerks parroting "Have a nice day." Each worked an eight-hour shift; altogether they made a day.

Beth worked the afternoons and was responsible for my daily massage, pulling gently on my joints and rubbing my muscles. Even these modest manipulations brought intense pain, all the way through the morphine. "If we don't do this, the skin will tighten and you won't be able to move your joints at all. We've been doing this all through your coma." Her explanation did not make it hurt any less.

"Contracture is a huge problem. If you could see your remaining toes, you'd see the splints on them. Can you push against my hand?"

I tried to push but couldn't tell if I succeeded or not; the sensation—actually, the lack of it—was simply too confusing. I could no longer tell where my body ended.

Dr. Nan Edwards, my main physician and the head of the burn ward, explained that she had been operating regularly during my coma, cutting off damaged skin and wrapping me in various replacements. In addition to homografts (the skin from human cadavers) I'd had autografts, skin from undamaged areas of my body, and porcine heterografts, skin from pigs. One cannot help but wonder whether Jews or Muslims would receive the same treatment.

"It was really touch-and-go because your lungs were so badly injured. We had to keep raising the level of oxygen in your respirator, which is never a good sign," Dr. Edwards said. "But you pulled through. You must have something pretty good ahead."

What an idiot. I hadn't fought for my life, I hadn't realized that I was in a coma, and I certainly hadn't struggled to come out of it. Never once in my time in the blackness had it registered that I needed to return to the world.

Dr. Edwards said, "If not for the advances in burn treatment made during the Vietnam War . . ." Her voice trailed off, as if it were better for me to fill in the blanks and realize what a lucky age I was living in.

How I wished that my voice worked. I would have told her that I wished this had happened in the fourteenth century, when there would have been no hope for me.

• • •

I began my career as a porno actor specializing in heterosexual sex with multiple female partners in a short period of time, without ever losing my erection. But please don't think of me as one-dimensional;

as an artist, I was always looking for a new challenge. With con-
scientious practice, I increased my portfolio to include cunnilingus,
anilingus, threesomes, foursomes, moresomes. Homosexuality was
not for me, although I always rather admired the men who could
drill both ways. I wasn't particularly interested in S&M, even though
I did make some films with light bondage motifs. I was not disposed
towards any film promoting pedophiliac leanings. Ghastly stuff, although I must admit that Humbert Humbert makes me giggle. Scat-
ology was strictly out, as nowhere in my psyche do I harbor the
desire to shit on someone and even less do I have the inclination to
be shat upon. And if I am a snob for not participating in films that
involve sex with animals, then so be it: I am a snob.

• • •

I lay in my bed, intensely aware of the sensation of breathing. Compared with how I breathed before the accident, it was so . . . What
is the best word? "Labored" is not quite right. "Oppressed" is better
and is as close as I can come. My oppressed breathing was due in part
to my damaged face, in part to the tubes twisting down my throat,
and in part to my mask of bandages. Sometimes I imagined that the
air was afraid to enter my body.

I peeked under my body bandages, curious to see what was left
of me. The birth scar that had spent its entire life above my heart
was no longer lonely. In fact, I could hardly even find it anymore, so
snugly was it nestled in the gnarled mess of my chest. Each day a
procession of nurses, doctors, and therapists waltzed into my room
to ply me with their ointments and salves, massaging the Pompeian
red landslide of my skin. "Passive stretching," they would tell me, "is
extremely important." *Passive stretching,* I would think, *hurts like hell.*

I buzzered the nurses relentlessly, begging for extra morphine to
satiate the snake, only to be told that it was not yet time. I demanded,
pleaded, bargained, and cried; they insisted that they—fuck them—
had my best interests at heart. Too much medication would prevent

my internal organs from working properly. Too much medication would make me dependent. Too much medication would, somehow, make things worse.

A snake lived inside me. I was enclosed in a skeleton's rib cage. The Vietnam War, apparently, had existed for my benefit. My fingers and toes had been lopped off, and I had recently learned that while doctors might be able to perform a phalloplasty, to build a new penis out of tissue taken from my arm or leg, I'd never be able to achieve an erection again.

In what way, I wondered, *could more morphine possibly make things worse?*

. . .

When the nurses got tired of my pleas for more dope, they told me they were sending in a psychiatrist. The blue gown he wore over his clothing, for the protection of the burn patients, did not quite fit properly and I could hear his corduroys rubbing at the thighs as he walked. He had a balding dome, wore an unkempt goatee in an unsuccessful effort to distract from his double chin, and sported the puffy cheeks of a man whose entire diet came from vending machines. His animal equivalent would have been a chipmunk with a glandular problem, and he extended his paw like he was my new best friend. "I'm Gregor Hnatiuk."

"No thanks."

Gregor smiled widely. "Not even going to give me a chance?"

I told him to write down whatever he wanted on the evaluation form and we could pretend that we'd made an effort. Normally, I would have had some fun with him—told him that I'd breast-fed too long and missed my mommy, or that aliens had abducted me—but my throat couldn't handle the strain of speaking so many words in a row. Still, I got the point across that I had little interest in whatever treatment he thought he could provide.

Gregor sat down and settled his clipboard like a schoolboy trying to hide an erection. He assured me that he only wanted to help, then actually used his fingers to air-quote the fact that he was not there to "get inside" my head. When he was a child, the neighborhood bullies must have beaten him incessantly.

I did manage to get a few final words out: "More painkillers." He said he couldn't give me them, so I told him to go away. He told me that I didn't have to talk if I didn't want to, but he would share some methods for creative visualization to cope with the pain. I took his suggestion to heart and creatively visualized that he'd left the room.

"Close your eyes and think about a place you want to go," he said. "This place can be a memory, or a destination that you want to visit in the future. Any place that makes you happy."

Sweet Jesus.

• • •

Dr. Edwards had warned me that the first time I was conscious during a débridement session would be painful beyond the ability of the morphine to alleviate, even with an increased dosage. But all I heard was "increased dosage," and it brought a smile to my face, although no one could see it under the bandages.

The extra dope started to take effect shortly before I was to be moved, and I was floating on a beautiful high when I heard Dr. Edwards' clipped footsteps, from sensible shoes, coming at me from down the hall before she arrived.

Dr. Edwards was, in every way, average looking. Neither pretty nor ugly, she could fix her face to look adequately pleasing but she rarely bothered. Her hair could have had more body if she'd brushed it out each morning, but she usually just pulled it back, perhaps out of practical concerns, as it is hardly advisable for loose strands to fall into burn wounds. She was slightly overweight and if one were to make a guess, it would be a good bet that at some point she'd simply grown tired of counting calories. She looked as if she had grown into her commonness and accepted it; or perhaps she'd decided that, since she was working among burn survivors, too much attention to her appearance might even be an insult.

Dr. Edwards gestured to the orderly she'd brought with her, a ruddy chunk of a man whose muscles flexed when he reached out for me. Together, they transferred me from my bed to a stretcher. I squealed like a stuck pig, learning in a moment just how much my body had grown to accept its stillness.

The burn unit is often the most distant wing of a hospital, because burn victims are so susceptible to infection that they must be kept away from other patients. More important, perhaps, is that the placement minimizes the chance of visitors stumbling across a Kentucky Fried Human. The débridement room, I could not help but notice, was in the farthest room of this farthest wing. By the time my session was finished, I realized this was so the other burn patients couldn't hear the screams.

The orderly laid me out on a slanted steel table where warm water, with medical agents added to balance my body chemistry, flowed across the slick surface. Dr. Edwards removed my bandages to expose the bloody pulp of my body. They echoed with flat thuds as she dropped them into a metal bucket. As she washed me, there was disgust in the down-turned edges of her mouth and unhappiness in her fingertips. The water flowing over me swirled pink. Then dark pink, light red, dark red. The murky water eddied around the little chunks of my flesh that looked like fish entrails on a cutting board.

All this was but a prelude to the main event.

Débridement is the ripping apart of a person, the cutting away of as much as can possibly be endured. Technically, it is removal of dead or contaminated tissue from a wound so that healthy skin may grow in its place. The word itself comes intact from the French noun débridement, which literally means "unbridling." The etymology is easy to construct: the removal of contaminated tissue from

the body—the removal of constricting matter—evokes the image of
taking the bridle off a horse, as the bridle itself is a constriction. The
débrided person shall be set free of the contaminant, as it were.

So much of my skin was damaged that removing the putrefy-
ing tissue meant more or less scrubbing away everything. My blood
squirted up onto Dr. Edwards, leaving streams of red across her
gowned chest, as she used a razorlike apparatus to take the dermis
off my body, not unlike the way a vegetable peeler removes the skin
from food.

Dr. Edwards made long— No, that's too formal. Our situation
made us more intimate than the cruelest of lovers, so why not use
her given name? *Nan* made long swooping passes over my back. I
could hear the blade as it slid along my body, disengaging the skin.
The only way she'd know that she'd reached the good tissue was to
actually slice into it. If I screamed in pain, she had burrowed deeply
enough to find functioning nerve endings. As Blake wrote in *The
Marriage of Heaven and Hell:* "You never know what is enough unless
you know what is more than enough."

Nan deposited the thin sheets of my flesh in the same metal
bucket that held my dirty bandages. It was like seeing myself disappear, the flags of my existence being blown away a millimeter at a
time. The pain, mixed with the morphine, caused the most interesting images to flash through my mind: Senator Joe McCarthy bellow-
ing "Better dead than red"; a carpenter assembling the crosses upon
which the crucified would be nailed; dissection in biology class, with
eighth-grade scalpels cutting into frog stomachs.

Once I was fully débrided, the exposed sites needed to be covered
with grafts, be they cadaver or pig. It never mattered much, because
my body rejected them all. This was expected, as the grafts were
never meant to be permanent; they were there mostly to prevent
infection.

During my stay in the hospital, I was skinned alive over and over.
In many ways débridement is more overwhelming than the original
burning because, whereas the accident came as a surprise, I always

knew when a débridement was scheduled. I would lie in the skeleton's belly and dread each future sweep of the knife, previewing it a hundred times in my imagination for each actual occurrence.

The dispensing of morphine was self-regulated—to "empower" me, they said—and I worked that button furiously. But there was a goddamn block on the overall amount so I couldn't overdose myself: so much for empowerment.

. . .

By the time I was twenty-three, I'd acted in more than a hundred pornos, of varying quality. Most of the early ones are primitive but there are a few, from the later years, that I consider genuinely decent work.

Pornography is like any other job: you start with lower-end companies but, as your résumé improves, you move up. In the beginning, I worked with directors who were only a step above amateurs—but, then again, so was I, not yet having embraced the fact that sex, cinematic or otherwise, was not about jackhammering away until orgasm.

I learned sex the way anyone does, by doing; for once the library was useless. Practice, not theory, taught me that a performer cannot race to climax without disappointing the viewer—but neither can he fuck indefinitely without becoming boring, and this was the balance that must be achieved. Likewise, I learned there is no standard set of maneuvers, and that readjustments can only be properly made when listening to the commands of the other's body.

I do not wish to brag, but the increase in my proficiency was admirable. Others noticed: demand for my services grew, my directors became more reputable, the women with whom I worked more talented, and my payments increased. My reputation, for performance and dedication, became known both to consumers and to those in the industry.

Eventually, I was no longer satisfied to work only one side of the camera and asked for other production responsibilities. The over-worked crews were happy for the assistance; I would help set up the lighting equipment while asking the cameramen how they knew where the shadows would fall. I would watch how the directors set the scene and, by this point, I had performed often enough that I could occasionally make a good suggestion. If the producer ran into a problem—an actress canceling at the last moment or a camera breaking down—I had enough friends in the industry that after a few quick calls, I could often solve it.

Before long, I branched into the role of writer, as much as one can claim to write a porn film. The writer can establish a situation, but when it comes to the action, he can only write SEX SCENE HERE. Different performers do different things: some refuse to do anal, some refuse to do girl-on-girl, and so forth, and because you're never really sure in advance which performer is going to do which scene, you can't get too specific. Final decisions are always made on the set.

Despite a coke habit that grew so severe giant white mosquitoes came for early morning visits, I was not an unintelligent young man. I was aware of the financial advantages of porn—no matter the economy, there's always a market—but there was more to it than this. I liked to write and act, and viewed my work to be a satisfaction of my artistic urges at least as much as it was a matter of commerce. After directing a few films, I figured out that the real money wasn't in acting in someone else's films but in getting others to act in *mine*. So I formed my own production company at a relatively young age and became a "successful executive in the movie business with a substantial income."

At times, I found this to be a better way to introduce myself than as a pornographer.

· · ·

Naturally I wasn't the only victim in the burn unit. Sufferers came and went. Some finished their treatments and moved on, while others died. To illustrate: one patient was Thérèse, a completely precious child with blond hair and sapphire eyes.

To look at Thérèse, you wouldn't have even known that she'd been burned, because she wore her destruction inside. Thérèse had experienced an allergic reaction—not unlike a chemical fire in her lungs—to antibiotics administered to alleviate asthma attacks. I overheard one doctor explain it to an intern: "For her, it was like taking a big gulp of Agent Orange."

Thérèse's mother, wearing a dark green gown that marked her as a visitor, brought in many overflowing arrangements of plastic flowers. (Real flowers, which carry bacteria by the million, could be agents of our death.) The mother was devout and always telling the little girl that each earthly occurrence was a part of God's Grand Design. "We can't know why things happen, only that God has a tremendous plan for each of us. His reasons are just, though we might not be able to understand them." Personally, I believe it's a poor idea to tell a seven-year-old girl that God's tremendous plan is to incinerate her lungs.

Howard was another patient in the ward. He'd been burned long before I arrived, in a house fire after his Alzheimer's-stricken grandmother fell asleep with a lit cigarette between her fingers. She didn't survive but he did, and now he was working diligently on every aspect of his rehabilitation. He used the walkers, he arm-curled his small silver dumbbells, and he walked ten steps one day and twelve the next. He beamed with each achievement, constantly telling me that he would "beat this thing" and "get his life back." These proclamations only intensified after his fiancée informed him that they'd no longer be getting married.

When he was discharged, Howard's entire family and a dozen friends (including the ex-fiancée) came to the burn unit to celebrate. They brought a cake and everyone told him how great he looked and how proud they were. Howard talked about this being "the first day of the rest of his life." It was a big fucking show, even the way they dramatically packed up his stuff. Howard shuffled over to my bed and took my good hand. "I told you I'd beat this thing. I told you. You can do it, too!" He winked in an effort to inspire me but, because of the skin contracture around his eyes, it only made me think of a housefly struggling to get out of a toilet bowl.

As he exited the room, his mother and father on each side of him, he didn't turn around to take a final look at the burn ward that had been his home for so many months; I could tell he was determined never to look back.

It is, I suppose, a heartwarming story of human triumph: determination, the love of family and friends, and positive thinking! But, really, who was he kidding? Howard's ex-fiancée was rightfully gone—who would (could) love a goblin? Would he ever have sex again? Would he go through life with his parents holding his arms to balance him as if he were forever two years old? Where, I ask, is the victory in that?

Howard had worked much harder than I intended to. I'd listened to him talk about how he was going to get better. I'd listened to everyone say how good he looked when, in fact, he looked like the monster that any sane person would cross the street to avoid. I wanted to scream when he took my hand, because even I didn't want to be touched by him. He disgusted me, this thing, my brother.

My reaction had little to do with him, really; it sprang from the realization that no matter what I did, I would never be the same. I could exercise every day, I could endure a thousand surgeries, and I'd still be a blister of a human being. There is no cure for what I am. *That's* what I took from Howard's great achievement. *That's* what I understood as I lay in the skeleton's belly with the snake swallowing my spine. HE'S JUST LIKE YOU, she hissed, BUT WITH A BETTER SOUL.

The worse realization: even if I could have gone back to what I'd been before the accident, how much better would that have been? Yes, I'd been handsome. Yes, I'd had money and a career but (let's not mince words) I'd been a coke-addled pornographer. I was told that my friends, who had laughed at my jokes when I was sharing drugs at the side of my pool, came to visit while I was in my coma—but each looked at me for less than a minute before walking out, never to return. One glance was enough to convince them that our days of sniffing at spoons were finished forever.

After I woke, the only person who made a real effort was Candee Kisses, a sweet girl who ended up in porn only because the universe is an unjust place. At seventeen, she had become tired of her stepfather raping her; she was willing to do anything to get out from under him. So she did. She should've been living on a farm somewhere, married to a hardworking guy named Jack or Paul or Bill, instead of making her living by sucking cock in front of the camera.

Candee came a few times, bringing little gifts and trying to cheer me up by telling me how fortunate I was to still be alive, but mostly she just cried. Maybe it was because of how I looked; more likely, it was because of her own life. After three visits, I made her swear that she wouldn't come back. She kept her promise. Now here's the funny thing: I knew her for over five years, I had sex with her, and I had heard her stories about her stepfather, but I didn't know her real name. Perhaps there are just some things you leave behind when you choose a new life.

When Howard and his parents disappeared through the burn ward door, I lost my veil of control. My chest started to lurch as anger and self-pity all came up like vomit, and my damaged throat allowed my breaths to be expelled only as long reedy gasps.

Then the girl Thérèse came to me. It was an incredible, torturous effort for her, and with each suck of air, I could hear her lungs rattle. She was exhausted by the time she reached my bed. She crawled up onto it and took my hand. Not my unburned right hand but my ravaged left one with its finger and a half missing, and she held it as if it were normal. It hurt so much to be touched there and, although I was thankful for the touch despite the pain, I implored her to get away.

"No," she answered.

My chest was still jumping involuntarily. "Can't you see what I am?"

"Yes," she replied. "You're just like me."

Her large blue eyes, radiant through the pain, never left my damaged face.

"Leave," I commanded.

She said she needed to rest a bit before she returned to her own bed, before adding, "You're beautiful in God's eyes, you know."

Her eyes closed and I watched her face as exhaustion pulled her into sleep. Then my own eyes drifted shut, momentarily.

The nurses soon woke me up. Thérèse was there in my bed, her hand still in mine, not breathing.

It only takes an instant.

• • •

Okay, I admit it: I tried the creative visualization that Gregor had suggested.

I slowed my breathing and concentrated on making my body feel heavy, beginning with my two remaining toes: heavy, heavy. Then my feet, then my ankles. Next I thought about my heavy calves, my heavy knees, and my heavy thighs. All the way up, torso, chest, neck, head . . . concentrating on my breathing: in, out, in, out, steady, calm . . .

This is when I started thinking about vaginas. I suppose this was natural, as I'd been inside hundreds. There are those men who would have you believe that all women feel the same, but obviously these men have not been with many women. Each vagina has its own texture, its own depth and moistness: each has its own personality. That's a fact.

I was very good at sex. It was a hobby as well as a profession. Outside of office hours, my passion was to find women who were the opposite of those with whom I filmed. If you work at a French restaurant, do you want to eat escargot on your day off? Hardly. You'll step out for something at the neighborhood diner. If you work in television production, you end your day by reading books. And, as a professional fucker of silicone creamgirls, I found it enjoyable to try other types of women. With careful words, not sincerely felt but spoken as if they were, I could lay out the most majestic dreams and well-planned kismet. With this gift of speech, I presented myself with 1001 women, from Scheherazade to Southside Selma.

Intercourse before the camera provides little satisfaction because the set is dressed, the check is in the mail, and where's the romance? But the feeling I got from taking—from *winning*—women who were not in the game was an entirely different thing. Satisfaction lay with housewives, policewomen, and secretaries. Book editors. Cowgirls. Track athletes, fisherwomen, tree planters, feminist writers, pro wrestlers, artists, waitresses, bank tellers, Sunday school teachers, dressmakers, and civil servants. Your mother, your sister, your girlfriend. I'd say anything to possess a woman, if even for an hour. I pretended to be left-wing, right-wing, artistic, manly, sensitive, commanding, shy, rich, poor, Catholic, Muslim (only once), pro-choice, pro-life, homophobic, gay (fag hags put out), cynical, wildly optimistic, a Buddhist monk, and a Lutheran minister. Whatever the situation required.

I remember a woman named Michelle. My sex with her was the closest I ever came to perfection in intercourse. She was a waitress with a slight potbelly, who smelled faintly of fried eggs and gravy and sported a scar where her appendix had been removed. I'd watched her and her husband have a furious dispute outside her greasy spoon. The husband left and she sat down on a park bench, determined not to cry. I went over and soon we were talking, soon she was laughing, soon we were back at my place. We had some cocaine and we laughed a little more and then we started to playfully punch each other's shoulders. When we started to fuck, first there was urgency, and then there was surprise at how good it felt, and then there was moaning. She started to laugh again and so did I, and then she started to cry; she cried all the way through—not from sorrow, but from release.

We went for hours. It seemed that we wandered a precipice where every nerve was awake. She told me about everything that transpired in (and out of) her marriage bed. She told me that she was afraid that she'd never actually loved her husband. She told me about her fantasies of her husband's sister and how she touched herself in public when she thought—but wasn't sure—that no one was looking, and she told me that she stole small things from the corner store because it made her horny. She told me that she believed in God and that she liked thinking about Him watching her do these things. I told her that she had been a very busy girl. We never stopped fucking and I found myself crying, too, at the rawness of it all.

My skin will never work like that again, so aware of the other person that I'm unsure where she ends and I begin. Never again. Never again will my skin be a thing that can so perfectly communicate; in losing my skin to the fire, I also lost the opportunity to make it disappear with another person. Mostly I'm glad that I found such physical connection, if only once, but I certainly wish it had been with someone whom I've seen since.

Perhaps I was clearly and persistently in the wrong in my many sexual transactions. But, then again, perhaps not. Please consider that I provided considerable comfort to many downhearted women. What does it matter if Wanda Whatshername believed I was a recently divorced, misunderstood painter? Her husband was more interested in drinking beer with the boys than in taking her dancing, so it probably did her a world of good to fuck a stranger. The key to the whole endeavor was that I was able to fold myself instantly into the shape of each woman's fantasy. To do this, to decode a person so that you can provide her with what she wants and needs, is an art, and I was a fuck artist.

The women didn't want the real me, and they didn't want love. They wanted a carnal short story, one that they had already been heating up in the dew of their thighs, to disclose at their book clubs.

I was just a physical body—a most singular beauty, too—with which they could realize their true desires.

This is the truth: we all desire to conquer the comely one, because it affirms our own worth. Speaking for the men of the world, we want to own the beauty of the woman we're fucking. We want to grasp that beauty, tightly in our greedy little fingers, to well and truly possess it, to make it ours. We want to do this as the woman shines her way through an orgasm. That's perfection. And while I can't speak for women, I imagine that they—whether they admit it or not—want the same thing: to possess the man, to own his rough handsomeness, if only for a few seconds.

All in all, what difference did my deceptions make? I didn't have AIDS or herpes, and while it's true that I've taken my share of needles in the ass, who hasn't? A little penicillin goes a long way. But then again, it's easy to fondly recall the days of minor genital infections after your penis has been removed.

Creative visualization is probably not for me.

• • •

Connie, of the morning shift, was the youngest, blondest, and cutest of my three nurses, and she checked my bandages when I awoke. Generally far too perky for my liking, she did have an adorable smile with just slightly crooked teeth and an always genuine "Good morning!" When I asked her once why she was always so gosh-darn nice—a difficult sentence but I got it out of my mouth—Connie answered that she "didn't want to be mean." There was great charm in the fact that she couldn't even imagine why I'd bother to ask such a question in the first place. In her efforts to be unfailingly kind, it was rare that she came onto the shift without bringing me some small gift—a can of soda that she held while I sipped through a straw, or a newspaper article she would read aloud because she guessed it might interest me.

Beth, by not just a few years the oldest of the three nurses, massaged me in the afternoon. She was too thin and too serious about everything. Her hair was curly, at times even slightly unruly, but you could tell that she would never let it get away from her. Perhaps it was from too many years working burn units, but she refused to become even the slightest bit personal in her dealings.

Maddy, of the night shift, looked like she'd rather be in a bar teasing a horny frat boy. Not necessarily satisfying, but definitely teasing. Even while tending to us burn victims, she made certain that her hips moved suggestively under her white skirt. She had what I'd always called a lemming ass—that is, an ass that you would follow right over the edge of a cliff. She was a naughty, naughty girl and it crossed my mind that she might've become a nurse simply so she would have that whole bad-girl-in-nurse's-outfit look working for her. She caught me staring at her once and said, "You were a real bastard before the accident, weren't you?" It was more a statement than a question and she didn't seem angry, just amused.

. . .

Thérèse's mother came by later in the week to pick up her daughter's effects. She told me about the funeral; apparently the mayor had sent a "magnificent bouquet of lilies" and everyone sang prayers "with their voices raised to Heaven." Then she lost her train of thought and looked longingly out the window at the park down the block, from which the voices of children playing baseball drifted up. She suddenly looked a dozen years older than the moment before, and when her trance broke she became terribly self-conscious that I'd seen it.

"Did Thé—" she started. "I understand that my daughter died in your bed. Did she . . . ?"

"No," I answered, "she didn't suffer."

"Why did she go . . . to you?"

"I don't know. She told me God thinks I'm beautiful."

The mother nodded, then burst into a sob that she tried to shove back into her mouth. "She was such a good girl. She deserved so much—"

The mother couldn't finish her sentence. She turned her back to me and the more she tried to remain still, the more her shoulders lurched. When she was finally able to look at me again, she said, "The Good Lord never gives us anything that we can't handle. You'll be all right."

She walked towards the door, then stopped. " 'Is not this a brand plucked out of the fire?' " She straightened her back. "That's Zechariah 3:2. The world is good."

Then she tucked the plastic flowers under her arm and left.

• • •

Anyone who's spent a long period in the hospital knows that one's nose loses its discernment in the atmosphere of ammonia. During one débridement session with Nan I asked, "What do I smell like?"

She wiped the sweat from her brow with the back of her white sleeve and I could tell that she was making the decision between telling me the truth or attempting something more pleasant. I knew her by this point: she'd choose the truth. She always did.

"Not as bad as you might think. It—I mean, you—your smell is musty and old. Like a house that everyone has left and no windows have been opened in a long time."

Then she went back to work, scraping and refurbishing this house that the owner had deserted. I wanted to tell her not to bother, but I knew that Nan would just turn down the corners of her mouth and continue her work.

• • •

Unable to tend yourself in a hospital, strangers plague you: strangers who skin you alive; strangers who cannot possibly slather you in enough Eucerin to keep your itching in check; strangers who insist on calling you honey or darlin' when the last thing in the world that you are is a honey or a darlin'; strangers who presume that plastering a smile like drywall across their obnoxious faces will bring you cheer; strangers who talk at you as if your brain were more fried than your body; strangers who are trying to feel good about themselves by "doing something for the less fortunate"; strangers who weep simply because they have eyes that see; and strangers who want to weep but can't, and thus become more afraid of themselves than of burnt you.

When I could stand no more television, I counted the holes of the perforated ceiling. I counted again to verify my findings. I memorized the stealth movement of the setting sun's shadows crawling down the walls. I learned to tell whether each nurse was having a good or bad day by the click of her steps. Boredom was my bedmate and it was hogging the sheets. The snake kept kissing the base of my skull, the bitch. **I AM COMING.** I was overwhelmed by whiteness and choking on antiseptic. I wanted to crawl through my urinary tube and drown in my piss.

As bad as it was, it became worse when Nan explained that at the end of my hospital stay—which would not come for many more months—I'd be placed in a halfway house for "reintegration" into society. Eventually, she said, I'd be able to look after most of my own needs and live on my own.

Seventeen years after release from one government home, I would find my way back into a different one—but at least when I was a penniless child, I had had my life ahead of me. At thirty-five I was a spent, struck match.

So I listened to the doctors and I nodded yeses when they told me about upcoming surgeries, but they might as well have been telling me about my upcoming trip to the city at the bottom of the sea. I signed consent forms; I signed away my house and all my personal possessions. A burn such as mine can easily cost half a million dollars to treat, and without much more effort can climb its way to more than a million.

My lawyer came to visit, uncomfortable in his gown. Unlike the other visitors, he had also decided to wear a surgical mask; it would be charitable to think this was for my protection, but it was more likely his own paranoia that he might catch something. In any case, I thought it appropriate: I could not look upon his masked face without thinking of a thief come to rob me.

He said a few words about how sorry he was about my accident; then, this formality dispensed with, he launched into an explanation of the serious trouble that my production company was experiencing. At the root, the problem was nonfulfillment of contracts to deliver new content to sales outlets; filming had ceased the moment I wasn't around to run operations, but delivery commitments had already been signed. He ran through a number of options, but because I had never trained anyone to fulfill my duties if I was incapacitated, only one scenario was truly viable: bankruptcy. He didn't want to bother me continually in my "difficult time," he explained, so he had already prepared the documents enabling my creditors to seize and liquidate my assets. Of course, he had ensured that the bankruptcy filing fees would be paid up front.

I just signed everything he placed in front of me, in order to get him out of the room quicker. The irony was not lost upon me that after making all my money in the skin trade, I was now trading all my money for skin. The deed done and my company instantly folded, the lawyer didn't know what to do other than say he was sorry one more time and exit the ward as quickly as possible.

And so my life went. When the doctors told me that I was improving, I did my best imitation of a smile. The nurses were proud of me as I squeezed the therapy ball with my burnt hand. They thought I was doing it to improve my strength, but I only wanted to shut them up. I was tired of Maddy's teasing, Beth's seriousness, and Connie's optimism.

I lay patiently during the Eucerin rubs, each one a tour of duty. I would pray, in the foxhole of my mind, for the opportunity to desert. At one point, Nan nonchalantly stated that my wounds were a "classic challenge" for a doctor such as herself. I pointed out that I was not a problem to be solved. She stammered. "That's not what I meant, I—I, uh . . . You're right. I was out of line, and I'm truly sorry."

I felt a brief sense of victory, but the funny thing was that I agreed with her completely: I *was* a problem to be solved, although we saw it from opposing angles. She saw my bandages as a larval cocoon from which I would emerge, while I saw them as a funeral shroud.

The bitchsnake of my spine kept swishing her tail around in my guts and churning out the sentence I AM COMING AND THERE IS NOTHING YOU CAN DO ABOUT IT. I didn't even care anymore. The snake was coming. So what? Just one more problem in an endless list. There was the Dachau of my face. There was my body, a real-life version of Dante's *Inferno*, constantly threatening to collapse in upon itself. The mantle of my skin over the hollowed-out Hell of my soul could not continue to support its own weight; my integrity had been compromised in every way. One doctor, hearing about the loss of my penis, visited to explain the most recent developments in erectile prosthetics, should I get a rebuilt cock. Whereas once there were only rods on hinges that allowed the penis to stand up or hang limp, it was now possible to install sophisticated pumping systems.

Such technological advances were little consolation to a man once admired for his ability to maintain an erection for ungodly periods of time. How the mighty are fallen.

I would simply get well enough to be released and, within twenty-four hours of leaving the hospital, I would be dead. This was my promise to myself, and it was the only thing that kept me going.

• • •

I am an atheist.

I do not believe there is a God who will punish me for self-slaughter.

Because I lack religious belief, I have never considered my accident to be divine retribution for my "immoral" activities. I know *exactly* why my accident occurred. Because I was high, I had a hallucination of arrows coming at me. To avoid the imaginary arrows, I drove my car over the side of a real cliff. The gasoline in my tank only did what gasoline does, which is to ignite when introduced to sparks. When flames engulfed my body, my body started to burn according to the laws of thermodynamics and biology. There is no deeper meaning.

I understand that some people find God after misfortune, although this seems to me even more ridiculous than finding Him in good times. "God smote me. He *must* love me." It's like not wanting a romantic relationship until a member of the opposite sex punches you in the face. My "miraculous survival" will not change my opinion that Heaven is an idea constructed by man to help him cope with the fact that life on earth is both brutally short and, paradoxically, far too long.

In the spirit of full disclosure, however, I should reveal something that many theists will insist *must* inform my disbelief in God. They will argue that I forgo the idea of Heaven because if I accepted it, I would have to admit that I am destined for Hell.

Because I have murdered someone.

• • •

There's a gentle sigh which descends like billowing silk upon the soul that accepts its coming death. It's a gentle pocket of air in the turbulence of everyday life. The silk of this feeling flutters—no, "flutters" is too active a word—the silk settles around you as if it has been drifting towards the earth forever and has finally found its target. The flag of defeat has been mercifully dropped and, in this action, the loss is not so bad. Defeat itself is defeated by the embrace of defeat, and death is swallowed up in victory.

The hiss of the snake fades away and death touches lovingly, possessively: it's a master who pets the head of the dog, or a parent who consoles the crying child. The hours begin to roll and the days scarcely separate themselves from the nights. Darkness swells like a beautiful, hushed tsunami, and the body craves calming lullabies and final psalms.

I can state this with authority: nothing compares with deciding to die. I had an excellent plan and it made me smile. It made me drift more lightly on my air flotation bed.

I was an unbeloved monster. No one would mourn my loss; for all intents and purposes, I was already gone. Who would miss me— the doctors who pretended to care? Nan did her best to say all the right things and showed a hopeful face, but she was kind enough not to lie. I lied to her, though, when I pretended that I wanted to heal. I was perfecting my plan, working on it as the nurses tended to my grossness, their tender hands skittering around my body like the most graceful of insects landing upon feces.

A suicide is not something you want to screw up. Especially if, like me, you're already facing the prospect of spending your entire life looking like last week's dim sum. The only way to make it worse would be to wind up brain dead or quadriplegic, which can happen if you miscalculate. So, let me repeat: a suicide is not something you want to screw up.

My plan would begin immediately upon release from the hospital, because in the burn ward they watched me too carefully. At the halfway house, there would be no locks or security guards. Why would there be? Those places are designed to put people back into society, not to secure them from it.

I still had a few thousand dollars stashed away in a bank account under a false name; this would be more than enough. I'd leave the halfway house, hobble down the street, find a bank and get this money. At a clothing shop, I'd buy a hooded coat so that I could move about undetected in the land of mortals. And then a most interesting scavenger hunt would commence.

Buying a shotgun would be easy. I'd already decided to approach

Tod "Trash" White, a small-time fence who would gladly sell his grandmother for a buck. Moving a shotgun at a handsome profit would put a shit-eating grin on his pockmarked face, and he'd probably even throw in a few extra cartridges for good measure.

The other items would be even easier. Razor blades are available at any convenience store. Rope is found at the corner hardware depot. Sleeping pills at the local pharmacy. Scotch at the liquor mart.

After procuring my supplies, I'd check into a hotel. Once alone in my room, I'd take a few antihistamine tablets, although not for hay fever. I'd settle in to watch a few adult movies on the hotel's blue channel, just for old times' sake. Who knows, I might even see myself in a farewell performance.

While watching the movies, I'd crack open the hinge of the shotgun to insert a couple of cartridges. Next I'd fashion a noose, paying particular attention to the knot. The object is not to strangle, but to break the neck: a large, strong knot facilitates a clean break. Having constructed a splendid loop, I'd turn the noose over in my hands a few times to admire my work and pull at it proudly, because you know how men love to yank their knots.

I'd wander out onto the balcony with my gun and my noose. Sunset. I'd breathe in the evening air. Throw out my arms to embrace the city. Bring my fists back in and thump my chest twice. Feeling strong and manly, I'd fasten the rope securely to the balcony railing. I'd drop the noose over the side, making sure there was ample length for a nice little fall before a sharp, satisfying jerk. Then I'd reel the rope back in, wishing that I could do the same thing to the damn bitchsnake living in my spine.

I'd spin the lid off the pill container and remove five sleeping tablets, sailing them down my throat with a glass of Scotch. This cocktail would be followed with a few more of the same. It's always nice to enjoy a drink while watching the sun go down. While ingesting these refreshing beverages, I'd remove a razor blade from its package and cut partway through the rope. This operation would involve a certain amount of educated guesswork, to cut the rope in a way that it would not immediately break with the jerk of my fall. I wanted it to hold me, at least for a while, when I reached the end of the line.

I'd have another glass of Scotch and another five sleeping pills. Now, here's the reason that I took the antihistamine: sleeping pills can cause vomiting when taken in excess and antihistamine counteracts that effect, making sure the sleepy stuff stays down. Pretty smart, huh? Next, I'd take the weekly supply of morphine given to combat the painsnake and inject it in a single satisfying plunge of the syringe. To complete my toxic cocktail, I'd wash down the remainder of my sleeping pills with a final shot of Scotch. By now, you can see how my plan is coming together.

I'd put the noose around my neck, working quickly because I'd be getting dizzy, Miss Frizzy. I'd take another shiny new razor blade out of its package. See how it sparkles in the light, like the wink of an imaginary God! With a single deft stroke I'd slash my right wrist, deep and clean, and then I'd slash my left wrist in the same manner. This is important: I'd cut along the length of the veins instead of across them. People who cut across the wrists either don't really want to die, or are too stupid to pull it off.

I'd sit on the edge of the balcony. With bloody hands, I'd lift the loaded shotgun and place the muzzle into my mouth. I'd carefully angle the barrel so that the blast would travel through the roof of my mouth and into the meaty gumbo of my brain. The advantage of a shotgun, as compared to a handgun, is that your aim doesn't really matter. The hundred pellets will immediately spread out to rip your damn head right apart. This is a beautiful thing.

My body would be positioned, back to the city, so that the blast would send me over the edge of the balcony's railing. As my brain was shredded, I'd fall, but this fall would be brought to an abrupt halt by the noose snapping my neck. For a while, I'd just hang there, feet bobbing. Actually, perhaps I'd jerk around spasmodically; it's hard to say. My wrists would be flowing red and my skull would be a gooey gray-matter mess, something like Picasso's very worst painting. What was left of my brain would start to starve for oxygen. My stomach would be brimming with Scotch and sleeping pills. My veins would run the happily morphined blood right out of the gashes of my wrists. Now, if I'd cut the rope just right, it would begin to unravel. The braided strands would spin away from each other and, in a few minutes, let go entirely. My body would fall twenty floors to the sidewalk below. Beautiful. Completion. Now *that's* a suicide, so much better than a cry for help.

Anyway, that was my plan. Never has a man looked forward to his death more than I.

III.

Let me begin with a description of her hair—because, really, it would be impossible to start with anything else. Her hair was like Tartarean vines that grow in the night, reaching up from a place so dark that the sun is only a rumor. It spread wildly everywhere, dark curls so cascadingly alluring that they looked as if they would swallow your hand if you were lucky enough to run your fingers through them. Her hair was so outlandish that even now, years later, I am compelled to create these ridiculous metaphors, which I know I'll regret in the morning.

Her eyes, also, are going to force me to embarrass myself. They burned like the green hearts of jealous lovers who accuse each other at midnight. No, I'm wrong, they were not green: they were blue. Ocean waves tossed around her irises, like an unexpected storm ready to steal a sailor from his wife. No, wait . . . maybe her eyes *were* green: mood eyes, perhaps, like the bejeweled rings that purportedly change color according to one's frame of mind.

She appeared in the burn ward door dressed in a light green hospital gown, with those unsolvable eyes and that riotously entangled hair, and I waited for the gasp that inevitably came whenever someone saw me for the first time. I waited for her to cover her mouth with her hand, in shock and dismay. She disappointed me by only smiling.

"You've been burned. Again."

Generally I make it a rule not to respond to bizarre proclamations by strangers, but, honestly, in this case my silence was because I didn't want her to hear my broken toilet of a voice. My throat was healing, but my ear (the one that still worked) was not yet used to the corrupted quality. I wanted her to know only the voice I had had before, the one that could talk a woman into bed.

In the face of my silence, she spoke again. "This is the third time you've been burned."

I steeled my courage and corrected her. "Once."

A look of confusion crossed her face. "Maybe you're not you."

She moved towards my bed, her eyes never breaking contact with mine, and drew shut the thick plastic curtains around us so that our privacy was assured. She leaned in, within inches of my face, studying me. Nobody had ever looked at me like this, not before the burn and certainly not since. Her eyes, dancing between the blue and the green, had dark bags underneath them, as though she had not slept in weeks. When her lips were almost touching mine, she whispered a word. "Engelthal."

No doubt, reader, you have at some point in your life been face-to-face with an insane person. You can sense the madness immediately, usually even before the person says anything at all, but this nonsensical word clinched it for me. Meeting lunatics is not really that notable, as the world abounds with them; what interested me more was my reaction. Usually upon such a meeting, you only want to get away. If you're walking on the street you avert your eyes and quicken your step, but in the burn ward the only recourse I had was to ring the nurse's call button. But I did not do this. My only response to this possibly dangerous situation was nonresponse. So who was less rational, the wild-haired woman or me?

She took a step back. "You don't remember."

"No." Whatever she thought I should be remembering, clearly I was not.

"That will make it more interesting," she said. "Are you aware that they're trying to poison my hearts?"

"No," I answered again, but I was interested in where such a comment might lead. "Are they?"

"Yes. I can't let them, because I have my penance to complete." She looked around, as if she were worried about being overheard. "How were you burned this time?"

I could form a number of short sentences in a row, as long as I remembered to pause and breathe, so I told her a few quick details about my accident—when, where, how long ago. Then I asked her name.

"You know my name." She kept reaching to her chest as if she were expecting to find something there, which was obviously missing. Her movements reminded me of the way I had always stroked my birth-scar.

"What are you doing?" I asked.

"They took away my necklace. They said it could be used to harm someone," she answered. "A young girl died here recently."

I thought about Thérèse. "How did you know?"

"Oh, I know some things about the dead"—she laughed—"but I suppose we're lucky."

"How so?"

"We've outlived a seven-year-old. We've outlived her a hundredfold."

"What are you talking about?"

"I have a dog named Bougatsa." Her fingers, now hanging at her sides, were twitching. "He'll like you."

"I don't like dogs."

"You will."

"They don't like me."

"Oh. Because you're so tough and mean, right?"

Was she really mocking a burn victim?

"What does the name mean?" I asked. "Bougatsa?"

"It's filling in Greek pastry, and my dog's exactly that color. Maybe I could bring him for a visit."

"Dogs aren't allowed here." Breath. "Even flowers can kill me."

"Ha! Don't try to sell me for dumb. You know you've worse things to fear than a dog." She placed her hand lightly upon my chest, with gentleness. I shivered, not only at the touch but also at the gleam in her eye. "You're sorely tempted to kill yourself and I can't say that I blame you. But there is a time and a place for such things, and this is not it."

Why would she say such a thing? I needed to change the subject. "You look good for seven hundred years old."

"You don't," she said, looking down the length of my body. It was the first time that anyone had made a joke about my burns. "So, what do you think I should do with my hearts?"

"I think . . ." I paused momentarily, to make her think I was carefully considering the issue, when really I was preparing for the length of the next sentence. "I think you should give them to their rightful owners."

Her eyes opened wide, as if I had inserted a key into a secret lock, and it made me wonder whether I had just pushed the wrong button on the insanity panel. But, just as quickly, her elated look was replaced by one of suspicion. She moved to one corner of my bed, where she intoned something in another language. *"Jube, Domine benedicere."* Latin? A short conversation followed, with her talking into the thin air, in a language that I couldn't understand, waiting for responses I couldn't hear. After the first imaginary conversation was completed, she bowed deeply and walked to a second corner of the bed to repeat the performance. And then, a third corner. She concluded each conversation the same way she started it—*"Jube, Domine benedicere"*—and she returned to her original position, with the look of suspicion gone.

"My Three Masters confirmed that it really is you. It is for you that I've been perfecting my final heart."

The very act of saying this clearly caused great emotion to well up inside of her. She looked on the verge of tears as she said, "I've been waiting such a long time."

Just then Beth drew open the curtains. She seemed shocked to find that I had a visitor after so many weeks without, but her surprise quickly turned to concern when she noted the gleam of insane happiness in the woman's eyes. Then Beth registered that while my visitor was clad in a gown, it wasn't the visitor's shade of green but the lighter shade of a patient, and that she had the color-coded bracelet that indicated a psychiatric patient. Beth, professional as always, did not engage my visitor directly but refused to leave me alone with her. She called an orderly immediately to "escort" the woman back to the psych ward.

I felt that I had nothing to fear and, in fact, that it was nice to have a little wildness injected into an atmosphere so oppressively sterile. In the few minutes before the orderly arrived, the woman and I continued talking, calmly, while Beth stood in a far corner with a watchful eye. My visitor whispered so that she would not be overheard. "We have a common acquaintance."

"I doubt that."

"You only saw her once, in a crowd. She can't speak," she said, leaning in closer, "but she gave you a clue."

"A clue?"

" 'Haven't you ever wondered where your scar really came from?' " My visitor reached up to her chest and I thought that she was going to point to the spot where my scar was on my body, but she was only reaching in vain for her missing necklace.

How could this woman guess precisely the words of the note that had been passed to me at the air show? Still, I am a rational man—this was a strange coincidence, nothing more. To prove it, I tried a little misdirection: "My entire body is a scar."

"Not your burns. The scar that you were born with, the one over your heart."

At this very moment, the orderly arrived and began the process of cajoling the woman to leave. Beth helped, using her body to deflect my visitor towards the door.

My voice was not yet strong but I raised it as much as I could. "How did you know?"

The woman turned back towards me, ignoring the arms pulling at her elbows. "The problem with people like us is that we don't die properly."

With that, the orderly took her from the room.

• • •

There is a logical explanation for everything; therefore, there was a logical explanation for the woman's knowledge of my scar.

First explanation: lucky guess.

Second explanation: a joke was being played on me by a friend, someone who thought it would be funny to send in an actress playing a psychotic woman with intimate knowledge of my life. The problems with this hypothesis were that I'd never told any of my friends about the Asian woman at the airfield, and that I no longer had any friends left to play tricks on me.

Third explanation: this woman liked my pornographic films and knew about the scar on my chest. It was a well-documented celluloid fact, as I'd never bothered with makeup to cover it. (Too much sweat in my genre.) Except that I was registered in the hospital not under my porn name but under my real one, and given the way I looked it would have been impossible to recognize me as the man I once had been.

Final explanation: this woman *loved* my pornographic films and was a stalker who had tracked down my now-defunct production company. Someone, probably my bastard lawyer, had informed her of my accident and pointed her in the direction of the burn ward.

But if she was an obsessed fan, why didn't she mention my former career? And if she had come looking for the actor that she'd seen, how could she have seemed so pleased to meet the new me?

And, finally, while much about the woman's behavior was odd, there was certainly nothing to suggest a hardcore porn addiction. Trust me, I've seen enough perverts in my life to pick them out of any crowd.

I supposed I would just have to ask her when she came again, because somehow I knew that she would. When I informed my nurses that I would welcome any future visits from the woman in the psychiatric ward, they all smiled strangely at me. How sad, they must have thought, that I looked forward to visits from a madwoman. But this did not deter me, and I even asked Beth to find out the woman's name. She refused to do any such thing, so I asked Connie. She also said it was against hospital policy to divulge the specifics of another patient. To this, I suggested that it would be "very, very mean" if Connie did not help me learn the name of the only person who had visited me in so long. As she wanted more than anything else to be kind, Connie soon came back with the information I'd requested.

The woman's name was Marianne Engel.

• • •

I was taller before the accident. The fire contracted me like beef jerky during the curing process. I had once been as lean and adorable as a third-century Greek boy, with buttocks ripe like the plump half-melons for which Japanese businessmen will pay a small fortune. My skin was as soft and clean as undisturbed yogurt, my stomach was divided into symmetrical pads, and my arms were sleekly muscular. But it was my face that was my coat-of-arms. I had cheekbones that would have been at home in Verlaine's wet dreams. My eyes were dark and deep enough for a small spelunking club to make a day expedition of them. A gay man once told me how much he yearned to let the plum of his penis rest softly upon my bottom lip. I laughed at him but secretly regarded it as a wonderful compliment.

Since my accident, I've tried to lose my vanity, but I still struggle with it. I remember the past, when my face was perfect, and when the wind would lift my hair so that it looked like the soft under-feathers of a bird's wing. I remember when women turned on the streets to smile at me, wondering what it might be like to own my beauty for even one shining moment.

If you accept the description of the beast that I am now, you should also accept the description of the beauty that I was. And since meeting Marianne Engel, I had felt that loss—especially at the empty juncture between my legs—all the more acutely.

• • •

She again graced my doorway about ten days later, dressed in a cloak that appeared to be of the finest medieval cut. This is not me having a little fun at your expense; she really was wearing just such a thing. The hood hung over her face and her eyes shone like aquamarine in a mine. She drew a finger to her lips, warning me to be quiet, and moved to my bedside stealthily. I wanted to laugh but I could tell that this, for her, was serious business. As soon as she was at my side, she pulled shut the curtains so that we might, again, have our privacy. She needn't have worried, because at that time there were only two other patients in the ward and one was out of the room for rehabilitation exercises and the other was snoring.

Behind the plastic barrier, she felt safe to pull back her hood— just a bit, not all the way off—and I could see that the bags had disappeared from under her eyes. She looked much sharper than she had during our first meeting, and there was the strong smell of tobacco upon her. I wondered if she'd actually been able to sneak by the nurses, or if they'd simply let her pass. By the fact she was without the proper visitor's gown, I suspected she had entered without their knowledge. She kept her hands at the corners of her hood, as if ready to draw it back up over her head at a moment's notice.

"I don't want them to know that I'm here."

"The doctors?"

Marianne Engel nodded. I told her that she didn't have much to fear, that they were good people.

"You don't know much about doctors." She reached inside her neckline and pulled out a leather strand with an arrowhead dangling from it. "Look, I got my necklace back." She lifted it up over her head and held it out, above my chest, so that the arrowhead hung like a magical amulet dowsing for my heart. "May I?"

I didn't know what she meant, but nodded anyway.

Marianne Engel lowered her hand, slackening the leather so that the arrowhead came to rest on my chest. "How does it feel?"

"Like it belongs there."

"It does."

"How did you know about the scar on my chest?"

"Don't rush. Explaining things like that takes time." She lifted her necklace from my chest and returned it to her own. "For now, may I tell you a story about a dragon?"

• • •

"Once upon a time, there was a dragon named La Gargouille who lived in France, close to the River Seine. La Gargouille was a quite ordinary dragon with green scales, a long neck, sharp claws, and little wings that couldn't possibly support flight but did anyway. Like most dragons, he could breathe fire, spout gallons of water, and rip up large trees with his talons.

"The residents of the nearby town, Rouen, hated the dragon and lived in fear. But what could they do? He was much more powerful than they, so each year they made a sacrifice in the hope that he'd be appeased. La Gargouille preferred virgin girls, as dragons are wont to do, but the villagers tended to offer criminals. In any case, people were eaten, which made it a generally appalling situation.

"This continued for decades. Finally, around A.D. 600 a priest named Romanus came to the city. He'd heard about La Gargouille and wanted to try his hand at subduing the beast. If the people would build a church, Romanus offered, and if every villager agreed to be baptized, he would dispatch the dragon. The villagers, no fools, thought this was a good deal. What did they have to lose, other than the dragon?

"So Romanus went to the Seine, taking with him a bell, a Bible, a candle, and a cross. He lit the candle and placed it on the ground, then opened the Bible before calling out to La Gargouille. The beast emerged from his cave with no real concern; he was a dragon, after all, so what did he have to fear from a mere human? If anything, such a visitor was nothing more than fresh meat.

"As soon as the dragon appeared, Romanus rang the bell—as if announcing a death—and began to read aloud the words of the Lord.

"The dragon snorted little puffs of smoke when he heard the sound, as if it amused him, until he realized that he could not have exhaled fire if he had wanted. There was a pain in his lungs which, after a few more moments, began to feel deflated and drained of breath.

"Realizing that he could not dispatch the priest with a burst of fire, La Gargouille lunged towards the man. Romanus lifted the cross and held it staunchly in front of the beast, which found it could go no further, as if an invisible hand were pushing it back. No matter which way the creature turned, the priest mirrored the action, and La Gargouille could move no closer to his tormentor. Cross in one hand and Bible in the other, Romanus continued to read with simple faith; each verse was like an arrow under the dragon's scales, and each chapter like a lance in its side.

"La Gargouille had never experienced anything like this in all its years, and began a retreat. It looked from side to side but Romanus used the cross to drive the beast directly back. Once the dragon was trapped inside its cave, the priest continued with unrelenting verse until the creature slumped defeated to its knees. The concluding act was when Romanus closed the Bible and blew out the candle; the ceremony was complete and the beast made docile.

"With no fight left in it, La Gargouille bowed its head and allowed Romanus to slip his vestments over its neck. The priest then used his cross to twist this leash tightly shut, and lead the defeated dragon back into town.

"The only way to kill a dragon is to burn it at the stake, everyone knew, and so this was done. La Gargouille cried in agony but to the villagers it sounded like sweet music. The shrieking continued until the very end because La Gargouille's head and neck wouldn't burn—the dragon's ability to breathe fire had tempered these areas against heat. But eventually the beast did die, and the villagers were freed from their great curse.

"The townspeople were honorable and fulfilled their end of the bargain. Each and every one submitted to baptism, and they built the church. La Gargouille's unburned head was mounted upon it and, for centuries to come, served as the original model for chimeras and gargoyles."

· · ·

Marianne Engel became completely involved in telling the story, allowing me the opportunity to observe her a little more closely. Her eyes, on this day blue, stopped darting around looking for doctors. She stared so intently, so directly, at me that it made me feel bashful. It was sensual and unnerving.

She was not what anyone would call a classical beauty. Her teeth were perhaps a little too small for her mouth, but I've always found microdontia rather sexy. I suppose her eyebrows might be too bushy for some men but, to be frank, those men are idiots. The only acceptable point of contention would be her nose, which was not too large, mind you, but certainly not delicate. A small bump on the bridge indicated that there had been a break at one time, but I thought it gave her character. A case could be made that her nostrils were slightly too flared, but any reasonable judge would have thrown that case out of court.

Her skin was pale, as if she did not get out in the sun often. She seemed closer to thin than fat, although her cloak made it difficult to imagine the dimensions of her curves. She was taller than most women, but not tall enough to push at the outer edges that defined the norm. Agreeably tall, one might say. How old was she? Hard to say, exactly, but she looked in her late thirties.

Long after she stopped talking, I realized that I was still staring at her and she was smiling back, not offended but pleased. I said the first thing that popped into my mind. "Did you make that up?"

"No, it's an old legend." She laughed. "I have *no* ability for making up stories, but I do know history. For example, did you know Jeanne d'Arc was burned at Rouen and her ashes thrown into the Seine?"

"I didn't, no."

"It pleases me to think that her body is still part of the water."

We talked more, about a number of things. Then Dr. Edwards, whose footsteps I recognized, entered the room on her regular rounds and pulled open the curtain.

"Oh!" she said, surprised to find a visitor. "Is this a bad time?"

Marianne Engel pulled her hood into place and bolted, almost becoming tangled in the plastic curtain as she pushed her way past Dr. Edwards. On her way out, she looked back at me and implored, "Don't tell!"

• • •

In the days that followed Marianne Engel's visit, Nan began using an electric dermatome to harvest my own good skin and relocate it to the damaged areas. She told me that this was a step forward in my treatment, but it didn't feel like one. The good skin still had working nerves, so each harvest literally ripped the covering from my body, leaving behind sites that were open wounds. It took about two weeks for each donor area to replenish itself before the procedure could be repeated. I was growing new skin only to have it removed again; I was a dermis farm, and the dermatome was the threshing machine.

After each harvest, I was smothered with creams and wrapped in loose bandages. A few days later, one of the nurses, usually Beth, would do the first dressing change after the procedure. Nan would stand off to the side checking the percentage of the graft that had adhered—the "take"—and a rough estimate was used to gauge whether the procedure was a success or failure. A take of eighty-five percent was good; anything below this would cause Nan to make a clicking sound with her tongue. Less than sixty percent meant she needed to perform another patch job.

Even when the skin did take, the absence of oil glands in the transplanted tissue resulted in extreme dryness. "Ants beneath the skin" is not only too clichéd a description of how it felt, but also not graphic enough. Lumberjack termites brandishing little chainsaws, maybe; or fiddler crabs wearing hairshirts and fiberglass shoes; or a legion of baby rats dragging tiny barbed-wire plows. Tap-dancing, subepidermal cockroaches wearing soccer cleats and cowboy spurs? Perhaps.

· · ·

I waited days for Marianne Engel to reappear.

I thought about her too much, and thinking stole time that could otherwise have been allotted to fearing débridement or formulating suicide plans. When my stomach started to ache, I wondered if I was actually missing her, this woman I barely knew. Was this longing? I honestly didn't know, as the only times I'd ever felt anything like this were when the town's cocaine pipeline had run dry.

As it turned out, the sensation in my stomach was not longing. My nervous intestines soon flamenco-danced themselves into sizzling pain. My bowels became chili pepper hot and there were snapping castanets in my anus. Nan poked at my abdomen and asked whether it hurt. I told her it was the site of the goddamned Spanish Civil War. Soon other doctors popped up in my room, in white-frocked rows that made me think of Flanders Fields. They performed scans, they took X rays, and they murmured things like "Interesting" and

"Hmmm." (No matter how interesting something actually is, a doctor should never, ever, say "Interesting" or "Hmmm" in front of a patient.) Soon enough, this murmuration of physicians determined that I had severe pancreatitis, which had caused much of the tissue in my pancreas to die.

Pancreatic necrosis comes in two types: sterile or infected. Mine was infected. Without immediate surgery, there was a good chance that I would not survive. So the doctors told me that I had little choice but to lose, as quickly as possible, a man-sized portion of my pancreas. Why not, I shrugged. Within five hours of my diagnosis, I was wheeled into an operating room, where the anesthesiologist told me to count backwards from ten. I made it only to six.

Burn patients cannot use regular anesthesia and what we are given instead—ketamine anesthesia—often causes delusions. For once, I had a most pleasing hallucination, an unexpected bonus in an otherwise woeful experience. I was looking over the ocean, a lovely English woman at my side, and what could be better for a burn victim than a dream of water?

• • •

I awoke to learn that half my pancreas had been removed. For good measure, the surgeon also took out a handful of nearby intestinal tissue that had also been damaged. I guess he decided that since he was in there already, he might as well grab everything he could. Piece by piece, I was becoming medical waste. Who knows, maybe someday the doctors will strip-mine me into complete nothingness.

Marianne Engel was in a chair in the corner of my room, reading, wearing something drab. After a few moments of my eyes adjusting, I could see that it was a visitor's gown. When she realized I was awake, she came towards me, the cover of her book proclaiming *Non Omnis Moriar.*

"Why are you here?" I was hoping for an answer that would stroke my considerable ego.

"I came to see your suffering."

"What?"

"I envy it."

Forget her mental illness: it's impossible for a burn victim to abide a person who says that she envies his suffering. I fought through my anesthetic fog to mount as angry an attack as I could muster. I can't remember exactly what I said, but it was not pleasant.

When she understood how her words had offended me, she tried to explain. "I envy all suffering, because suffering is necessary to become spiritually beautiful. It brings one closer to Christ. Those who suffer are the elect of God."

"So why don't you set yourself on fire," I spat, "and see how beautiful you become?"

"I am far too weak," she answered, not seeming to register my sarcasm. "I'm afraid not only of the flames, but of dying before my suffering becomes complete."

The braindope pulled me back into the darkness. I was glad to be removed from this conversation.

· · ·

The exact nature of Marianne Engel's illness was still unclear but when she suggested that "those who suffer are the elect of God," my best guess became schizophrenia.

Schizophrenics often have a particularly difficult time with religion, and some doctors suggest this relates to the age of onset: the condition most commonly develops between seventeen and twenty-five, a period when many people are first confronting their religious beliefs. Schizophrenics often have intense periods of heightened awareness—or outright delusions, such as auditory hallucinations—that can lead them to believe they've been specifically chosen by God. The situation is exacerbated by the fact that they often have trouble understanding that the symbolism of religion is metaphoric.

Christianity is based upon the idea that Jesus died for the sins of all mankind: to redeem us, Christ was tortured and nailed to a cross. A schizophrenic, attempting to understand the story, might reason thus: Jesus is the beloved Son of God, and Jesus endured incredible suffering, so those who endure the most pain are God's most beloved.

There is a long tradition of devout believers who feel that suffering brings one closer to the Savior, but a human face is always better than a general theory. For this reason, allow me to present the life of one Heinrich Seuse, German religious mystic. Born in 1295, Seuse would become one of the most important religious figures of the time, known as the Minnesänger—the "singer of courtly love"—because of the poetic quality of his writings.

Seuse entered the Dominican house in Konstanz at age thirteen and, by his own account, was completely unexceptional for the first five years of his religious life. At eighteen, however, he experienced a sudden illumination—a feeling of heavenly delight so intense he was unsure whether his soul was separated from his body. He considered this event so important that it was with this that he begins his life story, *The Life of the Servant*.

Some scholars claim that *The Life of the Servant* is the first autobiography in the German language, while others argue it's not an autobiography at all. Much of the actual writing appears to have been done by Elsbeth Stagel, a young woman from the convent of Töss, who was the most favored of Seuse's spiritual daughters. She apparently documented many of their conversations to use as the basis of the *Life* without Seuse's knowledge, and when he discovered what she'd done, he burned part of the manuscript before a "message from God" instructed him to preserve what remained. No one knows how much of the *Life* was written by Stagel and how much by Seuse.

The *Life* is a fascinating narrative, and provides wonderful details of the visions Seuse received throughout his life: God showed him representations of Heaven, Hell, and Purgatory, and departed souls appeared to him to give updates on their afterlives. Good stuff, and terrifically dramatic! But the most striking writing in the *Life* is Seuse's—or Stagel's—descriptions of his self-inflicted tortures.

As an adherent of the belief that bodily comfort makes one spiritually weak, Seuse claimed he did not go into a heated room for twenty-five years and that he refrained from drinking water until his tongue cracked from the dryness, after which it took a full year to heal. He restricted his intake of food—eating once a day and never meat, fish, or eggs—and once had a vision in which his desire for an apple was stronger than his desire for Eternal Wisdom, so to punish himself he went two years without consuming any fruit. (One wonders whether he could not simply have recognized the moral of the story and continued to eat actual—as opposed to metaphorically forbidden—fruit.)

On his lower body, Seuse wore an undergarment that had one hundred and fifty sharpened brass nails pointed inwards, at his skin. On his upper body, he wore a hairshirt with an iron chain, and under that a wooden cross the size of a man's outstretched hand and studded with thirty more brass nails. With this fastened between his shoulder blades, every movement—especially kneeling to pray— forced the nails to dig into his flesh, and later he would rub vinegar into his wounds. Seuse wore this spiked cross for eight years before God intervened in a vision, forbidding him to continue.

He wore these punishing garments even when he slept—upon an old door. When he lay down he shackled himself with rings of leather because if his hands were free, he could use them to swat away the rats that gnawed at him during the night. Sometimes he broke the restraints in his sleep, so he started wearing leather gloves covered in more sharpened brass tacks that would slice up his skin as effectively as if he'd run a cheese grater over it. Seuse kept these habits for sixteen years until another vision from God instructed him to throw these sleeping aids into a nearby river.

Rather than bring Seuse relief at being forbidden to keep punishing himself, these divine interventions bothered him greatly. When a nun asked how he was doing, Seuse replied that things were going quite badly because it had been a month since he'd known pain and he was afraid that God had forgotten him.

Such physical torments, Seuse realized, were only a beginning; they didn't allow for a tangible sign of his great love for the Lord. To remedy this, he opened his robes one evening and used a sharpened stylus to carve the letters *IHS* into the flesh above his heart. (If that's Greek to you, don't worry: *IHS* is the abbreviated name of Christ in the Greek language.) Blood poured out of his ripped flesh but he claimed he barely felt the pain, such was his ecstasy. The scarified letters never vanished and he wore the wound in secret until the end of his life; it soothed him in times of struggle, he claimed, to know that the very name of Christ moved with each beat of his heart.

Seuse died in 1366 after a long life which, one can only surmise, must have seemed even longer than it actually was.

I find it interesting that Seuse had his "illumination" at age eighteen, just when schizophrenia most commonly manifests. If you were a schizophrenic, you could do worse than religious life in fourteenth-century Germany. In the Age of Mysticism, your visions would not be feared but revered. If you beat yourself senseless, you were not self-destructive but emulating Christ. If you heard voices, you had direct communication with God.

But for all this, there is one event in the life of Heinrich Seuse that I find particularly interesting, although it is something I have never been able to verify in my library research.

Marianne Engel insisted that, once upon a time, she met him.

• • •

When I woke again, Marianne Engel was gone, but she had left behind a gift on the nightstand, a small stone gargoyle.

I turned the little fiend over in my hands. About six inches high, the gargoyle looked like a semi-human dumpling, cooked the color of a melancholic rain cloud. His potbelly drooped on crossed legs, his elbows were propped on his knees, and his chin rested upon three-fingered hands. His back sprouted short thick wings, presumably for show rather than flight. A blocky head was perched on his slumped shoulders like a boulder waiting to be pushed from the top of a cliff. He had enormous eyes that loomed underneath a Neanderthal brow, and a mouthful of uneven teeth. The gargoyle seemed to be trying hard to scowl, but he couldn't quite pull it off. His expression was sweet and sad and somehow all too human, like that of a forlorn man who has spent his entire life dragging himself from one tiny accident to another until the cumulative effect has crushed him under the weight of words he can no longer speak.

My physical condition improved markedly in the days after the surgery. The garbage scow that is my stomach learned to float again, although it could no longer carry as full a load as it once did. My right leg, with its mangled knee and blasted hip, was also beginning to mend, and the doctors promised that they would soon remove the mechanical spider cast. Each day, I seemed to lie in the skeleton bed a little less awkwardly.

Nan poked me and wrote little messages to herself on my chart. She always remained professional, but I found myself calling her Nan more often than Dr. Edwards. I don't know if she disliked this familiarity but she never asked me to stop. I suppose this emboldened me and in a moment of curiosity I asked her whether she was married. She hesitated and thought about answering, but in the end decided against it.

• • •

The seat beside the skeleton bed remained empty, save for the visits from the nurses and Nan. One Marianneless day became two Marianneless days, two became three, five Marianneless days, until they formed a Marianneless week. I wanted to ask her about the little gargoyle, why she had given it to me, what it meant.

I was reading a lot, mostly lawyer mysteries that I didn't actually enjoy. I needed something to replace them, so I requested of Nan that she loan me some textbooks on abnormal psychology. "You must have something on schizophrenia, manic depression, bipolar disorder, anything like that?"

"It's not my area of expertise," she replied. "Besides, you should be reading about burns."

Nan had already brought a number of books on burn recovery that sat untouched on my bedside table. I was not reading them simply *because* they were what I should be reading. We made a deal: for every psychology book she brought, I'd read one of the burn books. Nan considered this a victory and insisted that I read one of her books first.

After I had, Gregor arrived at my room, his corduroy thighs rubbing together, with a psychology text in his hands. He handed it over and said that Dr. Edwards had asked him to deliver it, from the private collection in his office.

"The place isn't driving you nuts, is it?" The way he chuckled to himself, I wondered if he'd been thinking that up all the way from the psychiatric ward. When I asked him whether psychiatrists were really supposed to refer to patients as nuts, he dabbed a bead of sweat from his brow with a tartan handkerchief, and didn't answer. Instead, he asked why I was so interested in schizophrenia and manic depression.

"None of your business," I said.

Gregor opened his mouth as if to say something more, but instead he just smiled and tapped my little gargoyle once on the head. "I like this," he said, before padding his way out of my room in his tasseled loafers.

◆ ◆ ◆

The following day, a very small Asian woman, who upon first glance looked more like a doll than a real person, entered my room.

Please don't jump to the conclusion that I'm attempting to further the stereotype that all Asian women resemble china dolls. That's not the kind of doll I have in mind. This woman had a broad face, a flat nose, and a most amazing smile. (I've always hated people who can smile widely without looking stupid.) Her cheeks were like ripe apples, which, when taken with the striped shirt and denim overalls under her gown, created an overall effect of an Oriental Raggedy Ann.

"Hi! My name is Sayuri Mizumoto. I'm pleased to meet you." She thrust her hand into mine for a hearty shake. And while I might not write that every time she spoke, she did so with a large grin, please take it as a given from this point forward.

"What kind of name is Sayuri?"

"A beautiful one," she answered with a touch of Australian in her accent. "Now sit up."

I asked why she expected me to do what she told me.

"Because I'm your new physical therapist and now you're going to sit up."

"You don't even know—"

"I've spoken with Dr. Edwards, and you can do it!" There was a strange combination of cheer and proclamation in the way that she told me I could *do it*! She placed her hands underneath my back and widened her stance to help me. She warned me that I would probably feel a little dizzy when the blood rushed to my head, and I protested that I wasn't sure this was such a good idea.

"Sure it is," she cheered. "Three, two, one, go!"

Up I went; she was pretty strong for a doll. For a moment I was fine, her hands steadying me. Then the vertigo hit and the room began to turn in strange circles. Sayuri moved a hand to the back of my neck to keep my head from lolling around. "You're doing *great*! Steady."

When she lowered me back down, she commented, "That wasn't so bad, was it?"

"It was fucking awful."

"*Shock!*" She lifted her hand to her open mouth in mock horror.

"You really are like they said. Didn't anyone ever tell you that the mouth is the front gate of all misfortune?"

• • •

When I opened my eyes after an afternoon nap, Marianne Engel was standing above me, the curtains shut. On my bedside chair hung one of the visitor's gowns; she had worn it into the room, I discovered later, to appease the nurse who had caught her sneaking in, and then promptly removed it. So she was in her street clothing: a billowy white shirt tucked into her faded jeans with a belt of small silver disks. Her hair hung loose over her shoulders, down her back. Her face was calm and her eyes were bright—green, definitely green. An embroidered dragon lived on her right pant leg.

Finally I knew that I'd been correct in guessing that Marianne Engel's figure was pleasing. The dragon seemed to think so also, for it crawled upwards from ankle to hip, twisting around and caressing her thigh. Each scale was a colored sequin; the ruby eyes were bulbous fake jewels. The tongue twisted outwards in playful licks across her buttocks. The claws, black stitches, dug into the delicious meat of her leg. "I like your pants," I said. "Where have you been?"

"I was busy," she answered. "The pants were a gift."

"Doing what? From whom?"

"Working, but then I got sick for a bit." She pulled a chair next to the bed and sat down. "Jack gave me the pants."

"Sorry to hear you were under the weather. Who's Jack?"

"I'm recovering. Jealous?"

"Glad to hear it. You're not hiding from the doctors today?"

"Nope. Jealous?"

"Of Jack?" I pshawed her. "So you're getting on with them?"

"Wouldn't go that far. Don't want to talk about it."

"The doctors or Jack?"

"Doctors," she answered. "You want to talk about Jack?"

"Of course not. Your private life is private, right?"

"The relationship is complicated."

"With Jack?"

"With doctors." Marianne Engel drummed her fingertips on her pantdragon's bejeweled eyes. "But Dr. Edwards seems okay, I guess."

"Yeah. So you're all healed from your, whatever, sickness?"

"Exhaustion, mostly." She tilted her head to one side. "Tell me about your accident."

"I was stoned, and I drove off a cliff."

"He who eats fire, shits sparks."

I indicated the little statue on the bedside table. "I like the gargoyle."

"Not a gargoyle. It's a grotesque."

"You say oyster, I say erster."

"I ain't gonna to stop eating ersters," Marianne Engel replied, "but that's a grotesque. A gargoyle's a waterspout."

"Everyone calls these things gargoyles."

"Everyone's wrong." She pulled a cigarette out of a pack and, after not lighting it, began to roll it between her thumb and forefinger. "Gargoyles throw water from the walls of cathedrals so the foundations don't wash away. The Germans call them *Wasserspeier*. Do you remember that?"

"Remember what?"

" 'Water spitter.' That's the literal translation."

"Why do you know so much about them?"

"Grotesques or languages?"

"Both."

"Grotesques are what I do," Marianne Engel answered. "Languages are a hobby."

"What do you mean, you 'do' grotesques?"

"I carve." She nodded towards the stunted monster in my hand. "I did that."

"My psychiatrist likes it."

"Which shrink?"

"Dr. Hnatiuk."

"He's better than most."

I was slightly surprised. "You know him?"

"I know most of them."

"Tell me about your carving."

"I became interested while watching you do it." Her other hand was now fidgeting with her arrowhead necklace.

"I don't carve."

"You did."

"No, I never have," I insisted. "Tell me why you like carving."

"It's backwards art. You end up with less than what you started with." She paused. "It's too bad you can't remember carving. I still have something you did."

"What?"

"My *Morgengabe.*" Marianne Engel looked at me intently, as if waiting for a nonexistent memory to enter my mind. When she saw that none was coming, she shrugged and leaned back into her chair. "Jack's my manager."

A professional acquaintance. Good. "Tell me about him."

"I think I'll keep you guessing." She was definitely in fine spirits on this day. "How about I tell you a story?"

"About what, this time?"

"About me."

IV.

The exact date of my birth hardly matters now, but as far as I know it was sometime in the year 1300. I never knew my birth parents, who left me in a basket at the front gate of Engelthal monastery in mid-April when I was only a few days old. Normally an abandoned child wouldn't have been taken in and raised—Engelthal wasn't an orphanage, after all—but as fate would have it, I was found by Sister Christina Ebner and Father Friedrich Sunder on the very evening that they'd been discussing what constituted a sign from God.

Sister Christina had entered the monastery at the age of twelve and started having visions two years after that. When she found me she was in her early twenties, and her reputation as a mystic was already secure. Father Sunder was approaching fifty, a chaplain of the area, who had entered the religious life much later than most. By this time, he'd been serving as confessor to the Engelthal nuns for about twenty years. But the most important thing to know about them was their basic natures, because if they had not been so sympathetic, everything would have turned out much differently.

There were two notes in my basket. One was in Latin and the other in German, but both read the same. *A destined child, tenth-born of a good family, given as a gift to our Savior Jesus Christ and Engelthal monastery. Do with her as God pleases.* It was rare at that time to find a commoner who could write one language, much less two, so I suppose the very existence of these notes supported their claim that I was from a good family.

From what I understand, Sister Christina and Father Sunder quickly decided that the appearance of a child on that evening, of all evenings, was not a coincidence, and it didn't hurt either that Sister Christina was herself a tenth child. When they took me to the prioress, she was hesitant to stand against their combined arguments. Could the prioress ignore the possibility that my appearance at the gate had been ordained from above? When dealing with messages from the Lord, it's always best to err on the side of caution. This was the general feeling among the sisters of the monastery, although there was one who argued strenuously against keeping me. This was Sister Gertrud, the armarius—that's the "master scribe"—of the Engelthal scriptorium. You should remember her name, as well as the name of her assistant, Sister Agletrudis. Both would prove instrumental in my life, and usually not for the better.

Engelthal was considered one of the most important spiritual centers in Germany. You might think this would make for a forbidding childhood, but in truth it did not. The nuns treated me well, probably because I was a distraction from everyday chores. I always loved it when I made one of them smile, because as soon as they realized they were doing it, they'd make all efforts to stop. I felt as if I'd broken a rule.

I was always closest to Sister Christina and Father Sunder, who became a kind of surrogate mother and father to me, a fact that was reflected in the name that I used for Sunder. Properly, he could have been called "father" by all, but his humility was such that he always required others to call him "brother." So to everyone else he was Brother Sunder, but to me he was always Father. He allowed it, I suppose, because I saw a side of him that no one else saw—well, except for Brother Heinrich, with whom he shared a small house near a ridge in the forest. In any case, I heard Father Sunder's laughter when almost everyone else only saw his intensity.

All the other nuns came to the monastery after having had their childhoods elsewhere, but I spoke my first word to Father Sunder. "*Gott.*" God, what a glorious introduction to language. Given this, how could he possibly wear the same mask of fierce piety in front of me that he showed to everyone else? It didn't fit his face when he was playing with an infant, and by the time he thought to put that mask on with me, it was too late. But I understood, even as a child, that he had an image to keep up, and his secret was safe with me.

Father Sunder always wore a hairshirt and berated himself constantly, calling himself a sinner—mostly for the "transgressions of his youth," whatever they were—and praying for mercy. He believed he was "polluted" by the things he'd done before entering religious life. He didn't often go on these rants in front of me but, when he did, Brother Heinrich would stand silently in the corner of their home and roll his eyes.

Though he condemned himself, Father Sunder never hesitated in forgiving others. And he had this voice, the sweetest voice that you could possibly imagine. When he spoke, you couldn't help but feel that not only did he love you but that God did too.

Sister Christina—I don't even know where to begin. She was an astonishing woman. She had been born on Good Friday, which was the first sign of the blessedness that was to come in her life. People said that of all God's representatives on earth, she was among the fifteen most blessed. As a little girl, I never once doubted it was true, and it was only much later in life that I asked myself how such a thing could be measured. Sister Christina's visions and literary talents brought fame to the monastery. She was always writing, and would go on to produce two masterpieces—*Revelations* and *The Sister-Book of Engelthal,* a history of the important nuns who had come before us. Her work inspired others in the monastery to also write. For example, Gertrud of the scriptorium wrote *The Life of Sister Gertrud of*

Engelthal with the help of Brother Heinrich and Brother Cunrat but, to tell the truth, I always felt this book was little more than an effort to increase her own legend.

Gertrud had a strange habit of incessantly sucking at the air. It was impossible not to notice and equally impossible not to hate. It was said that her mother had given birth to eight boys before her, all painful deliveries, but that Gertrud's birth was effortless. You might wonder what that has to do with anything, but from the beginning it equated Gertrud with the Christ child because His birth was also reputed to have been painless—a delivery as immaculate as the conception. People said that baby Gertrud never suckled at her mother's breast; she just preferred to slurp away at the air as if extracting divine sweetness directly from it. I always suspected she kept sucking at the air throughout her life simply so that no one would forget the story.

Of all the books that came from this period of inspiration, the one that I love most is *The Gnaden-vita of Friedrich Sunder.* Well, I love it but I don't love what was done to it. After Father Sunder's death it was sanitized and, among other things, all references to me were removed. Not that my vanity is offended, but I was—I am—offended by the destruction of his intent.

Anyway, these were the people around me when I was a child. The one time that I asked Sister Christina when I'd be allowed to live in the outside world, she said I never would—but that this was not a problem to be lamented, it was a gift to be celebrated. God had been generous to reveal His plan for me from my very birth, placing me immediately into Engelthal. None of the other nuns, even Christina herself, had been allowed to spend their entire lives in the glory of God's service. "What a lucky little girl you are," she said, signaling the end of the conversation.

It was widely expected that when I grew into a woman I'd also take up the pen. This expectation only grew when I began to speak at an extremely early age and took to Latin as easily as my mother tongue. Obviously I can't remember, but they say that I barely both-

ered with individual words before I started speaking in complete sentences. In those days, you must understand, children were basically
thought to be inadequate adults. A child's nature was not something
that could be developed, because character was set at birth; childhood was a period of revelation, not development, so when my language abilities appeared they were thought to have always existed,
placed there by God, waiting to be made known.

I loved the visitors who came to Engelthal. Locals came for medical treatment in our infirmary, and it was only proper that we accept
them. Not only from a standpoint of mercy, but also as a political
necessity. The monastery was expanding rapidly as nobles donated
surrounding lands, and we inherited the tenants as well. There were
other visitors, too, traveling priests who wanted to see what it was
about Engelthal that produced such exceptional visions in the nuns
or who, more practically, just desired shelter for the night. I was just
as interested in a sick farmer as in a nobleman, because each brought
stories about the world outside.

Sister Christina indulged me when these visitors came. I'd sit
quietly in the corner of the room, concentrating intensely upon the
conversation, perfecting the art of being overlooked. Gertrud disapproved, of course, and would look down her long thin nose at me.
She was already losing her eyesight, and it was a chore for her to
keep her disdain in focus.

Gertrud saw these visitors as intruders on her real work because,
as armarius, it fell within her duties to translate occasionally. She
wasn't particularly skilled at it—her French and Italian were sketchy
at best—but her position required it. Most of our visitors could
speak in Latin or German, but I liked the ones best who brought
exotic tongues. It was during these conversations that I sharpened
my listening. The challenge was not only to understand the foreign
words but also to grasp the foreign concepts. For example, I knew
that Pope Clement had moved the papacy to Avignon—but why?
And where was that? And what was it like? One night, I overheard

my first argument. A foreign guest dared to question the righteous-
ness of the late Pope Boniface and Gertrud jumped staunchly to the
defense of His Holiness. For a little girl, it was shocking stuff.

I remember distinctly the evening that my talent was revealed. A
foreign visitor was among us and Gertrud, as usual, was struggling
with the translation. I could never understand what the problem was,
because I could grasp everything that was said. It didn't matter which
language it was, I simply understood. On this evening the visitor was
Italian, an old, poor, unwashed man. Anyone could see that he was
not long for this world, and he was trying so desperately to make
his situation understood. Gertrud threw up her arms in disgust and
proclaimed that his accent was too vulgar to decipher.

Maybe it was because the old man looked so very frail, or maybe
it was because of the rattle in his chest. Maybe it was because he
thanked the nuns between every spoonful of his porridge, uttering
not a single bad word despite the fact that no one could understand
him. Or maybe it was because I felt that if someone didn't talk with
him that very night, it was possible that no one ever would again.
Whatever the reason, I broke my code of silence and stepped out of
the corner. In the Italian of his dialect, I asked, "What's your name?"

He looked up over his spoon with such joy on his face. "Paolo,"
he answered, then asked how I knew his Italian. I didn't know how
or why, I said, I just did. I told him that I listened to foreigners and
after they left I'd have conversations in their languages, in my mind,
before going to sleep. He thought this was wonderful. When I asked
where he was from, he answered that he'd lived much of his life in
Firenze but that he'd been born in the far south in an area notorious for its coarse vernacular. His own accent, he explained, was an
awful mix of the two places. He laughed when he said this, and the
laugh shocked Sister Christina out of her astonishment. She started
feeding me questions, which I suppose was as much to test my translation skills as to uncover information. Through me, the old man's
story was told.

Paolo had spent his entire life married to a woman he'd loved dearly. She'd recently died and he knew that he would follow her soon. This was why he was traveling, because he'd never seen countries outside his own and he did not want to die knowing nothing of the world. He was not afraid of death, as he'd been a good Christian and expected his final reward. He asked if he might have just one night's rest at the monastery before continuing his journey. Sister Christina granted this, as she had the power to act on behalf of the prioress, and Paolo thanked her for her kindness. For the first time in my life, I felt important.

Paolo took a book from his bag and held it in my direction. It was obvious that he wanted me to have it. "I won't be needing this much longer."

Sister Christina stepped forward to decline on my behalf. "Tell him he has so little that we cannot take from him what he does have. But thank him." I translated, and Paolo nodded his understanding. He thanked the nuns once more before heading to the bed that was made available.

Sister Christina told me that I was to meet with her and the prioress in the chapter room the following day after matins. I asked if I was in trouble for speaking up, but Sister Christina assured me that I was not.

When I arrived the next morning, the prioress was sitting at her desk, with Sister Christina behind her. Gertrud stood at the side of the room with a detached air. The prioress was a good woman but she scared me nonetheless. She was just so old, with wrinkled jowls like a hunting dog's.

"I take it on the authority of Sister Christina that we had a revelation last night," she growled. "Child Marianne, there is no conceivable reason for you to know the Italian language. By what method did you accomplish this feat?"

Sister Christina gave me a reassuring nod, which bolstered my courage. "When I listen to languages, I just understand," I said. "I don't know why everyone can't do it."

"You can do this with other languages, as well? Truly, it is a show-ing."

"If I may speak," Gertrud interjected. The old woman nodded. "Your judgment is sound, Prioress. As always. Still, I think it would be prudent to ask from where such an unusual ability might come. I urge that we be on our guard, as we know so little about this child's birth. What assurance do we have that this ability comes through the Lord, and not through . . . some other Entity?"

I was in no position to challenge Gertrud on such a suggestion but, luckily, Sister Christina was. "Where might *you* suggest it comes from, Sister Gertrud?"

"It is best that such names not cross the lips, but you are well aware that there are forces against which the righteous soul must be vigilant. I am not saying that this *is* the case, I am simply suggesting that we would be wise to consider all possibilities."

The prioress answered the charge. "Until we have reason to be-lieve otherwise, we shall assume that this is indeed a revelation from God and not a trick of the Enemy."

I could tell Gertrud wanted to say more, but stopped herself. "Yes, Prioress. Of course."

The old woman continued. "I propose that we consider this not only a revelation but also a calling. Do all speak with tongues? Do all interpret? No. When such a gift is recognized, it is our duty to see that it serves God's honor. Do you not agree, Sister Gertrud?"

"I agree that we should, every one, do what we can to serve." Gertrud squeezed these words out of her mouth as a miser might squeeze coins from her purse.

"It gladdens me to hear you say that," the prioress continued, "for I have decided that you will take the child into the scriptorium. It is clear that her gifts exist in the realm of language, and her training shall commence immediately."

My heart fell heavily into my stomach. If I could have foreseen that I'd be assigned to Gertrud's tutelage, I would never have stepped out of the corner. What the prioress thought of as my "reward" was actually the harshest of all possible punishments, and I'm certain my disgust was exceeded only by Gertrud's. At least we were finally united in a common belief: that this was a horrible idea.

"Marianne is but a child," Gertrud protested, "and is certainly not ready for such responsibilities. While she may have displayed some rudimentary skills, there are other traits necessary for such work. Patience, for example, and an attention to detail that a child cannot possibly possess."

"But she will learn," the prioress responded, "by your example."

"I beg to discuss the matter further. I understand your thinking, but—"

The prioress cut her words short. "I am pleased that you understand. You would not want me to go against the Lord's will, would you, Sister Gertrud?"

"Of course not, Prioress." Gertrud had her hands behind her back, and I could hear her fingernails digging into the fabric of her robe. Sister Christina stepped forward, laid her hand on my shoulder, and asked whether—with the kind permission of the prioress—we might have a few moments alone. The prioress granted the request and exited. Gertrud also left, sucking angrily at the air and doing her best not to slam the door on her way out. She was not successful.

Sister Christina spoke. "I know you do not think much of the idea, but I do believe that Sister Gertrud is a good and holy woman, and that there is much you can learn from her. Though you cannot understand it now, your gifts are as exceptional as they are unexpected. The Lord obviously has great plans for you and I could not in good conscience allow this to go unaddressed. We must trust in this revelation and remember that the Lord allows no accidents."

You can imagine how any child would take such an explanation, even a child raised in a monastery. How could God's design involve training under Gertrud? I howled until my cheeks were red and tears rolled down my face. Sister Christina let me get it all out and even took my childish blows. She did, however, dodge my kicks, so I suppose there was a limit to her self-sacrifice. When I had finally drained myself of energy and crumpled to the floor, she sat down beside me.

I told her that I hated her, but we both knew it was not true. She stroked my hair and whispered to me that everything would be all right, if only I trusted in God. And then she took something out of the folds of her robe, a book that she had secreted there.

"When I went to wake Paolo this morning, I found that he had died in his sleep. He went without pain, I believe, and the look on his face was serene. But it was clear that he wanted you to have this last night, so I am fulfilling his final wish by passing it along now."

Sister Christina handed me an Italian prayer book, the first book that I could call my own. Then she took me to the scriptorium, so that I might begin serving God's will.

V.

How do I best present the medieval life that Marianne Engel claimed was hers, when—of course—she no more lived in the fourteenth century than I did? The challenge lies not only in her story's inherent lack of truth, but also in the fact that I can no longer continue to write solely in my own voice: I now must consider hers. I have attempted to re-create the Engelthal story exactly as she spoke it, but if my rendering of her voice is sometimes flawed, please forgive me. I have done my best.

The tale also brought forth the question of just how crazy Marianne Engel actually was. Did she really believe she had been raised in a medieval monastery, or was she simply trying to entertain a burn patient? When I tried to get her to admit that she was making it all up, she looked at me as if I were the insane one and, since I wanted her to keep coming back, I could hardly insist she had it backwards. In the end, I decided I would let her keep telling the story until the facts tripped her up.

I was not the only one musing on the state of my visitor's sanity. Dr. Edwards paid me a visit with the unambiguous goal of discouraging further visits from this new woman in my life. The conversation opened with a warning about the physical risks that came with Marianne Engel; as she was sneaking in when the nurses weren't looking and was disregarding the rules about gowns for visitors, who knew what germs she might be bringing? I conceded the point but countered that it certainly could not harm my recovery to have something—*someone*—to look forward to seeing.

"That may be, but you need to focus on your recovery, and not deal with . . ." Nan took a moment to compose a politic phrasing. ". . . Other issues that won't help you get better."

She was very quick, I suggested, to tell me what I needed.

"I've been doing this a long time and I've seen what extra stress can do to a patient."

I asked whether her concern arose because my visitor was an occasional psychiatric patient at the hospital, and Nan affirmed the fact did not play in Marianne Engel's favor. However, she was also quick to add that this would not, or could not, be used to keep Marianne Engel away; as she had been judged competent to live in society, thus she was also competent to visit a hospital. Still, I could see that Nan might use her influence to make it as difficult as possible.

"I'll tell you what," I proposed, "if you allow her to keep coming, I'll work harder with Sayuri."

"You should be doing that anyway."

"But I'm not," I said, "and you should take what you can get."

Nan must have judged that she would not be getting a better deal than the one I was offering, because she accepted. However, she could not stop herself from adding, "I don't have to like it."

"No, you don't," I said. "You just have to leave her alone."

• • •

It was not long after the meeting with Dr. Edwards that Connie arrived with an orderly to take me to a private room, away from the other burn patients. I asked her what was going on—surely this was a mistake. No, she assured me, I was supposed to get my own room, on Dr. Edwards' orders, although she didn't know why. She told me that I should just enjoy the privacy while it lasted because if it was a mistake, it would be sorted out soon enough. Rather than taking me out of the skeleton bed, they simply wheeled the whole contraption down the hall and into a smaller, but beautifully empty, room.

Empty, that is, until Sayuri arrived to demonstrate an exercise that she wanted me to start doing daily. "Dr. Edwards tells me that you are excited about working harder," she said as she laid a board lengthwise on my bed, tilted up and away from me. This board had a groove cut into it, into which she placed a two-pound silver ball. I was to push the ball up the board until it reached the top, and then gently support it as it rolled back down to the bottom. Repeat.

I used to haul hundreds of pounds of camera equipment around bedrooms on every movie shoot, and now I was relegated to pushing a ball up a wooden plank. Worse yet, even this simple task took all my concentration. I could see my bandaged face reflected in the curved silver, and the farther away I would push the ball, the farther away my reflection would move. Sayuri commended me for each success. "Perfect!" When we were finished, she effortlessly whisked away the ball as if it was—well, as if it was a two-pound ball. This tiny Japanese woman pissed me off by being stronger than I, and then pissed me off further by bowing slightly when she left my room.

• • •

When Dr. Edwards next came to my bedside, I asked about the private room. How, I quizzed, could I possibly rate such an extravagance? It was not as though I was being rewarded for good behavior, or for the hard work that I had just started and needed to continue.

Nan was running a study that she hoped to publish, she claimed, about the effects of private versus shared rooms in the treatment of burn patients. She was hoping that my case might provide some insight into patients who are switched during the process, and it was a happy accident that a room had become available. I asked if this meant I might be switched back into the shared ward at some point, and she said that she wasn't sure yet.

I assured her I would happily be her isolated little guinea pig for as long as she wanted, but added: "Are you sure there's no more to the story?"

She considered, and decided to speak a further truth—one that I had already guessed: "It is all well and good that you'll continue to accept visits from Ms. Engel, but I see no reason to subject the other patients to her as well."

I said that I respected her concern for others, and she nodded. When it was clear that neither of us had anything more to say, she nodded a second time and promptly left the room.

Visits with Marianne Engel were more enjoyable now that it was just the two of us, with no plastic curtain necessary, and since the doctors had stopped trying to force her to wear protective gowns. In part, her regular wardrobe was accepted because I was becoming healthier and the need for gowns was not as great, but, perhaps more important, it was because the medical staff had tired of having arguments with her. Marianne Engel was a visitor of whom they didn't altogether approve but for whose visits I had fought, so I suppose they decided that any risk was mine to take.

Now that we had more privacy, my talks with Marianne Engel grew more varied: how to cook vegetarian lasagna; what carnival games are played in Hamburg; the beautiful melancholy of Marcello's Oboe Concerto in D Minor; the settlement habits of West Coast Indians; why people sing in rock bands; the merits of Canadian literature as contrasted with Russian literature; how harsh winter climates shape personality; the history of European prostitution; why men are fascinated by the concept of "Heavyweight Champion of the World!"; the conversations that might occur between a Jehovah's Witness and an archaeologist; and how long chewing gum remains fresh in the mouth. My years of library visits served me well.

I asked about her Three Masters, and teasingly inquired whether such protectors were common for medieval nuns. She seriously answered that they were not but that, in fact, Heinrich Seuse also had Three Masters whose consent he needed to gain (with the same Latin prayer that she used) when he wished to speak.

My response was the obvious one: "Are yours and his the same?"

"No." Seuse's first master was St. Dominic, founder of the Dominicans, who would grant permission to speak only if the time and place were proper. The second master, St. Arsenius, would allow a conversation only if it did not promote attachment to material things. The third, St. Bernard of Clairvaux, would allow Seuse to speak only if doing so would not cause him to become disturbed emotionally.

"And your masters?"

She answered that hers were Meister Eckhart, a prominent theologian who was active during the time of Sister Marianne's youth; Mechthild von Magdeburg, the spiritual leader of the Beguines, the order that had established Engelthal; and Father Sunder, of whom she had already spoken.

When our conversation finally came around to my career in pornography, it hardly seemed like an exotic topic at all; it was just one more subject in a long conversation that seemed to include everything. Still, she was curious about the work and asked many questions that I answered as well as I could. When I finished, I asked whether it bothered her, what I had done for a career.

"Not at all," she answered, and reminded me that even St. Augustine had lived a life of pleasure before famously imploring the Lord to "make me chaste—but not yet."

The difference, I pointed out, was that I was not going to find religion as a result of my past. Marianne Engel shrugged noncommittally. I couldn't tell whether she thought that I was wrong and I would find God, or if she didn't care. But the turn in our conversation had also brought forth the subject of chastity and I asked, tentatively, whether she knew what had happened to my penis in the fire.

"I have been informed by the medical staff," she answered, "that it was lost."

So she knew, but what did she think? "And . . . ?"

"And it is a pity."

Yes, a pity, indeed. "I thought you didn't like talking to doctors."

"It was important enough to learn about your wounds that I couldn't avoid it."

That was the end of that day's discussion about my missing penis; already more than I had intended to say.

Each time she visited, Marianne Engel was more elaborately dressed than the time before, blooming into a new woman. Her wrists jangled with bracelets from the world over: Aztec, Mayan, Tonka Toy, Ojibwa. She wore plastic rings on her fingers, yellow elephants named Duke Elliphant and Ellaphant Gerald. Her sneakers were covered in sequins that made me think of a fluttering school of tropical fish. When she left my room for a cigarette, she would hold out the edges of her purple dress in a curtsey. I asked what caused the change in her fashion sense and she answered that since everyone thought she was crazy, she might as well dress the part.

It was interesting: this was her first humorous comment regarding her own mental state. I thought it might be the opening I'd been waiting for, and I asked her—pointing out that she had already discussed my burns with my doctor—with what condition she had been diagnosed. She shut down the topic by stating that the doctors simply didn't understand her particular brand of charm.

She reached into her rucksack and pulled out a small leatherbound book. She wanted to start reading it aloud to me, she said. *The Inferno,* by Dante. An interesting choice for the burn ward, I commented, and added that despite my love of literature, this was one classic that I had never read.

She smiled as if she knew something that I did not. She had a very strong feeling, she said, that I would find the story not only to my liking, but very familiar.

• • •

Marianne Engel was telling a story of her life that dated back to the fourteenth century. Now, if she could do this, surely the reader will excuse me for providing some information on Sayuri's life that I did not yet have at this point of my hospital convalescence. In defense of my jump out of the timeline, I will plead that Ms. Mizumoto told me all this later in our acquaintanceship—and at least her story is true.

Sayuri was the third child, the second daughter, of Toshiaki and Ayako Mizumoto. Her birth position was most unfortunate, because it meant that as a child she was the fifth person to bathe each night. It is tradition that Japanese family members share a single tub of bathwater and, although they rinse before getting in, the water darkens with each bather. The father goes first, and then the male members from oldest to youngest. Only then will the women bathe, again from oldest to youngest. This meant that the father, the older brother, the mother, and the older sister all used the bathwater before Sayuri. Throughout her entire childhood, she was forced every night to soak in the accumulated filth of her entire family.

Toshiaki and Ayako's union was the product of *omiai,* an arranged marriage. If not a union brimming with love, it was at least functional, as evidenced by the three children. Toshiaki worked hard hours at the office, followed by drinking and karaoke; Ayako ran the home, looking after the household finances and making sure that there was food waiting for her husband when he came home intoxicated and sung-out. They fulfilled the requirements necessary to be classified as a normal Japanese family, and all Toshiaki and Ayako wished for their children was that they meet the same requirements.

The first son, Ichiro—a name which, incidentally, means First Son—attended a good university. Therefore, he got a good job with a good salary at a good company after graduation; that's how these things work. In fact, Ichiro didn't even need to apply himself to his schoolwork after he'd been accepted, because simply attending the right university was the important thing; learning, less so. After he got his good job, he worked for a few years before he married a good Japanese girl from a good family at a good age. Coincidentally, a good age for a Japanese girl is younger than twenty-five, because that's when she turns into a "Christmas cake." Christmas cakes, as everyone knows, are desirable before the twenty-fifth but afterward quickly become stale and are put on the shelf. Ichiro's wife was twenty-three, so she was still well before her expiration date. Toshiaki and Ayako were pleased; Ichiro would inherit the family house and would tend to the parents' graves after they died.

Sayuri's sister, Chinatsu—a lovely name, meaning A Thousand Summers—also went to a good university, then got a job as an office lady for a few years, and got married at the age of twenty-four and a half. Just in time. She quit her job and embarked upon babymaking. Again, the parents were pleased.

Then it was the turn of their youngest daughter, the somewhat troublesome Sayuri. (Her name means Small Lily. If nothing else, the Japanese are expert namers.)

Sayuri was some years younger than Chinatsu. Her parents would never have gone so far as to call her an accident, but they would, on occasion, let slip that she was "not planned." Her parents would also, if pressed, admit that unplanned things can be problematic but, on the other hand, if two children were good then a third child must be one third better. So never let it be said that Sayuri's parents regretted her birth. However, Sayuri's math skills were advanced enough to tell her that adding one to two actually increases the amount by half, not one-third.

Ichiro and Chinatsu had both walked the appropriate path and had done what was expected. The pattern had been firmly established, folded neatly and put away like a fine kimono; this pattern of proper behavior was practically a family heirloom to be handed down. All Sayuri had to do, to continue the perfection of her parents' lives, was imitate the examples of her older siblings. But this, unfortunately, was the very last thing she wanted to do. If she did, she reasoned, she would be doomed to spend not only her childhood but her entire life in her family's dirty bathwater.

The problem was that Sayuri was unsure about what she *did* want to do, so she kept her mouth shut and bided her time. She worked hard enough at her high school studies, but when her parents had their backs turned, she spent all her extra time studying English. Unbeknownst to them, an Australian woman named Maggie tutored her on Tuesday nights when Sayuri's parents thought she was at volleyball practice. Sayuri went to the movies each Saturday, not for entertainment but to learn to speak like Jodie Foster, Susan Sarandon, and (unfortunately) Woody Allen. On Sunday afternoons, she went to the local museum to hunt American tourists and when she cornered one, she'd ask him whether he would speak with her for five minutes so she might practice her English. Invariably the tourist agreed, because who could refuse such cute enthusiasm? Meanwhile, Sayuri dutifully filled out applications for the correct Japanese universities and was accepted into one of them. Her parents were happy. Now Sayuri only had to graduate, work a few years as an office lady, and get off the shelf by twenty-five.

Right after her high school graduation, Sayuri visited the Australian embassy with Maggie to pick up a work visa. One week later, Sayuri called her parents long distance from the Sydney airport. Needless to say, they were less than pleased, not only with her rash and disrespectful actions but because she had not even had the courage to say goodbye before she left the country.

In truth, it was not a lack of courage that had dictated Sayuri's actions, but an excess of it. If she'd tried to reason with her parents, they never would have let her go. It would have been an argument that Sayuri could not win but one that she was unwilling to lose, so she simply did what she had to do to start a life on her own terms. At first Sayuri's parents thought she was joking—she couldn't really be calling them from Australia, could she? She couldn't really be planning to stay, could she? When they finally accepted the truth, they threatened and cajoled her. Sayuri hung up, because nothing would have changed if she'd stayed on the line.

She spent a year in Australia, moving from one job to another: waiting tables, painting houses, picking fruit, tutoring people in Japanese, and so on. All the while her tan deepened, her smile widened, and her English improved. The biggest problem with Western countries was that she often had to shop in the children's section to find clothes that fit her, as she was small even for a Japanese woman. (This was why she was destined to spend her life abroad looking like a child's doll.) Sayuri called her parents once a month—always from a different pay phone—to let them know that she was all right and to listen politely as they begged her to return. Sometimes, Ichiro lent the weight of his oldest-son voice to the argument. Sayuri ignored his commands as well.

When Sayuri's visa ran out, she returned to Japan. Her mother cried and her father yelled, even though a part of him admired what she had done. Sayuri informed them that she was going to attend an American university to study for a degree. Over the next year, she worked three part-time jobs, passed the necessary English-language proficiency exams, and got accepted by the department of physical therapy at the University of Michigan. When it was time to leave once more, her mother cried another Japanese river. The father, however, had by this point accepted the ridiculous ideas of his youngest daughter. When Toshiaki offered to cover some of the tuition, Sayuri hugged him long and hard. He didn't quite know what to do about that, so he stood as ramrod straight as he could.

Sayuri completed her degree with honors and accepted a job in the hospital where she would, eventually, meet me. Long before I came along, she had paid back every yen her father had given her for her education.

• • •

Dr. Hnatiuk came by my room every few days to pass along a new psychology book. I was starting to like him. It's not easy for me to pinpoint when my feelings turned, as there was no moment of revelation in which I exclaimed: "Hey, the chipmunk's not so bad after all." He crept up on me. The most important thing was that he stopped trying to relate to me in a doctor–patient capacity, and simply let the conversation flow naturally. There was also the fact that he liked the gargoyle statue that Marianne Engel had given me, while Beth had called it a "horrible little thing." What really sold me on Gregor, however, was that despite his milquetoast exterior, he was a passionate man who cared deeply about his job. One afternoon he spoke at length about how lawyers have, in his opinion, been the biggest enemy of psychiatric care over the last half century. He told me how they fought for the rights of the patient—which was good—but to the point that a patient who was eating his own excrement could no longer be held for observation. "Leave it to the lawyers to turn shit into health food."

As the weeks passed, a physical change occurred in Gregor. He lost his tasseled loafers and ill-advised corduroys and began wearing clothes that almost seemed to fit properly. Even if they couldn't be considered quite "stylish," they were at least passable. He'd been exercising to the point that the glow in his cheeks no longer looked as if it came from climbing a flight of stairs too quickly, and he was losing some of the excess fat from around his midsection.

Gregor never asked why I was reading psychology books, but he was willing to answer every question I had about schizophrenia. Although I had never mentioned her name in any of our discussions, one day I let it slip (not quite accidentally) that I was doing my research because I feared that a friend of mine SHE'S NOT YOUR FRIEND might be suffering from the condition. SHE'S JUST A CRAZY WOMAN.

"I know," Gregor said. "Marianne Engel."

Gregor seemed satisfied to have proven himself a step ahead of me, but I assumed he'd been consulted when Dr. Edwards tried to convince me not to encourage her visits. Gregor had actually treated her several times, he said, the last being when she had been admitted for "talking to ghosts" in public. SEE? I asked why he'd never told me before this. He cited the Hippocratic oath, and added that he'd say no more about her than he already had.

"Furthermore," he added, "I will neither confirm nor deny a diagnosis of schizophrenia."

Gregor also pointed out that he never mentioned the content of our conversations to anyone. I told him that he was free to repeat whatever he wanted, because I was not his patient. To this, he countered that we were still in a hospital where I was a patient and he was a doctor, so he considered this reason enough for confidentiality. I voiced my opinion that psychiatrists were generally useless and that I really didn't care what they (meaning *he*) thought about me.

"Oh, it might be true that many of us could do better," Gregor conceded, "but we have our moments. For example, out of your many personality flaws, I can diagnose your largest."

"And what's that?"

"You think you're smarter than everyone else."

• • •

With the exception of the periods when she disappeared for almost a week at a time, Marianne Engel was now coming to the burn ward almost every day. She started helping with my exercise sessions, placing her hands underneath the pad of my foot on the intact leg and providing resistance as I pushed like a one-legged bicyclist.

"I talked to Dr. Edwards," she said. "She's given me permission to bring you some food."

Since she was now talking to my doctor, I asked whether she would give me permission to discuss her case with one of the doctors who had treated her. Specifically, Dr. Hnatiuk.

She answered that she didn't want me discussing her case with anyone, and was offended that I would even ask. Of all people, she said, I should know that she was not crazy.

There was a moment of awkward silence between us, until Marianne Engel snapped it in half by saying, "Paracelsus wrote a recipe for a burn salve that included boar fat, worms from a hanged man's skull, and part of a mummy. The whole stew was roasted." She then proceeded to educate me about the history of skin grafting, from its beginnings with the ancient Hindus through to the present times. I pulled up one of the bandages on my legs to show her my current grafts, which included some black skin. Because a mesher had been used to cut the skin into a net so it could stretch over a larger area, the resulting pattern resembled a distorted chessboard.

"If ever you were a racist," she said, running her fingers over the game board of my body, "this would certainly be a hair in your soup."

Her fingers were gentle lingering over the wasteland. They moved across my torso and towards my neck, pausing at the shoulders to follow the curves. "What is it like to wear another person's skin?"

"I don't have a good answer for that," I said. "It hurts."

"Can you remember their stories? Can you feel the love that they felt?"

It was difficult, sometimes, to know whether Marianne Engel was actually looking for an answer, or just teasing me. "Are you serious?"

"It makes me think of us," she continued. "It makes me want to sew myself to you like skin."

I cleared my throat.

"Did you know," she asked, "that my body is marked too?"

I had some idea what she was talking about. When she wore T-shirts it was impossible not to notice the tattoos of Latin phrases that circled her upper biceps. On the left arm was the phrase *Certum est quia impossibile est.* I asked what it meant, and she said that it translated as "It is certain because it is impossible." On her right arm was the phrase *Quod me nutrit, me destruit.* This, she said, meant, "That which nourishes me also destroys me."

"I don't get it," I confessed.

She laughed. "Well, that's only because you haven't seen me carve yet."

Then Marianne Engel did this one small thing. She touched my face.

It's a tiny thing, to have your face touched. Isn't it? But think again about the burnt and unbeloved beasts of the world. Think about the people whose skin cannot remember affection. Her fingers moved gently over my disaster, reaching under the bandages to touch the remains of my face. Her fingers traveled lovingly across my bandaged cheek, making the arduous journey to my lips. They rested softly there, for only a moment. I closed my charred eyelids, little scars reconnecting at the places where weeks before they had been sewn shut. My heart danced clumsily in the cavern of my chest and, all the while, my sealed pores were working overtime, not sweating.

"What does my face feel like?"

"Like the desert after a windstorm."

I had an overwhelming urge to tell her that I was beautiful before the accident, but I didn't. What would be the point? And then, I reached out with my good hand to touch her cheek. She didn't pull back: no. Not even in the least.

"There are good things happening," Marianne Engel whispered, before she stood up to go into the corners of my room to speak with her invisible Three Masters. It was apparent, even in Latin, that she was asking for permission to do something. *"Jube, Domine benedicere."*

When she returned to my bedside, her smile indicated that her request had been granted. "Would you like to see my other tattoos?"

I nodded, and she began by sweeping at the unruly mess of her hair, pulling it up so the back of her neck was exposed. A small cross was inked there, an intertwining of three braided ropes without end. She asked me to touch it. I did. I ran my fingers over its height, then its width; literally making the sign of the cross, on her skin.

She took off her shoes. Around her left ankle was the tattooed chain of a beaded rosary, inked so the cross lay across the bridge of her foot. This way, she said, she'd always be prepared when she needed to do penance. But she was smiling, and it was clear that even she didn't take this statement too seriously.

Next, she removed her pants—which I did not expect, because somehow the movies have conditioned me to think that women always undress from the top down. She was not wearing underwear, so she was left only in her white T-shirt with a picture of Beethoven drinking himself under a table. (The caption? "Beethoven's Ninth.")

There was a snake tattooed along the full length of her right leg, in exactly the same spot where the dragon had been embroidered on her pants. It twisted around her, just the way biblical representations invariably have the snake wrapped around the trunk of the Tree of Knowledge of Good and Evil. Marianne Engel was facing me, and I could see the body of the snake first appear at the knee, crawling upwards and wrapping itself twice around the thigh, with its diamond head coming to rest at her pelvis, angled in towards her vagina.

Her eyes were fixed upon me. She pulled off her Beethoven shirt, though it was a struggle to get it over her hair, until she was standing in the middle of my room entirely nude, save the arrowhead necklace that dangled around her throat.

There had been moments in the burn ward that I had felt the pangs of arousal. Maddy had done her best to tease me with her lilting ass, and sometimes she even twisted her head around to check if it was having an effect. But this was the first time that I found myself fully sexually aroused. Mentally, at least; I still produced the hormones that direct blood to produce an erection, I just didn't have anywhere into which that blood could rush. I imagined it collecting there, making my groin blush.

There was another cross, much larger than the one on the back of her neck, drawn on her stomach. It was Celtic in shape, its four arms meeting in a round joint at the center. The entire thing was enclosed in an oval, longer in height than width, covering the area from the top of her pelvic bone to the bottom of her rib cage. Three large block letters—"IHS"—were scripted directly above the oval's upper curve.

On her left breast was a large tattoo of the Sacred Heart, bright red and encircled with a crown of thorns. The heart was engulfed in yellow flames that burned upwards, towards her shoulder.

She came to my bed, so that I might study the details of her well-inked body, and she told me to touch the name of Christ. I did, and goose pimples spread across her skin under my good hand.

She turned so that she was sitting on the edge of my bed with her back to me. Angel wings extended from her upper shoulders to her buttocks, where the pointed tips came to rest. The wings filled the entirety of her back and I could not help but lift my hand towards them. It was as if I felt I had the right to touch her skin, as if it were mine to touch. It took a moment before I realized this was not—could not be—the case, and my arm paused in midair. It hung there unsure until Marianne Engel said, without turning around: "I want you to touch me."

So I reached the rest of the way, and I traced my fingers along the lines of her inky plumage. They were a combination of bold and intensely delicate strokes, detailed with such skill that you'd swear they were downy. Now the flesh of her back quivered, and my heart did the same.

After a few moments, she looked shyly over her shoulder. She smiled—nervously, excitedly—and I broke my fingertip contact. She got up and began putting her clothes back on. We did not speak. When she was dressed, she left the room.

◆ ◆ ◆

There are no conclusive studies on the best time to remove casts from burn patients, as muscle atrophy inevitably complicates matters. In the end, Dr. Edwards had to go with her gut in choosing a day to remove the mechaspider from my leg.

The removal brought great glee to Sayuri, who had been itching to get me out of bed. She smacked her hands together twice with a great dramatic flourish. "Are you ready? Are you *genki*? It's time!"

Maddy and Beth were there to help, dressed in blue gowns and big yellow gloves. They stretched out my muscles for a few minutes before pedaling my feet to lessen the stiffness in my legs. Then each nurse looped an arm behind my back to lift me into a standing position, and held me while the dizziness dispelled. Gradually, they loosened their grips until I was supporting my own weight.

For the first time since the accident, I was standing. Sayuri called out the seconds that passed with a too-loud voice—"... six ... seven ... eight!"—before my legs turned from uncooked to cooked spaghetti. All in a moment, blood rushed down my body as if remembering how gravity works, and gushed from my donor sites. My leg bandages blushed, embarrassed by their ineffectiveness; the moment of my swooning had arrived.

The women laid me back into the bed and cheered my efforts. When my mind calmed from its vertical lift, I saw that Dr. Edwards was standing in the doorway with a delighted smile.

Before the attempt, I would have said—in my best macho, smart-ass manner—that the results wouldn't matter much. Standing was too stupid to be even a child's game. If you allowed yourself to care about standing, who knew what you'd care about next? Although I didn't want to feel good about the cheers, they sounded genuine. The women were proud of me and, against my better judgment, I was proud of myself as well.

Instead of brushing my accomplishment off, I became a grinning idiot. I thanked everyone for their help and my only regret was that Marianne Engel hadn't been there to see it.

◆ ◆ ◆

I expected to sleep soundly that evening, but I did not. With sleep came the nastiness.

That night I dreamt that Sayuri had stood me up and then abruptly let me go. My tumbledown body crumpled; I could feel the snake of my spine coil and twist. YOU THINK YOU CAN

`STAND ON YOUR OWN?` Nan threw darts at my neutralized bulk while the nurses high-fived my failure. I looked under the skeleton bed. There were flames, a thousand candles. I wanted to reach out to extinguish them but it was as if someone had disconnected the muscles in my arms, rendering me a stringless puppet. The flames made angry smiling faces at me and their blazing cloven tongues licked the sheets on the skeleton bed, sparking them like a burning shroud. Bones crashed down around me, rattling furiously like a collapsing scaffold.

The medical staff continued laughing. One of them announced in a harsh German voice: "𝔄lles brennt, wenn die 𝔉lamme nur heiß genug ist. 𝔇ie 𝔚elt ist nichts als ein 𝔖chmelztiegel." Apparently in dreams, I am like Marianne Engel in real life: multilingual. *Everything burns if the flame is hot enough. The world is nothing but a crucible.*

I was trapped under the bones as the shroud continued burning. The faces in the flames kept smiling their hateful smiles, their treacherous tongues licking, licking, licking. `I AM COMING AND THERE IS NOTHING YOU CAN DO ABOUT IT.` I heard the whiz of arrows. I felt them hit my hands, and I felt them hit my feet.

I dreamed a long, long time of burning and when it finally ended and I awoke, the hovering effect created by the air flotation bed confused me. It took a few moments before I became certain about which side of consciousness I lay on.

♦ ♦ ♦

I told Marianne Engel about my success in standing for eight seconds on the first day I tried, and my even greater success in standing for thirteen seconds on the second. She attempted to give proper respect to my achievements, but it was apparent that she was distracted by something.

"What's wrong?"

"Hmm? No, no, nothing is pinching me." She ran her fingers over the very noticeable bump, which had been growing larger by the day, on my shoulder. "What's this?"

"It's called tissue expansion."

I explained that under the skin was a small silicone balloon, and every day the doctors were injecting a little more salt water into it. As the balloon inflated my skin stretched with it, just as when a person puts on weight. Eventually, the balloon would be drained and I'd be left with a flap of extra skin, which would then be transplanted from my shoulder to a recipient site on my neck.

"How fascinating. I wish I could've done something like that for you the first time."

"What?"

"Never mind." She touched the bump again, and smiled. "Do you know, that growth makes me think of the boils that come with the Black Plague."

"What?"

"I have this friend. . . ." Her words trailed off, and she lost her thoughts in the air. For a few minutes she sat, staring into space, but rather than being still, her hands fluttered more than they did when she was flipping unlit cigarettes or touching her necklace. They looked as if they wanted to open up and release a story that she was withholding from me.

Eventually, she nodded in the direction of my bedside table. On it was the stack of psychology books that she always had made a pointed effort of not asking about. "You're studying up on me," she said. "Should I rent one of your porn films to understand you better?"

This—though I thought I'd not indicated it to her in any way—was something I hoped she would never do. I asked her to promise that she would never view one of my films.

"I have told you that I don't care," she said. "Are you ashamed?"

I assured her I wasn't; I just didn't want her to watch them. This was the truth, but not all of it: I didn't want her to watch them because I didn't want her to see what I had been, and compare it with what I had become. I didn't want her to see my handsomeness, my smooth skin, my toned body, and then have to look upon the hideousness blotted across the bed in front of her. I realized this was unreasonable, and that of course she knew there was a time when I was unburned, but I didn't want it to become more real to her. If she could accept me as I was, perhaps it was only because she had no point of comparison.

Marianne Engel went to my window and stared out it for a moment, before she turned and blurted, "I hate leaving you, and I wish I could always be at your bedside. I need you to understand that it's beyond my control when I get my instructions."

This was one of the rare instances in which I understood exactly what was going on inside her: she had a secret that she wanted to share, but knew it was the kind of secret that most people could not understand. It was vital to say it aloud, but she was worried that it would sound absurd. Like, for example, explaining that you have a snake living in your spine.

"When I'm about to work, I sleep on the stone," Marianne Engel began, with a deep breath, "for twelve hours at least, but usually more. It's preparation. When I lie on the stone, I can feel it. I can feel *all* of it, everything inside. It's . . . warm. My body sinks into the contours and then I feel weightless, like I'm floating. I sort of—lose the ability to move. But it's wonderful; it's the opposite of numbness. It's more like being so aware, so hyperaware, that I can't move because it's so overwhelming."

"What do you mean," I asked, "when you say you can feel what's inside the stone?"

"I absorb the dreams of the stone, and the gargoyles inside tell me what I need to do to free them. They reveal their faces and show me what I must take away to make them whole. When I have enough information, I begin. My body wakes but there is no sense of time, there's nothing but the work. Days pass before I realize that I haven't slept and I've barely eaten. It's like I'm digging a survivor out from underneath the avalanche of time, which has been collecting for

eons and all at once has come sliding down the mountain. The gargoyles have always been in the stone but, at this precise instant, it becomes unbearable for them to remain. They've been hibernating in
the winter of the stone, and the spring is in my chisel. If I can carve
away the right pieces the gargoyle comes forth like a flower out of
a rocky embankment. I'm the only one who can do it, because I
understand their languages and I'm the only one who can give them
the hearts necessary to begin their new lives."

She paused and seemed to be waiting for me to say something,
anything—but how does one respond to proclamations such as
these? Because she wanted a prompt and I wanted her to continue
talking, I said it sounded like an extremely creative process.

"No, it's the opposite. I'm a vessel that water is poured into and
splashes out of. It's a circle, a flowing circle between God and the
gargoyles and me, because that is what God is—a circle whose center
is everywhere and whose circumference is nowhere. And the entire
time I'm carving, the gargoyle's voice becomes louder and louder. I
work as fast as I can because I want the voice to stop, but it keeps urging me on, demanding that I help it achieve its freedom. The voice
goes silent only when I'm finished, and then I'm so exhausted that
it's my turn to sleep. So that's why I disappear for five or six days at a
time. It takes that long to free a gargoyle and then recover myself. I
have no say in when a gargoyle will be ready, and I cannot refuse. So
forgive my disappearances, because I have no choice."

• • •

Okay, fine. At least now I knew what she was doing with the multiple hearts she thought were in her chest. They were going into the
statues she carved.

I had been certain that Marianne Engel was schizophrenic, but
given her description of her work habits I now had to consider that
she might be manic-depressive instead. Evidence was mounting in
that direction: when I first met her, she was fatigued and darkly at-

tired; now she was bright in both dress and personality. Schizophrenics tend to eschew talking, sometimes remaining completely silent for hours on end, but Marianne Engel was just the opposite. And there was the nature of her work. Many manic-depressives achieve fame in the arts because the condition itself provides the fervor necessary to create something monumental. Which, of course, was exactly what Marianne Engel did: create monuments. If her account of her carving habits was not a description of a manic at work, I can't imagine what is.

But there was also so much evidence for schizophrenia. She described the voices that came out of the stone, giving her instructions. She saw herself as a channel of the Divine, and her work as a circle of communication between God, the gargoyles, and herself. This is not to mention her Engelthal "past" and her belief that *Inferno* was appropriate reading material for the burn ward. In short, there was very little in her life that was not touched in some way by Christianity, and, as previously noted, schizophrenics are often preoccupied with religion.

Statistics could argue for either condition. Schizophrenia tends to affect men more often than women, but more than eighty percent of schizophrenics smoke heavily, and Marianne Engel was constantly popping out of the burn ward for a nicotine hit. And while speaking to me, she always had that unnerving stare, which kept her eyes locked upon mine: this only started to make sense after I read in one of Gregor's books that schizophrenics rarely blink.

Refusal to take one's medication is common to both conditions, but for different reasons. A manic-depressive is likely to refuse her meds because in her high she becomes convinced that a low is no longer possible, or she is so addicted to the high that the low becomes simply the price that must be paid. Schizophrenics, on the other hand, tend to refuse medication because they believe they're being poisoned—a claim that Marianne Engel had made on more than one occasion.

Many doctors are now convinced that the two conditions co-exist far more often than commonly diagnosed, so maybe both diagnoses applied.

In the hours I spent leafing through mental health texts in an effort to understand her better, I came to understand myself better as well—and I was not altogether pleased with what I learned.

I was constantly measuring her pain against my own, telling myself that she couldn't possibly understand my physical anguish while I *did* understand the nature of mental pain. And while many mental illnesses are treatable with the correct medication, there was no pill that would allow me to pass for normal. A medicated wack job could blend into the crowd but I would always stand out like a burnt thumb from the fist of humanity: this made me feel like the winner in a competition that didn't really exist.

◆ ◆ ◆

Marianne Engel arrived the next day in a simple white dress with open-toed sandals, and she might have passed for a woman from a seaside village on the Mediterranean. She appeared with two food hampers, one blue and one white, and I could tell they were heavy from the way she lugged them into the room. Bent over as she was, the arrowhead on her necklace bobbed in and out of the V-neck of her dress like a lure on a fishing line. "I'm finally going to live up to my promise to feed you."

I'll take a moment to explain why Dr. Edwards would allow a visitor to bring food into the burn ward. In addition to the psychological benefits of a picnic (as it were), there was also a physical one. With my healing came a condition known as hypermetabolism: a body that normally requires two thousand calories a day can consume seven thousand after a severe burn. Despite the nasogastric tube that constantly delivered nourishment directly into my stomach, I was still not getting enough and I was allowed, even encouraged, to eat extra food.

Marianne Engel had previously brought me snacks, but it was obvious that this meal was far more substantial. She opened the hampers—one for hot items and the other, packed with ice, for cool—and started to lay out the food. There was a freshly baked round of focaccia, still smelling of wood smoke, and bottles of olive oil and balsamic vinegar. She danced a swirl of black across the surface of the yellow, and then dipped a chunk of the focaccia into the leoparded liquid. She said the familiar prayer before she lifted the bread to my mouth: *"Jube, Domine benedicere."*

She'd also brought cheeses: Camembert, Gouda, blue, Iranian goat. She asked my favorite and when I picked the goat, she smiled broadly. Next, some steaming wraps that looked like crepes but had a most bawdy smell. Gorgonzola pancakes were not for everyone, she explained, but she hoped I liked them. I did. There were cantaloupe balls wrapped in thin slices of prosciutto, the fruity orange peeking through the meaty pink.

She continued to excavate the hampers. Bastardly plump green olives, fat with red pimiento stuffing, lounged contentedly in a yellow bowl. A plateful of tomatoes soaked in black vinegar with snowy nuggets of bocconcini. Sheaves of pita and cups brimming with hummus and tzatziki. Oysters, crabs, and scallops drowning a wonderful death in a marinara ocean; little wedges of lemon balanced on the plate's edge like life preservers waiting to be thrown in. Pork sausages with peppercorn rims. Dolmathes, trying hard to be swarthy and macho in their little green suits, scented with sweet red wine. Thick rings of calamari. Souvlaki shared skewers with sweet buttered onions and braised peppers. There was a shoulder of lamb so well cooked it fell apart if you only looked at it while thinking about a fork, surrounded by a happy little family of roast potatoes.

I sat trapped under the culinary avalanche, unable to move for fear of tipping a plate over. "There's no way we can eat all this."

"Finishing isn't the point." She pulled a bottle out of the chilled hamper. "Besides, I'm sure the nurses will be happy to help with the leftovers. You won't tell them I was drinking alcohol, will you? I like retsina because you can taste the earth in it."

The nurses soon hovered around the door like a flock of hungry seagulls. I felt a strange manly pride, the one we get when being seen on a date with a beautiful woman. The nurses giggled and made a few comments before dispersing to their rounds. Marianne Engel lifted morsel after morsel to my lips. "Try this. . . . You're going to love it. . . . Have more."

We made a determined effort, but it was predestined that we'd never be able to finish the meal. When we gave up, she brought out a slim metal thermos and poured Greek coffee into two demitasses. It was so chuggingly thick that it took a good thirty seconds to pour out. Then she brought out the dessert: baklava so honey-dense that it oozed like a charitable beehive. Tricolor gelato, green white red. And of course bougatsa, her dog's namesake—light brown pastry with custard between layers of phyllo.

"Would you like to hear a story?" Marianne Engel asked. "It's got true love, brotherly devotion, and arrows that find the mark."

"Is it about you again?"

"No, it's about my good friend Francesco Corsellini."

VI.

If there was one thing that Graziana knew for certain, it was that her beloved Francesco was a good man. He was a blacksmith in their hometown of Firenze and he toiled at his craft, always trying to forge a better horseshoe or a stronger sword. Sometimes he lost track of the hours and stopped only when Graziana appeared in the door of his shop to suggest that he pay a little less attention to his fire and more attention to his wife. She joked that he must have done something very bad in his past life to be preparing so diligently for Hell. He would laugh, promising to come right away, and Graziana would laugh, too. She knew that Hell was the last place her husband would end up.

Francesco would never be known as "the finest sword maker in all of Italy" or "the great metal worker of Firenze," but this didn't matter to him. He wanted to be a good tradesman, a dependable blacksmith with honest prices, but his real desire was to be a great husband. He crafted beautiful gifts for Graziana in his metal shop—candleholders, cutlery, and the most wondrous jewelry. He always claimed that his greatest achievements as a metal worker were the wedding rings that he had forged for himself and Graziana. In one room of their home, there was a collection of metal toys for the baby they were attempting to conceive. He dreamed of the day that he would be the loving father to her children.

He was no great beauty, this Francesco Corsellini, but then again neither was his wife. He was a little too hairy for some women, and his steely arms extended from a body built on too much pasta and beer. Graziana would call him L'Orsacchiotto—The Bear—and poke his stomach, and Francesco would respond, "I have earned this. It is relaxed muscle!"

Graziana had thick hair and dark eyes but the rest of her was undistinguished. Still, when Francesco told her she was the most beautiful woman in all of Italy, he believed it. They had been childhood sweethearts and there was rarely a day that he did not thank God for having her as his wife.

They were happy. She was kind. He was devoted. Need more be said?

Unfortunately, yes.

The year was 1347 and a new disease had just arrived from China, the most horrible disease that anyone had ever seen. It swept outward from the ports, into the cities and the Italian countryside, killing people as a forest fire destroys trees. In towns, church bells rang incessantly because it was believed the sound would drive out the illness. Many people thought that the smell of the dead carried the disease, so they walked about with scented handkerchiefs over their faces. Incense burned everywhere, mingling with the stench of death. . . .

And one day, Graziana felt a fever in the afternoon. She retired to her bedroom for a nap. When she woke up that evening, she discovered a boil the size of an egg in her groin, and swelling under her armpits. She knew that the Black Death was upon her.

In the kitchen, Francesco was preparing food. She yelled at him to leave, immediately, because she had the illness. *"Gavoccioli!"* she yelled. Buboes. She demanded that he save himself, because everyone knew that there was no cure, no hope. She implored, "Leave! Leave now!"

There was a stillness in the kitchen. Graziana lay in her bed, listening to the silence that covered the distance between her and her husband. Then she heard him begin to clank the pots and pans to cover the sound of his crying. This continued for some minutes; then Francesco's footsteps came down the hall towards her. She yelled and cursed and insisted that he stay away, but he appeared in the doorway with a tray of pasta and some wine.

"You will feel better if you eat, even just a little," Francesco said. He entered the room, put the tray down, and sat beside her. And then he moved to kiss her.

Graziana tried to pull away. It was the first and only time in her life she attempted to refuse him but Francesco used his blacksmith's strength to force himself upon her and kissed all her protests back into her mouth. After a few seconds, she realized it was useless to fight and she accepted him. It was done.

They ate a little that night and lay down. Through the window, the full moon looked in on them. *"La luna è tenera,"* Francesco said. The moon is tender. He closed his eyes and held her tighter. The last thing Graziana saw that night was his sleeping face. When she awoke the next morning, his face was the first thing she saw in the new day. She had a terrible fever, a sheen of sweat upon her, and a galloping pulse.

"Look," he said gently, "the dark spots have come to your skin." Graziana began to weep, but Francesco smiled and stroked her hair. "Don't cry. We don't have time for tears. Let us love while we still can."

That very afternoon, Graziana fell into the worst of it. For three days, they lay together. For three days, Graziana went about dying horrendously in his arms while he told her stories about swans and miracles and great loves. On the third midnight of her illness, Francesco awoke to her tortured breathing. She turned her face to his.

"This is it."

He said, "I will see you soon."

Francesco kissed Graziana one final time, taking her final breath deep into his chest. *"Ti amo,"* she said. I love you.

After she passed, Francesco slipped the wedding ring from her finger. He, too, was now deeply ill, but he pulled himself out of bed. He could barely stand, crippled by the nausea and fever, but he forced himself into his blacksmith shop. There was one thing left to do.

He lit the fire and heated the forge. He melted both wedding rings, his and hers, and poured them into an arrowhead mold. When the arrowhead was completed, he set it onto a shaft. He looked down the length of the arrow, ensuring it was as straight and true as any he had ever made.

Francesco pulled down the crossbow that was pinned to his wall. It had belonged to his father, a great archer who had been killed in battle when Francesco and his brother Bernardo were still babies. This crossbow, which had been returned to Firenze by a fellow warrior, was the only possession of his father's that Francesco had owned. Beyond this one thing, he did not even have memories of the man.

He returned to the bedroom, to Graziana's body. He reached through the open window and placed the arrow and the crossbow outside. It was now dawn and he called out to a passing boy, so that he could send a message to his brother who lived in another part of town. Within the hour, Bernardo was standing outside the bedroom window.

Francesco implored his brother to come no closer, for fear that he'd pass on the disease. Francesco asked one final favor.

"Anything," Bernardo said. "I will honor your final request."

After Francesco made his appeal, he sat on the bed, facing the window. Between heaving sobs, Bernardo lifted the crossbow and put the arrow into place. He took a deep breath, braced his body, and asked the spirit of his father to guide the arrow to its target. Bernardo released the string and let the arrow fly. The shot was precise and death was instant.

Francesco fell backwards into the bed, beside his Graziana, with the arrowhead made of their wedding rings lodged solidly in his heart. He died as he lived, in love.

VII.

No one will ever accuse me of being overly romantic, because after Marianne Engel finished telling the story the first thing I said was "Don't you find it depressing that they both died from the plague?"

I leave to your imagination the tone of her voice when she said that no, she did not find this story of love "depressing."

After she left, I examined the story from a number of different angles. It was quixotic: old Italy, sacrifice, devotion, and wedding rings shot clean through the Heart of the Soul's True Husband. Intellectually, I came to the conclusion that the point of the story probably wasn't that the pair died from a hideous illness but that there was something poignant in Francesco's gestures. Nevertheless, if it were I in the kitchen making noodles and my wife started shrieking about her elephantine boils, I'd be out the back door before you could say Jack Robinson.

• • •

I waited a few days for Marianne Engel to return, anxious to report that upon reflection I had decided Francesco was not a complete moron. I wanted to show her that I was growing as a person, as they say in clichéd psychojargon, because she needed to be kept abreast of these developments. When she didn't come, I wondered whether she had been called into the service of the gargoyles or whether I had blown it with my unromantic comments. And then my walnut-sized brain started working again: *Blown what?* How could I have allowed myself, even for a moment, to imagine us a couple? IDIOT.

Beth came to my bed with a package that she said just had been delivered by courier. I ripped it open to find a note on brown parchment. The handwriting looked as though it had been done with a quill, centuries before, and the letters swooped with a kind of penmanship no longer taught.

Dear One,

I will be working for the next few days.
The spirit has inhabited me once more.
Gargoyles ache to be born.

Be with you soon,
M.

It pleased me to discover that she was not absent because of anything that I had done to keep her away; the reason was simply another carving session.

There was a soap opera on television. Edward had amnesia again, and Pamela's long-lost sister had just returned from her missionary work in Africa. I pushed my ball bearing up the board. I watched my silver face roll away. I pedaled my feet. More skin was harvested. The morphine continued to drip. The snake continued to lick at the base of my skull. I AM COMING, AND THERE IS NOTHING YOU CAN DO ABOUT IT. And there was more: ASSHOLE, LOSER, WHINER, ADDICT, DEMON, MONSTER, DEVIL, FIEND, BEAST, BRUTE, GOBLIN, HAS-

BEEN, NEVER-WAS, NEVER-WILL-BE, UNLOVED, UNLOVABLE, UNPERSON.

Ah, what did the fucking bitchsnake know? Marianne Engel had called me "Dear One."

I thought about Francesco working in the heat of his metal shop. I thought about Graziana eating pasta on her bubonic bed, just a little bit so that she would feel better. I thought about lovers in their time of dying. I tried to imagine being so thoroughly devoted that I would die for someone else; I, who found it difficult enough to imagine living for myself. And then I tried to envision what might happen when I was finally released from the burn unit, and how my relationship with Marianne Engel would change.

The hospital was an insular environment in which I found her eccentricities colorful, but where they had no real ability to affect my daily life in a negative way. I was protected by the regularity of my schedule, and the staff tolerated her because I had fought for her visits and because I had no other friends—except, perhaps, Gregor. As I had only seen her in such a limited, and limiting, environment, I had to wonder: in the real world, how much further might Marianne Engel's weirdness go?

When she spoke about the multiple hearts in her chest, or her life seven hundred years previous, it was a nice diversion from the monotony. Sometimes it made me uneasy, but mostly it gave me a secret thrill to think that she felt a "magic connection" with me. But how would I have reacted to her if I had met her before the accident? No doubt, I would have dismissed her with a wave of my hand and continued on my way. Just another lunatic. In the hospital, of course, I couldn't walk away.

A time would come when I could, if I wanted to.

• • •

The monastic Marianne Engel, last seen as a child in the early fourteenth century, had been about to start her training in the Engelthal

scriptorium. Such institutions had been around for several hundred
years, since Charlemagne had ordered that copying rooms be established for the preservation of important written works. In the beginning, of course, bookmaking was almost exclusively devoted to
preserving the Word of the Lord.

The scribe's task was not easy. He—or, at Engelthal, *she*—had
only simple tools: knives, inkhorns, chalk, razors, sponges, lead
points, rulers, and awls. Out of concern for the safety of the books,
no candles were allowed in the scriptorium. If it was a cold time of
year, the scribe could not even warm her hands. The value of the
books was such that the writing rooms were often set at the top
of an attack-proof tower; the books themselves carried inscriptions
warning about the consequences of theft or vandalism. A typical
passage might suggest that a book thief would fall into sickness, be
seized by fever, be broken on the wheel, *and* be hanged. Not just one
of these fates, but all in succession.

It was a rigorous life, but the scribe could remind herself that
each word she copied was both a mark that would count in her favor on Judgment Day and a weapon against Satan. The Archenemy,
however, is not the kind to take such attacks without retribution,
and so He sent Titivillus, the patron demon of calligraphy, to strike
back.

Titivillus was a tricky little bastard. Despite the scribe's best intentions, the work itself was repetitive and boring. The mind would
wander and mistakes would be made. It was the duty of Titivillus to
fill his sack a thousand times each day with manuscript errors. These
were hauled to Satan, where they would be recorded in The Book of
Errors and used against the scribe on Judgment Day. Thus, the work
of copying came with a risk to the scribe: while properly transcribed
words were positive marks, incorrectly transcribed words were negative marks.

But the Devil's ploy backfired. The knowledge that Titivillus was
at work inspired the scribes to produce more accurate transcriptions.
Eventually, Titivillus was no longer able to fill his sacks and was de-

moted to lurking in churches, recording the names of women who gossiped during Mass.

In any case, the typical script employed by a medieval scribe was called Gothic minuscule—interestingly enough, the same script that Marianne Engel used in her everyday penmanship. Which doesn't necessarily prove anything, but I would be remiss if I didn't mention the fact.

• • •

Six days since Marianne Engel had sent the note. Five days since the most recent patch of flesh had been moved from one part of my body to another. Four days since I had stood for thirty-seven seconds. Three days since my last conversation with Gregor. Two days since I had stood for forty-six seconds, propped up by the ever energetic Sayuri Mizumoto. One day since I'd reverted to spending most of my time thinking about suicide.

When Gregor dropped in, I could see he was still exercising, but there remained a little flab under his chin that he could not get rid of. His newly trimmed goatee helped to hide it, and I complimented him on his improving appearance and asked who the woman was.

He quickly responded that there was no woman. Too quickly, in fact. Sensing that he had tipped his hand, he changed his strategy and tried to shrug it off as casual, but only came across as guilty.

It's a strange but consistent trait of people who consider themselves unattractive. They look embarrassed if you suggest that they might be interested in someone; because they feel unworthy of receiving attention, they also deny that they would dare to give it.

We were not yet close enough for me to pry, so when Gregor attempted to change the topic, I let him.

• • •

Sayuri came bouncing into my room, speaking in italics. *"Good morning! Do you have a moment to talk about your treatment?"*

I told her I did not. My voice was a dull thud that jangled with metallic edges, like a cutlery tray being dropped to the ground. It was precisely the effect I'd hoped to achieve.

"Shock!" Sayuri exclaimed, covering her mouth with her hand before assuring me that laughter is indeed the best medicine, and began explaining that she was there to conduct a series of tests on my strength and dexterity. My body's abilities, she explained, were "yet to be determined," so she would use an instrument called a goniometer to measure the range of motion in my joints. She took hold of my arms and bent them at the elbows, jotting down the results in a little book. She then tested my legs, discovering that my right knee (the one that had been so badly busted) did not have much give. She duly noted this also in her little book. "A bit of a problem."

Next, to gauge sensation in various parts of my body, she jabbed at me with a goddamn stick and asked how it felt. I told her it felt like she was jabbing me with a goddamn stick. Oh, how she laughed; what a fine comedian I was.

Sayuri handed over her pen to my undamaged hand and asked me to write a phrase into her book. I wrote, unsteadily, *Where is she?* (It is another example of my stellar luck that the fire spared my right hand, when I was born left-handed.) Sayuri paid no attention to the words I wrote; she was interested only in my dexterity. She moved the pen to my left hand, the one missing a finger and a half, and asked me to write another sentence. I managed to scribble out the words *Fuck this.* Sayuri looked at my literary undertaking, and commented that at least it was legible.

She wrapped things up by saying that I'd soon have an exercise program, and that was pretty exciting! "We'll have you on your feet, strolling around, before you even know it!"

I said that I already goddamn well know how to walk, so how could I possibly get excited about that?

Sayuri pointed out—in a most gentle manner—that while I had known how to walk in my old body, I would have to learn how to do it in my new one. When I asked whether I'd ever be able to walk like a normal person again, she suggested that perhaps I was looking at the process in the wrong way and that I should just concentrate on the first steps rather than the entire journey.

"That's just the kind of cheap Oriental wisdom I don't need in my life."

I suppose it was then that she realized I was looking for a fight and she took a step closer. She said that how well I would eventually walk depended on many things, but mostly on my willingness to work. "Your fate is in your own hands."

I said I doubted it really mattered to her one way or the other how my progress went, as she'd get her paycheck just the same.

"That's not fair," Sayuri replied, providing just the opening that I was hoping for. I took the opportunity to explain to her what "not fair" really was. "Not fair" was the fact that when she went home in the evening to eat sushi and watch *Godzilla* on the late night show, I'd still be lying in my hospital bed with a tube sucking piss out of my body. *That*, I pointed out, was unfair.

Sayuri realized there was no point in continuing to talk to me, but still she was graceful. "You're scared and I understand that. I know it's difficult because you want to imagine the ending but you can't even imagine the beginning. But everything will be okay. It just takes time."

To which I replied: "Wipe that condescending look off your face, you Jap bitch."

• • •

Marianne Engel arrived at my bedside the next day with a small sheet of paper that she shoved into my hands. "Learn this," she said, and drilled me on the words until I had committed them to memory.

An hour later, Sayuri Mizumoto came into the room, her head held high. She glanced at Marianne Engel, but then focused her eyes on mine. "The nurses said you wanted to see me."

I did my best to affect a small bow in her direction, though it wasn't easy lying down. I started to speak the words I'd memorized: "Mizumoto san, konoaidawa hidoi kotoba o tsukatte hontouni gomenasai. Yurushite kudasai." (This roughly translates as *I'm truly sorry that I spoke such terrible words to you the other day. Please forgive me.*)

It was obvious that I'd caught her off guard. She replied. "I accept your apology. How did you learn the words?"

"This is my—friend, Marianne. She taught me." Which was true, but it did not explain how Marianne Engel knew Japanese. I had asked, of course, but for the preceding hour she'd refused to discuss anything other than the mistakes in my pronunciation. I also did not know how, after seven days away from the hospital, she knew that I'd insulted Sayuri. Perhaps one of the nurses had told her, or Dr. Edwards.

It was sheer coincidence that this was the first time the two women had met. Marianne Engel stepped towards Sayuri, bowed deeply, and said, " 水元さま、会えて嬉しいです。マリアンヌ・エンゲルです。"

Sayuri's eyes opened with astonished delight and she bowed back. "そうですか？　初めまして。　どうぞ宜しくお願いします。日本語ができるのですか？"

Marianne Engel nodded. "少し。北海道のラベンダー農場に数年住んでいました。　あなたの名前は漢字で小さな百合になりますか？"

"ええ、そうです。" Sayuri smiled. "日本語が上手ですね。"

"いいえ、それほどでも。" Marianne Engel shook her head in disagreement. "あなたの名前は水の元という意味ですか？"

"ええ、そうです。"

Marianne Engel bowed once more. "あなたの名前は私の友人にとって良い前兆ですね。　彼を宜しくお願いします。マナーの悪いのは許してあげて下さい。"

Sayuri stifled a giggle with a hand raised to her mouth. "ええ、最善を尽します。"

Sayuri looked deeply pleased that my vile behavior the day before had produced such an unexpected meeting. She excused herself from the room with a wide smile, bowing one final time towards Marianne Engel.

Marianne Engel brought her mouth close to my ear, and whispered, "I don't want to hear about you spitting black toads at Mizumoto san ever again. Talking with the mouth of a beast won't ease your pain. You have to keep your heart open with love, and trust me. I promise that we're moving towards freedom but I can't do this alone."

She moved away from my bed, pulled a chair from the corner, and sat heavily, with the tired look of a wife disappointed in her husband's failure. Her strange little speech drove me to voice a question that I'd long wanted to ask but had been too afraid to: "What do you want from me?"

"Nothing," she answered. "I want you to do absolutely nothing for me."

"Why?" I asked. "What does that even mean?"

"Only by doing nothing will you truly be able to prove your love."

"I don't understand."

"You will," she said. "I promise."

With this, Marianne Engel stopped talking about things that were going to happen in the future and decided to return to telling the story of her past. I did not believe any of it—how could I?—but at least it didn't leave me, like our conversation, feeling dumb.

VIII.

Growing up in Engelthal, I found my most difficult challenge was to keep my voice down. I understood that silence was an integral part of our spiritual welfare, but nevertheless I received many reprimands for my "excessive exuberance." Really, I was simply acting as a child does.

It was not only sound that was muted at Engelthal, it was everything. All aspects of our lives were outlined by the Constitutions of the Order, a document so thorough that it had a full five chapters devoted just to clothing and washing. Even our buildings could have no elegance, for fear it might taint our souls. We had to sit in the dining hall in the same order that we took our places in the choir. During the meal, readings were given so we received spiritual nourishment as well as physical. We'd listen to passages from the Bible and a lot of St. Augustine, and sometimes *The Life of St. Dominic*, the *Legenda Aurea*, or *Das St. Trudperter Hohelied*. At least the readings distracted from the food, which was flavorless—spices were prohibited and we couldn't eat meat without special permission, given only for health reasons.

Whenever I wasn't in the central chapel for Mass, I spent my time in the scriptorium. Gertrud made it clear from the start that she didn't appreciate my presence. Because of her position as armarius, however, it would have been improper for her to vent her frustrations directly. For this, she had her minion Sister Agletrudis.

Agletrudis was a chubby little planet that orbited around Gertrud, the scriptorium's largest star; her every action was calculated to please her mistress by torturing me. Her only goal in life was to take over the scriptorium when Gertrud finally died. What was I, except an obstacle upon that path?

Well before I arrived, a financial consideration had infiltrated the scriptorium. It was common practice to produce books for wealthy citizens, often in exchange for land upon their deaths. Gertrud, despite all her self-professed holiness, never took offense at the economic terms of this arrangement but disliked the sale of books for a different reason altogether: it interfered with using the scriptorium to achieve her own ends. Early in her career, Gertrud had decided that she would produce one great work upon which her legend would forever rest: a definitive German-language version of the Bible. Though she never said it aloud, I'm certain she imagined it would come to be known as *Die Gertrud Bibel*.

This was the basic problem with my presence: I was a young girl—an incomplete adult—who would take precious time away from her real work. I remember Gertrud's words when she put me under the tutelage of Agletrudis. "The prioress seems to believe this child will be able to offer something. Demonstrate for her some of the basics of the craft, preferably on the other side of the room, but she is not to touch anything. Those fat little fingers are undeserving of God's instruments. And above all, keep her away from my Bible."

So, in the beginning, I was only allowed to watch. You'd imagine this to be incredibly boring for a child but, as I'd spent much of my young life gathering information while sitting quietly in the corner, this was nothing new for me. I was hypnotized by the way the quills worked as an extension of the scribes' fingers. I learned the recipe for ink and that adding vermilion or cinnabar would make it red. I watched the way the nuns used a blade to sharpen their nibs, whenever the lettering threatened to lose its definition. I knew instantly that I was in the right place.

Things that we take for granted today were extraordinary at the time. Take paper, for example. We didn't make our own but received delivery from a local parchmenter. Then we had to ready the parchment for use. The nuns sorted it by quality and then arranged the sheets by hair and flesh sides, so the grains of the pages would match when the volume sat open on its spine, and sometimes Gertrud would instruct that the parchment should have some color added "just for a touch of drama." A single book required the skins of several hundred animals. How could a girl not be fascinated by that?

I can criticize Gertrud for many things but not her devotion to the craft. If the work was a translation, discussions about the phrasing of a single sentence sometimes lasted for over an hour. Most nuns in that room, despite the grumblings about Gertrud's dictatorial attitude, felt that she was completing a task God had specifically chosen her to do. The sisters never flagged, not even during the most intense periods of working on *Die Gertrud Bibel*.

There were a few scribes who wondered under what authority such a grand translation was being attempted and whether the undertaking were not sacrilegious, but these sisters knew better than to question the scriptorium's armarius—or simply feared to do it. So they didn't complain, but focused instead on the rare pages of the Bible that received Gertrud's approval. While everyone had input into the process, she always had the final say.

Gertrud allowed only the most skillful scribes to work on the most perfect vellum. She hovered over the work, jerking her scrawny neck each time she feared that a word might be misspelled or that the ink might be smudged. When the final period was dotted on the page's final sentence, you could see Gertrud's shoulders let go and you could hear the air that had been trapped in her lungs exit in relief. Then she would loudly slurp in another mouthful.

These moments of relaxation never lasted long. Gertrud would take the leaf to the rubricator so that the chapter and verse numbers could be highlighted in red, and while this was being done, the illuminator would make dozens of trial sketches for the blank spaces on the page. When the final decisions were made, the image was laid into place.

The completed pages were magnificent. Gertrud would spend a good hour, checking and double-checking it, before she would file it away and start the next page. Leaf by leaf, the book was coming into existence, but there were always other jobs to be completed. Whenever we had a backlog of manuscript requests from the nobility, Gertrud would glance longingly in the direction of her first love. But she had her orders from the prioress just like everyone else.

Somehow word reached the prioress that I wasn't being allowed to participate in any scriptorium duties. I imagine Sister Christina was probably behind this. With a great sigh of resignation and a lengthy explanation that she was against it, Gertrud explained that "under order of the prioress, I now have to allow your stupid little hands to start practicing." She gave over some old parchment, ruined by copying errors, and told me to start my efforts.

I immersed myself in it. I worked on any discarded vellum I could find and, as my skills improved, I was grudgingly given better quills and greater leeway to practice my translations. I could already understand German, Latin, Greek and Aramaic, the Italian of Paolo's prayer book, and some French. I was reading my way through every volume in the scriptorium and my development was a constant source of amazement to the sisters, although I never received a word of praise from Gertrud. Sister Agletrudis always took great pleasure in pointing out my every mistake and when I turned my back on my work, my inkwells would mysteriously tip over, my books would mysteriously go missing, or my quills would somehow mysteriously snap. Each time I pointed out these "coincidences" to Gertrud, she'd only smirk and vouch for Sister Agletrudis' very fine character.

Eventually, however, Gertrud and her acolyte could no longer continue to deny my talent. I was becoming the most versatile of the translators, and I was also the fastest and most accurate. Agletrudis' annoyance with me moved beyond simple dislike, into feelings of jealousy and threat, and there was a disturbed look in Gertrud's eyes as she started to realize how valuable I could be to *Die Gertrud Bibel*. She was no longer a young woman, and if she wanted to ensure that the Bible was completed in her lifetime, she needed to hurry the process along. Eventually, she allowed me to start contributing.

There was also life outside the scriptorium. As I grew older, I discovered a way to climb over the monastery gates and finally gain access to the world outside. I wasn't looking for trouble; I only wanted to see what was out there. Naturally my first stop was the small home that belonged to Father Sunder and Brother Heinrich. When I appeared, Father Sunder let his displeasure in my actions be known. He threatened to haul me back to the monastery and report me to the prioress, but somehow we ended up having a cup of juice instead. And then we had something to eat. And before he knew it, so much time had passed that it would have been awkward to try to explain why he had not brought me back immediately. So, after I promised not to come again, Brother Heinrich and Father Sunder allowed me to sneak back into the monastery. I returned the following night. Again I was severely chastised, but we ended up having more food and drinks. This pattern of my broken promises and their half-hearted scoldings continued for some weeks before we gave up the pretense altogether.

Each time I arrived at the ridge that overlooked their house, I was delighted. Their cabin became like a second, secret home to me. On summer evenings we sometimes played hide-and-seek amongst the trees. These were the best times for me, peering out from behind the brush at the two fatherly men in their fifties pretending they couldn't find me.

Engelthal was a small community, so it was inevitable that others knew about my "covert" visits. I suppose no one could see any real harm in them and, although they were an open secret among the nuns, I honestly believe that Gertrud, Agletrudis, and the prioress never knew. If they had, my visits would have been put to an abrupt end simply for propriety's sake.

The prioress died one night when I was in my teens, and a new prioress needed to be chosen as soon as possible. Dominican monasteries were democratic institutions; Sister Christina, who was just then finishing the *Sister-Book of Engelthal* and starting her *Revelations*, was elected in a nearly unanimous vote. Just like that, she took possession of the title Mother Christina. Obviously, I was pleased by this turn of events, but it was another matter altogether for Sister Agletrudis. How quickly events had turned against her, in regard to her desire to ascend as the next armarius. Not only had a wunderkind appeared in the scriptorium, but the new prioress had long been the girl's greatest champion. When I took my formal vows into the sisterhood not long after Mother Christina's election, this must have been the drop that made Sister Agletrudis' barrel overflow. I could feel the burning hatred in her eyes as I professed my obedience to the Blessed Dominic and to all the prioresses until my death.

In the eyes of the other nuns, however, I saw approval and affection. To them, it must have looked as if everything in my life was falling perfectly into place—but this is not what I felt. I felt like an imposter in the house of the Lord.

I had been raised in an atmosphere of intense holiness, but I felt anything but holy. So many of our sisters, including Gertrud and Agletrudis, had mystic visions, but I did not. This created a constant sense of inadequacy in me. I had skills with languages, yes, but that was what they felt like—skills, not gifts or revelations. It was not only a lack of communication from God that made me feel less worthy, it was also that the other nuns seemed so sure of their paths when there was so much I didn't understand. I was bewildered in heart and mind; I was deficient in the certainty the others seemed to have.

Mother Christina assured me that I should not worry about my lack of visions. Each sister receives her message only when she is ready, she said, and it is not a matter of calling the Lord to oneself but of making oneself purer so that the Lord would want to come. When I responded that I did not know what else I could possibly do to make myself more pure, Mother Christina advised that I should prepare myself for the Eternal Godhead by losing the creatureliness that adhered to my soul. I nodded my head, as if to indicate that this explanation clarified everything, but in truth it left me feeling as confused as a cow standing in front of a new gate.

I'd been studying these ideas all my life, but that's what they remained. Ideas, concepts. Vague generalities I couldn't really grasp. Mother Christina must have seen the look on my face, because she reminded me that I did have my inexplicable ability for languages and while this capability was not a mystical visitation, it did make me unique. It was increasingly clear, she maintained, that God must have a wonderful plan for me. Why else would he bless me with such gifts? I promised that I would try to do better, and silently hoped that I would someday grow to have the same belief in myself that she had.

Shortly after I entered my twenties, I met Heinrich Seuse for the first and only time. He was traveling from Straßburg to Köln, where he was to study at the *studium generale* under Meister Eckhart. Though our monastery was not directly on the path, he said he could hardly pass up the opportunity to visit the great Engelthal. Those were his very words.

It was obvious that he knew what to say to charm Mother Christina, but Gertrud was another matter. As soon as she heard that Seuse was going to study under Eckhart, she refused to meet him.

The subject of Eckhart was a touchy one. Although an accomplished writer in Latin on theological matters he was perhaps better known, or more *notorious,* for the unusual sermons he gave in the vernacular German. When Eckhart spoke on the metaphysical sameness between God's nature and the human soul, his ideas often seemed to stray from the orthodox path, and it was not a good time for ideas to do that. There was already much unease among the monastic orders and clergy because of the move of the papacy to Avignon.

When I came across Eckhart in my readings and asked Gertrud about him, her reaction had been severe. While she admitted that she hadn't actually read any of his works, she stated emphatically that neither did she need to. She'd heard enough of Eckhart's filthy views that she did not need to go to the filthy source. She spat his name out of her mouth as if it were rotten fruit. "Eckhart was a man with such promise, but he has allowed himself to fall to ruin. He will be found a heretic yet, mark my words. He will not even admit that God is good."

Gertrud's attitude worked out well for me, strangely enough. Because of her refusal to meet Seuse, it was I who was appointed to show him the scriptorium. I was shocked by his appearance. He was so slight that I could barely believe that his bones could support his weight, as little as that was. His skin was sallow and blotchy, and I could see every vein in his face running just below the surface. Dark bags hung under his eyes, and it looked as if he had never been to sleep. His hands, covered with scabs that he picked at habitually, were like fleshy gloves filled with loosely connected bones.

My description makes him sound gruesome, but in truth he was the exact opposite. The thinness of his skin only seemed to allow the light of his soul to shine through. The way he waved his slender fingers around while speaking made me think of saplings blowing in a breeze. And if it looked as if he never slept, the way he spoke suggested this was only because he was constantly receiving messages too important to ignore. While he was only a few years older than I was, I couldn't help but feel he knew secrets that I never would.

I walked him through the scriptorium and then, later, through the outlying lands belonging to Engelthal. When we were safely removed from the ears that could be found in every corner of the monastery, I brought up the topic of Meister Eckhart, and Seuse's eyes danced as if I had just handed him the keys to Heaven. He raced through everything he knew about the man who would soon be his master. I'd never before heard such a brilliant jumble of ideas fall from a mouth, and Seuse's voice was wild with ecclesiastical joy.

I asked why Sister Gertrud claimed that Meister Eckhart would not even admit that God was good. Seuse explained that Eckhart's position was that anything that is good can become better, and whatever may become better may become best. God cannot be referred to as "good," "better," or "best" because He is above all things. If a man says that God is wise, the man is lying because anything that is wise can become wiser. Anything that a man might say about God is incorrect, even calling Him by the name of God. God is "superessential nothingness" and "transcendent Being," said Seuse, beyond all words and beyond all understanding. The best a man can do is to remain silent, because any time he prates on about God, he is committing the sin of lying. The true master knows that if he had a God he could understand, he would never hold Him to be God.

That afternoon my mind opened to new possibilities, and my heart to new understandings. I could not imagine why Gertrud would want to prevent Eckhart's writings from entering our collection of books. What some would call heretical, I saw only as reasonable suppositions about the nature of God. I came away convinced that the teachings of my youth had been limited. If the arguments of Eckhart had not been allowed to cross my ears, what else had I not heard? As Seuse said that afternoon, with a brilliant gleam in his eyes, "That which is painful sharpens one's love."

In a moment of candor, I confessed to Seuse that I desperately wished I could read something by Eckhart. This caused a slightly wicked smile to cross his lips, but he said nothing. I wondered if he was amused that I would speak a desire that ran contrary to the monastery's stance, but I thought no more of it until he left us a few days later. I very much wanted to spend more time with him, but Gertrud, perhaps sensing this, ensured that my scriptorium duties were doubly heavy.

I was allowed to bid farewell to Seuse at the gates, as he set out again towards Köln. When he was certain that no one was looking at us, he slipped a small book into the folds of my robe.

IX.

Since the moment I wrote the words, they have haunted me. *Wipe that condescending look off your face, you Jap bitch.* The urge is always with me to retouch yesterday's canvas with today's paintbrush and cover the things that fill me with regret, but I want so desperately to remove these words that I am convinced I must leave them in.

Sayuri Mizumoto is not a bitch and she did not have a condescending look on her face. That much should be obvious. I said those horrible words because I was mad at Marianne Engel for not visiting me in a week.

I am ashamed of how I treated Sayuri and afraid that leaving that sentence in will make me appear racist. How could it not? But I assure you I chose the word "Jap" only because I was looking for any advantage that might make Sayuri feel vulnerable. I used the word not because *I* think Japanese people are inferior, but on the possibility that *Sayuri* might feel herself inferior, being Japanese in a non-Japanese culture. (As I've gotten to know her better, I've discovered that she absolutely does not have an ethnic inferiority complex.) And just as the word "Jap" suggests racism, so the word "bitch" suggests misogyny, but the truth is that I dislike most men as much as I dislike most women. If anything, I am an equal opportunity misanthropist.

Or rather, I *was.* I believe that I have changed since the day I attacked Sayuri. While I'm not claiming that I now feel great love for all people, I can state with some confidence that I hate fewer people than I used to. This may seem like a weak claim to personal growth, but sometimes these things should be judged by distance traveled rather than by current position.

◆ ◆ ◆

Dr. Gregor Hnatiuk, in righteous anger, was beautiful to behold. He stormed into my room to demand that I apologize to Ms. Mizumoto. Apparently he was behind the times: he'd heard of my insult, but not about my Japanese-speaking act of contrition. But still, it was breathtaking to see the shine on his sweaty brow as he defended the honor of the fair lady.

It was then that I understood upon whom he had his crush.

I explained that all the necessary fences had been mended and added that in the process Sayuri had even found a new companion with whom to speak Japanese. This placated Gregor somewhat, but he still felt it necessary to throw one final barb. "Someday you'll have to learn that your big mouth is the front gate of all misfortune."

"Yes, Gregor, I've heard that before," I said. "From Sayuri."

His chipmunk cheeks turned red. It was obvious that just hearing her name spoken aloud was enough to unsettle him, and the way he spun on his heel to exit confirmed all my suspicions.

At the door he stopped suddenly, turned back around, and said: "Marianne can speak Japanese?"

◆ ◆ ◆

What follows is a translation of the conversation between Marianne Engel and Sayuri Mizumoto.

Marianne Engel: Ms. Mizumoto. It's nice to meet you. I'm Marianne Engel.

Sayuri Mizumoto: Is it so? It's nice to meet you, too. Please
    treat me favorably. You can speak Japanese?
Marianne Engel: A little bit. I lived on a lavender farm in
    Hokkaido for a number of years. May I ask, is your first
    name the Chinese character for "Small Lily"?
Sayuri Mizumoto: Yes, it is. Your Japanese is very good.
Marianne Engel: No, it's not. And your family name means
    "Source of the Water," doesn't it?
Sayuri Mizumoto: Yes, it does.
Marianne Engel: Your name bodes very well for my friend.
    Please take good care of him. Please forgive his very
    bad manners.
Sayuri Mizumoto: Yes, I will do my best.

The question: how can I include a translation of a conversation
that I did not understand when it was first spoken?

The answer: Sayuri helped me. She assures me that it's faithful to
the original conversation but I really have no way of knowing that it
is, other than to trust her. Which I do, mostly, although I still have a
nagging fear that the whole thing is a massive manuscript error that
Titivillus will throw into his sack for Satan to use against me on Judgment Day. But this is a chance I'll have to take.

I'm pleased to report that my cruel words did not fatally sabotage
what has grown into a friendship between us. In the many hours that
we've spent together, I've learned the truth of Sayuri's childhood (or,
at least, her version of it), as I reported earlier.

But what I have learned above all else, in the years that have
passed, is that Sayuri Mizumoto is an exceptional woman. What
other word could be used to describe a woman who has helped with
translations for a book in which she's called a Jap bitch?

· · ·

Sayuri and Marianne Engel decided to work together on my rehabilitation program. Dr. Edwards had some reservations about the idea,
but acquiesced when Sayuri suggested that a partner would make
the program both easier and more enjoyable for me.

I had stood and even taken a few steps, but Sayuri wanted me
walking. The process was not going to be as simple as me jumping
out of bed and lurching down the hall. She brought in a special chair
that allowed my legs to dangle while she crouched in front of me,
pedaling my legs in circles. She, or Marianne Engel, would press her
hands against my soles to mimic the resistance of the ground, and I
was to push back against them. Sounds simple; wasn't.

At the end of each session, Sayuri would make me stand for as
many seconds as I could. It was never very long, but she'd yell "Fight!
Fight! Fight!" to encourage me. When I could take it no more, I was
placed back in bed and we'd review the day's progress.

Sometimes Marianne Engel would hold my hand and I'd have
trouble concentrating on what Sayuri was saying.

◆ ◆ ◆

Marianne Engel arrived in clothes so dusty I was surprised they'd let
her in. She must have sneaked past the nurses' station, although I
don't know how that was entirely possible, as she was dragging her
two hampers. When she squatted to start unloading them, I saw a
little cloud of dust cough out of the crook of her knee.

"I've been thinking about the story of Francesco and Graziana,"
I blurted, remembering that I had never updated Marianne Engel
about the improvement to the idealistic aspects of my personality.
"It's romantic."

She laughed at me while pulling bottles of Scotch out of the cold
hamper. "These are for Dr. Edwards, Mizumoto san, and the nurses.
I'd prefer that you don't lie to me, but maybe you'll like tonight's
story better."

I noticed the dried blood clinging around the edges of her battered fingernails as she took food from the coolers. Fish 'n' chips, bangers 'n' mash. Prime rib with pudgy Yorkshire puddings. Finger sandwiches: ham and egg, cheese and vegetables. Scones with strawberry jam. Kaiser buns. Garlic and onion bagels. Herb cream cheese. German butter cheese, Swiss, Gouda, smoked Gruyère, and Emmenthal. Fresh cucumber salad with yogurt sauce in a delightful little bowl adorned with images of Hänsel and Gretel. Chunky red potatoes, quartered to show their white interiors; chubby green stems of asparagus, sweating butter; a plump eggplant's fecund belly pregnant with stuffing. There were fat mutton slices piled up in an obscene monument to arterial sclerosis. A lonely pile of sauerkraut that seemed to have been added at the last moment only because someone had thought there weren't enough vegetables. Roasted eggs, even though who the hell eats roasted eggs? Then, an abrupt culinary turn towards the Russian states: varenyky (pirogies, in layman's terms), cavorting with candy-blackened circles of onions, and holubtsi (cabbage rolls, fat with rice) in tangy tomato sauce.

Marianne Engel popped an egg whole into her mouth, as if she hadn't eaten in days, and devoured it in a manner that was almost bestial. How could someone this hungry not have sampled the meal while preparing it? When she had tamed the worst of her hunger, she announced, "The story of Vicky Wennington has great storms, vigilant love, and saltwater death!"

I settled in, anxious to hear it, and took another bite of the holubtsi.

X.

In London society, nothing was more important than a revered family name, and Victoria D'Arbanville was born with one of the oldest and most respected. Her childhood was a series of lessons for her improvement: she was taught to speak French, Italian, German, Latin, and a smattering of Russian; she could discuss Darwin's theories without overtly suggesting any relationship between men and monkeys; and she could sing the best of Monteverdi, though she preferred Cavalli. Her parents didn't really care what music she liked; they only cared that she marry a gentleman, because this is what Victorian ladies did.

Victoria never doubted that she would do just that, until the day that she met Tom Wennington. Not a Thomas, this man was every inch a Tom. They were attending the same formal dinner, with Tom—in an ill-fitting suit—accompanying a city friend. After the meal, the men retreated to a drawing room where the main topics were Parliament and the Bible. Tom didn't have much to say about those things although, if pressed, he could have offered his opinions about dirt. He was a farmer, through and through, as his forefathers had been.

Tom was a rougher sort of man than Victoria generally knew but there was no denying the delight she felt each time she ran into him, accidentally on purpose, during the following weeks. And for his part, Tom extended his stay in London a month longer than he had originally intended; he put up with the parties, the teas, and the operas just on the chance that he might see Victoria. Eventually Tom's friend, well-heeled and generous though he was, began to run out of suits to loan him. Tom, knowing full well that his fields weren't likely to plant themselves, had a decision to make—go home alone or screw his courage to the sticking place. Which was, by the way, a phrase that Victoria had taught him.

The D'Arbanvilles were horrified when they first guessed their daughter's interest in this, this, this—farmer! But by then, it was already far too late. Victoria had not only been quoting Lady Macbeth, but channeling her efficiency (if not her criminal intent) in planning. When it quickly became apparent that Tom didn't understand the language of flowers, Victoria arranged a private tour of London's foremost factory producing steam-driven barn machinery.

Tom had been navigating the foreign world that was London only because he was besotted with Victoria, but it never left his mind that she knew nothing of his life. With this tour, she showed him that she was willing to learn about agriculture. Her questions to the plant manager demonstrated that she had done a good deal of research on the equipment before she ever set foot in the factory, and *this* was what convinced Tom there could be no other woman for him.

When Tom proposed, she knew that her days in the drawing room were over. Yes, she answered immediately, not playing any game of hesitation. She was finished as Victoria, and ready to start her new life as his beloved Vicky.

Her parents' objections weakened considerably when they learned the vast acreage of Tom's land, and the couple married in a ceremony that was too grand for Tom's liking. Vicky moved into the large Wennington farmhouse, which overlooked their fields on one side and the North Sea on the other. It was a rather strange location for the house, but Tom's great-grandmother had insisted on a view of "the very spot where the earth ends and falls into the sea."

Vicky would admonish Tom when he forgot to shave, and Tom would tease Vicky that her heels were too high for a farmer's wife, but she secretly thrilled at the rugged angles of his stubbled jaw and he loved the way her city boots made her hips sway. The smell of his sweat could bring her skin to gooseflesh, and the hint of her perfume could make him wipe the back of his neck with his well-stained handkerchief. In London, her body had been a muted thing, but on their farm, Vicky was plugged directly into the elements of the earth. She would stoke the fire to heat giant kettles for Tom's evening bath. She squeezed the bellows, smiling, sweating, and imagining how he would feel under her touch. It was during these evening baths that Vicky loved her hands for the first time in her life. She forgot her childhood piano lessons as she scrubbed the dirt from her husband's body.

At harvest time, Vicky conceived. She grew fat over the winter and gave birth in the spring. Vicky called the boy Alexander; Tom called him Al. The country air was even sweeter than before.

On their cliff they would stand in the mornings, baby in arms, watching the fishermen come and go. They had done this often through their marriage, and things did not change over the baby's first summer. Tom would close his eyes and imagine that it was he who was on the water. When he was younger, he had flirted with the idea of enlisting in the Royal Navy, but had abandoned the notion when his father died and left him the farm.

Still, Tom had a small boat that he took out on Sundays. On one such day in early November, much like any other, he asked Vicky to come with him. The crops had recently been harvested and they had the time to take a day for themselves. She told him that she was feeling under the weather and wanted to stay with the baby. "But go," she said. "Enjoy yourself."

From the cliff Vicky, with Alexander in her arms, watched as Tom steered the boat out of the harbor and into the ocean, becoming smaller and smaller until he disappeared. She pulled her coat tighter and tucked the baby's blanket under his chin. There was a chill wind coming; she felt it in her bones as she hurried back to the house. *It's November,* she thought, *wind's to be expected.*

The wind brought a storm upon its cold breath, very suddenly and very violently. Inside the farmhouse, Vicky was sleeping off her headache with the baby pressed to her bosom. She tossed and turned until they were startled awake by a vicious slap of lightning against their fields. Vicky sat bolt upright and Alexander burst into tears. She threw on her clothes and headed for the edge of the cliff, handing the child to the housemaid.

Vicky scanned the horizon for her husband's little boat. There was nothing but the water's churning gray anger.

Soon, one of the farmhands came to bring Vicky back to the house, afraid that the wind might pull her over the cliff's edge. At the bottom were rocks that could shred a person. Once Vicky was inside, the hands tried to reassure her. "Mr. Wennington's a good sailor. He'll find shelter in an inlet and wait out the storm in a safe place. He'll return when it's over." Vicky nodded distractedly, wanting to believe it.

The storm was the worst in living memory and raged for three obscene days. Vicky wandered from farmhouse to cliff, where she would stand until a farmworker forced her back to the house by telling her that Alexander was crying and needed attention.

The storm finally passed. The dark skies opened and sunlight poured through the cracks in the clouds. Vicky resumed her place at the cliff's edge, and there she stood for an entire day, awaiting her husband's return. But he did not appear.

The next day she organized a search party. Tom was well liked and all available boats ran up and down the coast looking for him.

There was no sign of Tom. No sign of anything. Just long, lonely expanses of water. It was as if the ocean had removed all evidence of his existence. After three days of searching, the fishermen reluctantly called off their efforts. They had families of their own to feed. They promised Vicky that they would continue to keep a good eye out.

She would not—could not—give up so easily. She hired a sailor and his boat, and together they spent six more weeks looking. Vicky became intimately acquainted with every rocky crag of the shoreline. In mid-December, however, the icy winds blew Vicky and her hired man right off the ocean. It was time to return from the search for the lost to the care of the living. The child Alexander needed his mother.

The farmhands continued their duties but lacked the direction that Tom had provided. They were only thankful that the crops had been brought in before the storm. Christmas was an awful affair, with no tree erected and no goose cooked. The year, which had started so promisingly with Alexander's birth in the spring, ended in sadness.

Gradually Vicky resumed her life but, still, she wore only black. The locals called her the Widow Wennington. She received some decent offers for the farm, but decided not to sell. It did not feel right to release the land that had been in Tom's family for generations, and she did not want to give up the home where she had loved and been loved so well. Besides, she could not return to London society life now. There was too much dirt under her fingernails.

But most of all, this land would be all that Alexander ever knew of his father. This land was Tom. Over that first lonely winter, Vicky studied farming operations, learning all she could, for the sake of her missing husband and her infant son. She needed to do something, anything, to minimize her brooding over Tom's unjust theft by the sea. But every morning, while the sun rose, Vicky stood at the cliff's edge for one hour. "Tom's dead," the locals said. "Why can't she accept it? Poor thing!"

When spring came, Vicky mobilized operations. At first the laborers were hesitant to follow her lead but when it became apparent that she knew what she was doing, they stopped muttering. They decided that Wennington money was as good out of Vicky's hand as it ever had been out of Tom's. She worked hard to prove herself, and while the harvest was not as good as that of the year before, it was good enough. On the first anniversary of Tom's disappearance,

Vicky removed her widow's weeds, but each morning she still visited the cliff's edge. It was not anything that she could ever explain to anyone else, but she believed that somehow the return sweep of the tide took her love out to Tom.

Over the years, the farm flourished. Vicky became known as a fine farmer and a shrewd businesswoman. She got the best hands because she always paid the best wages. She always paid the most because she always made the most. Eventually she started to buy out neighboring farmers, at a fair price, and when she brought new land under her management, its yield invariably increased.

For twenty-two years, Vicky worked. She became the greatest landowner in the region, and Alexander became a healthy young man, strong in body, spirit, and values. Then one day, he met a bright, energetic young woman from a nearby town. He fell in love, proposed marriage, and was accepted. Vicky knew that her son would be happy.

For twenty-two years, she had spent an hour every morning looking from the cliff at the crooked, inviting fingers of the surf. Three hundred and sixty-five days a year. Everyone knew she was waiting for her husband. Eight thousand days. Rain, wind, sleet, snow, sun; it did not matter to the Widow Wennington. Eight thousand hours. Never once did she desert her lonely command post at the edge of the world, where the earth fell into the sea.

In the autumn after Alexander's wedding, there was a terrible storm. It was, in fact, the worst since the one that had claimed Tom. Strangely enough, it occurred during the same weekend, in early November, in which she'd lost him. The wind raged, but not even a storm of such magnitude could keep Vicky from the cliff's edge. In truth, she liked stormy days best, because they made her feel closest to her missing husband. Vicky stood with her arms out, embracing the rain as it pounded into her skin. She whispered his name, "Tom, Tom, Tom, Tom . . ." Her hair leapt about in mad directions, and then she yelled into the gale. "I love you, I love you, I love you. I will always love you."

Alexander watched from the farmhouse, fascinated and dismayed. He had accepted his mother's ritual because he had never known a life without it, but this was different. Usually, she was quiet and contemplative in her lookout; this day, she was jerking about as if she were the storm's marionette. Alexander rushed out to confront her. "Mother! I've never asked you to stop before. Come in, this is dangerous!"

Vicky shouted back over the storm, "No!"

Alexander braced himself against the winds. Against his mother. "It doesn't matter how long you watch."

Vicky shook her head. "Of course it does."

Alexander pulled the neck of his raincoat tight. He shouted from under his yellow rubber hood. "No one doubts your love."

Vicky turned her face away from her son, towards the sea. She spoke softly, too softly for him to hear. "I only want to remember him."

The thrashing of the rain had dug tiny gutters around her feet. The ground had begun to loosen and Alexander felt it shift. A crack opened between them: twenty-two years of standing in the same spot had undermined the cliff's foundation. Alexander reached out frantically towards his mother, his eyes wide with fright. He screamed for her to take his hand. Vicky reached out towards her son but when her hand was almost in his, she stopped. Her fear left her and she smiled. She let her hand drop to her side.

"For God's sake, Mother!"

Alexander could say nothing more. The wind and rain howled, and blasts of thunder and lightning crashed everywhere, but he had never seen his mother so calm, so beautiful. It was as if she had been waiting for her turn, and it had finally come. The ground gave out under her and he watched his mother disappear with the cliff's crumbling edge.

Her body was never found. All the villagers said that she was finally returned to her beloved Tom, beneath the ocean's waves.

XI.

Next to my bed, on the small table, I found a glass lily the morning following Vicky's story. I was at a loss to explain how it had gotten there, as Marianne Engel had left the hospital well before I fell asleep. When I asked the nurses whether any of them had left the glass lily, they all swore that they had not. Furthermore, Maddy firmly held that no one had passed by the nurses' station during the night. Which meant that either the nurses were lying, or Marianne Engel had sneaked back in under the cover of darkness.

The second question about the glass lily was: what did it represent?

Why, you might be asking, do I assume that it had any meaning at all? Some things, blown-glass objects among them, are simply pleasing to look at. (And need I remind you that real flowers were not allowed in the burn unit?) Nevertheless, I was certain that it *did* have meaning; the more time I spent with Marianne Engel, the more certain I became that all things are inexplicably connected.

"Well," Dr. Edwards said, "a little mystery is not always a bad thing. It forces a person to have faith."

"Don't tell me that you're religious, Nan. I don't think I could stand it."

"My religion, or lack of it, is none of your business. You have your life, like last night's big feast, and I have my life." There was a touch of—jealousy, anger, disdain? what?—in her voice.

It was odd that Nan would resent a meal she herself had authorized. Ever the opportunist, I saw this as an opening to ask a question that had been bothering me: yes, I knew that hypermetabolism required me to take in an inordinate number of calories, but what was the *real* reason she had authorized Marianne Engel to bring meals for me?

"Everybody needs to eat," Nan said simply.

Her answer, of course, was not an answer. So I asked again. Nan, as she sometimes did, took a moment to weigh the benefits against the drawbacks of speaking the truth. I liked it when she did this. True to form, she didn't lie. "I allow these meals for a number of reasons. First, it *is* good for you to take in as much nourishment as possible. I'm doing it for the nurses, too, because you're a nicer person after Ms. Engel visits. But most of all, I'm doing it because I've never met anyone who needs a friend as badly as you do."

It must have felt good for Nan to get that off her chest. I asked what she thought about Marianne Engel helping with my physical therapy, and she admitted exactly what I suspected, that she did not like the idea very much.

"You worry I'm going to come to start depending on her too much," I said, "and that she'll let me down."

"Doesn't that worry you, too?"

"Yes," I answered.

Since Nan had chosen to tell me the truth, the least I could do was reply in kind.

· · ·

Everything seemed to be progressing more or less exactly as it should. Now that I actually had a desire to improve my body and was working to do so, I could feel myself becoming stronger. `ARE YOU SURE?` But preparation for the real world included the mental as well as the physical.

Maddy put me in a wheelchair and pushed me into a common area with four other burn patients. A man stood at the podium in a dress shirt and tie: Lance Whitmore was a former patient who had survived burns that were almost (but not quite) as bad as mine. His damage was less visible—only the right side of his jaw and neck revealed that he had been burned—but he said he had extensive keloid scarring on his torso that he could show us at the end of the lecture, should we desire to see what we could expect a few years into our recoveries. I didn't; it was enough to deal with the present day.

Lance's presence was intended to be both inspirational and informative. He'd been on the outside for three years and he was ready to pass along some hints for a successful transition, just like an AA speaker.

"Look up the word *insult* in the dictionary," Lance began, "and you'll find a number of definitions. In the medical sense, the word refers to harm brought to the body from an outside force, which in our case was fire. Of course, there's also the more common meaning, and you're going to get your share of insults—both intentional and not—when you leave this place. People don't quite know what to make of us."

Lance's speech went as one might expect: he talked about the "challenges" and "opportunities" he'd faced, and what he'd done to reclaim his life. When he was finished, he opened the floor to discussion.

The first question was from a female patient who'd been scratching herself through the entire talk. She wanted to know if her "damn donor sites" would always itch "so damn much."

"The itching will eventually go away. I promise." There was a general murmur of relief through the group. Even I, who had vowed to remain quiet, let out a thankful sigh. "There's nothing you can do but tough it out, unfortunately, but I always found it helpful to remember what Winston Churchill once said."

" 'We shall never surrender'?" suggested the itchy female.

"Well, yeah," laughed Lance, "but I was thinking about 'If you're going through Hell . . . keep going.' "

Another patient asked, "What's it like when you go out in public?"

"It's really hard, especially the first couple of times. Most people pretend they can't see you, but they whisper. Some will mock you openly, usually young men. The interesting thing is that a lot of people think that if you're burnt, you must've done something to deserve it. The teaching of the ages, right? Fire as a sign of divine retribution. It's difficult for people to face something as illogical as us—burned, but alive—so we must have done something wrong, or otherwise they'd have to accept that it could happen to them." He paused. "Who here thinks their burns are some kind of punishment?"

We looked at each other before one patient tentatively raised his hand, followed by a second. I was not going to raise my arm, no matter how long Lance waited.

"It's completely normal," he assured us. "*Why me?* I asked the question every day but never got an answer. I lived a good life. I went to church, paid my taxes, volunteered on weekends with a boys' club. I was, and am, a good person. *So—why—me?*" Pause. "There is no reason. A moment of bad luck, with lifelong consequences."

Another patient asked, "Do people ask about your burn?"

"Children, because they haven't learned tact. Some adults do, too, and to be honest I appreciate it. Every single person you meet for the rest of your life will be wondering about it, so sometimes it's good to get it out of the way so you can move onto other things."

A timid hand went up. "What about sex?"

"I like it." Lance's delivery of the line earned some laughs, and I guessed that he had given this speech often enough to perfect his answers to the questions that always came. "It'll be different for everyone. Your skin was a pretty amazing part of the experience, right? The largest organ of the body, a surface area of about three square meters, and that's a lot of possibility for pleasure. Now we've lost a lot of our nerve endings, and that really sucks."

The patient who had asked the question sighed heavily, but Lance held up his hand to indicate that he still had a few more things to say. "Skin is the dividing line between people, where you end and others begin. But in sex, all that changes. If skin is a fence that divides people, sex is the gate that opens your body to the other person."

Never again would I have that option, not with anyone. Not with Marianne Engel.

Lance cleared his throat. "I'm lucky: my wife stayed with me. In fact, the burn brought us closer together emotionally, and that's translated into our sexual activity as well. It forced me to become a better lover, because I've had to become more, umm, creative. That's all I'll say about that."

"What was hardest for you, after your release?"

"That's a tough one, but I think it was wearing the pressure garments twenty-three hours a day. They're amazing, you know, for limiting the scarring but—Jesus Christ!—it's like being buried alive. You look forward to your bath, even though it hurts, just to get out of the damn thing." Lance held my eyes for a moment, and I had the feeling that he was speaking to me specifically. "I wore mine for the first ten months after release but for some of you it'll be a year, or longer."

He continued, "It's only after you get out of here that you'll finally realize that a burn lasts forever. It's a continual event, one that constantly reinvents itself. You'll swoop from incredible highs when you're just glad to be alive, to those lows when you wish you were dead. And just when you start thinking that you've accepted who you are, that changes, too. Because who you are is not permanent."

Lance looked a little embarrassed, as if he'd talked himself into an area where he didn't want to go. He moved his gaze around the room, engaging all eyes for a few moments, before beginning the big wind-up. "Modern burn treatment is incredible, and the doctors are amazing, and I'm so thankful to be alive. But none of that is enough. Your skin was the emblem of your identity, the image that you presented to the world. But it was never who you really *are*. Being burned doesn't make you any less—or more—human. It only makes you burnt. So you're in a unique position to understand what most people never will, that skin is the clothing but not the essence of a person. Society pays lip service to the idea that beauty is only skin deep, but who understands like we do?

"Some day soon," Lance said, "you'll walk out of here and have to decide how you're going to live the rest of your lives. Will you be defined by what other people see, or by the essence of your soul?"

`TWO VERY POOR CHOICES.`

• • •

Gregor brought an assortment of goodies to wish me a happy Halloween. Because we are men, we didn't mention our previous conversation, and the candy was his way of saying that we should pick up where we'd left off before our spat. If the place hadn't been a hospital, I'm certain he would have brought a six-pack of beer.

The evening proved to be a breakthrough in our friendship. Gregor told me a somewhat embarrassing story about his very worst Halloween, when he'd dressed—in a misguided effort to impress a medical student he fancied—as a human liver. He'd gone to great lengths to make his costume as realistic as possible, including a rubber hose that was supposed to approximate the hepatic tube, which he hooked to a hidden bag of vodka in the organ's left lobe. His rationale was that he could take sips throughout the evening, whenever his nervousness with the woman became too much. (For perhaps the first time in history, a man filtered alcohol out of his liver to put into his body.) Unfortunately, his shyness was so great that he soon became completely drunk. At the end of the evening, Gregor and his date found themselves in the loft of an artist who made a living imitating the works of Jackson Pollock. The story ended with Gregor paying the artist several hundred dollars after vomiting onto one of his canvases, although I don't know how it could have made any difference to the work.

I tried to one-up Gregor with my most embarrassing Christmas story, of a failed attempt at seducing a department store elf who was married to a steroid-abusing Santa. Gregor responded with a yuletide tale of his own, in which he accidentally shot his mother with the BB gun he'd received after months of swearing that safety would be his primary concern. In the end, we somehow decided to share the single most embarrassing stories of our childhoods, holidays or not. I went first.

As a normal young boy I discovered it was pleasurable to stroke my penis, but as I was living with my addict aunt and addict uncle at the time, I had no one with whom to discuss my biological discovery.

I had a vague understanding, from eavesdropping on the meth-smoking adults, that there were such things as venereal diseases. You certainly did not want to contract one, as nasty things would happen to your jigger if you did. (Aunt Debi, when she found herself unable to avoid referring to my penis, always called it a jigger.) I also knew that venereal diseases were passed in the fluids that resulted from sexual acts. I could have done some research, I suppose, but I knew the librarians too well to risk being caught looking through such books. Besides, it was all pretty straightforward: since there was venereal disease in ejaculate and I was now capable of ejaculating, I would have to be careful not to infect myself. So I reviewed my options.

I could stop masturbating. But it felt too good.

I could cover my stomach with a towel to catch the offending fluid. But the towels were too large to hide and too difficult to clean discreetly.

I could masturbate into a sock. But all my socks were of a loose

cotton weave, through which seepage threatened to enter the pores of my skin.

I could masturbate into zip-lock sandwich bags. Yes: not only was this approach medically sound, but also it offered an unusual level of convenience. Clearly, this was the way to go.

Before long I had a large collection of brimming Baggies under my bed, but I couldn't simply bundle them up with our regular trash—what if someone discovered them, or if a scrounging dog spread the salty bags across the front lawn? So I decided the best option was to place them in another family's garbage can; the farther away from our trailer, the better.

The ideal location would be the rich area of town, removed from the trailer park both in distance and social standing. What I failed to consider, however, is that moneyed folk react suspiciously to young boys sneaking around their trash bins. Before long a police car arrived and I was standing in front of two burly officers trying to explain my surreptitious actions.

I desperately wanted not to betray the true nature of my mission, but the police demanded that I hand over the shopping bag in my possession. I begged them to let me go, stating there was nothing in the bag but "my lunch." When they took the package by force, they found forty little parcels of an unknown white substance and demanded to know exactly what kind of liquid narcotic I was dealing.

Afraid of being questioned at the local police station while they ran a chemical analysis on the milky fluid, I confessed that I was walking around with zip-locked sandwich bags filled with my own semen.

The officers didn't believe me, at first, but as the details of my story piled up, they stood in stunned silence—until they began to laugh. Needless to say, I was unimpressed with their reaction to my health crisis. When their amusement subsided, the officers deposited my junk in the nearest trash can and drove me home.

In our newfound spirit of male bonding, Gregor boasted that he had a story that could equal mine, if not better it.

As a lad, Gregor was likewise uneducated, although I give him full marks for never believing that he could infect himself with an STD. When he discovered self-pleasure, his thoughts ran somewhat like this: *If masturbating with a dry fist is this enjoyable, what would it feel like to use something that better approximated a vagina?*

So Gregor began his experiments. He tried liquid soap in the shower until he discovered the harsh reality of soap burn. His next attempt involved hand lotion, which worked well until his father began to question the boy's unusual commitment to supple skin. Eventually Gregor, who had a creative mind and a kitchen with a fully stocked fruit bowl, began to speculate on the possibilities afforded by a banana peel. Had not nature itself designed the peel specifically to house a fleshy cylinder?

The peel had an unfortunate tendency to rip during the act but, not to be defeated, Gregor decided to shore up this natural weakness with duct tape. This worked well, but he was faced with the same predicament that had stymied me: disposal of the evidence.

He decided upon flushing the remains down the toilet, but the fourth peel caused the pipes to back up. When Gregor's father discovered the clog, he naturally set to work with the plunger. Gregor hid in his bedroom, praying feverishly to God to send the peels down the tube instead of back up. *If you help me, Lord, I will never masturbate into a fruit skin again.* When Gregor's father was unable to unplug the pipes, the local plumber was called in, bringing a toilet snake and the potential for disaster.

God answered Gregor's prayers. The incriminating fruit did indeed go down, and the plumber's only comment was that Gregor's mother might consider adding more fiber to the family diet. Gregor kept his promise to the Lord by abandoning his fruit-abusing ways forever—or so he assured me, at my hospital bedside.

We were laughing at ourselves and promising to keep each other's secrets safe when Marianne Engel entered the room, wrapped in a mummy's bandages, her blue/green eyes beaming out from between the white strips on her face, her dark hair cascading down her back. She was obviously not expecting to encounter a psychiatrist in my room, much less one who had treated her in the past. It stopped her un/dead in her tracks, as if three thousand (or seven hundred) years of rigor mortis had set in all at once. Gregor, recognizing her unmistakable hair and eyes, spoke first. "Marianne, it's wonderful to see you again. How are you?"

"I'm fine." The words came tersely. Perhaps she was afraid her costume would put her right back in the loony bin, as wandering through the burn ward in bandages was whimsical at best and a bad joke at worst.

In an effort to put her at ease, Gregor said, "Halloween's my favorite holiday, even more than Christmas. Your costume is great." He paused to give her the chance to respond but she didn't, so he continued, "It's very appealing for psychiatrists, you know. Seeing everyone's costume is kind of a peek into their deepest fantasies. Me, I'm going to dress up as a murderous Bolshevik."

Marianne Engel was pulling nervously at the bandages twisted around her waist. Gregor saw that his attempts at conversation were going nowhere, so he politely excused himself and headed out the door.

She loosened up after he left, feeding me chocolate bars and telling ghost stories—the traditional kind, not those which featured her personal acquaintances. She told the famous story of the two young kids who, after hearing a radio announcement about a hook-handed escapee from a nearby insane asylum, speed away from Lovers' Lane only to find a severed hook hanging from the door handle when they arrive home; the story of the young female hitchhiker picked up and delivered home only to forget her coat which, when returned by the driver to the house a few days later, brings forward the revelation that the hitchhiker died ten years earlier, along the same stretch of road where she'd been picked up; the story of the man who sits at his kitchen table working on a jigsaw puzzle, which, as it comes into focus, reveals a picture of him sitting at his kitchen table completing the jigsaw puzzle, with the last piece revealing a hideous face looking in through the window; the story of the young babysitter who gets increasingly disturbing phone calls alerting her to the danger to the child she is looking after until, upon calling the operator for a call-trace, she is told that the call is coming from inside the house; and so forth.

While talking, Marianne Engel covered her head with an extra bedsheet and lit her face from the underside with a flashlight she'd borrowed from the nurse's desk. It was all so hokey that it became charming. She stayed well past the end of visiting hours—the nurses had long since stopped trying to enforce the rules with respect to Marianne Engel—and at midnight, she seemed perturbed by the lack of a grandfather clock to count out the dozen (or perhaps thirteen) strokes.

The last thing she said, before leaving in the early hours of the morning, was "Just wait until Halloween next year. We're going to go to a wonderful party. . . ."

• • •

The harvesting of my skin was occurring less often. Surgeries still marked my days, which was only to be expected, but my suicidal daydreams were now almost completely gone and I had become Sayuri's star pupil. I could lie and say this was because of my strong sense of character, and that I was determined to keep my deal with Nan. I could lie and say I was doing it for myself. I could lie and say I was doing it because I'd seen the light. But mostly I was doing it to impress Marianne Engel.

HOW CUTE. My bitchsnake flicked its tail and tongue, cheerfully caressing me at both ends. I WONDER WHAT IT WILL BE LIKE WHEN YOU LEAVE THE HOSPITAL?

I'd graduated to shuffling a few steps at a time, using an alumi-

num walker. I felt foolish, but Sayuri assured me that I'd soon be moving up to canes that wrapped around the forearms.

One thing that helped immensely was a pair of orthopedic shoes that had been designed specifically for me. The first pair made my feet ache so the expert cobbled together a second pair that worked out the problems. The greatest advantage of the shoes, however, was mental rather than physical. Shoes are a great equalizer for a man with lost toes: they are like leather disguises that make one's ruined feet look normal.

I had to admit that Sayuri knew precisely what she was doing. In the beginning my exercises had a heavy emphasis on stretching to regain my lost range of motion. Then we moved to Thera-Bands, elastic straps used for resistance, before switching to a simple weight-training program. The weights grew larger with each week that passed, and sometimes I even asked Sayuri if I could do a few more lifts than were demanded by my routine.

Now that I could take a few steps out of the bed, I started shuffling off to my washroom when I needed to relieve myself. One would imagine this to be a great step forward in the feeling of self-reliance but it was a psychological blow to discover I could no longer pee while standing up. I found this state of affairs unreasonably emasculating.

◆ ◆ ◆

I was nearing the eight-month mark of my hospitalization, and Christmas was coming. Marianne Engel did what she could, putting up wreaths, playing Handel, and lamenting the fact that she wasn't allowed to light Advent candles in the burn ward.

On the evening of December sixth, Marianne Engel lifted my new orthopedic shoes onto the windowsill and explained that on this night St. Nicholas left treats in the shoes of children. When I said that we had never practiced this tradition in the trailer park, she reminded me that the world did not begin and end with my personal experiences. Fair enough. When I pointed out that I was no longer a child, she just shushed me. "In the eyes of God, we're all children."

When Connie took down my shoes the next morning—"What the heck are *these* doing here?"—she found them stuffed with hundred-dollar bills.

I was touched by the incident, more than I would have expected. My reaction was not so much to the gift of money itself, but to the thought that Marianne Engel had put into my situation. The holidays left me in a quandary: how could I pay for any Christmas gifts? While it was true that I had a small amount of money hidden in a bank account under a false name, I had no way to access it. Probably, in fact, I would never be able to withdraw the money, even when I got out, for the false identification I had used to set up the account bore a photo that no longer matched my face.

Marianne Engel had realized what I needed and, rather than forcing me to ask for cash or do without, found a way to deliver it to me in a charming manner. A gift! From St. Nicholas! And so my dilemma was solved. Almost. I still had to find a way to get the presents from a store to my bedside, but I had a plan for that.

I requested that Gregor drop by at the end of one of my exercise sessions with Sayuri. When both were there, I began: "Feel free to say no, but the two of you could really help me out. I hope you can do some shopping for me."

Gregor asked why I needed both of them. Because I wanted to give each of them a gift, I explained, and I could hardly ask them to buy their own. Sayuri would purchase my gift for Gregor, and Gregor could buy my gift for Sayuri. The remainder of the gifts, they could shop for together.

"No worries," Sayuri said. "I *love* Christmas shopping."

Hearing this, Gregor also quickly agreed. I gave each an envelope that included what I wanted them to buy, on my behalf, for the other. As they left the room Gregor glanced back at me, a strange little smile on his face.

• • •

Marianne Engel had not yet finished reading *Inferno* to me. In part, it was going so slowly because she never read too much in a single sitting, preferring to savor the beauty of the writing, but also because she kept slipping into Italian. I never had the heart to stop her when she did this because she was so deep into the story and, besides, the Italian sounded wonderful from her mouth. At the end of the canto, I would have to point out that I had understood nothing, and the next day she would repeat the section, usually making it all the way through in English.

Voltaire wrote that Dante was a madman who had many commentators, and whose reputation would continue to grow mostly because almost no one actually reads the *Commedia*. I suggest the reason that so few people read Dante is because no one actually needs to. In the Western world, *Inferno* is everyone's idea of Hell; as literature, only the Bible is more deeply woven into society's collective consciousness.

"Did you know," Marianne Engel asked, "that Dante's Hell was based upon *The Flowing Light of the Godhead,* by Mechthild von Magdeburg?"

"One of your Three Masters, right?"

"Yes," she answered.

I admitted that, not surprisingly, I knew very little (in truth: nothing) about this woman, so Marianne Engel proceeded to educate me. Mechthild was born in Saxony near the start of the thirteenth century and as a child experienced daily visits from no less a figure than the Holy Ghost itself. At twenty she became a Beguine at Magdeburg, living a dutiful life of prayer and mortification; interestingly, as she increased the severity of her self-punishment, her visions became correspondingly more frequent. When she described them to her confessor, he became certain of their divine origins and impelled Mechthild to write them down.

Das fließende Licht der Gottheit, as the masterwork is known in German, influenced countless writers who followed, including

Meister Eckhart and Christina Ebner. It is also clear that Dante Alighieri read the Latin translation, and many scholars are convinced he used Mechthild's ordering of the afterlife as the conceptual basis for the *Divine Comedy:* Heaven at the top, Purgatory directly below, and Hell at the bottom. In the very abyss of Mechthild's Hell, Satan is chained by his own sins while anguish, plague, and ruin flow from his burning heart and mouth. This sounds suspiciously similar to Dante's Satan, a three-faced beast trapped in a block of ice at the lowest center of Hell chewing at a frothy trio of sinners (Judas, Cassius, and Brutus) whose pus flows from his three mouths for all eternity.

"There are those who believe," said Marianne Engel, "that the 'Matilda' Dante encounters in *Purgatorio* is in fact Mechthild."

"Is that what you think?" I asked.

"I believe," she answered with a slight smile, "that in his work, Dante often wrote in appearances by those who influenced him."

As she read me the tale of Dante's journey, I found it deeply familiar and I loved it despite (or perhaps because of?) my burn ward surroundings. There was something comforting in having Marianne Engel read it to me, and in the way she curled her fingers into mine as she did. I marveled at the twisting mix of our glorious and ghastly hands, and I wanted her reading of the story to never end—perhaps because I was afraid that when it did, she would no longer continue to lead me, hand in hand, though my own Hell.

When I presented Marianne Engel my theory that no one needs to read *Inferno* to know its representation of Hell, she was quick to correct me. "While that may be true for most people, you know it so well because I read you my German translation."

"Uh-huh." I hadn't seen that coming. "When did you translate it?"

"I suppose about ten or twenty years after Dante finished writing it. It took me quite a while. I'm pretty sure I was *Inferno's* first translator, but you can never be positive about these things."

"And when did you read it to me?" I asked.

"When you were recovering from your first burn."

• • •

Inferno was first published in A.D. 1314. If Marianne Engel completed her translation twenty years later, the year would have been approximately 1334. Given her earlier claim that she was born in the year 1300, this would put her in her mid-thirties at the time.

As I detail these numbers, I'm not forgetting that this is ludicrous and could not have actually occurred. I'm simply pointing out that, at least, the impossible things were occurring in a possible timeline. This is what I find rather amazing about her mental state: her wild statements were held together by internal consistency.

Because I didn't live in the Middle Ages, I needed to do a lot of research during the writing of this book to check what she said, or what I remember her saying, against facts. The interesting thing is that all the events she claimed were true *could have* happened exactly as she described them, had she not been talking about ancient events in the first person.

Despite being under the control of the Church, Engelthal *was* a democratic institution whose prioress was elected. All daily activities *were* outlined in the Orders of the Constitution. Marianne Engel's descriptions of the architecture, the prayers, the books studied, and the rituals for eating *were* accurate. Christina Ebner *was* in that monastery and she did write *The Sister-book of Engelthal* and *Revelations*. Friedrich Sunder *was* a local priest, the confessor to the nuns, and he did write *Gnaden-vita*. There *was* a book called *The Vita of Sister Gertrud of Engelthal*, written with the help of a Brother Heinrich and Cunrat Fridrich.

While there is no record of Heinrich Seuse having visited Engelthal, there is also no way to prove that he did not do so. If he did come during the early 1320s, as Marianne Engel claimed, this *was* when he was traveling from Straßburg to Köln to study under Meister Eckhart. So who's to say he didn't visit the monastery that was widely regarded as the foremost center of German mysticism?

Still. No matter how perfectly she constructed her timelines or researched German religious figures, Marianne Engel was either schizophrenic or manic depressive, or both. I cannot forget this. Creating and managing imaginary universes is the province of such people: it's not only what they do, it's who they are. And there *were* some seeming discrepancies in Marianne Engel's account; for example, there is no record of a Sister Marianne in any of the extant writings from Engelthal, nor is there any mention of *Die Gertrud Bibel,* and I tried to use these omissions to force Marianne Engel into admitting her story was not true.

"You are studious, aren't you?" she said. "Don't worry, there's a reason you can't find information on me or on Gertrud's Bible. We'll get to it, I promise."

• • •

Goodwill carolers dropped in to sing about silent nights, holy nights. A Sally Ann Santa brought cookies and books. Decorations went up along the hallways.

How strange it was to be looking forward to the holiday season. Traditionally, I'd hated Christmas; it always left a taste in my mouth akin to moldy fruitcake. (By this, I do not mean an elderly Japanese spinster.) In my childhood, I'd had a succession of Christmases when the Graces spent the money originally intended for my presents on methamphetamine; in my adulthood, Christmas meant fucking a woman who was wearing a red felt hat.

I still had my exercise sessions, my regular medical procedures, but the most interesting event was to be a meeting of the important women of my life: Nan, Sayuri, and Marianne Engel. I had no clue as to its agenda and, strangely, no one wanted to tell me. In my egocentric little heart, I imagined it might be a surprise party. I couldn't have been more wrong.

Sayuri arrived first. I've mentioned before that she always seemed to carry her tiny body behind a gigantic smile, but on this day only the tiny body was present. When I asked whether everything was okay, she answered unpersuasively that it was. Rather than push the subject, I asked whether she'd bought my gift for Gregor yet. She replied that she had and in this, at least, I believed her. I was going to ask a few more questions when Marianne Engel and Nan entered the room like horses jockeying for position. Marianne Engel looked directly at me and stated: "When you get out of here, you're coming with me."

"Not so fast," Nan said sharply, before turning her attention on me. "As you know, you'll probably be released in a few months—"

"—and then you're coming to live in my house." The impatience in Marianne Engel's voice betrayed that she thought this meeting was unnecessary.

"Calm down." Nan held up her hand while shooting Marianne Engel an exasperated look. "That's not your decision to make."

"He doesn't have anywhere else to go."

Nan countered, "I've already arranged for a place in Phoenix Hall."

"He doesn't want to live there." Which was true, I didn't, but Dr. Edwards had long been recommending it because of its highly trained workers, job placement programs, and proper medical supplies. In addition, it had counselors, not to mention other burn patients who would be facing the same challenges as I.

"I work with the patients at Phoenix," Sayuri said, "so if you go there, we can continue your gait training."

"I'll hire you," Marianne Engel said. "Money isn't a problem. You can do it at my house."

This suggestion made Sayuri look towards Dr. Edwards uneasily. "I don't know hospital policy on that."

Nan replied that beyond policy issues, Phoenix Hall had a host of professionals, *all* ready to offer their expertise. Marianne Engel reiterated that she was willing to provide whatever I needed. "If Mizumoto san is too busy, we'll hire someone else. But we'd prefer to have her, because we like her."

She wheeled around to look directly at me, and finally asked what I wanted. "Do you want to go to this Phoenix place?"

"No."

"Do you want to come to my house?"

"Yes."

Marianne Engel turned her attention back to Dr. Edwards. "There. Discussion finished."

It might have been prudent to claim that I needed time to think. After all, I had just chosen Marianne Engel over the doctor who'd been expertly guiding my recovery for months. My hasty answer was, to say the least, illogical.

If there was one thing I could be certain about, however, it was that everyone in the room truly had my best interests at heart. I hadn't known that Marianne Engel and Nan had been arguing about my living arrangements for weeks; since I saw both of them almost daily, this could only have occurred if they were working together to hide it in order to keep my stress level as low as possible.

"There's still plenty of time to make an informed decision," Nan said, indicating that this discussion was anything but finished. It was not lost on anyone how heavily she stressed the word *informed*.

◆ ◆ ◆

There were practical concerns that I could not ignore in regard to living with Marianne Engel. One was that, although she said she had plenty of money, she probably couldn't afford me.

Housing a burn patient is incredibly expensive. Beyond my treat-ment costs—Sayuri's fees, medical supplies, exercise equipment—there would be regular living expenses. Food. Clothes. Entertainment.

Utilities. She would have to pay the costs of my life not only as a patient, but as a man as well. While there might be government programs or charities that would contribute to my care, I doubted Marianne Engel would ask for their assistance; her personality being what it was, I expected pride, paperwork, and privacy issues would prevent her from even looking into it. She claimed to have the resources to support me, but I could hardly accept this as fact—a shoeful of hundred-dollar bills was not enough to convince me of her fortune. Was this money as much a fantasy as most other aspects of her life? Was I to believe that she had been saving her pennies for seven hundred years?

Not only was living with her fiscally questionable, it was also morally suspect. As the basis of the offer was her belief that her "last heart" was for me, I would clearly be taking advantage, under false pretenses, of a confused woman. As the sane one, not only did I know better, I was obligated to act upon the fact that I knew better. And in any case, why should I put myself in the position of depending upon a mentally ill woman whom I hardly knew? Although my circumstances had changed and I was less physically able than previously, I had been on my own since my teens. Before that, even: as guardians, the Graces had been competent only at guarding their drug stashes. For all intents and purposes, I had looked after myself since I was six years old.

So I had been mistaken in accepting Marianne Engel's offer, and Nan had been correct. I would reverse my rash decision and enter Phoenix Hall after all.

When Gregor came by that afternoon to drop off Sayuri's present, he congratulated me on my decision to move in with Marianne Engel. When I informed him that I'd changed my mind, he backtracked and said that I had made the only logical decision. "I think your progress has been fantastic under the guidance of Dr. Edwards. I hold her in the highest esteem."

I knew Gregor well enough to recognize when he was not saying all that he was thinking. This was one of those times. "But . . . ?"

Gregor looked to the left, and then to the right, to ensure that no one was around to overhear him. "But even monkeys fall from trees."

I had no idea what this meant, so Gregor explained: *Even experts make mistakes.* "While Dr. Edwards is your physician, and a good one, I don't think you should underestimate Marianne's effect on your recovery, either. She comes every day, she helps with your exercises, and it's obvious that she cares deeply about you. God knows why. But I'm not telling you anything you don't know."

`HE THINKS YOUR NUTJOB GIRLFRIEND IS SE-RIOUS ABOUT YOU.`

Shut up, fuck. I corrected Gregor. "She's delusional."

"Go ahead and deny it," he said, "but it's obvious."

`THAT'S SO CUTE.`

I wasn't going to bother arguing the point; I didn't feel up to that. "What would you do?"

"I'd be worried about living with Marianne, too," he said, "but you're no prize, either. If you can put up with each other, I think you should do it."

"Even if she is fond of me—and I'm not saying that she is—I'm not really sure how.I feel about her." I paused. "I don't know."

"If you don't accept her invitation, you're the biggest idiot I've ever met," Gregor said. "In addition to being a lousy liar."

When you lie in a hospital bed long enough, you start a mental catalogue of all human contact. I touched Gregor on the back of his hand, the first time we'd ever touched, and said, "Thank you for bringing Sayuri's present."

`A TOUCHING MOMENT . . .`

I buzzed the nurse to ask for more morphine.

`. . . BETWEEN LOSERS.`

· · ·

On Christmas morning, Marianne Engel appeared in my room with a sack of presents and a silver briefcase that she immediately slid under my bed. We passed a few hours, speaking as we often did about everything/nothing, while she fed me mandarin oranges and marzipan. As usual, she made her regular trips outside to smoke cigarettes, but I noticed that sometimes when she came back, she didn't have the telltale smell of fresh smoke upon her. When I asked her if she had something else going on, she shook her head no. Her smile, however, betrayed her.

In the early afternoon, Sayuri and Gregor arrived, followed by Connie, who'd just finished her rounds. Dr. Edwards never worked on Christmas Day, and Maddy and Beth had both booked the day off to spend with their families. With no one left to arrive, Marianne Engel dragged her sack out of the corner and we began to exchange gifts.

The nurses had pitched in to buy me some books on subjects that had recently taken my interest, such as the inner workings of medieval German monasteries and the writings of Heinrich Seuse and Meister Eckhart.

"You aren't easy to buy for, that's for sure. I had to go to three different bookshops," Connie said. As soon as she realized this might sound like a complaint, she hastily added, "Not that I minded, of course!"

Gregor gave me a stationery set, as I'd confided to him that I'd been working on some writing in recent weeks, and Sayuri gave me some lavender ice cream that I happily shared with everyone. Marianne Engel seemed to enjoy it the most, and was tickled by the fact that it turned her tongue purple.

To the nurses I gave compact discs by their favorite artists. While this was not particularly personal, I didn't know much about their nonhospital lives. To Sayuri, I gave the gift that I'd asked Gregor to pick up on my behalf: two tickets for an upcoming Akira Kurosawa film festival.

"I got the idea when Dr. Hnatiuk was telling me about it. He loves Kurosawa, you know."

Marianne Engel looked at me, raising an accusatory eyebrow, because subtle I'm not.

Next came my gift to Gregor, as picked up by Sayuri: coupons for a dinner for two at a Russian restaurant with the highly unoriginal name of Rasputin's. I asked Sayuri whether she'd ever eaten authentic Russian food, and she answered that she had not. It was now I who raised an eyebrow in the direction of Gregor. When they thanked me for their gifts, I grumbled that "Christmas wouldn't be Christmas without any fucking presents." No one seemed to understand what I was talking about, which only proves that more people should read Louisa May Alcott.

Next, Marianne Engel gave her gifts. The nurses got day passes to a spa, which Connie tucked away with the CDs. Sayuri received an intricate blown-glass Buddhist temple, while Gregor received a pair of wrought-iron candlesticks. They were impressed with the handmade quality of the items, and Marianne Engel boasted that the gifts were the work of two of her friends.

As for Marianne Engel and I, we had already decided to exchange our gifts later, in private. And maybe I was the only one who'd noticed, but apparently Sayuri and Gregor had also come to the same understanding.

After a while, Gregor said, "Are we ready to move along?" Everyone looked at Marianne Engel, who nodded. Christmas truly was a time for miracles, if the medical staff was looking to the schizophrenic to provide guidance. Sayuri put me into a wheelchair and Gregor pushed me down the hall, and when I asked where we were going, no one would answer directly. Soon I figured out that we were heading to the cafeteria. Perhaps there was some sort of Christmas function, a hired Santa or volunteer carolers, although the fact that I'd heard nothing about it struck me as odd. After so many months in the hospital, very little escaped my attention.

When the doors of the cafeteria slid open, I was battered by the smell of every food in the world. Against the far wall, a small task force of caterers was tending to a series of heavily laden tables. Thirty or forty people were milling around the room, under red crepe streamers that hung from the roof, and a few of them gestured in our direction. At first, I thought they were all pointing at my appearance but when the caterers waved to Marianne Engel, I realized that she was the center of attention, not I. The patients started ambling towards us: an old man with a cough, a curly-haired woman with bandages on her arms, a handsome boy with a limp. Bringing up the rear was a preteen girl with no hair, a fistful of balloons, and a cheering section of relatives.

Everyone thanked Marianne Engel for what she'd done; at this point, I still didn't know what that was. After Gregor pushed me to the catering tables and helped me out of the wheelchair, he explained that she had arranged and funded the entire party. This, in accordance with her general lack of restraint, was no small undertaking. Even having seen the outsized dinners that she brought to my room, I could scarcely comprehend what was available.

Turkey, ham, roast goose, chicken, meat dumplings, curried goat, boar, venison, meatloaf, carp (carp? who eats carp?), cod, haddock, lutefish, shellfish, cold cuts, a dozen types of sausage, roasted eggs, oxtail soup, meat broths, onion soup, more cheeses than you could shake a cow's udder at, brown beans, gungo peas, onions, pickles, rutabaga, potatoes, sweet potatoes, sweeter potatoes, sweetest potatoes, cabbage, carrots, parsnips, squash, pumpkin, basmati, white rice, brown rice, wild rice, tame rice, antipasto, stuffing, assorted breads, bagels, buns, cheese scones, green salad, Caesar salad, bean salad, pasta salad, jellied salad, whipped-cream-and-apple salad, spaghetti, fettuccini, macaroni, rigatoni, cannelloni, tortellini, guglielmo marconi (just checking to see if you're still reading), bananas, apples, oranges, pineapples, strawberries, blueberries, mixed nuts, mincemeat pies, Christmas pudding, Christmas bread, coconut shortbread, pecan pie, chocolates, chocolate logs, chocolate frogs, Bertie Bott's Every Flavour Beans, fudge, sugar, spice, everything nice, epiphany cake, fruitcake, gingerbread men, Torte Vigilia di Natale, snips, snails, puppydog tails, cranberry punch, eggnog, milk, grape juice, apple juice, orange juice, soft drinks, coffee, tea, you say to-may-to juice, I say to-mah-to juice, and bottled water.

Everyone in the hospital must have filled up their plates once, twice, thrice, and Marianne Engel charmed each guest with her grace and eccentricity. It didn't hurt that she had slipped into an elf costume and looked astoundingly cute. Music played and people talked merrily to each other, everyone partaking in the spirit of the event. Patients who otherwise would never have met were speaking at length, probably comparing illnesses. Coughs were drowned out by laughs, and there were squeals of delight from the children, who each received a gift from under the plastic Christmas tree. Apparently Marianne Engel couldn't obtain permission for a genuine pine, but an artificial one was more than good enough. If flowers might kill a man, just imagine what a conifer could do.

For this one afternoon, I was a hospital celebrity, as the word spread that it was my friend who'd done all this. An old man came to talk with me with such a large grin on his face that it was a shock when he mentioned that his wife of sixty years had recently died. When I told him I was sorry to hear it, he shook his head and clasped his hand on my shoulder. "Don't be wasting your sympathy on me, kid. I did pretty damn well, I'll tell you what. You snag a woman like that, you don't ask what you did to deserve it. You just hope she never wises up and changes her mind."

During the party, a feeling of strange relief had come over me. From our first meeting, Marianne Engel had shown such irrational affection towards me that I expected it to disappear as abruptly as it had started. Relationships fall apart, that's their nature. We've all seen it a thousand times, even between couples who we were certain were "going to make it."

I once knew a woman who liked to imagine Love in the guise of a sturdy dog, one that would always chase down the stick after it was thrown and return with his ears flopping around happily. Completely loyal, completely unconditional. And I laughed at her, because even I knew that love is not like that. Love is a delicate thing that needs to be cosseted and protected. Love is not robust and love is not unyielding. Love can crumble under a few harsh words, or be tossed away with a handful of careless actions. Love isn't a steadfast dog at all; love is more like a pygmy mouse lemur.

Yes, that's *exactly* what love is: a tiny, jittery primate with eyes that are permanently peeled open in fear. For those of you who cannot quite picture a pygmy mouse lemur, imagine a miniature Don Knotts or Steve Buscemi wearing a fur coat. Imagine the cutest animal that you can, after it has been squeezed so hard that all its stuffing has been pushed up into an oversized head and its eyes are now popping out in overflow. The lemur looks so vulnerable that one cannot help but worry that a predator might swoop in at any instant to snatch it away.

Marianne Engel's love for me seemed built on so flimsy a premise that I assumed it would come apart the moment we stepped through the hospital doors. How could a love based on a fictional past survive into an actual future? It was impossible. That kind of love was a thing to be snatched up and crushed in the jaws of real life.

That was my fear, but this Christmas Day had shown me that Marianne Engel's love was not feeble. It was strapping, it was muscular, it was massive. I thought that it could fill only my room in the burn ward, but it filled the entire hospital. More important, her love was not reserved only for me; it was shared generously with strangers—people she didn't think were friends from the fourteenth century.

All my life I had heard foolish stories about love: that the more you give away, the more you have. This had always struck me as nothing more than a violation of basic mathematical principles. But watching Marianne Engel share her love so widely awakened in me the weirdest of romantic feelings: the opposite of jealousy.

It comforted me that love was her soul's natural condition and not an aberration built on fantasies. Her love was not a lemur, an animal so named because Portuguese explorers in Madagascar noted large shining eyes peering out of the forest when they sat around their campfires. Convinced that these eyes belonged to the spirits of their departed companions, they christened the animals with the Latin word meaning "spirits of the dead."

◆ ◆ ◆

When the last turkey leg had been eaten, Marianne Engel thanked each caterer and passed out envelopes that contained "just a little something extra for working on the holidays." While she was wheeling me back to my room, she claimed that this was the best Christmas she'd ever had. I pointed out that that was quite a claim, given that she'd had seven hundred.

After she helped me into bed, Marianne Engel sat with a satisfied thud. I observed that the party must have cost her a fortune; she dismissed this with a wave of her hand and pulled the silver briefcase from under my bed. "Open it."

The briefcase was fat with sleeves of bills, fifties and hundreds. In my days of pornography and drugs, I'd seen the occasional satchel of cash, but nothing like this. I spun the numbers around my skull, trying to come up with a rough estimate. It was difficult to do the math—I was still too stunned by the *fact* of the money—so Marianne Engel saved me the trouble. "Two hundred thousand."

Two hundred thousand dollars. Which she'd left sitting under the bed all day. Which anyone could have walked away with. I called her stupid; she laughed and replied that against stupidity even the gods struggle in vain. And really, she asked, who would look under a hospital bed on Christmas Day for a briefcase of money?

"You think I can't afford you." She stated it as if there were no possibility that she might be wrong. She wasn't. When I nodded, she said, "I'm ready for my present now."

Over the previous weeks I'd fashioned dozens of versions of the same little speech, like a high school boy plotting how to ask his favorite girl to a dance, but now that the moment was upon me, I felt only uncertainty. Timidity. Embarrassment. I wanted to be suave but, just like that high school boy, I was struck dumb. It was too late to escape, and I knew that my gifts—there were three—were too personal. Too stupid. My hours of labor had been to no avail: what prideful delusions had convinced me to make these gifts? She'd think them childish; she'd think me too forward, or not forward enough. I wished for lightning bolts to blitz my room, to pierce the bedside table where my silly little offerings were hidden in a drawer.

I had written three poems for her. The spinesnake laughed at the sheer arrogance of my efforts.

All my life, I had written poetry, but I'd never shown it to anyone. I hid my writing, and hid myself within the writing that I kept hidden—only a man unable to handle the actual world would create another one in which to hide. Sometimes when I realize that I couldn't stop writing even if I wanted, a wave of discomfort shudders down my back, as if another man were standing too close to me at the public urinals.

Sometimes I feel there is something profoundly unmanly about any writing, but poetry is the worst of all. When I was gripped by fits of cocaine paranoia, I would burn my poetry journals and watch the burning pages peel off one another in layers, the flames spitting little gray flakes into the air. As my ashen words swirled into the heavens, it pleased me to know that my inner self was once again safe: a team of the FBI's best forensic scientists couldn't put my emotions back together again. The beauty of keeping my truest emotions hidden in my writing was that I could incinerate them at a moment's notice.

Speaking a woman into bed was safe, because my words disappeared with the vapor of my spoken breath; writing a poem for a woman was fashioning a weapon that she could later use to assault me. Giving away one's writing meant that it would be out there in the universe forever, ready to come back to wreak vengeance at any moment.

So I'd blown it. It was Christmas Day, I was stuck in the skeleton bed, I owed Marianne Engel a present, and I had no backup gift. I had only the childish scrawls that blackened the pages' white pu-

rity. My words were Egyptian hieroglyphics before the discovery of
the Rosetta stone; my words were wounded soldiers limping home,
guns spent, from a lost battle; my words were dying fish, flipping
hysterically as the net is opened and the pile spreads across the boat
deck like a slippery mountain trying to become a prairie.

My words were, and are, unworthy of Marianne Engel.

But I had no choice, so I reached into the desk drawer and—
LOSER—screwed my pale imitation of courage to an imaginary
sticking place. I pulled out the three single sheets of paper, closed
my eyes, and held the poems in Marianne Engel's direction, hoping
they wouldn't rot in my hands.

"Read them to me," she said.

I protested that I couldn't. These were poems, and my voice was
a deal at the crossroads gone horribly wrong. A fiery hellhound had
broken into my throat and left behind a busted guitar with rusty
strings. My voice was—is—majestically unfit for poetry.

"Read them to me."

Now it is years later. You have this book in your hands, so obviously I've overcome my fear about giving away written words. But
the three poems I read to Marianne Engel on that Christmas Day will
not be included in the pages of this story. You already have enough
incriminating evidence against me.

When I finished, she crawled into my bed. "That was lovely.
Thank you. Now I'll tell you how we first met."

XII.

fter I began reading the writings of Meister Eckhart, a change came into my way of thinking. It wasn't huge but it was enough, and I finally started to understand some of what Mother Christina had meant about losing the creatureliness of my soul in an effort to come closer to the Godhead. But I kept the book secret, because sisters like Gertrud would never even consider his more radical ideas. And while it was Eckhart who acted as the catalyst, it was someone else who accelerated my questioning. When one of our older nuns died, Gertrud assigned me her duties, which included dealing with the tradesman who supplied our parchment.

The parchmenter was rougher than the men I was used to, so it surprised me that we got along so well. The first thing he asked me to do was pray for him. He explained that the previous nun had done so, and it was my first lesson in how one hand washes the other. If I did, he'd give the monastery a discount. He admitted that he had sinned, but added with a sly smile that he "hadn't sinned in such a way as to afford indulgences."

He loved to talk about everything and I was impressed with his grasp of politics, but perhaps only because I didn't realize his complaints were standard in any tavern at the end of the day. During our monthly dealings, I learned much about the Germany that ex-

isted outside the monastery walls. Pope John was engaged in a feud
with Louis the Bavarian. Wars were breaking out, and local lords had
taken to hiring mercenary troops known as condotta; the linguist in
me recognized that the word was borrowed from the Italian. Death
was being sold for profit, completely without ideology or belief, and
this turned my stomach. I couldn't understand how men could do
such things, and yet the parchmenter only shrugged and assured me
it was happening everywhere.

In the scriptorium, Gertrud kept us working late into the night
on *Die Gertrud Bibel,* and the efforts were paying off. Even with her
passionate attention to detail, and even with all our other chores, I
could see that only a few more years of work remained. She was old,
but I knew that she would force herself to hold on. As pious as she
claimed to be, she would have argued with Christ Himself if He had
had the gall to try to take her away before her task was completed.

It was late one night, just like any other, when one of the nuns
arrived at the scriptorium and whispered of the arrival of two men,
one covered in such severe burns that he looked as though "he might
have battled the Enemy!" It all sounded interesting enough, but I
had work to do.

The following morning, Sister Mathildis, one of the monastery's
nurses, woke me in my cell and said that my presence was requested
in the infirmary, on Mother Christina's orders. I threw on my cloak
and we crossed the cloister garden together while she informed me
that she and the other infirmary nuns—Sisters Elisabeth and Constantia—had been up all night treating the burn victim. Everyone
was surprised he'd held on as long as he had.

Mother Christina met us at the infirmary door. Across the room,
Father Sunder and the nun-nurses were attending to a man under a
white sheet. An exhausted soldier, still in the ripped clothes of battle,
was slumped in a corner. When he saw me, he jumped up and asked,
"Can you help him?"

"Sister Marianne, this is Brandeis, who brought the burnt man to
us. We have consulted all our medical texts"—Mother Christina nod-

ded at the open books on a counter—"but there is no information sufficient for dealing with this type of injury."

I was at a loss as to what was expected of me. "Have you considered the Hospital of the Holy Spirit in Mainz? I am told it is one of the best."

Father Sunder now came forward. "We've considered it, of course, but his condition is too fragile to risk the journey. Whatever is done must be done here."

"If anyone knows the entire contents of the scriptorium, it is you," Mother Christina said. As a political afterthought, she added, "And Sister Gertrud, of course. But she has many pressing tasks, as befits her position, so I will ask you to scour the library for any information that might be of use."

Two things were immediately clear. First, this measure was being undertaken primarily to appease Brandeis: there was little chance that any of our books would actually contain useful information. Second, Mother Christina did not believe Gertrud would devote the necessary concentration to the search. While there was small hope that I'd find anything, small hope is better than none, and Mother Christina had apparently decided a man's life was more important than Gertrud's pride. Which, I admit, delighted me. But it would have been improper to show it, so I only bowed humbly and said that I was pleased to serve my prioress before God. My sole request was that I might check the soldier's wounds, so that I might know what remedy I was looking for.

As I approached the table, I saw your face for the first time. It was burned then, as it is now, although less severely, and there was a great puddle of blood at your chest, seeping through the white sheet. I couldn't help but think of a rose breaking through the snow. Even in the moment, I knew it was an inappropriate thought. Father Sunder looked to Mother Christina, who nodded her consent, and he gently peeled back the sheet. I could hear a slight tearing sound as the bloody fabric untacked itself from your body.

My reaction surprised me. I was fascinated more than anything else, and certainly not repulsed. While everyone else in the room, even the soldier Brandeis, took a step backward, I took a step forward.

There was scorched skin, of course, and your body was exuding more liquid than the bandages could absorb. I asked for a cloth to wipe away the excess. Black and red and gray all flowed into each other, but as I wiped away the charred residue, I made an amazing discovery. There was actually a rectangle of unburned flesh on your chest. It was on the left, just above your heart, and it stood out starkly in contrast to the destruction of the skin around it. Directly in its center was a single wound, a slit where some sharp instrument had cut into you. I asked Brandeis about this, and he answered that it was the entry point of the arrow that had hit you. He said that the arrow had not cut deeply and it was the fire that had caused the real damage.

I asked to know exactly what had happened. Brandeis' face dropped, because he had already told this story to the nurses and telling it again was the last thing he wanted to do. But he braced himself and began talking.

You and Brandeis belonged to a condotta, as mercenary archers, and he looked down at the floor as if ashamed to admit his profession in a house of the Lord. There had been a battle the day previous. One moment the two of you were side by side with your crossbows, and the next moment you were struck by a flaming arrow. Brandeis reacted quickly, but the fire was already spreading. Because the shaft was sticking straight out of your chest, you couldn't roll on the ground to extinguish the flames, so Brandeis broke the arrow near the head. At this point, he paused to hold out his palms and display his own considerable burns. He peeled away your burning clothes, but it was too late. The damage had been done.

He stayed at your side throughout the battle, using his crossbow to take down any attackers who dared to venture too close. Eventually, your troop prevailed and the fighting drew to a close. When your opponents had retreated, your fellow soldiers began to comb the carnage looking for survivors.

There were rules that everyone understood. If a wounded opponent was found, he would be executed. If one of your own was wounded but could be treated, treatment would be given. But if one of your soldiers was alive but injured past help, he too would be killed. This was considered an act of both mercy and economy. It was unbefitting for a good man to die a slow death, and it was not practical to waste resources to keep alive a useless soldier.

When you and Brandeis were discovered by your fellow mercenaries, a general consensus was quickly reached. You were too far gone and would be put out of your misery. And theirs.

A young warrior named Kuonrat stepped forward to offer his arm as the one to bring down the fatal sword, but do not think for a moment that this was a task he would regret. Kuonrat was an ambitious and bloodthirsty man with little in the way of conscience; he already had fixed his eye on the highest position, and your death would simply remove another of the old guard who was hindering his ascent to the position of condottiere, the troop's leader.

But it was Herwald who was still in command that day, and your history with him had been long. In fact, it was he who had brought you into the troop when you were still just a teenager. You were one of his longest-serving soldiers, and over the years he'd come to respect you greatly. He was not looking forward to ordering your execution but, without a choice, he knew that the responsibility could not fall to a man like Kuonrat. So Herwald offered it to Brandeis, your closest friend. If Brandeis declined, Herwald would do it himself.

Brandeis would hear no talk about killing you. He drew himself up to his full height and pulled out his sword. "I will take down any man who dares step forward. My friend will not be cut down like some lame horse."

Why couldn't Brandeis just take you somewhere to look after

you himself? The reason lies with the motto of the condotta. Once a soldier was in, he was in for life. That's the way it was, the way it had always been, and the way it always would be. A soldier needed to know that he could count on the man next to him, and there could be no desertion in times of trouble. To enforce this rule, anyone who attempted to leave was hunted down and brutally killed, with no exceptions. If Brandeis were allowed to leave to care for you, who would claim the same privilege next?

So Brandeis was standing over you, his sword raised against the entire troop and against a tradition that could not be broken. It was incredibly brave and incredibly stupid. But, perhaps, the other soldiers felt a grudging respect for someone who would risk his own life for a friend. The stalemate could be resolved only if Brandeis was able to offer a workable solution and, amazingly, he did just that.

Brandeis knew the proximity of Engelthal to the battle, and he knew of the monastery's reputation as a place where miracles occurred routinely. Brandeis swore, on his honor, that he would rejoin the troop before their next battle if he were allowed to bring you to the monastery. He put forward that—since everyone was convinced you would die anyway—you should at least be allowed to die under the protection of the Lord.

Herwald accepted the proposition, a rare concession on his part. Personally and politically, this was an astute decision. It illustrated that loyal soldiers would be rewarded, while at the same time it saved him from ordering the execution of an old friend. And no one could charge that he would be letting an able soldier leave the ranks, as Brandeis had promised to return.

Kuonrat the Ambitious knew better than to attack Herwald publicly when goodwill was high, but he did whisper to anyone who would listen that this was actually the second time that the condotta's supposedly unbreakable rule had been disregarded. "Does no one remember the Italian bowman Benedetto? We let him escape without sending soldiers to track him. Again Herwald has betrayed us with his weakness. How long can we allow this to continue?"

Only a few listened. Most agreed that after your years of service you should be allowed to die close to God, under the care of the sisters at Engelthal.

When Brandeis finished the story, he rubbed his exhausted face. It's possible that I saw a tear, but it might just have been sweat. And that's how you came to the monastery. How you came to me.

Brandeis' story had entranced everyone in the room, even those who'd heard it before. Father Sunder finally broke the silence, commending him for his most proper actions. Mother Christina said that she did not approve of mercenaries but recognized true brotherly love when she saw it. She assured Brandeis once more that we would do everything we could, and the nurse-nuns nodded their agreement. These were all good words, of course, but every face in the room was written with the same expression of pity. Everyone thought you would die.

I did not. I wanted to run my fingers over your wounds; I wanted your blood on me. Where everyone else saw a dying man, I saw a man awaiting resurrection. I thought of Christ's wounds in His finest hour.

Brandeis straightened his spine, the way men do when they think it'll give them greater strength than they actually possess. He bowed stiffly and said that he had to honor his promise to return to his troop. He had confidence in our abilities, he said, and in the goodness of the Lord. At the door he looked over his shoulder at you, one final time.

After Brandeis' departure, I spent the day poring through the scriptorium's volumes looking for anything that might be of service in your treatment. But as urgent as my task was, I had trouble keeping my focus. I tried to imagine the two of you in battle, but I couldn't. Brandeis seemed too concerned with your life to also be a killer, and the calm expression on your face as you lay on the table haunted me. I didn't realize it then, but you were in shock. At the time, it seemed to me as if your spirit had slipped out of the casing of your body. As a nun, I found this deeply disconcerting. It did not help my concentration to realize that I hadn't asked Brandeis why the rectangular area above your heart was not burned, in the midst of such damage to the rest of your torso.

Our books presented no remedies for your terrible burns. No shaft of light through a window illuminated a relevant passage, nor did the wind flow through an opened casement to flip a book to the correct page. In the evening, I felt obligated to return to the infirmary, if only to inform the nun-nurses that I'd made absolutely no progress.

The scene was markedly different from what I had seen earlier. You were screaming with a fury that I'd never heard in my life. My years of monastic silence had rendered me unable to imagine that a human body could produce such noises. The nuns were trying to hold you still, but it was a losing battle. Sister Elisabeth was more than happy to yield her place to me. You were drenched in your body's escaping fluids, and your eyes darted from side to side as if following a demon that only you could see. I placed my hands around your head, but you wouldn't stop thrashing. I stroked your hair and spoke soothing words as the others poured water over you. Each cool splash induced another jerk of your body. I grabbed a jug also, and tried my best to force liquid down your throat. When you finally opened your mouth to accept it, your eyes fluttered for a moment before going completely still.

A minute passed in eerie silence, and I could see in the way they glanced from face to face that everyone was certain you'd died. The nurses tentatively allowed themselves to sit down, exhausted from dealing with you.

And then you jolted awake with a gasp, your eyes filled with terror as if you had seen everything there was to know about death. You began to scream again, so I slapped your face and tried to force you to focus, but your eyes kept darting in search of that demon again. I grabbed you as vigorously as I dared and brought my face inches from yours, yelling. When you were finally able to concentrate upon me, your fear seemed to fly away.

The look in your eyes was more like recognition than anything else. We studied each other. I don't know how many moments passed. You tried to say something, but it was so soft I thought I must be imagining your voice. I brought my ear nearer to your mouth. The other nuns had taken a few steps back and could not hear that in a garbled voice, you said a few words.

"My heart . . . Locked . . . The key."

Then you closed your eyes and drifted back into unconsciousness.

I had no idea what you meant by these words, but they somehow strengthened my certainty that I was meant to help you. It is not in the nature of any nun to accept the idea of a man's heart being locked, especially the heart of a man who might so soon be at the threshold of Heaven—or, though I did not want to admit it to myself, Hell. One must be realistic about the final destination of a mercenary.

I stayed with you through the night and washed away the murky fluids that ran from your chest. I was as gentle as I could be, but your flesh still leapt beneath my touch. As difficult as it was to look upon your pain, I was certain—for the very first time in my life—that Engelthal was *exactly* the place for me to be. My lack of mystic visions, my lack of understanding about the Eternal Godhead, these things were now completely unimportant.

The following morning, on the way back to my cell, I met Gertrud. She inquired, with a fakely sweet voice, when I "might find a few moments away from the killer" to resume my scriptorium duties and continue God's work. I informed her that Mother Christina had specifically requested my help with the burn patient, and that was my primary responsibility at the moment. I also let it slip that Mother Christina thought I was uniquely qualified to find any relevant information in our scriptorium. I could see anger pass across Gertrud's face, but only for a moment.

When she regained her composure, Gertrud said, "It is most kind of Mother Christina to devote such resources to aiding this man. However, I think you would be wise to remember that only God can help this soldier. It is out of the hands of a bastard child left at the gate."

These were by far the harshest words she'd ever spoken to me. I was shocked, but I assured her that she was quite right, of course. I added that, nevertheless, I should excuse myself to say my prayers and get some sleep, just in case God did decide to grace a bastard child such as myself with the ability to assist a man in need.

When I returned to the infirmary later that day, I discovered that you'd had a very rough time in my absence. You'd been babbling incoherently, tossing violently. Mother Christina and Father Sunder were there, consulting with the nurses, but no one knew what to do next.

Without warning, you lifted an arm and pointed at me. All your confused talk fell away and you called out in a clear voice: "This one."

Everyone was stunned. Except for the few words that only I had heard, this was the first time you had spoken. There was a perfect dramatic pause in the room before you added, "I had a vision."

The nuns gasped and Mother Christina uttered an immediate prayer for guidance. A soldier having a vision: truly Engelthal was a mystical and wonderful place! But I didn't believe it. You'd been in the monastery for a short time, I thought, but somehow you'd managed to learn that the only currency which mattered was heavenly revelations.

Mother Christina took a tentative step forward. "What kind of vision?"

You pointed at me again and whispered, "God said this one would heal me."

Mother Christina clutched tightly at Father Sunder's arm. "Are you certain?"

You nodded almost imperceptibly and closed your eyes, exactly the way the nuns did to show just how deeply they were in contemplation.

The nun-nurses clasped their hands in holy fear and kneeled in reverence, while Father Sunder and Mother Christina withdrew into a corner to confer. Shortly after, Mother Christina took my hands into her own. "It is highly strange, Sister Marianne, but we must take him at his word. Have I not always known there was something more to you than meets the eye?"

Perhaps Mother Christina, bless her, was anticipating a marvelous new chapter in her Engelthal chronicles. Who was I to disappoint? I nodded, as though the mantle of chosen healer was a heavy burden for an unexceptional sister such as I, but one that I would shoulder for the sake of our monastery. Behind Mother Christina, you appeared to have lapsed back into unconsciousness, but there was the trace of a smile on your lips.

The other nuns gave me great leeway in your treatment after the revelation. No doubt, they didn't want their earthly mistakes to sully divine remedy. I cleaned your wounds with cold water and changed your bandages, but I also took to cutting away bad flesh, a procedure that drew protests from the others until I reminded them of your vision. Perhaps they didn't have the stomach for it, or perhaps they thought we had no right to desecrate a body created by the Lord, but whatever the reason, they always left the room when I did it.

Why I decided cutting was the correct course of action, I'll never know. From my birth, it had been ingrained in me that one had to separate the bad from the good, so maybe I was only taking this idea to its most literal level. And why you allowed me to cut at your skin, I also don't know, but you did. You screamed, and slipped in and out of consciousness, but you never once told me to stop using the knife. I was amazed by your courage.

In that first week you were consistently delirious. On the seventh day, your fever broke and you finally woke fully into the world. I was dabbing the sweat from your brow when you looked up and began to sing in a weak voice.

Dû bist mîn, ich bin dîn:
des solt dû gewis sîn;
dû bist beslozzen in mînem herzen,
verlorn ist daz slüzzelîn:
dû muost och immer darinne sîn.

It did not matter, the fact that you coughed fitfully in the middle of your singing. Simply because it came from the throat of a recovering man, it was more beautiful than any song that I had heard ever lifted on the nuns' voices in salute to the glory of the Lord.

Word of your awakening traveled the length of Engelthal. "Truly a miracle has been worked through the hands of Sister Marianne!" I thought that common sense would prevail, but you can't argue with a monastery of elated nuns. Even Gertrud and Agletrudis stopped whispering into the ear of Mother Christina that I needed to get back to my scriptorium duties.

XIII.

o what did the song mean?"

"How strange that you no longer remember your mother tongue," Marianne Engel mused. *"You are mine, I am yours: you may be sure of this. You've been locked inside my heart, the key has been thrown away; within it, you must always stay.* It's a traditional love ballad."

"Why that one?" I asked.

"You were a warrior, not a singer. Maybe it was the only song you knew."

We spoke more—mostly she talked, explaining the tradition of the Minnelieder—medieval love songs—to me, until it came time for her to leave. After gathering her belongings, she asked me to close my eyes.

When I did, she slipped over my head a thin strand of leather, with a hanging coin as its pendant. "The proper name for that is an 'angel.' They were issued in England in the sixteenth century. Please allow me to make a gift of it to you."

On one side of the coin was the image of someone killing a dragon; Marianne Engel explained its history. "It's the Archangel Michael, from Revelation. 'And there was war in Heaven: Michael and his angels fought against the dragon. . . . And the great dragon was cast out.' "

"Thank you," I said.

"When the time comes, you'll know what to do with that coin."

Such comments from Marianne Engel, nonsensical at worst and cryptic at best, were so common that I had stopped asking what they meant. Trying to get her to explain herself in these matters usually brought our conversations to a halt and, ultimately, she never really explained anyway.

Marianne Engel informed me that she'd not be able to return until after the New Year because she had a basement full of neglected grotesques. As she headed towards the door, she patted the briefcase containing the two hundred grand. "Don't forget, you're coming to live with me."

· · ·

DO YOU THINK SHE WILL EMPTY YOUR CATHE-TER'S DRAINAGE BAG?

I concentrated on the emptiness of the room. I would not allow my serpentine tormentor to succeed in her efforts.

I WONDER IF SHE WILL BRING HOME MEN WITH PENISES?

The most useful function of my old drug habit was the ability to write off entire days. I longed for the whiteout that cocaine and booze could always provide.

WOMEN HAVE NEEDS WHICH YOU CANNOT FUL-FILL.

Dr. Edwards entered, wearing a bright red sweater for the holidays. I'd never seen her in anything other than her lab coat. "I hear the party was a good time."

I was pleased to see Nan, because her appearance meant the snake would disappear for a while. The snake liked to confront me when we were alone. "It's too bad you weren't there."

She checked my medical chart. "Maybe next year."

"Did you have anything to do with it?" I asked. "I mean, there must have been a lot of forms to fill out. Legal documents, disclaimers, that sort of thing."

"The hospital did have to consider its position," Nan admitted, "and demand legal indemnity on a lot of issues. What if someone got food poisoning?"

"I can't imagine Marianne navigated the paperwork by herself."

"I acted as a liaison between her and the board," Nan said, "but only because I thought it would be good for all the patients. Not just you."

"Thank you. I know you don't like her very much."

Dr. Edwards' back straightened, slightly. "I think she is a fine person."

"It's only as a caregiver that you have doubts."

"It doesn't matter much what I think."

"Of course it does," I said. "I like your sweater. Are you going out?"

She looked down as if she had forgotten that she was wearing it, but it was bad pantomime. "I'd prefer to keep my personal life personal."

"Fair enough," I said. "Why did you become a doctor?"

"That's a personal question."

"No," I corrected, "it's about your profession."

She tilted her head to one side. "For the same reason anyone does, I guess. To help people."

"And I thought some doctors did it for the money," I said. "Why the burn ward? There are easier places to work."

"I like it here."

"Why?"

"When people leave here, there's a . . ." Nan paused, thinking about the best choice of words. "When I was a resident, they taught me to consider everyone who came here to be already dead. It's a trick, you know, because so many burn patients die in the first few days. But if you consider the patient to be dead when he arrives, and then he manages to somehow make it . . ."

"It's a way to think you only save people and never lose them," I said. "Does it work?"

"Sometimes I hate it here."

"Me, too." I wanted to reach out to take her hand, but I knew better. So instead I said, "I think you're an excellent doctor."

"I'm selfish. I just want that feeling I get every time a patient walks out of here." She looked up from her feet and back into my eyes. "Did anyone ever tell you that your heart stopped twice during your emergency surgeries?"

"No. I guess it's safe to assume it started again."

"They don't always."

"I am going to live with Marianne."

"I just don't want you to make a mistake after you've come this far."

"If I don't go to her, I have no idea why you saved my life."

Nan thought about this statement, taking a few moments before speaking again. "I can't save anyone's life. The very best I can do is help a few not die before their time, and I can't even do that very often."

"Well," I said, "I'm still here."

"Yes, you are." She reached down and took my hand in hers, but only for a moment. She then turned to leave the room but at the door spun around and added, almost impulsively, "I'm meeting my ex-husband for a glass of brandy. That's why I'm wearing the sweater."

"I didn't know you'd been married."

"I was, and I'm not now." She fidgeted with the door handle, turning it a couple of times. "My husband is a good person but we were a bad match. It happens."

• • •

After New Year's, Marianne Engel stepped up her participation in my physical therapy sessions. I was being trained in the arts of brushing my teeth, buttoning shirts, and using utensils, practicing these ADLs—activities of daily living—for the time that I would be released. Each time I used my good hand to manage these tasks, Sayuri rebuked me. While it would be easier in the short term, she argued, it would give my damaged hand license to wither. Even such simple activities were "exercise."

I was scheduled for a tutorial on bathing, one more thing that I would have to learn all over again, and I had a great deal of discomfort with the idea of Marianne Engel's attendance at this lesson. Though she had been helping with most aspects of my rehabilitation, she had not yet been present when my bandages were fully removed. She knew that my penis was gone; she simply had not *not* seen it yet. When I moved into her house, she would be the one to help me bathe, and obviously that would be impossible with my clothing on. Still, I was not ready for her to witness this specific lack in my physique.

A compromise was reached. Even though Sayuri thought it would be best if Marianne Engel were involved in the practice from the start, we would do the first few baths without her, while I was given more time to adjust to the idea.

• • •

Gregor was ecstatic about his evening with Akira Kurosawa and Sayuri Mizumoto.

He regaled me with stories about what they had bought at the concession stand (popcorn + licorice twists); how Sayuri did not like licorice (apparently a cultural thing, as most Japanese people think it tastes like bad Chinese medicine); how their fingers had accidentally touched while they were reaching for popcorn at the same time; how they held hands after the popcorn was gone; how all he could think about was the buttery residue on his fingers; how he was praying she didn't think the butter grease was sweat; how he wiped his fingers on his pants so as not to offend her with his greasy hands; how for the remainder of the evening there were four greasy finger streaks on his pants; how he was certain that she would find the streaks a disgusting indication of his poor hygiene; and so forth. It was all very cute. Gregor told me everything except the name of the movie, which I suppose was the least important aspect of the event.

At the end of their evening, Sayuri agreed to eat dinner with Gregor at Rasputin's on the following weekend.

• • •

Marianne Engel pushed my wheelchair into a room where a large group of interns was waiting. Sayuri introduced me to everyone and then asked a seemingly innocent question: "What is my job?"

The interns looked to each other, sensing a trick. A young man in the back suggested, obviously, that Sayuri was a physical therapist. Her ever-wide smile spread ever wider as she shook her head. "Today I'm a tailor. These measurements are extremely important, because the suit we're making will be worn twenty-four hours a day, for a year."

She pulled out a tape measure and asked who wanted to help. Two interns stepped forward and were soon laying out scraps of fabric, the kind used to make pressure garments, along the contours of my body. The work took longer than I expected, mostly because they were so unsure of themselves. Sayuri patiently dealt with all their questions and it was obvious that not only was she a good teacher, she enjoyed it as well. When the measurements were finished, she was glowing as she exclaimed that what came next—making the first impression for the plexiglass mask I'd need to wear—was far more challenging.

"Most of his head surgeries have already been performed and the swelling in his face has subsided, so the primary function of the mask is to minimize scarring. What do we do first?"

"We make a negative impression of the face," answered one of the students.

"Nope," Sayuri said, holding up a camera. "We take photographs for reference when we're preparing the inside of the mask. How would you like to wear a mask for a year if it didn't fit properly?"

Sayuri took the pictures herself, shooting from all angles to capture every nuance of my face. I hated that she was making a permanent record of how I looked. When she put the camera down, she said, "*Now* it's time for the impression. What do we do first?"

At least one student had read the correct chapter in the book. "We pour GelTrate over the face, and then we lay on plaster strips."

"Excellent. You come help." Sayuri pulled a white sheet off a nearby table; underneath were all the materials necessary for the job. Little circles of cloth were placed over my eyes, and small tubes were put into my nostrils so that I could breathe. The student applied the first squirts of GelTrate into his hands and began spreading it around my face. "This is the same material that's used to take dental impressions. It's good to remember that, because no one likes that stuff. Be gentle when applying it."

The intern's fingers were tentative, compared with Sayuri's, but she praised him anyway, and then she asked a few others to "step forward and give it a go." The feeling of so many hands touching me was overwhelming. Sayuri kept explaining as they worked, "It's important that we get the natural shape of the head, the cheekbones, around the eyes. . . . Remember to be gentle. . . ."

After the GelTrate came a neck splint to hold me steady as the interns laid the strips of plaster into place. Sayuri instructed them on the proper angles, occasionally smoothing out a mistake but mostly just reminding them to take care. "This is not only skin, it's burnt skin. Remember that."

When the plaster was finally in place, we had to wait for it to harden. Sayuri used this time to answer questions on my recovery; with my head covered in plaster, I was unable to add anything to the conversation. In a whisper, so as not to disturb the students, Marianne Engel suggested that she could read me the final canto of *Inferno*. The offer pleased me greatly; I wanted to hear her voice in the darkness.

She began:

"On march the banners of the King of Hell,"
my Master said. "Toward us. Look straight ahead:
can you make him out at the core of the frozen shell?"

Satan, the King of Hell, trapped in a frozen shell in the very bowels of the *Inferno:* how fitting an image, I mused, as I lay wrapped in my own shell of plaster. Dante's master was Virgil, leading him ever forwards, while my guide was Marianne Engel. She slipped twice into the Italian, catching herself and laughing before reverting to English. In the background were the muffled voices of the interns, still learning about the tribulations of burn treatment. When Sayuri decided it was time to remove the mask, I could feel her fingers peeling away the plaster. Just as I was reintroduced to the room's light, Marianne Engel read Dante's final line softly into my better ear:

. . . And we walked out once more beneath the Stars.

♦ ♦ ♦

"Only wear short-sleeved white cotton shirts," Dr. Edwards said, "and run them through the laundry cycle a few extra times with only water. Soap residue is horrible for healing skin."

I was scheduled to leave the hospital; I had made such good progress that I was being released in mid-February, almost two months earlier than expected. Nan pointed towards the thick book of rehabilitation instructions in Marianne Engel's hands. "The tub needs to be sterilized before every bath, and chemicals added to the water. The list of chemicals is in the book. We'll give you enough for the first week, but then you'll have to buy your own. There's also a list of appropriate soaps. Don't forget to apply the salves after bathing, and then apply new bandages. Your pressure garments will be ready in about a month, but until then it's still bandages. Oh, and if you used cologne or deodorant before the accident, they're absolutely forbidden now."

"Anything else?" asked Marianne Engel.

Nan thought for a moment. "Be careful of insects. A sting can result in a nasty infection. There aren't any insects in your house, are there?"

"Of course not," Marianne Engel said, before adding, "but one of my friends was stung by a wasp once and was mistaken for dead. It was horrible."

There was a pause in the conversation as both Dr. Edwards and I tried to figure out what Marianne Engel was talking about. We looked at each other and came to an unspoken agreement that to ask would be futile, so Nan simply commented that anaphylactic shock is certainly common in such cases and continued her instructions on my care. She reminded me to pay as much attention to hidden damage as to that which was readily apparent. Skin is the organ that regulates body temperature, releasing excess heat through sweat on a hot day or during exercise, and my body had lost much of that ability. Because of the damage to my sweat glands and pores, my brain would face severe challenges in managing the nervous and endocrine controls. Theoretically, my body could revolt and fry itself from the inside out; if I didn't take care, I might become my own spontaneous human combustion.

"We've kept things at a good temperature for you here in your room," Dr. Edwards said, "but you'll probably have to play with the air conditioning to find what works. You *do* have air conditioning, don't you, Marianne?"

"I'll get it installed as soon as possible."

"Good. Any final questions?"

I asked how much morphine they would provide. (I was certain that the bitchsnake wouldn't slither out of my spine as I exited the hospital.)

"A month's worth," Nan answered, "but be careful. A little pain now is better than going through life as an addict. Do I make myself understood?"

"Of course," I said. But I was THIRSTY thinking about my next delicious dose.

Now that the treatment instructions were completed, I was placed into a wheelchair, in keeping with hospital policy, and Nan pushed me to the front door. Marianne Engel didn't even protest that she should be the one pushing; perhaps she thought that Dr. Edwards needed to do it for her patients, as a ritual to let them go.

At the front entrance, I stood up while Nan gave a final warning. "People think that when a burn patient goes home, the worst part's over. Really, what happens is that you lose the hospital's everyday support system. But we're still here, so don't hesitate to call if you need anything at all."

Unlike Howard, I did not have a contingent of friends, family, and ex-fiancées to see me off. But I could hardly complain; unlike Thérèse, I was leaving alive. The hospital staff and Marianne Engel gathered around for a hearty exchange of "Thank you"s and "Good luck"s. Connie gave me a hug, Beth gave me a strong handshake, and while Maddy was not there, I'm sure that if she had been, she would have shaken her ass. Sayuri promised to come over soon to continue my gait training, and apologized for Gregor's absence at my farewell. An emergency with one of his patients, she explained.

I expected Nan to extend her hand, but she did not. She hugged Marianne Engel, telling her to look after me. Then she kissed me on my cheek and told me to look after Marianne Engel as well.

◆ ◆ ◆

They let schizophrenics drive? Apparently so. Marianne Engel owned a '70s muscle car, which was the last vehicle I would have imagined for her; therefore, it was perfect. She bragged that it had once belonged to the winner of the Medicine Hat Beauty Pageant, 1967.

YOU CAN'T EVEN BE IN A CAR WITH HER . . .

During the last moments before I was committed to the hospital, I was being extracted from a smoldering car wreck. Now here I was, first thing upon discharge, getting into a vehicle. I knew I couldn't walk but I wished there was another way to go.

. . . WITHOUT WONDERING IF SHE SHOULD BE DRIVING.

The engine turned over like a grouchy bear yawning his way out of hibernation. The ancient eight-track was busted and so, to keep herself amused as she drove, Marianne Engel sang. At first, Edith Piaf flew out of her mouth like a beautifully wrecked little sparrow; after this, she sang herself "so long" in the Leonard Cohen song.

At a traffic light, we pulled up alongside a couple in an old Ford truck. The woman in the passenger seat saw me—I was still in bandages, and would be until the pressure garments were ready—and she bleated out a little scream before swiveling her head back to the road in an effort to pretend that her reaction had never happened.

The woman had looked at us and thought Marianne Engel was the normal one.

NEITHER OF YOU IS NORMAL.

This was what it was going to be like, and I guess I should have been prepared. But I wasn't.

XIV.

I shouldn't have been surprised that the first building I saw when we turned onto Lemuria Drive was a church. St. Romanus of Condat was a large structure trying hard to look more respectable than it really was. It didn't look as if it had been mistreated, but rather as if the money had simply run out. The paint was peeling, the bricks were chipped, and the cracks in the windows were covered with transparent packing tape. There was a sign beside the concrete walkway leading to the front doors, proclaiming in black letters on a white plastic background that Father Shanahan invited everyone to Sunday Mass. Behind St. Romanus was a crumbling graveyard with row upon row of weathered gray slabs that poked out of the ground like Alka-Seltzer tablets dropped on edge. The brown grass was like uncut hair and remembrance flowers were decaying upon the plots. A few of the larger gravestones depicted angels carrying the dead heavenward. I asked Marianne Engel whether she had sculpted any of these. No, she said, she didn't do that kind of work.

Her house, on the next lot over from St. Romanus, was actually more like a fortress: a great stone stronghold that looked as if it could withstand a siege by Huns. She could see that I was impressed into a stupor by the solidness of the place, and explained that she couldn't imagine living in a building that wouldn't stand against the passage of time.

As she helped me out of the car, I asked whether it ever bothered her that she lived next to a graveyard. She just shrugged and suggested that I be careful of the cobblestones on the path, because some of them were loose. A gnarled excuse for a tree stood over a wheelbarrow serving as a planter, its rusty front wheel disappearing into the earth. There was a mailbox that allowed letters to be inserted into the gaping mouth of a dragon.

At the side of the house were two massive oak doors on great steel hinges that opened into her basement workshop, specifically installed to receive her stone slabs. "A lot of the renovations were tax writeoffs. That's what Jack told me, anyway." YOU DIDN'T FORGET ABOUT JACK, DID YOU?

A creamy brown dog came running out of the backyard, the famous Bougatsa. Marianne Engel bent down to massage his big stupid head, bending his ears back. "Boogie!" It only took a moment to decide that this pooch confirmed everything I disliked about dogs. It was obtuse in the way only a dog can be, a retarded tongue slopping from side to side, its head bobbing around like a plastic hula dancer on the dashboard of a pimp's car.

I BET JACK IS A NORMAL MAN, WITH LOTS TO OFFER.

"How about we sing the nice man a song?" Marianne Engel produced a groan such as a chain-smoking Sasquatch might make, and Bougatsa joined in, trying to mimic it. I already knew that she could sing well, so it was clear she sang this way only to play with the dog. Now, my ears are fleshy little stubs, somewhat like dried apricots that stick out from my closed fist of a head. The right ear is mostly deaf but the left ear remains sensitive enough to know how truly awful they sounded. The upward tilt of their heads suggested that they could imagine high notes floating above them, waiting to be jumped up on. They missed. No wonder Marianne Engel lived next to a graveyard: who but the dead could put up with her?

LIKE A JOB. Reptilian bitch. LIKE A FUTURE.

As they caterwauled, I drank in the oddity of her home. The windowsills were of heavy wood, and the windows of such thick-leaded glass that an errant baseball would probably have bounced off. The stone blocks looked as if men with hairy arms and fat bellies had lifted them into place, one by one, and then whacked them into position with heavy mallets. Green tentacles of ivy climbed the walls towards the most striking aspect of the entire place: the carved monstrosities that lined the gutters. As a way to get Marianne Engel to stop yodeling, I pointed out that you didn't see many gargoyles on private residences.

"If you did, I'd be rich. They're good promotion, even got me an article in the paper. Besides, I've got more of the little guys than I know what to do with."

The fiends gazed down, their oversized eyes bulging in my direction no matter the little steps I took to the right or the left. Their twisted bodies mesmerized me: the upper body of a man disappeared into a fishtail without quite turning him into a proper merman; an ape's torso lurched out of a horse's haunches; the head of a bull jutted from the body of a winged lion. A snake grew out of a bat. A woman's face spat an angry mouthful of frogs. In every body, disparate beasts coexisted; it was difficult to determine where one ended and the next began, and it was impossible to know which beasts—or which parts of which beasts—were good and which bad.

"We need them up there," Marianne Engel said.

"For what?"

"To keep away the evil spirits." She took me by the hand to lead me through the front door. I asked why she didn't have a drawbridge and a moat. Zoning regulations, she explained.

I expected that the interior would be all velvet tapestries and thrones, but there were vast expanses of emptiness. Square wooden pillars held up the roof, and the floor consisted of wide planks. She placed her jacket on an iron coatrack just inside the door and said, noticing my interest in the wood, "The beams are cedar and the rafters are fir."

She started my tour of the house in the living room, which was painted bright red. There was a great fireplace with an interlaced pattern of angels and demons around its stony mouth. There were two armchairs, with a grand rug between, which looked as if they were awaiting regents to sit in them and have serious conversations.

The dining room had large paintings on the walls, mostly intense splashes of color across flowing shapes. They were more abstract than I'd expected; if someone had asked me to guess, I would have said that she'd have paintings with religious themes. But not so. There was an expansive oak table with a fresh display of purple flowers at the center, and candles in iron holders on either side. "Francesco made those. When you see metalwork in this house, you can assume that he did it." I nodded my head: Sure, why not? Aren't most homes furnished by Italian ghosts?

In the kitchen were a fat silver stove, an ancient refrigerator, and rows of copper pots hanging from the ceiling. Glass jars with pastas and spices lined the shelves, and sunflower-yellow paint kept the room relentlessly upbeat. Everything was in its place, and the only sign of disarray was an overflowing ashtray. Her house once again surprised me: not the ashtray, but the order.

Her study was dominated by a large wooden desk, which she claimed had once belonged to a king of Spain. I just nodded again: Sure, why not? Italian ghosts can't do everything. Behind the desk was a very sturdy chair, and to its right side was a leather couch that looked as if it were waiting for one of Dr. Freud's patients.

Bookshelves, heavy with serious volumes, lined three of the walls. Spenser, Milton, Donne, Blake, and the Venerable Bede represented the English. The German authors included Hartmann von Aue, Wolfram von Eschenbach, Ulrich von Türheim, Walther von der Vogelweide, and Patrick Süskind. Russian books included *The Life of Archpriest Avvakum*, Mikhail Lermontov's *Demon*, and *Dead*

Souls by Nikolai Gogol. Spain supplied the masterpieces of St. Teresa of Ávila: *The Interior Castle* and *The Way of Perfection*. The Greeks were not going to allow themselves to be forgotten: Homer, Plato, Aristotle, Euripides, and Sophocles took up most of the bottom shelf, as if they had long ago decided that bookshelves would be incomplete without everyone else standing on their shoulders. There was a half-wall of Latin volumes, but the only ones that caught my eye were Cicero's *Dream of Scipio* and Ovid's *Metamorphoses*. Looking a little out of place, but not wanting to be left off the world stage, were a number of books from Asia. I couldn't tell the Chinese characters from the Japanese, and often even the translated English title couldn't give the book's homeland away. Finally, there were copies of all the major religious texts: the Bible, the Talmud, the Qur'an, the four Vedas, and so on.

The most striking thing about the collection was that there were two copies, side by side, of every foreign book: the original, and an English translation. Naturally, I asked Marianne Engel about this.

"The English versions are for you," she said. "That way we can talk about them."

"And the originals?"

"Why would I read translations?"

Marianne Engel reached among the books to withdraw two that were not professionally published, but handwritten on thick paper and bound with uneven stitching. The penmanship was her own and the text was, thankfully, in English rather than German. Christina Ebner's *Revelations* and *The Gnaden-vita of Friedrich Sunder*.

"I thought you might want to read these," she said, "so I translated them."

There was another item of interest on the bookshelf: a small stone angel whose wings reached heavenward. I inquired whether she had carved it but my question, so innocently asked, seemed to hurt her. She blinked a few times, as if trying to keep herself from crying, and puckered her mouth in an effort to calm her quivering lower lip. "You carved that for me," she said with a cracking voice. "It was my *Morgengabe*."

That concluded the tour of the main floor. Her workshop was in the basement, but I didn't have the legs to go down. My first day out of the hospital had been long enough and, in truth, the freedom was overwhelming. I'd grown accustomed to knowing every inch of my surroundings and every minute of my schedule, but now I was confronted with endless new sensations. We passed the remainder of the afternoon sitting in the living room, talking, but she couldn't seem to put back on her face the smile that had been wiped away by my question about the stone angel.

THIS WON'T LAST, YOU KNOW. The snake swished its tail around my intestines. YOU WILL CRUSH HER UNDER YOUR INSENSITIVITY.

In the early evening, I climbed the stairs to the upper floor with Marianne Engel walking behind to make sure I didn't tumble. I was aching for a needle of morphine that would shut up the bitchsnake. I had a choice of two rooms: one was the visitor's room, already made up, the other an atticlike recess that overlooked the graveyard behind St. Romanus. Marianne Engel was concerned that the odd shape of the room, wedged as it was in the corner of the roof, might be too oppressive after months in the hospital, but I instantly took a liking to it. "It's like a belfry. It's perfect."

She fixed me with morphine that was sweeter than the desert's first rainfall, and the snake slithered silently into her hole. I assumed I would sleep through until the next morning, but it didn't work out that way. It was February and not yet warm outside, but for some reason it seemed ridiculously hot inside. Perhaps the effect was partially psychological, from the stress of sleeping in a new place for the first time in ten months.

My unbreathing skin revolted in the feverish night and I dreamed of concentration camps, of human ovens, of people with matchstick bodies. Their hunger was transforming them into something too thin to be human. Their eyes bulged and accused; they were hunting me with their stares. Someone said in German, "𝕬𝖑𝖑𝖊𝖘 𝖇𝖗𝖊𝖓𝖓𝖙, 𝖜𝖊𝖓𝖓 𝖉𝖎𝖊 𝕱𝖑𝖆𝖒𝖒𝖊 𝖓𝖚𝖗 𝖍𝖊𝖎𝖟 𝖌𝖊𝖓𝖚𝖌 𝖎𝖘𝖙. 𝕯𝖎𝖊 𝖂𝖊𝖑𝖙 𝖎𝖘𝖙 𝖓𝖎𝖈𝖍𝖙𝖘 𝖆𝖑𝖘 𝖊𝖎𝖓 𝕾𝖈𝖍𝖒𝖊𝖑𝖟𝖙𝖎𝖊𝖌𝖊𝖑." *Everything burns if the flame is hot enough. The world is nothing but a crucible.* It was the same phrase I'd heard in my hospital nightmare about the skeleton bed going up in a shrouded flame.

I awoke suddenly upright in my thin sheets, wishing I could sweat. I heard the snake chanting the word `HOLOCAUST. HO-` `LOCAUST. HOLOCAUST. HOLOCAUST.` The word, I am told, literally means "burning everything." The belfry was cooking me; Dr. Edwards had been correct, we needed air conditioning. `I` `AM COMING AND THERE IS NOTHING YOU CAN DO` `ABOUT IT.` There could be no denying that the snake was persistent; it was like having a Jehovah's Witness living in my spine. `I` `AM COMING AND THERE IS NOTHING YOU CAN DO` `ABOUT IT.`

I looked at Friedrich Sunder's *Gnaden-vita* (which means "Mercy-life") on my bedside table. I decided that I didn't have it in me to do any reading, especially not something that challenging. I got up on uncooperative legs and, with a little persuasion, was able to point them in the direction of the master bedroom, from which—to my surprise—Marianne Engel was absent. I listened to the house. From below, I heard faint strains of classical music that I didn't recognize but that, for some reason, made me think about field workers. I struggled down both flights of stairs, from belfry to main floor, then from main floor to basement workshop.

There were a hundred candles, a hundred dots of fire in the room. I did not like this. Rivers of lush red wax flowed down iron candleholders; little splashes blotted the stone floor like an upside-down canopy of ruby stars. I could make out the grand oak doors on one side of the room and a considerable wooden workbench on the other. Tools on hooks lined the wall, and a coffeemaker sat on a shelf next to the stereo that was playing the music. A push broom leaned against the wall near a pile of carelessly swept stone fragments. But these were the unimportant details.

Everywhere there were incomplete monsters. It was generally the bottom halves of the grotesques that remained unfinished, as if the hobgoblin mafia had given them the proverbial cement shoes. A half sea-savage was using her webbed hands to claw out of a granite ocean. The upper body of a terrified monkey burst out of a lion whose legs were not yet carved. A bird's head sat on the shoulders of a human, but everything below the chest was untouched marble. The shimmer of the candlelight only amplified the beasts' already exaggerated features.

The workshop was a symphony of unwholeness, with grotesques caught between existence and nonexistence. It was difficult to tell whether they were ecstatic or melancholic, fearful or fearless, soulful or soulless; perhaps they themselves didn't know yet. There wasn't even enough light to decide whether they were beautiful or disgusting. And in the midst of these rough gargoyles, Marianne Engel was sleeping upon a huge slab of stone, undressed except for the necklace whose arrowhead, resting in the valley of her breasts, moved slightly up and down with the rhythm of her breath. She was at home here, the nude one danced upon by the shadows and light, her hair twisted around her body like wings woven from black rope. She clung to her rock like moss waiting to absorb the rain, and I couldn't remove my eyes from her glorious body. I didn't want to stare; I just couldn't force myself to stop.

I was aware that I was invading something intensely personal; something about the scene was more vulnerable than her nudity. I felt as if I were interrupting a private conversation, and I knew I should leave immediately.

I climbed back up to the main floor and decided to sleep in the study because it was cooler than the belfry. I placed towels on the leather couch because I still shed skin, and lay down. I administered another generous shot of morphine, because one man's poison is another man's warm milk. There were no more dreams of holocausts that night.

◆ ◆ ◆

I awoke to find Marianne Engel, wearing a white robe, standing over me. We talked for a few minutes before she bundled me off to the washroom, where a bath had already been drawn with the proper chemicals added and a thermometer hung over the tub's edge. "Take off your clothes."

I had managed to avoid bathing practice with her at the hospital through a combination of luck and deceit, but my luck had run out. My benefactor was now demanding to see my exposed body, so I played the only card left in my deck: I told her that my naked-ness in front of her would make me feel self-conscious, and asked whether she could understand that. She told me she could, but it didn't change the fact that I needed to be washed. I told her that she needed to respect my privacy. She laughed and told me about an es-pecially vivid dream she'd had the night before in which I'd stood in the middle of her workshop, looking upon her nude body.

I could hardly talk my way out of that. The best I could do was cut a new deal: I agreed to allow her to bathe me if she'd fix me with more dope first. Compromise accepted. Soon I stood unclothed, looking as if I were made out of rubber that hadn't set properly in the mold, while she searched my abominable body for an appropri-ate morphine-hungry vein.

THIS IS WHERE SHE SEES YOU FOR YOUR LACK.

Her hand rested on my hip and my left arm was presented for the drugs, but my right arm hung strategically in front of my groin.

She prepared the needle, placed the tip where it might enter, and asked, "Is this a good place?" SHE CAN ENTER YOU . . . I nodded. The needle penetrated and I wasn't even thinking about the morphine that was coming; I was only thinking . . . BUT YOU

CAN'T ENTER HER that I had to make sure I did not move my right arm.

"Into the tub," she said. But I was unable to climb into it without moving my right arm. So I just stood there, concealing the blank space between my hips.

"I will help you wash each day," she said gently. "It'll be difficult to keep hiding it."

There is nothing to hide, I thought.

"I already know it is missing."

I didn't say anything.

"You think I will be repulsed," continued Marianne Engel, "or my feelings will change."

Finally I spoke. "Yes."

"You are mistaken."

I dropped my arm as if challenging her, as if I expected her reaction to prove her words wrong. I wanted her to recoil at the closed scar where one could imagine that my body had been cut open, the penis pushed in, and the slit sewn shut. I wanted her to recoil at the sight of my lonely scrotum, which looked for all the world like a tumbleweed on the abandoned street of a ghost town.

But she did not pull back; instead, she kneeled in front of my naked body, and leaned in. Her head even with my groin, she narrowed her eyes and studied the faint scratch-lines of stitches, long since pulled out, that closed up the place where my penis had been. She lifted her hand and pulled it back, but not in revulsion: she seemed to be acting on the instinct that my body was hers to touch before realizing that it was not, not in this century at least. So she looked up at me and requested permission.

I cleared my throat, once, twice, and then nodded weakly.

Marianne Engel reached out again, and this time her fingertips grazed my crinkled wasteland. I could not feel the touch at all, because the scarring was too dense, too complete; I only knew her fingertips were upon me because I could see them there.

"Stop now," I said.

"Does it hurt?"

"No." Third clearing of my throat. "Haven't you seen enough?"

SHE'S SEEN NOTHING.

She removed her fingers and stood. She looked directly into my eyes with hers, green this day, and they worked the way they sometimes did, unsettling me. "I don't mean to make you feel uncomfortable."

"You do," I said. "Sometimes."

"Do you really believe," she asked, "that I ever loved you because of your body?"

"I don't . . ." Fourth, fifth; damn my throat. "I guess not." And to show that I meant it, I climbed into the bath without any more argument.

The tub was a massive thing with lion's paws for feet, and soon Marianne Engel was scrubbing away the dead outer layers of my skin. It was a painful process, so she distracted me—and demonstrated she was ready to move on in our conversation—by asking why I'd had so much trouble sleeping. I explained that the heat was a bit much, causing bad dreams. Then I asked why she'd been stretched out on the stone. "Instructions?"

"I thought a grotesque was ready," she admitted, "but I was wrong."

"You once told me that you carve as fast as you can to get the grotesque out of the stone, but the basement is full of half-finished work."

"Sometimes we get halfway through the process before they realize that they aren't ready. So we pause for a little while." She cupped some water into her hands and showered my head. "When I get the call again, I'll finish them."

"What if," I asked, "you were to refuse to carve when they called?"

"I couldn't do that. My carving pleases God."

"How do you know?"

She pressed the sponge harder into an area of my skin that did not want to give. "Because God gave me ears that can hear the voices in the stone."

"How does that work, exactly?"

She stumbled over her words; for all her language skills, she could not articulate precisely what she wanted to say.

"I just empty myself. I used to be so anxious to receive God's instructions that I couldn't. Now I clear myself, and that's when the gargoyles can most easily talk to me. If I'm not empty, I bring my own ideas, and they're always wrong. It's much easier for the gargoyles, you see, because they've been emptying themselves for a million years. In the rock, He entered them and informed them. Then they inform me of God's plan for us. I have to"—she paused for a good five seconds—"I have to empty myself of potency to become as close as I can to pure act. But only God is pure act."

I will not pretend that I understood this perfectly, but here is my best interpretation: God acted upon the "buried gargoyles" (meaning the gargoyles still encased in stone) by informing them of the shapes they should assume. The buried gargoyles acted upon Marianne Engel, instructing her how to realize these shapes. Marianne Engel then became the agent of action, chipping away the stone. In this way, she allowed the gargoyles to realize the shapes God intended for them. The now unburied gargoyles (the finished carvings) were therefore a realization of God's instructions. They were not Marianne Engel's creations, because she wasn't the sculptor; God was. She was only the tool in His hand.

She kept scrubbing hard on my body the entire time that she was explaining. When she was finished, I could see the chips of my skin floating in the bathwater.

• • •

It was not long before a work crew arrived to install air conditioning and I found myself able to sleep comfortably in the belfry. I assembled a few shelves in the room—one for books, and one for the small stone grotesque and the glass lily that I'd received in the hospital. There was a desk in one corner, which I equipped with the stationery set that Gregor had given me. In another corner were the television and video player that Marianne Engel had bought for me, despite her own aversion to these too-modern items.

The scene in the basement did not repeat itself any time soon after that, and we quickly developed a routine. When I woke in the morning, she'd inject me first and scrub me second. Following this, there was a series of exercises that Sayuri had prescribed. In the afternoon I'd take a nap, and while I slept, Marianne Engel shopped for my recovery supplies or took Bougatsa for a walk. In the early evening I'd get up again and we'd play cards, or drink coffee and talk. Occasionally, if she had something to do, I'd call Gregor and we'd spend a few minutes on the phone. I found I missed the visits he had made to my hospital bedside and we usually ended our calls by promising to get together soon. It was not easy, though, because his schedule was busy and it seemed that whatever free time he had was spent with Sayuri.

At the end of most evenings, Marianne Engel would go to bed before I was ready to sleep, and I'd stay up to read Friedrich Sunder or Sister Christina.

The *Gnaden-vita* was fascinating even though, for reasons I couldn't fathom, the writing included several occurrences of gender reversal. Sunder would be writing in the proper masculine sense and then—whoops!—he'd be a woman. These mistakes might have been inserted by female editors after Friedrich's death, or by various female scriveners over the years, or even by Marianne Engel as she finally brought the work into English. (Imagine the glee in Titivillus' eye!) However, I doubted this was actually the case, because the feminine qualities were beyond mere typographical slips: they were integral to the content.

A particularly striking example is in Father Sunder's description of his marriage to Christ. The idea of such a union seems—to my modern mind—strange, but apparently "marriage" to Christ was common among men of Friedrich's position. Even allowing for this, however, there can be no denying the enormously erotic nature of the bridal imagery. The marriage is consummated in an ornate bed covered with flowers, in the middle of a court, and watched by many figures from Heaven, including Mother Mary. Sunder writes that Christ embraces him and kisses him, and that they take their pleasures with each other. (You read that correctly.) When Christ is finished with Friedrich, He tells the angels to take up their instruments and play them with as much pleasure as He has just played His beloved spouse. Jesus even claims that through this consummation a multitude of souls has been freed from Purgatory, which really does suggest that it was quite a wedding night.

It crossed my mind that Marianne Engel might have included this passage in the translation simply to have a good laugh at my expense. Because—c'mon!—this episode *couldn't* really have existed in Sunder's original text, right? But in the interval I've checked other sources and found it to be accurate.

As interesting as that is, more notable to me is the fact that the *Gnaden-vita* includes no mention of a Sister Marianne who'd been dropped off as a babe at the Engelthal gates. When I pointed this out, Marianne Engel assured me that her omission from Sunder's book would be explained before she finished telling me the story of our past lives.

• • •

"I know that you don't like the idea of going out in public," she said, "so let's go now, under the cover of night."

I resisted nominally, but was too curious about where a midnight excursion with Marianne Engel (and Bougatsa) might lead. Soon we found ourselves in her car, heading towards a beach at which I'd never bothered to stop. I wondered whether anyone else would be there and decided probably not, on a cold night in late February. But

I was wrong. The sandy shoreline was speckled with small bonfires around which teenagers sat drinking beer. They were equidistant in the darkness, affording everyone a degree of anonymity. I liked this.

Marianne Engel laid out a blanket. I wanted to take off my shoes, because they were full of sand, but even in the dark I was too bashful about my missing toes. She said she wished that I could go swimming with her, or at least wade out to my knees, but she had no idea what saltwater would do to my skin. My gut feeling was that it would not be pleasant. It didn't really matter, because as a child I had never learned to swim. "That's a shame," she said. "I love the water."

I laid my head in her lap and she told me about the great wolf named Sköll that chases the sun every day, trying to eat it. It is said that at Ragnarök, the battle at the end of the world, he will finally succeed, devouring the sun while his brother Hati eats the moon, and the stars will disappear from the sky. She told me about the terrible earthquakes that will rip the earth apart as Miðgarðsormur, the Midgard Serpent, twists his immense body in the ocean and causes towering tidal waves. All the gods will be involved in a tremendous war, and eventually fire will be flung in all directions. The world, Marianne Engel said, will burn before the charred remains sink into the sea. "At least that's what my friend Sigurðr believes."

She hopped up from our blanket and started stripping off her clothes. "I'm going swimming now."

Though I usually accepted her idiosyncrasies, I was shocked by this announcement. It was obviously and immediately dangerous, and I protested that the weather was far too cold.

"It's fine," she insisted. "People do it all the time, you know, in polar bear plunges."

I had heard of such events—people jumping into the freezing ocean for a few minutes, usually for charity—and knew they were closely monitored by dozens of volunteers, not to mention doctors. Any one of a hundred participants could help to pull out a swimmer in trouble, but here, she would be alone.

"I love that you're so worried about me," she said, "but I've done it plenty of times before."

"Yeah?" I challenged. "When? Where?"

"Finland. Often."

Finland. "That doesn't make it a good idea today." *We weren't in Finland.*

"You're sweet. I'll only stay in for a few minutes, and I won't swim past where my feet can touch bottom." Her clothes were now off, heaped in a pile on the beach, and I asked her one more time not to do it. "Only a few minutes. Not in deep water."

I'M SURE IT'LL BE FINE.

"I really am touched by your concern," she added, "but you needn't be worried."

She headed out into the ocean, calmly. The moon cast a splintered glow over the waves. She did not pause, nor shiver, nor splash, nor scoop up water to smooth over her stomach to acclimate to the cold. No, she just walked out until she was up to her chest and then leaned forward to slide THERE SHE GOES into the water.

Down the beach, I heard some of the teenagers laughing about the fact that anyone was stupid enough to go swimming at this VERY COLD time of year. I watched the small wake that formed behind her as she headed away from me, but parallel to the shore. At least she was keeping her promise not to head into deeper water. I followed her progress, hobbling along the shore to keep abreast, although I didn't know what I could do if she encountered trouble in any case. SAY "BYE BYE." Yell to the teenagers, I supposed; since my accident there was no chance that my body could handle the chill of a winter ocean.

She cut the surface smoothly; it was apparent that she was good at this and, despite her smoking, her body was strong from the physical labor of carving. Occasionally she would look towards the shore, towards me. I thought I saw her smile, but she was too far out for me to know for sure. I nervously clutched at my angel coin necklace until I saw her turn around and start back to where she had entered the water.

When she started returning to the shore—to my relief, only a few minutes after leaving it—she exited the water the same way that she went in. She did not rush out, or shake her body to dispel the wet. She just calmly emerged and walked to me, shivering from the night chill, although less than I would have imagined.

"Do you know what the best part of that swim was?"

"No."

"Knowing that you were on the shore waiting for me." She used a towel to squeeze the water from her hair—quite a job, I'll tell you—before she put back on the clothes that I was anxiously thrusting at her, lit a cigarette, and said it was time to tell me more of our story.

Each time she paused, perhaps to add a bit of drama to the telling, I was worried it signaled the delayed onset of hypothermia.

XV.

Now that you had come out of the worst of it, your condition was improving every day. There was still much healing that lay ahead, but I no longer worried about you slipping away each time I left the room.

In the beginning, you said that you didn't want to talk about your life. I was unsure if this was because you were ashamed of all your years as a mercenary, or if that final battle was simply too painful to remember. But since your life was not to be discussed, we talked about mine instead. You seemed fascinated by it, by *me*, which I couldn't quite fathom. What could possibly be interesting about life in the monastery? But your eyes lit up when I told you about my scriptorium duties, and you excitedly asked for your clothes. I retrieved them from the cupboard where we'd stored them. Even though they were mostly in tatters, the nuns couldn't bring themselves to throw out something that didn't belong to them.

The arrow had cut through the breast of your habergeon and much of the material around it was burnt away, but I could feel something heavy and rectangular in the inside pocket. You pulled out this item, which was wrapped in cloth. The broken shaft was still embedded in its front, with the arrow's tip just barely emerging from the back. You turned the object over in your hands a few times, amazed that this accidental shield had prevented the arrow from entering more deeply into your chest. After you pulled the arrowhead out, you pressed it into my palm and told me to do with it as I pleased.

I did not even have to think on the matter; I said instantly that I knew what I would do with it.

"And what is that?"

"I will return it to you," I answered, "after I have asked Father Sunder to bless it. Then your chest can accept it as protection rather than an assault."

"I look forward to that day," you said as you handed over the parcel. "I got this from a dead man."

I unwrapped it, revealing a hand-copied book with scorched edges that left charcoal on my fingertips. How, I wondered, could the book have remained undevoured by the flames?

I held it against your chest, and it lined up perfectly with your burns. The patch of unburnt skin was exactly where the book had been pinned to you by the arrow, and this also explained the small cut in the middle of that unburned rectangle.

I flipped through the book, noticing that the cut on the pages became smaller the deeper I went, and I asked you about the dead man. You answered, "We had two Italians in our ranks. One was killed in battle, a good man named Niccolò. The book was his."

It was not uncommon for the condotta to hire foreigners, provided they had special skills. Your mercenary troop had taken on Italian bowmen and that is, in fact, how the troop began calling itself a condotta in the first place; it was the Italian word for mercenary troop, and the soldiers just liked the way it sounded.

The Italians were among the best crossbowmen you'd ever seen, and they worked well with you and Brandeis. You couldn't speak much of their language, but both Benedetto—that was the other Italian—and Niccolò were able to struggle through in German, and during your years together, you came to respect each other as archers and as men. You trusted each other enough even to talk about the fact that you'd all grown weary of battle.

When Niccolò died, Benedetto decided that he'd had enough. Since he risked death every day on the battlefield, he might just as well risk it in an escape. The fear of being chased down by a team of trackers was finally outweighed by the fear of remaining. Rather than simply disappear without a word, Benedetto offered you and Brandeis the opportunity to join him.

You considered the idea, but in the end decided against it. Herwald might allow one foreigner to disappear, but if three crossbowmen vanished at the same time, the retribution would be inevitable and gruesome. But, more important, neither you nor Brandeis could make the same claim as Benedetto. The truth was that you were still more afraid of your own troop than of the enemy. Still, you both admired Benedetto and felt compelled to help him, partially out of friendship and partially for the vicarious thrill.

Benedetto felt it only proper to take whatever he could to Niccolò's wife and two young boys in Firenze. "The sons should have something that belonged to their father when they grow up." So, in the dark of night, the three of you laid out the dead man's effects and went through them. There was a bag of coins, his clothing, his boots, a book, and his crossbow. Benedetto picked the coins, so that he could pass along these items of value to the wife, and the crossbow, which he thought would make a fitting gift for the sons of a warrior.

Although you really had no need for a book, you pressed some money into Benedetto's hand to pay for it. "With the father gone, the family will need this more than words."

Benedetto agreed, saying that he didn't know why his friend had a book in the first place. "Apparently, it was written by a great poet of Firenze, but I always kidded Niccolò about it. What do men like us need with poetry?"

The following morning, you and Brandeis had to pretend that

you were as surprised as anyone that Benedetto had fled. Kuonrat the Ambitious was livid and demanded that a large expedition be immediately dispatched to "find and kill the traitor!" Herwald was more reasonable. He decided that only a small tracking crew would be sent after Benedetto, and only for a short time.

Herwald reasoned, "The Italian will return to his home country. Let him go. He is not German; he is not one of us. But do not think this represents a shift in policy. If a fellow German runs, we will not stop until he is found and killed. Even if it takes years."

This speech appeased the troop, most of whom had never liked the foreigners in their midst. For them, it was enough that both Italians were gone, however it had happened. Kuonrat the Ambitious remained angered at Benedetto's disappearance, but the renewed threat of death to German deserters brought a smile to his face. Still, he recognized this was the perfect opportunity to begin a campaign of whispered slander. "The old man Herwald is turning soft."

It was at this point that you abruptly stopped telling the story, and looked down at the floor of the Engelthal infirmary so bashfully that I had to ask what was wrong.

"This book," you said, "there's something strange about it. When I first saw it, it seemed to call to me. As if it wanted me to take it."

"That's not so odd. I feel that way about books all the time."

"But Sister Marianne," you confessed, "I cannot read."

I don't know why you would've thought that I expected you to be able to. I was well aware that my ability to read was the exception, not the rule. If you hadn't taken the book, I pointed out, the arrow would have pierced your heart and killed you. "Surely you have found more value in this book," I said, "than any that I will ever read."

You knew, or at least it was your best guess, that the book was in Italian rather than German. I confirmed the fact, but added that I could translate it. You were suitably impressed, because you didn't know anyone who could read one language, much less two. I promised that I would take a closer look at it, back in my cell, and would let you know what it was about. This pleased you, but you still asked for one more favor.

"Please pray for the soul of my dead friend Niccolò, and for his wife and children. And for Brandeis. I would do it myself, but my prayers are not worth as much as yours."

I assured you that everyone's prayers were worthy, if spoken with a sincere heart, but that I would certainly do as you'd requested.

That very evening, I commenced upon a translation. The book had an enormous amount of religious imagery in it, so Paolo's prayer book was a great help, but it seemed to be written in a rough vernacular, which I found quite challenging. It was apparent from the start that the writing was unlike anything I'd ever read. This was yet another book best kept secreted away from the eyes of the other nuns. *Inferno,* the cover proclaimed, by Dante Alighieri.

While it was clear that this Dante was a deeply religious man, it was equally clear that he had little regard for the Church's daily practices. I gasped when I came to the section of Hell that housed heretical popes. One of the popes was Boniface, who'd served during my lifetime. Gertrud and even Mother Christina had spoken highly of him.

By night I furiously translated, and by day I tended you. When the nun-nurses stepped out for their prayers, I'd read you what I had finished the night before. It felt as if we were sharing something wicked, but wonderfully wicked. The story took each of us to a different place. The rough language and the harsh imagery brought me towards your world, but the religious ideas brought you towards my life of spirituality. Somehow we met in the middle.

I'd always been taught that I would find God all around me, in every aspect of creation, but I never really did. I was told that if I was not finding God, I needed to pray for *more* guidance, or to make myself more pure so that He would give Himself to me. So imagine my surprise when I began to achieve a deeper understanding of the

Divine through the voice of Dante and, after a lifetime of immersing myself in the words of Heaven, I finally grasped God only after being given a vision of Hell.

Our moments alone were never long enough. The other sisters would return and we would have to turn our conversation to things other than the book. Over time you softened your original resolve not to discuss your life in the condotta. I found everything you told me fascinating, including how you became a mercenary in the first place.

As a child, you had always assumed that you'd follow your father into the masons' guild. You were training under him and your life seemed set until your early teens, when your father had a fatal seizure while moving stone, and your mother died shortly afterward, of a disease that no one could name, much less treat.

Just like that, you went from being the son of a good family to being an orphan. The city appropriated your home and, as you had no relatives, you taught yourself to live on the streets. Petty thievery didn't seem like much of a sin when it was your only option.

One day you tried to steal some coins from the purse of Herwald, who was in town for supplies. When he caught you, he was more impressed with your nerve than displeased with your offense. He offered you a position in his troop, and you could see no reason not to accept it. It offered excitement and, simply put, you couldn't imagine anything better coming along.

The choice to enter the condotta was not a particularly bad one, or so it seemed. The power struggle between the pope and Emperor Louis left princes all over the country in disarray. When the German military forces became exhausted, the nobility started to assemble private armies. The situation was so complicated that they often didn't know their allies from their enemies and the only thing certain was that there was always work for a mercenary troop. When I asked with whom you sided—Pope John or the Emperor—you answered that as soon as a man has chosen a side in war, he's already picked the wrong one. "All history is just one man trying to take something away from another man, and usually it doesn't really belong to either of them."

This attitude explained how you managed to go from day to day with a crossbow in your hands. It was simply a matter of practicality. I'd never heard anyone speak as plainly as you did, not even the parchmenter, and I'd certainly never had anyone speak *to me* the way you did. I hated the fact that it excited me, but it did. It had always comforted me to imagine soldiers as unthinking killers and nothing more, but you disproved that. I was probably a bit of a snob after spending my life in books, but I had to admit there was much you knew that I did not.

The flesh across your chest was tightening as it healed. You instructed me to cut it open so that it could expand. I didn't want to, and it was painful for me to see your agony coming from a knife in my hands. It was different from when I had cut away the bad flesh because, in those first days, I had still been able to divorce myself from my emotions.

But you insisted. You said that you could feel that the treatment was necessary, you could feel it in the way it hurt to lift your arms. So every few days you'd wedge a knot of fabric into your mouth and I'd cut new stripes across your chest to ease the tightening. It was horrible and I had to avert my eyes, but there was still the sound of your muffled screams. You have no idea how much I admired your courage. The treatment seemed to work: eventually, you were able to leave the infirmary bed for short walks, and sometimes our hands accidentally touched.

The inevitable rumors started to pass through Engelthal. The nurses, upon returning from prayers, had interrupted the story of *Inferno* enough times to know that we were sharing some kind of secret. And no one could miss that there was something more than the relationship between nurse and patient in the way we looked at each other. The time we spent together could no longer be explained away as simple medical treatment.

I was certain that Gertrud and Agletrudis were behind the stories. "The mercenary is corrupting our sweet Sister Marianne." I suppose this was even true, because I was learning it was possible to love more than just God. In fact, I was learning that it was *better* to love more than just God.

It had to happen. Mother Christina decided to remove you, but because you had not yet fully healed, she was sending you to stay with Father Sunder and Brother Heinrich. "To ease your transition back into the world," she said. "The arrangements have already been made."

There was nothing for me to say, as I was pledged for all my life to serve my prioress. So you gathered your few items and thanked us all, the other nun-nurses as much as me, for our kind ministrations. Your farewell was so businesslike that it hurt, but I suppose the best warriors know which battles not to fight. Just like that, you were taken out of my life and put into the care of others. I told myself that it was for the best, and I was even determined to make myself believe it.

It was time to move on. God had not bestowed my literary gifts to enable me to translate blasphemous Italian poets, so I locked *Inferno* away in my trunk. I told myself that my feelings for you were nothing more than a test, so that I might overcome my earthly longings and thus serve God better. I attended all my prayers and worked late each night at the scriptorium, concentrating on *Die Gertrud Bibel*. Gertrud had started to design a cover for the book and occasionally wondered aloud whether jewels were too much. I assured her that nothing was too extravagant in honoring the Lord.

This lasted for a week, and then it struck me. I couldn't keep *Inferno* locked away in my trunk, because it was not actually mine. It was only proper that I return it to you. Just as the nuns didn't have the right to destroy your clothing, neither could I keep your book. This would be a kind of thievery, and I knew that the Lord did not wish that I be a thief.

I decided to sneak a visit to Father Sunder, and why should I not? I'd been making midnight visits to him all my life, so why should things be any different because you were there? If I avoided my regular habits I'd be allowing your presence to alter my routine—which was exactly what the prioress was trying to prevent. So there it was. The only way to keep you from influencing my life was to sneak a visit to the house where you were staying.

Father Sunder answered the door and nodded to the corner where you were sitting. "This one," he said, "has spent the week trying not to mention your name."

There was more color in your cheeks than when I'd last seen you, and when you stood I could see that your upper body swung more freely. Soon you'd be well enough to leave, I thought, and in that instant, my heart almost stopped. I turned to Father Sunder and asked in a panic, "What am I going to do?"

He looked over at Brother Heinrich and something passed between them, a look or a memory, before he turned his attention to me and said with that sweet voice, "Sister Marianne. You're going to leave Engelthal, of course."

For as long as I could remember, Father Sunder had railed on about his regrets for the sins of his youth, and now he was advising me to flee the monastery to enter that same sinful world? It was the last thing that I ever would have expected so I whispered, too low for you to hear, "Why?"

"I was with Mother Christina the night you were found at the gates," Father Sunder answered in a return whisper, "and I argued that your appearance was a sign from God. I believed then that the Lord had special plans for you, and I still do. But I am no longer convinced these plans are meant to be fulfilled at Engelthal."

It was not enough, and I needed him to explain further.

"When this man arrived, again I was present for the event. I saw his condition, and he should have died—yet he did not. None can doubt you are the reason. I cannot help but think your journey with him is not finished, and that it is a journey upon which the Lord smiles."

"But to leave my vows is a sin."

"I do not believe," whispered Father Sunder, "in any God that considers love to be a sin."

Those words were exactly the permission I needed, and I didn't even have the words to thank him. I just threw my arms around him and squeezed, so tightly that he had to plead with me to loosen my grip.

I returned to my cell and gathered my few possessions. A couple of robes, my best footwear, and Paolo's prayer book: I had nothing else worth taking. It was raining as I started back towards Father Sunder's, through the garden. As was the custom for every nun walking along the cloister path, I recited the Miserere for the souls of the dead nuns buried below, but my thoughts of the future had me trembling with fear and anticipation. The rain was good, I thought, as if it had been sent to cleanse the monastery from me.

"You appear to have a bag packed, Sister Marianne." It was the voice of Agletrudis. "Have you at least said goodbye to your champion, the prioress?"

It was an immaculate swipe. It didn't matter to me what Agletrudis or Gertrud might think, but deep in my heart I felt that I was betraying Mother Christina. But what could I have said to her? I wouldn't have known how to deal with the hurt in her eyes. She had always believed in me, even when I had not, and she would never have anticipated my disloyalty.

I walked away from Agletrudis without answering, and she called out after me. "Don't worry about Mother Christina. I'll ensure that she never forgets you."

I almost turned around to ask what she meant, but what good would that have done? So I kept walking. I knew that Agletrudis would not raise the alarm on my departure. It was in her best interests to let me go quietly and reassume her position as armarius-in-waiting.

By the time I reached Father Sunder's house, I had banished Gertrud and Agletrudis from my mind. The face of Mother Christina, however, still lingered. Brother Heinrich packed some food and even though Father Sunder was nearing seventy, he insisted on walking part of the way with us. I protested because of the rain, but he simply pulled on his pluviale and came anyway.

As we walked, Father Sunder in the middle, my thoughts were not upon what lay ahead but what I was leaving behind. Despite Father Sunder's kind words, there could be no arguing against the simple and damning fact that it *was* a sin for me to break my holy covenant. I tried to rationalize it and, after great effort, even devised an argument that had some semblance of sense.

Of all the Engelthal nuns, I was the only one who had not made the decision to enter the life. Even if they arrived as young girls, they had known a life outside the monastery walls; they had lived in the secular world and knew what they were forfeiting when they entered the sisterhood. I had never had that opportunity. So if I left Engelthal with you and came back later, the religious life would be worth more. Finally, it would be my choice rather than that of the parents who abandoned me at the gate: to learn if my destiny lay within the monastery, I *had to* leave it.

After we had walked about a league, I could tell you were becoming fatigued. It was understandable, as your injuries were considerable and you'd had only limited activity since your accident, but you were determined to show as little weakness as possible—whether to convince yourself that you would be fine or to convince me, I was unsure. It was Father Sunder who had to stop first, however, too tired to continue because of his advanced years. He grasped your arm and warned you to love me well, and then he pulled me to the side so that we could speak a moment in private.

He brought out a necklace that he had been carrying inside his pluviale, and pressed it into my hands. Its pendant was the arrowhead that had been removed from the copy of *Inferno,* and he said, "I have done what you asked, Sister Marianne, and blessed it."

I started to thank him but he held up his hand. "I have something else for you." He reached into his pluviale again and pulled out some papers. "Mother Christina is neither blind nor stupid. She didn't think you'd actually leave, but she saw the possibility. She asked me to hold on to these, just in case."

He handed me the two notes that my parents had left in my basket at the gates. There, in Latin and German, were the words that had come to Engelthal with me. *A destined child, tenth-born of a good family, given as a gift to our Savior Jesus Christ and Engelthal monastery. Do with her as God pleases.*

Only then did I break into the tears that I'd been fighting since I'd made my decision. In a fit of doubt, I asked Father Sunder if he truly believed I was making the correct choice.

"Marianne, my dearest child," he said, "I believe that if you do not listen to your heart in this matter, you will regret it forever."

XVI.

Given an afternoon of solitude while Marianne Engel was shopping for groceries, I decided to spend it with the *Gnaden-vita*. I was in the kitchen reading when I heard someone enter through the fortress' front door, with footsteps that approximated those of a mother rhinoceros looking for its young.

"Marianne?" A woman's voice fired off the syllables like a gun emptying three shells. When she appeared in the frame of the kitchen door, she pulled back noticeably at my appearance. *"You're* him? Sweet Jesus! This is worse than I thought."

Short, but Napoleon short; the kind of short that's always pulling itself up by its bootstraps in an attempt to look taller. Fat, but water balloon fat; with flesh not flabby, but round like it's looking for a place to explode. Age, fifties? Hard to tell, but probably. She didn't have wrinkles; her face was too spherical. Cropped hair, too much rouge on her cheeks; a dark business suit with a white, broad-lapelled shirt poking out; well-polished shoes; hands on her hips. Her eyes were confrontational, as if she were daring me to pop her one on the chin. She said, "You're a helluva mess."

"Who are you?"

"Jack," she answered. I was finally in the presence of the man I'd feared, only to find that she was a woman. But barely: Jack Meredith was more like the cartoon of a woman who wished that she were a man.

"Marianne's agent, right?"

"You're never gonna see one red cent of her money." She one-handedly helped herself to a cup of coffee, while the other hand never stopped jabbing a finger at me. "She say you could live here?" Apparently Jack knew the answer, because she didn't give me time to answer. "How's she going to look after you? Tell me that, huh?"

"I don't need her to look after me," I said, "and I don't care about her money."

"What is it then? Sex?" She spat out the word with enough disdain to suggest that she thought sex was nothing more than an ugly argument between two opposing bodies.

"I have no penis."

"Well, thank God for that." She burned her lip with her first sip of coffee. "Lord love a duck!"

She grabbed a handful of tissues to wipe away the spill on her chin, as she eyed me with a combination of contempt and curiosity. "What happened to you, anyway?"

"I was burned."

"Well, I can see that, you think I'm stupid?" She wadded up the tissues and lobbed them towards the garbage can. She missed and, angry with herself for missing, took the few necessary steps to pick the tissue ball up and drop it in. "Burned, huh? That's a damn shame."

"Do you always just walk into this house?"

"I've been walking into this house since you were sneaking drinks at the high school dance," Jack barked, "and I don't much like you being here. You got a cigarette?"

"Don't smoke."

She headed towards a pack that Marianne Engel had left on the counter. "Probably a good idea in your condition."

"So you're Marianne's agent?" I never got an answer the first time.

"That and more, buddy boy, so watch your step." Jack inhaled deeply and now jabbed the cigarette towards me in a most accusatory manner. "This whatchamacallit, your living here, it's a horrible fucking idea. I'm going to talk her out of it, you little monster."

Perhaps you can guess that I liked Jack Meredith plenty. For one thing, she was the only person who spoke loudly enough that I never had to ask her to repeat herself. But more than that, I was taken with the general outsizeness of her personality: she was like an anthropomorphized butterball turkey, cast as the lead character in a Raymond Chandler novel. However, what I appreciated most was that she entirely dispensed with burn patient sympathy. We spent a few moments staring at each other over the table. She rolled her cigarette between her thumb and forefinger and squinted her eyes, real tough-like, before saying: "Whaddaya think you're looking at, Crispy Critter?"

. . .

A few days later, Marianne Engel and I were sitting on the back porch waiting for a delivery of new slabs of stone, and she told me that she'd instructed Jack to set up a credit card for me. When I said I couldn't imagine Jack being very happy about that, Marianne Engel said, "She'll do as she's told. Jack's all bark, no bite."

I KNOW WHAT WE CAN DO WITH A CREDIT CARD.

Our conversation wandered around a bit, before I asked a question that I had from the last part of our story: I wanted to know what a pluviale was. Marianne Engel explained that it was a type of raincoat that priests used to wear, decorated with scenes from the New Testament. I asked whether Father Sunder's pluviale had an image on it. She confirmed that it did. "And I'll tell you what it was," she said with a playful pause, "later in our story."

When the truck arrived, she clapped her hands like a child at the carnival and sprinted to her basement doors to insert a heavy key into the great lock. She laid down iron rollers that allowed the blocks of stone to slide into the house. Seeing the stones disappear into the opening made me think of a hungry parishioner receiving communion. She stood off to the side, imploring the deliverymen to be gentle with her friends. The deliverymen looked at her as if she was crazy but continued their work. As soon as they were gone, she took off all her clothes and lit candles. After putting on a recording of Gregorian chants, she stretched herself out over one of the new slabs and fell into a deep slumber that lasted until the next morning.

She came into my bedroom with a huge smile and proclaimed that she had received wonderful directions, but that she would wait until after my bath to begin her work. As she scrubbed me, I could tell she didn't want to be doing it—her fingers wanted stone, not flesh—but that she felt it was her duty. The moment she was finished with me, she raced to the basement. I sat in the living room on the middle floor of the house, trying to read, but was too distracted by the rhythm of her chisels. I moved up to the belfry to occupy myself with other things—videos, reading, teasing Bougatsa with a towel on a string—but after a few hours, my curiosity grew too great. I cracked the door to the basement and crept a few steps down the stairway to spy on Marianne Engel.

I needn't have worried that she'd find my presence intrusive, for she was working so intently that she didn't seem to notice me at all. To my surprise, she was carving in the nude; it was somewhat unsettling to see her working so swiftly with sharp metal tools. The instruments flew around furiously but her hands looked sure, and I sat hypnotized by the dance of metal, stone, and flesh.

To say that Marianne Engel "carved" is not enough: it was so much more than that. She caressed the stone until the stone could no longer stand it and gave up the grotesque inside. She coaxed the gargoyles out of their stony caverns. *She loved them out of the stone.*

Over the many hours that she didn't notice me, I became amazed by her stamina. She was still working when I went to sleep, and continued through the night. She went all the next day as well, and into the night again. In total, she labored for over seventy hours, drinking gallons of coffee, smoking hundreds of cigarettes. This was just how she had claimed to work—carving nonstop for days at a time—but I'd never quite believed her. I assumed it was a boastful exaggeration of her artistic discipline. But it wasn't. Skeptics might think that she waited for me to go to sleep before she herself took a nap, but her hammering kept waking me up. On the first morning, she did haul herself away from her work long enough to clean me, but I could see—could feel—that it was done grudgingly. There was an anxiousness in her eyes, a barely contained frenzy, as she raced the sponge over my skin.

Around the sixty-hour mark, she asked me to order two large vegetarian pizzas. Normally, she had no objection to eating meat, but I soon learned that when she was in her carving like this, she manically refused to do so. "No meat! No animals!" When I brought down the pizzas, she went to three corners of the room to ask her Three Masters for permission—*"Jube, Domine benedicere"*—and did not eat until they gave their consent. She sat haltingly unstill in the middle of the stone fragments and ate like a beast, barely seeming to notice that I was there. A cheese strand dangled from her mouth to the edge of her left nipple, and I wanted to rappel it like a mozzarella commando to storm her lovely breasts. The candlelight captured the chalky sheen of her body, and lines of sweat created tributaries through the stone dust that coated her angel wings. The combination of her tattoos and her ecstatic bearing made her seem part Hildegard von Bingen, part yakuza.

Over the hours, her stereo passed through the works of Carl Orff; Berlioz's *Symphonie Fantastique*; Beethoven's nine symphonies; Poe (the singer, not the writer); the first album by Milla Jovovich; the entire catalogue of The Doors; the recordings of Robert Johnson; *Cheap Thrills,* by Big Brother and the Holding Company (four times in a row); and a variety of Bessie Smith, Howlin' Wolf, and Son House. As the hours progressed, the music grew ever louder and her choice of singing voices more guttural. Even with my bad ears, by the end I had to retreat with earplugs to my belfry.

When she finished, she could barely stand. The completed monster was a human head with horns, atop a kneeling dragon's body, and she kissed its stony lips before crawling up the stairs to collapse into her bed, still covered in dust and sweat.

• • •

"Well, obviously manic depression is common among artists," Gregor said across the table, as he poured a shot of the bourbon that he had brought for us to drink. The sun was going down and we were sitting on the back porch; Marianne Engel was still sleeping off her efforts. After reaffirming that he could not address any specifics of her previous treatments, Gregor said that he'd be happy to answer general questions.

"After reading all those books," I said, "I decided that her symptoms were more consistent with schizophrenia than with manic depression."

"Well, maybe. Could be both," Gregor answered, "or neither. I don't know. Maybe it's obsessive-compulsive disorder. Did she ever say why she has to do so much carving all at one time?"

"She thinks she's following instructions from God. She thinks she's giving out the extra hearts she has in her chest."

"Well, that's weird." Gregor took a sip. "Hey, this stuff is good. It beats me what's wrong with Marianne."

"Aren't you supposed to know about these things?"

Gregor shrugged. "What I don't know could fill a warehouse. Is she taking her medicine?"

"No. She hates pills even more than she hates doctors. No offense."

I asked if she could be forced, by some sort of legal order, to take her meds. Gregor explained that only a guardian could take that step. I suggested Jack, who I had recently learned was Marianne Engel's conservator as well as her manager, but Gregor explained that a conservator only has jurisdiction over a patient's property, not her personal decisions. No one can force a patient into a hospital except a judge, Gregor said, and then only for a few days. I interjected that I didn't want Marianne Engel committed; I simply wanted her to take her drugs. Gregor said that all I could do was ask nicely. Then he asked me if we could stop talking about her condition; while he felt he hadn't gone over any line of doctor-patient confidentiality yet, he was worried he was getting dangerously close.

We left the topic at that. I asked him about Sayuri and he told me that they were seeing more of each other. Had a date that night, actually. Then he chastised me for always wanting to talk about his love life, while never giving up any details of my own. I laughed it off—*What love life?*—but he threw it right back at me. "You're not fooling anyone."

There was a pause in the conversation, but it was a good pause. Gregor took another sip of bourbon and we looked out into the sunset together. "Nice night," he said.

"She touched me," I blurted.

This caught Gregor off his guard. "What do you mean?"

"The first time she bathed me and saw . . . my groin"—Gregor knew, through his position at the hospital, about my amputation—"she inspected it. Ran her fingers over the scars."

"What did she say?"

"That the condition of my body is not relevant to her."

"Did you believe her?" he asked.

"I don't know." I swirled the bourbon in my glass. "Of course it matters. It's gone."

Gregor frowned. "I'm disappointed."

Now he had caught me off guard. "By what?"

"Your answer," he replied. "Because I believe her, and I think you should, too."

Another pause in the conversation, which this time I broke. "It is a nice night, isn't it?"

He nodded. I didn't mention that the brand of bourbon Gregor had bought was the same that had spilled into my lap, costing me the penis in question. Gregor's intentions in bringing the gift were good, so what profit was there in trying to make him feel bad about it?

I expected that the bourbon would taste like bad memories; instead, it just tasted like good alcohol. And it was nice to have: Marianne Engel quaintly clung to the idea that morphine and booze were a bad mix, but I suspect Gregor was trying to show me his wild side by allowing me a glass or two.

* * *

A few days later, after she had recovered, I asked Marianne Engel why she increased the music's volume throughout her carving. She reminded me that the gargoyles became louder the longer the process went on, and turning up the stereo was a way to drown out their screams. She explained that when she cut through the excess stone to find the grotesque's form, the only way to know whether she'd reached the monster's outline was to actually cut into it. If the grotesque screamed in pain, then Marianne Engel knew that she'd cut deep enough.

I asked whether she wasn't afraid that she was drowning out important instructions from God. She laughed and assured me that in the entire world, there was not music loud enough to drown out the sounds of His commands.

* * *

A major complaint of burn survivors is that only one pressure suit is covered by insurance, despite the fact that these garments cost thousands of dollars and must be worn up to twenty-three hours every single day. During the other hour, the patient is being cleaned, and if the caregiver is already busy washing the patient, how can she or he also be cleaning the pressure suit at the same time? This is why it's essential to have at least two. "But the cost!" cry the insurance companies as they deny the claim. Furthermore, even with proper care pressure garments last only about three months.

Insurance companies were not a problem for me, as my costs were being covered in full by Marianne Engel. But I had to wonder, briefcase of cash under the skeleton bed or not, how could she afford this? She kept reassuring me that her prominence as a carver had left her amply rewarded and that there was nothing she'd rather spend her money on. I was unsure but even if I tried to argue, what would be my case? That my scars should go untreated?

My pressure suits and mask were finally ready in mid-March. When Sayuri handed them over, I could immediately appreciate all the work that had gone into them. The mask had been sanded down so that it would sit comfortably along the contours of my face. Sayuri even pointed out how the students had paid special attention to where my scars were raised above the skin's surface, and had prepared the plastic accordingly.

"You'll need to use this as well." Sayuri held out a spring-loaded contraption. The way my face had been burned left me particularly susceptible to oral commissures—scar tissue around the corners of my mouth—which, if not treated, would make it difficult for me to eat or speak in the future. After I had properly wedged the retractor into my mouth, I raised the mask to my face. It was to remain in place all the time, except during cleaning and skin care, even while I was sleeping. I asked Marianne Engel how I looked (in the process discovering that the retractor made my already garbled voice sound even worse) and she answered that I looked like a man who was going to live for a long time.

I looked into the mirror. As if the scarred topography of my face were not enough, it was now smashed flat by the clear plastic. The areas that were normally red had turned white under the pressure and the retractor had peeled my mouth outwards in a grotesque grimace. Every imperfection was amplified, and I looked like the bastard child of Hannibal Lecter and the Phantomess of the Opera.

Sayuri assured me that a poor first reaction was normal, because all burn patients—including me, despite being specifically told otherwise—assume that the mask will hide their faces. But it did not. It would not shield me and help me cope; it was a Petri dish that would place my face under the microscope of the world.

Sayuri explained the proper order in which to put on the pressure garments and showed Marianne Engel how to fasten the straps in back. While they fussed with the technicalities, I was left to experience the sensation, which was like slipping into the tight fist of an angry god. *It's only fabric,* I told myself. *It's not who I am.* It sent shivers down my spine anyway. IT FEELS GOOD, DOES IT NOT? LIKE YOU ARE BEING BURIED ALIVE. The snake loved to laugh at me. I AM COMING.

• • •

I found Marianne Engel waiting for me in the dining room, wearing a kimono of jade silk. It bore an embroidered scene, impeccably stitched, of two lovers under a cherry blossom tree near a carp-filled stream. In the garment's starry sky, a full moon looked down on the lovers as if it were not only the source of their light, but also the protector of their love.

She asked whether I was ready to eat. I answered that I was. I went out on a limb to guess that Japanese was on the menu.

"*So desu ne.* How perceptive you are," she said with a slight bow. The stream on her kimono disappeared into the blue sash across her waist, drawn with an obi bow in back. "I've been reading *Makura no Sōshi*."

"Yeah, I saw that on your bookshelf. Pillow-something, right?"

"*The Pillow Book of Sei Shōnagon*. A very famous Japanese text, tenth century, and the first novel ever written. Or so they say, but who knows for sure? I've been thinking that I should do something with it. You'd be surprised how many great Japanese books don't have decent Latin translations."

"No, I wouldn't."

Marianne Engel retreated to the kitchen with short, sharp steps, as she'd even gone so far as to put on geta, traditional wooden slippers. She returned with multihued trays of sushi: slices of white (and orange and silver) fish lay on beds of compressed rice; beady red fish eggs lolled on seaweed beds; and shrimps curled into each other, as if hugging tightly during their final moments on earth. There were inarizushi, cubes of rice wrapped in thin sheets of sweet golden tofu. Gyoza, dumplings made of beef or pork, bathed in zesty black sauce. Yakitori, barbecued strips of chicken and beef, on wooden skewers. There were onigiri, triangles of rice wrapped in seaweed; each, she explained, contained something different, something delicious: plums, fish eggs, chicken, tuna, or shrimp.

We cleaned our hands with *o-shibori*, steaming napkins, and then she placed her palms together. She said, *"Itadakimas!"* (a Japanese blessing before eating), before adding her more familiar Latin invocation.

She showed me the proper way to stir my miso soup with chopsticks and demonstrated that ramen noodles must be slurped loudly, because this not only cools them but makes them taste better. While she drank sake, she insisted that I stick with oolong tea; she just wouldn't give up that silly idea that alcohol and morphine don't mix. Every time my cup was less than half-full, she refilled it with a slight but respectful bow. When I inserted my chopsticks into my bowl of rice so that they stood straight up like two trees growing out of a snowy hill, she immediately pulled them out. "It's disrespectful to the dead."

When the meal finally ended, she rubbed her hands together gleefully. "Tonight I'll tell you a story about another woman named Sei, although this one wasn't even born until hundreds of years after the writing of the *Pillow Book*."

XVII.

Long ago in old Japan, a girl named Sei was born to a glassblower named Yakichi. At first her father was disappointed that she was not a son, but his disappointment ended the second that he held her. From that moment on he was devoted to her, and she to him.

Yakichi watched with proud eyes as Sei grew from a spirited child into an intelligent young lady. That she was beautiful was beyond question and, in her fine features, Yakichi could see his late wife's eyelids and cheekbones. The mother died when Sei was just a child and this made the father and daughter hold each other all the tighter.

On the verge of adulthood, Sei decided to follow in her father's footsteps. Yakichi felt great joy in her decision and his happiness was now complete: his knowledge wouldn't die with him, after all. Sei adopted the title of Glassblower's Apprentice and showed remarkable potential and quick progress. She had a delicate touch and, more important, she could envision the object before it was blown. Technique can always be learned, Yakichi knew, but Sei was born with the gift of vision. She could see beauty where others saw only empty air.

Sei studied well under her father's tutelage, learning just how hot to stoke the fire and just how forcefully to blow. She learned to read the bright glow of the heated glass. She worked diligently to develop her understanding of breath; for she knew that with breath she could create a world. She imagined herself breathing life into the glass and, with every week that passed, Sei came closer to realizing the loveliness of the objects that she could picture in her imagination.

Yakichi began to bring Sei to the local weekend market, where he maintained a stand to sell their wares. Men started to come in swarms. They claimed they wanted to look at the glasswork but really, of course, they came to look at the captivating young woman. "How like glass you yourself are," one old man couldn't help but say, scuttling away like a crab across a beach when he realized that the words had actually slipped aloud from his claws.

Soon, their table was selling out before lunchtime. Almost all the pieces were purchased by men—even as gifts for their own wives—simply because they wanted to own a container of Sei's breath.

Yakichi was pleased. Business was stronger than ever, finances were good, and Sei was becoming a fine glassblower. But for all their success, Yakichi wished a husband for his daughter. Though he was a protective father, he wanted her to experience all that life had to offer and, he thought, a "beneficial" marriage would better their family line.

So Yakichi took stock of the men who frequented the stand. There were artisans, landowners, fishermen and farmers, soldiers and samurai. Certainly, he mused with a smile, there would be no shortage of suitors. After all, Sei had beauty, skill, health, a pleasing personality, and loyalty. She would be a fine wife and good mother, anyone could see that, and it would be easy to arrange an advantageous marriage.

When Yakichi approached his daughter to suggest this, she was quite shocked. "I know this is the tradition," she cried, "but I never thought that you would ask it of me. I will marry for love, and love alone."

The force of his daughter's conviction surprised Yakichi, for she had never before gone against his wishes. Marriage was for improving one's family position, the old man thought; marriage was not something to be undertaken for love. And yet Sei insisted and, because Yakichi adored her, he acquiesced. Still he worried, because there was no one in his daughter's heart.

But, as is often the case in these matters, Sei soon met a young man, and she did fall quite completely in love with him. At first, Yakichi was displeased because Sei had chosen Heisaku, a simple farm boy with neither money nor prospects. However, the boy had a pure, good heart. So, maybe . . .

Yakichi remembered his own departed wife. Although theirs had been an arranged marriage, they had been lucky and Sei had been conceived in love. Buoyed by the memory of his own good fortune, Yakichi decided that he could hope for nothing less for his daughter. He gave his blessings to Sei and Heisaku.

It was about this time that one of Sei's more inspired pieces—a glass flower—was given to a daimyo, a local feudal lord, by one of his servants. This daimyo was despised and feared for his brutal temper. He had no time for glass flowers and angrily asked the meaning of the trivial thing.

The servant, always looking for special favor, said, "I thought you might like to know, my lord, that this glass flower was created by the most beautiful girl in all the land." The daimyo's ears pricked up and the servant quickly added, "And she is unmarried." The servant, you see, had recently overheard the daimyo talking about his desire to start producing children, saying that only the most beautiful and skilled woman would suffice.

The daimyo quickly decided on a plan of action. He sent out a message that he had in mind a commission for a great glass statue, and that he'd heard Sei and her father were the most skilled glassblowers in all of Japan. For this reason, the message claimed, he was summoning them.

The daimyo had no more interest in commissioning a glass statue than he had in commissioning a ladder to the moon. He was interested in owning land and castles and cattle and rice fields. And a beautiful woman. Yes, that interested him very much. But Sei and Yakichi knew nothing of this, and were only excited. They imagined that this might be the first of many noble commissions—in short, the realization of their dreams. So the father and daughter loaded up their little cart and set off for the daimyo's castle.

They were admitted into the main court, where the daimyo was waiting, and his eyebrows went up at the sight of Sei. His gaze followed her around the room; to Sei, it felt like cockroaches upon her skin. She could tell immediately that this was not a good man, as he sat there turning one of her glass flowers over and over in his grubby fingers. But this was not about her feelings, she told herself, and all she could do was give the best presentation possible.

Sei and her father showed the daimyo their finest works and described them in detail. She showed crystal cranes and glass-bubble blowfish with translucent skin. She displayed tinted sake glasses and heavy goblets. She exhibited plates and toy horses and wind chimes that produced pure notes in the slightest breeze. When father and daughter were finished, a rainbow of glass lay before the daimyo.

The daimyo was impressed, sure enough, but by the artist, not the art. Sei was the most enticing girl that he'd ever seen. He clapped as Sei and Yakichi bowed deeply. "I have made my decision," he announced.

The father and daughter held their breath, which was highly uncommon for glassblowers. They waited hopefully but the words were not at all what they expected. As he fingered the glass flower, the daimyo said, "Sei is fit to be my wife and bear my children. She should be overjoyed with her good fortune."

Sei knew that this was a very powerful man and that to oppose him would be very difficult. Nonetheless, she could not stop herself. "But I love another."

Yakichi immediately begged pardon for his daughter's abruptness. When pressed, however, he did confirm the truth of her statement. The daimyo was livid and the glass flower snapped in the involuntary fist that he made. Who could compete with a lord? He demanded to know who this "other" was.

Sei spoke up. "He's only a farm boy, but my love for him is true."

The daimyo asked, "What is his name?"

Sei feared that if she told, Heisaku would be hunted down and killed. She looked at her feet for a moment and then lifted her head to meet the daimyo's gaze. "The name of a simple farm boy should be of no consequence to a lord."

The daimyo was shocked by the girl's audacity. Then he laughed, too loudly, too spitefully. "A farm boy? You dare to choose a farm boy over me? You dare to withhold his name?" The daimyo looked down at his hand and saw that he was bleeding where the broken glass flower had cut him. The blood calmed him because it reminded him who he was.

"You will not marry this farm boy," he stated with certainty, "and you should thank me now for the life that I have saved you from. You will marry me."

Sei spoke with equal certainty. "I will not marry you. I will marry the farm boy or I will marry no one."

The daimyo's counterargument was swift and merciless. "Very well. Marry, then. Marry this farm boy and I will execute your father. But marry me and your father shall live."

Sei stood dumbstruck, for never could she have imagined herself in such a position. Never could she have imagined a man such as this. The daimyo continued, "In one week, you will return to this court and speak a single word. 'Yes' means you will marry me and your father will live. 'No' means you refuse me and your father will die. A single word. Think well, Sei." With this, the daimyo threw the shards of flower at her feet and swept out of the courtyard.

Father and daughter were released from the castle to ponder their answer. There was nowhere they could hide; they could not just pack up and move, as they would be found wherever they went. Yakichi pleaded with Sei to say no. He was an old man with only a few more years to live, he argued, but she had her entire life ahead of her. The father was willing to die so that the daughter was not condemned to a lifetime of unhappiness.

Sei wouldn't hear of this. She refused to make a decision that would kill her father. And yet, she knew the unhappy waste that her life would become with the brutal daimyo.

That night, Sei was unable to sleep. She tossed in her bed, considering the problem from all sides, but there seemed to be no way out. Then, shortly before dawn, inspiration came and she knew what she must do. When Yakichi awoke, he found his daughter gone and, in her place, a note stating that she would be back in a week to face the daimyo.

First, Sei went to her farm boy and explained the situation. She told Heisaku that he was her one true love but that she would never be able to speak to him again. The last words she said to him were "If you listen to the wind very carefully, you'll be able to hear me whisper my love for you." Then she disappeared.

Days passed, and Yakichi began to think that his daughter must have run away. Though it saddened him that he would be unable to say goodbye, he was reassured that she would live. When a week had gone by, the father appeared before the daimyo to say that Sei had disappeared and that he was pleased to forfeit his life in her stead.

The daimyo was about to order the father's execution when two women, clothed in simple robes and with shaved heads, entered the courtyard. It took even Yakichi a moment to realize that the younger woman was Sei. He broke into tears now that Sei had reappeared to marry this awful man.

"What is this?" the daimyo demanded. "Why have you shaved your head? Who is this woman with you?"

But neither Sei nor the older woman spoke.

The daimyo raged, "What is this insolence? I command you to speak!"

Still, Sei and the older woman remained silent.

"What is your answer? Will you be my wife, and save your father's life? Or shall I kill him because of your selfishness? Answer my question—yes or no, will you marry me?"

And still, neither Sei nor the older woman responded.

The daimyo spat on the ground. "Execute the old man!" he commanded. But Sei raised her hand to stop the two soldiers who stepped forward to take her father. She approached the daimyo and held out a sheet.

He gestured to one of the others in the court to take the note, as if it were beneath him to handle it personally, and growled, "Read it aloud, so that everyone can hear the words of this most disrespectful girl!"

The courtier glanced over the note and cleared his throat. He did not want to read what it said. But he had no choice:

> One week ago, you asked me to be your wife. The word yes would seal our engagement, and the word no would ensure my father's death. I will speak no words, for I am now *mugon no gyo no ama-san.*

The final words got caught in the courtier's throat. He knew how this would displease the lord, as *mugon no gyo* meant "the discipline of not talking" and *ama-san* meant "nun."

The courtier cleared his throat again and continued to read:

> I have taken vows of silence and poverty, and I have shaved my head to show my dedication. I have moved to the temple on the highest mountain of the region. It is here that we feel closest to Buddha. I cannot marry you because I am already wed to the Universe. I cannot speak the answer to your question, because my vows will not allow it. Therefore, with no answer, you must release my father and I will return to the mountain temple to spend my life in devotion.

The daimyo was stunned. Though powerful, he knew better than to contradict the Great Buddha. He thought for a few moments and then made his response.

"I must commend you for your commitment," he said. "I would not think to stop you from returning to the temple. Please do so."

Sei bowed her head to hide the smile that might betray her sense of victory.

"But before I let you go," the daimyo continued, "I require that you confirm, yet again, your promise of eternal silence."

Sei bowed once more to indicate that she did. "Good," continued the daimyo, "for if you *ever* speak again, I promise you this: your father's life will be forfeit, and you will become my wife. And if your farm boy *ever* visits you at the temple, I will kill both him and your father and make you my wife. Is this clear?"

The daimyo let the proclamation sink in for a moment. "Do I have your word, your Holy Promise, that you shall never speak, nor ever see your farm boy, again?"

Sei stood silent for a moment, then nodded. The daimyo declared, "I am satisfied."

On her way out of the castle, Sei saw Heisaku hidden in the wooden rafters. How much he loved her, to risk such a foolhardy gesture. Heisaku looked down with the saddest of eyes, for now he truly understood the gravity of the situation. Sei looked up at him and silently mouthed the phrase Aishiteru, "I love you." Her glassblower's breath carried these words to the farm boy's ears, and it was just as Sei had promised: if he listened very hard, he could hear her whispers upon the wind.

Yakichi and Sei were taken by armed escort to the mountain temple. Her father said goodbye, but Sei, of course, could say nothing. She cried silent tears and Yakichi promised to send her a gift as soon as he could. And then he was gone.

Soon the present arrived: a full set of glassblowing tools. The other *ama-san* were happy to allow her this luxury, as they were deeply devoted to beauty and saw Sei's art as yet another way to

serve Buddha. Besides, the objects would provide a source of income to help meet their modest needs. Even nuns know that while poverty is a virtue, it is terribly inconvenient.

Sei was allowed to convert an empty room of the temple, and every day she worked to create all manner of objects, from dinnerware to artwork. The days became weeks and the weeks became months. Her work grew increasingly beautiful, as she perfected her techniques. And all the while, she was slowly crafting a statue in the likeness of Heisaku.

Sei would work on the statue each time she felt the need to speak, as a way to articulate her love. This meant that she worked on it daily. She created it lovingly, one minuscule section at a time. It began with the ball of his right foot. It expanded to the heel. Then, the toes. With each addition—ankle, lower shin, upper shin, knee—she would whisper while blowing the section. *Aishiteru.* The word was captured in the glass bubble. *Aishiteru.* "I love you."

Miles away, Heisaku would feel the words in his ears. They would travel his spine and into his heart. He'd stop his plow and turn his eyes towards the distant mountain. And so it continued for years. Each time Sei felt the need to speak her love, she would blow a section of the statue, encasing her whispered breath in Heisaku's hipbone, his finger, his shoulder, his ear . . . *Aishiteru, aishiteru, aishiteru.*

When the statue of the farm boy was completed, her love was not. So she started to create surroundings for him, beginning with a field of glass lilies in which he could stand. Later, when the lilies were completed, she would have to find something else. *Perhaps,* she thought, *I will make a tree for my beloved to stand under. . . . Creating the leaves alone would provide enough work to make my life bearable.*

And so her life went until one morning, like any other, when Sei was cleaning herself in the mountain stream. The cold water felt good on her skin but as she washed out her hair, she felt a sharp quick pain in her neck. Before she could even react, her arms and legs began to stiffen.

Sei had been bitten by insects many times, but this was the first time she had been stung by this particular species of wasp and, as fate would have it, she suffered a severe allergic reaction. Her throat tightened, her body would not respond, and she became unable to move. Her paralyzed body was washed down the stream until it became caught upon a rock. For two hours she lay there, as the intense cold of the stream seeped into every corner of her flesh.

Eventually, another *ama-san* found Sei and dragged her out of the water. Sei's eyes were unresponsive and the cold water had dropped her pulse so low as to be undetectable. More *ama-san* were called but none could find any sign of life and, despite their vows of silence, a chorus of tears broke the still mountain air that morning.

Sei's paralysis was total, but she could see everything, right up until the moment the nuns respectfully closed her eyelids, believing her to be dead. Even when she had warmed slightly, the venom still immobilized her. For three days, the *ama-san* prayed silently over her. Yakichi was alerted and came to bury the daughter who had sacrificed her life so that he might live.

The daimyo also came, to ensure that this was no hoax. He had heard that Sei was to be buried, which made him suspicious as it was a well-known fact that Buddhists were cremated so the flames would purify the soul. If flesh remained, the soul would still long for its existence on Earth and feel uneasy in Heaven. However it was Sei's own written request that she be buried, because she wanted to exist forever as a part of the earth that Heisaku would continue to till.

Yakichi had brought Heisaku with him, but introduced him as a new glassblowing apprentice. Fear of the daimyo made this lie necessary. Who knew what he might do if he realized that this was the youth who had bested him for Sei's affections?

The daimyo was the one who shut the lid to the coffin after ensuring that Sei was truly inside. Unable to move, Sei lay there listening to his horrible voice, "Yes, I am satisfied. She really is dead." Sei was thankful that her eyelids had been drawn shut, for how awful it would have been if her last sight had been this loathsome man's face.

Sei heard the sound of the stretching ropes as her coffin was lowered into the ground and her body given to the earth. Yakichi threw the first shovelful of dirt into the grave and Heisaku threw the next. All the while, Sei listened as the dirt thudded against the lid of her coffin.

And then there was a miracle. She felt the poison in her veins wear thin and her body begin to loosen. She was able to open her eyes but saw only darkness. She could wiggle her fingers and toes but was not yet recovered enough to lift her arms or legs, so she could not bang on the lid. But she knew that if she yelled, those above would be able to hear her. She could feel the ability creeping back into her throat, and felt elation that she would not die after all. All she had to do was yell. . . .

Then Sei remembered her promise. She would become the wife of the daimyo if she spoke even a word to save herself. Her father would be executed, and Heisaku as well. The daimyo was right there with them, so there could be no denying that she had broken her word. There could be no denying that Heisaku had visited the temple.

And so, Sei shut her mouth and allowed herself to be buried alive. She listened to the dirt being thrown into her grave, with the sound becoming more muffled as every shovelful piled up above her. When the sound stopped altogether, she knew that the hole had been filled and that she was sealed into the earth.

Above the ground, Yakichi and Heisaku cried at the unfairness of Sei's life. She had given up so much to protect the ones she loved, and this was her reward. As for the daimyo, he cared nothing about the woman who had been buried before him; he was simply satisfied to know that she had not tricked him once again.

As he'd never been to the temple before and it was unlikely he would ever return, the daimyo decided to explore the grounds before returning to his castle. The *ama-san* tried to prompt him along a path that would keep him away from Sei's workshop but they were unsuccessful. When he pushed his way into the shop, he was astonished to see the glass likeness of Yakichi's new "apprentice" standing there in a half-finished field of lilies. The daimyo was no fool: he immediately understood that this was a statue of the farm boy whom Sei had loved so well, and thus he also knew that the boy pretending to be the apprentice was Sei's great love.

Light poured in through the temple windows and lit the statue. The very beauty of it, the care and detail, mocked the daimyo. He picked up a wooden rod that lay upon the workbench and swore that he would destroy the statue first, and then destroy the real boy. The daimyo lunged forward, swinging the rod like a scythe to cut through the glass lilies that surrounded the statue. The swipe was mighty, and broke through dozens in a single stroke.

There was an enormous blast as glass petals and stems erupted everywhere, riding a massive wave of sound. All the whispers of love that Sei had encased in her lilies came rushing forth simultaneously. Their force was so great that the glass shards traveled outward as if on the wind of a hurricane. They cut the daimyo completely, disfiguring him beyond recognition. The sound was so thunderous that he was deafened and all his hair turned instantly white.

The noise exited the workshop and spread out across the sky over Japan. People in every corner of the country could hear it, and later all agreed that it was the most beautiful thing they'd ever heard. It sounded like pure love.

The daimyo lived, but as a hobbled little half-man, scarred and beaten. His own anger and jealousy had done him in. He no longer had the spirit for intimidation and never again attempted to harm Heisaku or Yakichi.

Heisaku and Yakichi, for their part, loaded the glass statue into a cart and took it back to their village. Heisaku moved into the old man's house as the son he never had, and they grew to be great friends. After all, they were bound by the love of the woman that they had both lost.

For the rest of their years, the glass statue sat in the middle of their house. It made Heisaku feel somewhat awkward to see his likeness every day, but it served a great purpose. When their grief for Sei's loss became overpowering, Heisaku or Yakichi would break off a small section of the statue—a fingertip, a lock of hair, the petal of a remaining lily.

Aishiteru, aishiteru, aishiteru. From each broken pocket of glass, Sei's voice would whisper out to ease their sorrow.

XVIII.

Even though she obviously knew the answer, Marianne Engel made a great show of asking me what day it was.

"Good Friday," I answered.

"Follow me." We climbed into her car and it was not a half-hour before I realized exactly where we were headed: to the hills where I'd crashed. When we arrived, there was nothing to indicate that the accident had ever occurred. The trees no longer looked as if they housed a dark troop of mercenaries sent to destroy me. The wooden posts had been replaced, restrung with new metal cable, and were now weathered enough to be indistinguishable from the rest. There were no tire tracks and no upturned dirt; it was just another curve. When I asked how she knew the exact site, Marianne Engel just smiled and let Bougatsa out of the backseat. He jumped around excitedly, and she had to scold him when he got dangerously close to the road's edge.

She pulled a small leather bag from the car trunk and took me by the hand to the boundary between road and cliff. Here I saw the first indication that my accident had, indeed, happened. There was a still-scorched area at the base of the gully, a small black circle not unlike the period you'll find at the end of this sentence, right beside the creek that had saved my life.

Motorists whizzed by, no doubt wondering what we were looking at. "Let's go down," she said, leading me past the new wooden
posts. Bougatsa ran ahead of us, happily finding a path to the bottom that we could follow, and off to one side I saw a broken wedge
of red plastic, a turn signal cover that had been ripped from a car. My
car. My stomach tightened.

As we climbed down, there were dozens of rocky slots into which
I could wedge my orthopedic shoes, but it was difficult to keep my
balance. I tried to command my legs to react the way they would
have before the accident, but it was not possible: my rebuilt knee
was too feeble. When I told Marianne Engel I couldn't make it down,
she refused to accept that. She placed herself directly in front of me,
her legs wedged against the slope, so that I could place my hands on
her back. This provided enough resistance that I could make it to the
bottom, and not claim otherwise.

When we reached the scorched area, I noticed a few small tufts
of grass within it, just starting to grow. *Someday this area will be green
and healthy again,* I thought.

"What is it?" she asked.

"Nothing," I said. "I just never expected to come back, that's all."

"It is good to return to the locations of one's sufferings."

"You're wrong." I could remember it all: the eruption of glass;
the steering column as it flew past me; the hiss of the engine settling; the tires spinning to a stop; the flash of blue flame across the
car roof; the way the flames looked as they jumped into existence;
the smell of my hair burning; and my flesh starting to bubble and
pop. I could remember everything that changed me from a man into
what I had become.

"It doesn't matter if you agree. One cannot become whole by
ignoring one's misfortunes." Marianne Engel unfastened her bag,
pulled out an iron candlestick that she claimed had been made by
Francesco, and crammed a candle into its open mouth. She handed
me a pack of matches and asked me to light it. "But it is also important to celebrate this year that you have lived."

I pointed out that it was not actually the one-year anniversary: while it was true that my accident had occurred on Good Friday, obviously that holiday fell on a different date each year.

"You should not regard time in such literal terms," Marianne Engel said with a kiss to my plexiglass face. "What does a single day matter in the vastness of eternity?"

"I thought every day mattered," I said. "Especially the ones when you almost die."

It would have sounded more dramatic, I think, if at that exact moment Bougatsa had not jumped into the air beside us to snap wildly at some bug buzzing around his head.

"But you didn't," Marianne Engel said. "Tell me, was your life good before the accident?"

"Not really."

"Then beginning again should be a gift to be embraced."

She believed sincerely that I was starting over, and I suppose I was: but not entirely, and I felt a twinge of shame at what I was doing with the cash I was advancing from the credit card Jack had set up for me.

• • •

A few days later, Marianne Engel was out of the fortress, walking Bougatsa, when I decided to proceed with a secret mission. I put a long gray raincoat over my pressure garments and, though I was not supposed to, removed my mask and mouth retractor. I donned a hat and sunglasses, turned up my collar with criminally gloved hands, and looked in the mirror to see the very caricature of a sexual deviant looking back at me. I supposed it was perfect, considering where I was headed.

"The nearest porno shop." My voice, revving like a rusted motor, made the taxi driver size me up in the rearview mirror. He seemed to have some second thoughts about taking the invisible man on a field trip, but they were dispelled when I held up my credit card. The

driver put the car into motion and we passed the front of St. Romanus, where Father Shanahan was changing the white plastic sign to
read: "Was Your Friday As Good As It Could Have Been?"

When we arrived at the Triple-XXX Velvet Palace, I asked the
driver to wait. He nodded; he had seen me hobble into the car and
knew that I couldn't run far. Entering the shop was like coming home.
There were the familiar smells of latex, leather, and lube. To my right
was a collection of anal probes and giant rubber cocks, and to my left
was an assortment of French maid and Japanese schoolgirl outfits.
Magazines lined the walls, but I was interested in the videos at the
back. Scanning the covers, I soon saw one of my own: *Doctor Giving
Bone, I Presume.* (I've always considered this one of my more amusing
titles.) I laid it down in front of the balding, bespectacled clerk. "Excellent choice," he said in a completely unenthusiastic voice.

Back in the belfry, I slid the movie into the player. There was the
warm blue glow of the television screen followed by the logo of my
old production company. The plot, as in most pornos, left something
to be desired; even to me—writer, actor, director, and producer—it
was muddled. The film opens with a woman, Annie, who's getting
a medical check-up. When she has difficulty putting on her hospital
gown, she asks the nurse for help and, as so often happens, hot les-
bian sex ensues. The doctor (me) happens upon these shenanigans
and, with nary a worry about ethics violations or venereal diseases,
decides the proper treatment for Annie is unprotected anal sex.

I thought of the day of the shoot. The catering came from Sun
Lee's Chinese Take-Out, just down the street, and the delivery arrived late. Boyce Burgess worked the camera and Irdman Dickson
did the sound and, despite the fact that we were shooting at one
in the afternoon, Irdman was plastered. As the director, I would've
reprimanded him if I had not been blasted on cocaine. In fact, if you
carefully scrutinize the film, you can see a small gold spoon on my
necklace bouncing out of my doctor's coat as I rear-end Annie over
the examining table. Because of Irdman's drunkenness, the sound
was particularly bad and, in some places, is completely unintelligible.

Occasionally a line is audible: something about taking Annie's tem-perature with "my big fat thermometer." It's probably for the best that most of the dialogue was lost.

This opening scene is, regrettably, the cleverest part of the film. From this point forward, the story becomes exponentially more lu-dicrous. One of my lovers is a psychiatrist, who continually prattles about my hostility towards women as I spank her. Meanwhile, Annie becomes a hypochondriac/nymphomaniac who believes that her al-lergy to cats is best treated with liberal doses of penis.

All this would seem laughable if not for the way I looked. My hair bounced with each thrust of my pelvis, and my skin shone beauti-fully as sweat crept down my neck onto my chest. The muscles of my arms flexed as I spanked my silly-stern mistress, letting her out and reeling her back in. My smile strained the corners of my re-tractorless mouth and my face tensed in wonderful anticipation as I neared orgasm.

I had to turn the video off: it sickened me to see the princely boy I'd been, compared with the wretched thing that I'd become. It sick-ened me to see, forever captured on film, the sweat on my smooth skin. I, who can no longer perspire. Is this how Fred Astaire felt as an old man unable to dance? Footage of one's athletic youth is a kind of tyranny in old age; such footage has doomed Fred Astaire and me.

When I hit the eject button, the tape came whirring from the machine like a tongue sticking out at me. I took it down to the fire-place in the living room, where I placed it on a pile of torn newspa-per. Taking a match to it, I watched the flames jump up to engulf the cassette.

That was the last time I ever looked at one of my old films.

• • •

Sayuri was coming once or twice a week, always smiling as she put me through my increasingly difficult paces. The results could not be denied: my body was starting to uncurl its contracted muscles, my back beginning to change from a question mark to an exclamation point. An emphasis of the therapy was on fighting my body's desire to move along the path of least resistance by using the strongest muscles instead of the correct ones. Sayuri concentrated on getting me to move with the proper technique and walked alongside me with a hand on each side of my torso, forcing me to keep my head up. She corrected the swing of my arms, enabling my balance to improve, and was constantly reminding me to put equal weight on both feet. This was especially difficult going up and down stairs.

Kinetic basics mastered, we set out on walks of greater speed and longer distance. Bougatsa demanded to come along as well, running around in yapping circles. Sayuri threw a ball for him to chase, but this was mainly to get him out of the way so she could pay proper attention to me. When we returned home, we used the exercise equipment Marianne Engel had bought for me. There was a weight bench, a Nautilus machine, and a stationary bike for conditioning. Sayuri took it upon herself to incorporate each into my rehabilitation.

She always checked my garments during her visits, and occasionally found something that needed modification. As the scars on my face healed under the constant pressure, the mask needed to be adjusted. Sayuri would sand it down accordingly, and a few times even took it to the hospital to be reshaped. Once, the mask came back having been altered incorrectly; when I pointed this out to Sayuri, she muttered to herself in Japanese: *"Saru mo ki kara ochiru."* When I asked what that meant, she answered, " 'Even monkeys fall from trees.' It means—"

I cut her off. "—that even experts make mistakes. Yeah, I've heard that before."

When she asked where, I told her she should ask her boyfriend. I must say, I don't believe I've ever met anyone who could turn such an adorable shade of red as Sayuri.

· · ·

One aspect of the medieval story had been bothering me more than
any other: the claim that Gertrud was producing a German version of the Bible. This was, remember, a full two centuries before
Martin Luther began work on his famous translation. The Church
vehemently disapproved of Luther's work, so how could they have
sanctioned Sister Gertrud?

I approached the problem as I always did, and the first surprise
of my research was the discovery that by the time *Die Luther Bibel*
appeared, there already existed numerous other German biblical
translations; Luther's was simply the first written with the language
of the common man in mind. Previous versions had been literal
translations rendered in obsolete idioms and were, for all intents and
purposes, understandable only to readers who could also read the
source Latin.

The earliest Germanic version of the Bible was a Gothic translation by Ulfilas in the fourth century, which predated the Latin
Vulgate by decades. A remarkable man, Ulfilas needed to devise an
entire alphabet to write his text and thus created much of contem-
porary German Christian vocabulary. Only one partial handwritten
copy of this Bible, known as the Codex Argenteus or Silver Bible,
still exists, at the University Library of Uppsala. After that there is
a ninth-century manuscript from Fulda, which contains Old High
German translations of the first four books of the New Testament,
and a suggestion of a fuller, but unsanctioned, biblical translation
from about 1260. Some passages from the Bible, such as the Lord's
Prayer, had long existed in German, but there is no compelling evidence that anyone had put together an entire German Bible at the
time Gertrud was reputedly working on it—although it is said that
shortly afterwards, in 1350, a complete New Testament surfaced in
Augsburg.

So far, so good: it would seem the time was right at the start of
the fourteenth century for someone to tackle the whole project, so
why not Sister Gertrud of Engelthal?

There are plenty of reasons, actually, but perhaps none more compelling than Gertrud's own intense piety—or at least, her attempts to appear pious. She would not have wanted to proceed in any manner that might be construed as sacrilegious, and few things were more heretical than producing an unsanctioned translation of the Bible. Before embarking on such an extraordinary task Gertrud would have needed permission from a higher authority, and such consent would have been nearly impossible to secure. But that is the crux of the matter—"nearly impossible" is not the same as "impossible."

Engelthal's prioress was an elderly woman; could senility have led her to permit a translation that any able-minded administrator would have rejected? Stranger things have been known to happen. However, this assumes that Gertrud's permission came from within the Engelthal monastery, which is not necessarily the case. Perhaps she had stepped outside the gates to find a church official with his, or her, own agenda; one needs to remember that the Church was notoriously a web of conflicting backroom politics. Conceivably a superior might have authorized Gertrud's work as a part of a larger scheme, and Gertrud might have been happy to overlook her position as a pawn so long as she was allowed her project. It would have been a most dubious arrangement, but it is always easier to skirt the rules when encouraged to do so by a higher-up.

This is all conjecture, of course. Why Gertrud thought she could progress with the project is a question with no clear answer, but I can forward another possibility: perhaps I have underestimated her desire to be remembered. Vanity is both a great motivator and a great deceiver, and the idea of leaving behind an everlasting legacy can spur even the most cautious person to proceed recklessly. Possibly she convinced herself that she was doing nothing wrong even if she lacked full consent. She was working from the Latin Vulgate, after all, and her unwavering belief in the excellence of her translation may well have pushed her to gamble that, in the end, her Bible would be too good to warrant punishment. One can imagine her rationalizing that *Die Gertrud Bibel*'s very existence would excuse its secret genesis and, as the work was being completed towards the end of her life, perhaps she was simply willing to take the risk. What could the authorities do to an old woman who believed that her place in Heaven was already reserved?

When I finally asked Marianne Engel on whose authority *Die Gertrud Bibel* was being produced, I was hoping to get either a definitive answer or a clear contradiction that would disprove the story once and for all. But her answer was neither.

"I was so young I never thought to ask, and Gertrud never said. But she was always very secretive about it and none of the nuns were allowed to talk about the work outside of the scriptorium."

"Wouldn't they have rebelled," I asked, "if they believed it wrong?"

"Perhaps they might have to answer in Heaven for what they had done," she said, "but I think they were more scared of Gertrud and Agletrudis here on earth."

Marianne Engel seemed quite pleased that I was so carefully considering these aspects of the story she had been telling, and it prompted her to ask whether I would like to hear more.

"Of course," said I.

XIX.

Behind me lay the only life I had ever known, and ahead of me stretched a life I could not even imagine. As we walked, I looked over my shoulder to see Father Sunder's figure disappear into the night. He'd been in my life since my first memories, and now he was gone. Only then did I realize that neither you nor I had any idea where we were going.

You led the way, pretending that you knew what you were doing, putting distance between us and Engelthal. I doubt you were worried about a posse of nuns chasing us down; you were probably more concerned that I'd lose my nerve and turn back. So you kept moving forward, despite the fact you were still suffering from your burns, and I had to struggle to keep up. My feet slid in the mud but I was determined to show that I could keep any pace that you set. I suppose it was important to me because I didn't know if it was true.

I could see that your battles had taught you to forget the physical body and push forward on willpower alone. I had assisted in your recovery, I knew this effort was far beyond anything you'd attempted since being brought to Engelthal, and I was amazed by your endurance—until, all at once, it failed utterly.

Your feet slipped in the mud and you went down awkwardly. You tried to jump up immediately, but it did not work: as soon as you were upright, you lost your balance again. This time, while falling, you put out your arms to brace yourself, but the contracted skin across your chest caused you to cry out in pain. You withdrew your arms instinctively and dropped face first into the mud.

I reached out to assist you and your first instinct was to push me away. Then, perhaps realizing that we needed to work together if we were to proceed, you allowed me to help you upright. You said, trying at a joke, "I think the devil pushed me down."

After a few moments, you had recovered enough that we could move together under a tree. There we sat, covered in mud, as the rain continued to fall. We huddled together for heat and it was the closest I had ever been to another body, a male body no less, but it was nothing like I had imagined. I knew this moment would eventually arrive and I had expected it to be thrilling and terrifying, but I only felt anxious fear that I had made the wrong decision in leaving Engelthal.

This was the start of our life together: in freezing rain, unable to move forward, waiting for the morning to arrive and perhaps— *perhaps*—bring some warmth with the sun. Maybe, I thought, this was the sign for me to turn back. I might arrive before anyone even knew I was missing, and I could feign illness in my cell. In a day or two, I could resume my duties, and life would be as it always had been.

But no. Agletrudis would not allow my actions to go unreported, and I could not leave a sick man at the side of the road, especially a man for whom I felt such great responsibility. Still, I could not help but think about the calmness of the monastery and my place there. I was at home in the scriptorium, among the books. But under a tree, in a storm, with a man I barely knew but upon whom I had pinned my future: how could that be the direction of my life?

And there was nothing to do but wait out the night.

When the morning broke into a dull gray, the rain slowed but did not stop. We started moving again, but all your pretense of vigor was gone. Each attempted step was a trial, and each completed step was a small triumph. I was at your side for each of these little victories, my arm wrapped around you, worried that if you fell again you would not get up.

Then came our first bit of luck, in the guise of a farmer's cart. The horse clopped up to us, and you waved for the man to stop. You asked where he was headed—the answer was Nürnberg, to market—but when you requested a ride, the farmer denied us. No room with the pigs, he said, pointing out the cargo with which his cart was loaded.

"How much for two of the animals?" you asked.

The farmer named his price and you drew out the coins necessary, handed them over, and slowly climbed up into the cart. You tried to lift out one of the pigs but found you were not quite able, so you beckoned me and our combined strength was enough. As soon as the pig's hooves hit the ground, it ran squealing into the forest, and then we unloaded a second animal to the same result. You turned to the bewildered driver and said, "Now you have room for us."

The farmer begrudgingly admitted that he supposed he did. I could tell he was not happy about having human companions, but he must have known you would not allow him to drive off without us. Since he already had the money, consenting was easier than arguing.

The pigs jostled for position the entire ride, curiously bumping into us, carrying out inspections with their snouts. At first I tried to shoo them away, but the effort was doomed by the fact they had nowhere to go. If I managed to force one to move, another immediately slid into its place. They squealed incessantly but the sound was inconsequential compared with the smell, and by the time we finally arrived at the outskirts of Nürnberg, I was certain that God had resorted to sending His messages through pig excrement.

The farmer dropped us at an inn, where I might speculate he had a personal dislike of the keeper. We were certainly a strange sight, and smell, as we tried to negotiate a room. The keeper was hesitant to take us in, having no idea what to make of a burned man and a nun who traveled with livestock, and intended to share a room. But you slipped him extra coins and I offered to say a few words of blessing for him, assuring him that despite my appearance God would hear my prayers all the same. Reluctantly he found us a room at the very back, far removed from his own lodgings, and we were only allowed that if we would first wash ourselves in a nearby stream, clothes and all.

There was only one bed in the room and this emphasized what I'd been trying desperately not to think about. There'd obviously been something sexual between us through all our conversations at Engelthal. I knew I was not running off to live as your sister, but I had no idea about the ways of men and women. The look on my face must have been obvious. You walked to the middle of the room and laid down some cloth, saying that you were used to sleeping on the ground from your mercenary days. You did not look upon me as I climbed out of my wet habit and into the bed, and I will always remember that kindness.

Despite how tired I was, I still could not sleep. Perhaps you heard the way my leg was jittering, or maybe it was that my breathing did not relax. Whatever the clue, after a few minutes you spoke again. "Marianne?"

I was almost afraid to answer, but I did. "Yes."

"It has not been a very good start, but it is a start nonetheless," you said. "I promise that it will get better. For tonight, just sleep and know that you are safe."

Those words reassured me in a way that you cannot imagine, and in return I did the one thing that I could do. I handed over the arrowhead necklace—lacking even the courage to slide it over your neck myself—and said that Father Sunder had blessed it for your protection.

"Then I shall wear it always, and proudly," you said, "and I thank you."

We slept until early the next morning, and decided to stay one more night to recover before setting out again. We still needed to set

our destination and even this scared me, because we had the freedom to choose what would happen next in our lives. Choice was
something you had not had since entering the condotta, and it was
something that I had never known.

The innkeeper prepared dinner for us and I was stunned that
food could be so tasty. Remember, the nuns always thought their
humility was measured by the blandness of their cooking. You and
I talked while we ate. We both wanted to go to a place of some size,
to blend into the crowd as much as we could, for obvious reasons.
The two large cities in the region were Nürnberg, on whose edge the
inn sat, and Mainz. There was a great deal of construction occurring
in Mainz, mostly on new churches, so that was an advantage. Your
only training other than archery had been in stonework, so this was
what you'd attempt for a living. It wouldn't be easy, as you'd been
out of the craft for over a decade and were still recovering from your
burns, but we lacked any better options. You had some money from
your mercenary days and Brother Heinrich had forced some coins
into my palm before we left, so we could hold out for a while.

There was another reason for choosing Mainz: it had a strange
balance of the religious and the secular. The citizens had earned the
right to elect their own government and manage their own financial
affairs, rather than have the Church do it for them. Though my place
in Engelthal hadn't been particularly important, I'd feel better knowing we were in a city that maintained a certain autonomy from the
Church. Nürnberg was too close to Engelthal both geographically
and historically—after all, it was from Nürnberg that Adelheit Rotter
had led the Beguines to establish the monastery.

Having decided upon Mainz, we now had to get there. I couldn't
travel any farther in my nun's habit, because I would feel as if I were
lying. Although I didn't yet know how to define myself, I knew I was
no longer a sister. We found a place that sold the current fashions,
and that was an education in itself. I tried on a surcot with large
openings at the arms, the kind that I'd been taught were "windows
to Hell" because they'd tempt men to reach inside. Such a garment

was not for me. In the end I decided upon woven tights and a simple tunic. I packed my nun's robes into my rucksack rather than throw them away. Even if I wanted to, there was no way I could toss them as garbage.

We entered Mainz on the east side, through the gates that opened onto the Rhine. You would not believe how fascinating it was for me. There were people shouting! I know that doesn't seem like much, but remember that I'd lived my entire life in a monastery. We pushed through the crowds by the food stalls, and past the drunks stumbling out of taverns. Not a single person bowed in my direction, as they'd always done when I was in my habit. I was just another citizen.

We headed for the poorer areas of town, in search of the cheapest accommodations we could find. Eventually we found decent lodgings in the Jewish section behind a shop run by an older couple. They were a little puzzled by why we'd want to live there, because it didn't take the woman long to place me as Christian. I assured them that the last thing I wanted to do was press for converts, and this was good enough. I suppose our sincerity was obvious and they could see that we were nothing more than an anxious couple in love. Whether we were or not was another story altogether—I certainly wasn't sure yet—but so we appeared to our landlady. We paid our first few months in advance and they even gave us some bread in welcome.

We took some time to explore the town, as you weren't ready to immediately throw yourself into the hunt for work. I had my fingers crossed during that entire first week, hoping that we'd like the city and, more important, that we'd continue to like each other. Mainz was only a kilometer or two across, not so large, but there must have been twenty thousand people. A good size at the time. There was a citizens' center with a market in the northeast corner, and the first time we visited we encountered a lively festival. The city hall was there, as well as the hospital dedicated to the Holy Spirit, the one that I'd suggested when you were first burned. There was an orchard on the west side, and a pig farm run by the Antonite monks.

For some reason, they believed that raising swine perfectly complemented their other work of caring for the sick.

The sheer number of religious orders in Mainz was remarkable. There were the Franciscans, the Augustinians, the Teutonic Order, the Carthusians, and the Magdalens, and . . . I don't know, too many to remember. But I was most interested in the Beguines, who were essentially nuns without any formal orders. Given my situation, you can imagine that I felt a kind of kinship with them—they were not quite of the Church but not quite of the world, either. They seemed to be everywhere on the streets and it lifted my heart a bit. Even though I had deserted Engelthal, I had no intention of deserting God.

The Cathedral of St. Martin towered over all the other churches in the city. It was built under the direction of Archbishop Willigis around the year 1000, because he needed someplace grand after securing the right for German kings to be crowned in Mainz. But on the day before its official consecration, St. Martin caught fire. It seemed to develop a taste for flames, in fact, because by the time that we arrived it had burned twice more. I always thought that there was something appropriate about that. Burned three times, resurrected three times.

St. Martin was a thing of great beauty. There were bronze doors and a stunning carving of the Crucifixion, and beautiful tracery windows that flooded the nave with amazing colors on sunny days. There was a main choir loft behind a transept and a secondary choir loft in the east. It contained the tombs of some of the archbishops—Siegfried von Epstein, I think, and Peter von Aspelt. During our years in Mainz, a tomb for Archbishop von Bucheck was added. You couldn't step into the place without feeling the weight of its history.

After we finished our exploration of the city, you set about finding work. You knew that you'd have to start at the bottom, but you were certain your work ethic would ensure that good things would follow. Every morning you got up early to visit all the churches under

construction, and every day you'd be turned away by them all. Then
you started visiting private houses being built, commercial buildings,
and new roads, but all these worksites turned you away as well. You
became as well known around the construction sites as a colorful
dog, but no matter what you did, no one would offer you a job.

Your first problem was that you refused to lie. When foremen
asked about your experience, you were always forthright that you'd
not practiced masonry for some time. When they asked about what
you'd done in the interval, you would say that you'd been a soldier.
If pressed about exactly what *type* of soldier, you'd remain quiet.
But the real reason you were turned away, time after time, was your
burns. They weren't nearly as extensive as they are today, but try to
imagine the superstition of the age. Who knew what a burned man
had been involved with, especially if he withheld the details? Something sinister, no doubt.

Every night you'd drag yourself home, but you'd take a moment
outside the door to our lodgings. You'd straighten your clothing, and
then clench your fists and splay your fingers a few times before shaking a smile onto your face. I know this because I used to watch you
through the little window. Before you entered, I'd reposition myself
so that you never knew that I'd seen it.

My pains in adjusting to our new life were different. I felt oppressed by the freedom. With no schedule of prayers to follow, I visited the churches around town on my own time, but it was different
praying when I really didn't have to. I started teaching myself to prepare food, something I'd never done in the monastery. I stuck with
fresh vegetables and fruits, thinking I couldn't go wrong, until, after
a few weeks, you indicated that you'd appreciate something more
"substantial." That meant something heated, something involving
meat. Overcooked, undercooked, mixed improperly, I managed to
destroy just about everything I lit a fire under. You smiled your way
through my efforts, hiding the scraps in your pockets and telling me
that I was getting better. More kindness on your part. In the end our

landlady, who could no longer stand the smells from my kitchen, finally showed me enough tricks to get by.

But cooking was simple, compared to playing the role of a lover. God, was that terrifying! But again you were patient, certainly more than I could have reasonably expected. Perhaps in part that was because of your burns; some nights you were too tender to be touched. You weren't innocent and it would have been naïve of me to expect that, but you never apologized for the fact that you'd known women before me. There was the time before we met and the time after, and that was that. Just as I'd left my previous life behind, I had to accept that you'd done the same. For the most part it wasn't too difficult, although sometimes I had to wrestle my jealousies into the closet when you weren't looking.

There was an advantage to your experience in the arena of physical love. Strangely enough, it was the same thing that I had spent my entire life trying, but failing, to perfect in spiritual love. I never had to lead, I only had to receive. You introduced me to a sensuality that I had no idea I possessed. I discovered that I . . . Look at me, all these years have passed, and I still blush. I still can't talk about it. Let's just say that I had always lived with my vows, but after a few months with you I realized that a life of chastity was hardly any life at all.

In any case, I adjusted to living outside the monastery. I still visited St. Martin but I was soon praying for your health and success in finding work, which meant I was praying for what I wanted to happen rather than for what God did. Outside the church, I found myself talking to the Beguines on the street, and I struck up friendships with a few.

The Church basically considered it unbecoming for amateurs to meddle in the affairs of God, but that's not how it appeared to me. The Beguines were working the streets and living out their vows of poverty; they presented quite a contrast to the churches, for I was discovering that the majority of priests were unqualified and even corrupt. The Beguines supported themselves on what they earned

from small crafts and hospital work, supplemented with people's do-
nations, rather than by imposing mandatory taxes. Each night they
returned to their beguinages so they could start the whole process
again the next morning, and their sincerity was beyond question.
It was not long before I came to believe that the main reason the
Church opposed the Beguines was because these amateurs made
them look bad.

The Beguines couldn't quite figure me out. I could speak at
length on the Bible and I could read both Latin and German. I had
studied all the biblical scholars and masters. I knew about Mechthild
von Magdeburg, a mystic of great importance to the Beguines, and
was familiar with her masterwork, *The Flowing Light of the Godhead*.
I knew all these things, but I couldn't—wouldn't—tell them how or
why. I was impressive but confusing. What interested them most,
however, was my extensive knowledge of bookmaking. I knew more
than their own experts, who made the Pauper's Bibles they handed
out on the streets.

Winter was approaching; you still hadn't found employment, and
the repeated rejections were taking their toll on you. The construction managers were becoming increasingly hostile to your repeat
visits, and each night you dragged yourself home with less energy.
You started berating yourself for the inability to "do what any decent
man should be able to do." I was learning yet another lesson about
the outside world, the lesson of male pride. I wanted to help you
but any suggestion I made was met with anger. It didn't make it any
easier that I knew you were angry with yourself, not me.

Another major impediment was that you lacked your journeyman's papers, which were expected of any worker your age. It didn't
matter that it wasn't your fault, that it was never your plan for both
your parents to die while you were still a boy. But there it was. The
Masonry Guild was strong and you simply didn't meet their requirements. Something had to be done, and quickly, because our funds
wouldn't last forever.

So I made two decisions, and told you about neither. The first thing I did was to offer my services to the Beguines. Not as a member, but as a freelance worker.

Their production of the Pauper's Bibles wasn't complicated, just woodblock printing of images and text, but I found them impressive nonetheless. So few people could read that the pictures were the only way to bring religious stories to the masses. Stories from the New and Old Testaments were placed side by side, so the reader could contemplate their connection: rather than underestimate the readers, the Beguines tried to engage them in reflection. Still, I knew that I could improve the quality of the writing and suggest better scene combinations. The Beguines were unconvinced, so I provided some samples and they had to admit I was good. When they remained leery about including an outsider in their work, however, I decided that it was time to tell them about my life at Engelthal.

Upon learning this, they could not bring me into their ranks fast enough. They didn't admit it aloud, of course, but I suppose they thought that if they rubbed up against me, maybe a little bit of Engelthal would rub off. While they couldn't afford to pay me, they made me gifts of bread and turnips. This actually made things easier because when you came home from job hunting I could tell you, honestly, that the food was a charitable donation. I didn't have to say that I was earning while you were not.

The second thing I did, I've never told you before now. Please remember that it was a long time ago, and I hope you'll forgive me.

You got up one morning and prepared for your daily search for work. I asked, casually, about which churches you'd visit, and you answered that you'd start with St. Christoph before moving on to the Poor Clares and then St. Quintin. After that, you really didn't know. When you went out the door, your heels dragging, I put on my nun's robes for the first time since leaving Engelthal. I headed to St. Quintin, knowing that it would take some time before you arrived there.

"It will be a beautiful church," I said to the construction manager. "The nave seems relatively short and the aisles are tall. It's an interesting effect."

He thanked me, but knew full well I wasn't there to talk about architecture. Politely—because who wants to insult a nun?—he asked about the real purpose of my visit. I'd come on behalf of a friend, I answered, a man in need of work. A man covered in burns. The manager rolled his eyes and answered that, yes, a man like that came by every goddamn day, pardon his language, but they had enough workers. Besides, the man's appearance unsettled the other workers.

I used my most soothing voice, the one I'd developed specifically to speak about God. "But surely a man must not be judged by appearance alone. I know for a fact that this man has an excellent heart and a history in stonework."

The manager responded, politely again, that your work history seemed to have been interrupted for many years while you were some sort of soldier, and a mercenary unless he guessed wrong.

I neither confirmed nor denied the construction manager's guess but I did suggest, rather cryptically, "There are soldiers who fight on God's behalf, men whose actions are necessary but not bragged about in public. So I ask you again, in constructing a church as fine as this, surely there must be room for one more worker? Even one with some holes in his history? I can personally vouch for his character."

He looked me over from top to bottom and asked where, exactly, I was from. I answered that I was from Engelthal, not indicating that I was no longer an active sister. I couldn't tell if the man was impressed or not. He'd obviously heard of Engelthal, because he nodded. He said that he'd see what he could do but that he wouldn't make any promises.

"I thank you for indulging me. Should you find a spot for him, please do not tell him that I was here. He's a proud man and it would be well if he believed his persistence had paid off." I bowed and, for good measure, mentioned to the manager that I'd pray for him.

After changing out of my habit, I headed directly to St. Martin. Not to pray for the construction manager's soul, as I'd suggested, but for my own. My deception in the clothing of the Church had made me sick to my stomach. When I left the cathedral, I did not have any feeling that I'd been forgiven. I had asked for a sign, but none was shown.

Until that evening, when you came through the door exhausted but smiling and covered in stone dust. "One of the managers took me on today."

Weeks passed, and you made a favorable impression at the site. When work ran out at St. Quintin's, the manager recommended you to St. Stephan's. It continued that way through the winter, you shuffling from one church to the next. You built a small reputation and made some friends, and each day you were overjoyed to bring home a handful of coins. I heated water and filled a large bucket so that I could wash you. You were still scarred and tight, and I massaged your body until the knots loosened. The work was difficult for any man, but because of your injuries it was twice as bad for you. Still, you were becoming stronger each day. I'd feed you whatever we could afford, usually only turnips or dark bread, cheap cuts of sidemeat, and whatever I'd secretly earned from the Beguines.

There was always just enough money to keep us in our lodgings. Our landlady continued to teach me about cooking and introduced me to some of her friends. It took time for them to accept me, because relations with Christians had always been complicated for the Mainz Jews—stories were still told about the massacre at the hands of Emich's Crusaders, and how the archbishop had once tried to expel all Jews from the city. But as they were living and conducting business within the city, it was impossible not to deal with all types of people. I suppose they decided that since I never pressed my religion upon them, they could accept me as an individual.

So now I had some Jewish acquaintances to go with my Beguine associates, and you had the construction workers at sites all over town. I stopped praying for a sign that I'd made the right choice in leaving Engelthal. I knew that I had.

In the spring, a mason you'd befriended made an unusual and unexpected offer. He said that he was "tired of training stupid little boys" and was longing for the company of a man. If you didn't mind the low pay, he'd petition the Masonry Guild for a special exemption to take you on as an apprentice. He warned that it would not be easy and that there'd be a cut in your current income, but in the end you'd receive your journeyman's papers. We only discussed it for a few minutes before deciding that an offer like this might never come along again. There was some difficulty in convincing the guild but in the end they agreed, and that's how you became the oldest apprentice in Mainz.

You threw yourself into the work, arriving early and leaving late. You did whatever was asked, never complained, and paid deep attention to all your instructions. It didn't hurt that you had a natural aptitude for stone. The lessons you had learned under your father had not been lost over the years.

Belief in a better future is an amazing gift. We still had no money, but we started talking about eventually getting a new place. "A small house, maybe." It gave us something to dream on and the dream was necessary because the loss in income was affecting all parts of our life, most noticeably our diet. Without the "charity" from the Beguines, we never would have made it.

Though our stomachs were empty, we'd walk around town and point out the houses that we'd move into. Someday.

"And when we do," you said, "I will ask you to honor me by becoming my wife."

XX.

Our past was paused here.

When I begged to know whether we got married, Marianne Engel said, "You'll have to wait and see."

• • •

I returned often to the hospital for more reconstructive surgeries. By this point, these were mostly cosmetic: attempts to make me look, rather than work, better. I asked Nan how much longer my resurfacings would continue, and she answered that she didn't know. I asked how much better I would look in the end, and she answered that it varied from patient to patient.

It was always my feeling that, as much as Marianne Engel cared for me, my absences from the fortress were welcome as breaks during which she could work uninterrupted. It was common for me to take a cab back after a few days in the hospital to find her stretched exhausted on her bed, still covered in stone dust, and I'd peek into the basement to see a new monster leering up at me. Then I would check the bowls of water and food I had left out for Bougatsa before leaving and they were always empty; I suspected he consumed everything the moment I stepped out the door, but there was nothing I

could do about that. All in all, these trips to the hospital worked out
well, because her carving in my absence meant we had more time
together when I was there.

But there were still times when she was carving and I was not in
the hospital, and I was becoming better at looking after myself—and
her. While she still managed to pull herself away from her work long
enough to bathe me, I could tell that she resented it: the further into
her statue she was, the harder she'd scrub at my body. When she
finished, she would retreat into the basement and I would bring her
food. "You know, you'd be able to carve better—and *faster*—if you'd
just eat something once in a while."

"It's not only a matter of getting the gargoyle out. It's also a matter of honing my spirit."

"What does that mean?"

"The world pampers the body with food and material comforts,"
she said. "They appease the flesh but are enemies of the spirit. Absti-
nence is a bridle that gives the spirit a chance in the eternal quarrel
with the body."

It was another argument in which logic was a stranger; therefore,
it was another argument that I was destined to lose. So I emptied her
ashtrays, refilled her water bottles, and left a plate of cut fruit that I
knew would still be untouched the next time I came down.

Marianne Engel's raptures always played themselves out after
a few days. She would apologize for her time away, but I knew I
didn't have much to complain about, really, as she usually had only
one—two, at most—of these sessions each month. They paid well,
including all my bills, and the rest of the time she was devoted
to me: anyone whose spouse has a nine-to-five job would tell me to
quit whining.

Besides, each work session was the perfect opportunity for me
to call up old acquaintances and arrange for the delivery of the extra
morphine I was buying with cash advances from my credit card.

• • •

The other customers in the supermarket tried not to look at us, but they failed. Marianne Engel waved at a slack-jawed grandmother, who scurried off as if she'd been caught doing something immoral but still could not prevent herself from looking back over her shoulder twice.

Intellectually I understood the fascination with me, but emotionally I hated it. My anonymity is forever lost, because I am now outstanding in the most literal sense of the word. The fact that my body was hidden behind plexiglass and pressure garments only made me, in a way, all the more compelling. As in any good horror movie, the thing you must imagine is scarier than the thing you actually see.

I heard a mother in aisle eight tell her child not to stare. The boy, five or six, curled his little body behind the safety of her leg but his eyes never left me. The mother said, "I'm sorry. He's, umm, curious and, ah, too friendly. . . ."

"You shouldn't apologize for that! You can't be *too* friendly!" Marianne Engel bent down to look the little guy in the eyes. "You're cute. What's your name?"

"Billy."

"Is that short for William?"

"Yes."

"That's a good name." Marianne Engel nodded in my direction. "William, do you think my friend is scary?"

"A little bit," Billy whispered.

"He's actually not that bad once you get to know him."

I wondered whom Marianne Engel was making most uncomfortable—Billy, Billy's mother, or me—and I said that we had to get going. I had forgotten the effect my croak had on people hearing it for the first time. After Billy was finished recoiling, he asked with a mixture of curiosity and awe, "What's wrong with you?"

The mother scolded him, explaining that this question wasn't very polite. I dismissed it with a wave of my hand, but Marianne Engel asked if she wasn't just a little bit curious about the very same thing. Billy's mother fumbled a mouthful of words until two fell out. "Well, sure. . . ."

"Of course you are. Look at him! William is only asking the question that everyone's thinking." Marianne Engel rubbed the boy's hair, so that he would know he wasn't being criticized.

"He's only in kindergarten," the mother said.

"I was burned in a fire." I only wanted to get the conversation over with, so we could move on, but Billy had another question: *"Did it hurt?"*

"Yes." I suppressed my natural urge to warn the boy not to play with matches. "I was in the hospital for a long time."

"Wow," Billy said, "you must be real happy you're not there anymore."

The mother pulled the boy's hand hard enough that he could not ignore her. "We really do have to go." She never looked back, but Billy turned and waved as she dragged him down the aisle.

When we left the supermarket, Marianne Engel emptied all her extra change into the hands of the beggars loitering outside. All the while she was talking about the half-finished statues in her workshop because, apparently, her Three Masters had recently informed her that she needed to complete them.

I was holding up well until we reached the car, but while I was getting in, I banged a large portion of my burned skin into the passenger door. My body immediately reacted to my mistake by sending intense jolts of pain skittering from one nerve cluster to the next, and the spinebitchsnake started snapping at the base of my skull as if it were a field mouse to be swallowed whole. FUCK YOU. FUCK YOU. FUCK YOU! My hands started to shake from an immediate thirst for morphine and I begged Marianne Engel to administer an injection as quickly as possible. She took the equipment from my kit (I never left home without it) and plugged a syringe into me.

Morphine is like a religious zealot on a mission; it searches for body parts to convert, offering milk-and-honeyed dreams to flow sluggishly through your veins. The snake became mired in the syrup and slowed into nonmovement, but I knew she'd be back. The snake always came back.

When was the last time that my blood had been free of contaminants? In my early twenties, I supposed.

. . .

Marianne Engel paced around our place for days with a coffee and a cigarette, berating herself for not being able to properly clear her physical instrument and receive new instructions. Eventually she accepted that the time really was upon her to complete the unfinished statues that had been collecting in her workshop. "Can't put it off forever, I guess. The Masters say so."

When she worked on these statues, she was not possessed with daimonic energy as she was when starting one from scratch. She would come upstairs to help with my exercises or take a walk with Bougatsa. When she cleaned me in the mornings, I didn't feel like an intruder on her real work. The difference, she explained, came not from herself but from the grotesques. Having stopped partway through the process once already, they now understood that there was more time available than they had originally believed. "They've learned that no matter what I do to them, they're still going to be stone. They know they don't have to yell at me to get what they want."

Over the course of a few weeks, she finished off a few of her lingering pieces. The bird's head, which had been sitting on human shoulders with everything below remaining untouched, was given a male torso and goat's haunches. The uncompleted sea-savage clawing its way out of a granite ocean got the rest of its body, as well as foam on the crests of the waves. Trucks came to pick up these statues and take them to Jack's gallery for sale, because cigarettes and pressure garments do not pay for themselves.

It was a bit of a surprise when, after a few weeks, Marianne Engel asked me to accompany her into the workshop, the one area of the house that was unequivocally hers. She puttered around for a few moments, not saying anything, not looking at me, trying hard to come across as casual. It was such a contrast to all the times I'd seen her immersed in her working rapture. She took the broom and swept a few rock crumbs into a corner, then blurted, "I hope you aren't mad."

She walked over to a block of stone that was covered with a white sheet. I hadn't given it much thought; amid all her other eccentricities, concealing a piece of artwork until it was finished seemed positively sane. I could see a somewhat human silhouette beneath the contours of the sheet, making me think of a child dressed up as a Halloween ghost. When she pulled away the cover, she said, "I've been doing you."

There was a half-completed statue of me. No, not half—more accurately, it was just the outline of my body. None of the detailing was done, but it was impossible not to recognize the vague perimeters of my bulk: the shoulders were properly hunched; the spine had a serpentine curl; the head looked correct, in the wrongness of its dimensions when compared to the rest of the body. It was like looking at myself in the mirror, in the morning, before my eyes had really opened. I stammered that I was not angry that she'd been "doing me," but confused. *Why?*

"God is acting through me," she said, quite seriously, before laughing so that I'd know she was joking. I laughed, too, but it didn't sound very convincing.

"I want you to sit for me, but think about it before committing," she said, indicating the half-finished gargoyles all around her. "I don't want you to suffer the same fate as these ones."

I nodded—to indicate that I'd think about it, not that I agreed—and we headed back up the stairs. I concentrated on climbing with correct form, but when I looked back over my shoulder at the stone figure in the corner, I couldn't help but think I really needed to work on my posture.

• • •

Jack came barging through the front door, straining under the weight of a leafy plant, which she slammed into a corner of the living room. "Last time I was here, I noticed you have no plants. Isn't anything alive in here?" Jack looked at me, then added, "Good Lord, you haven't got any better looking, have you?" She swung her attention quickly in the direction of Marianne Engel, who had been watching her entrance with amusement. "And you, I've got a couple of private buyers looking for originals. They're not crazy about anything at the shop, so they want to know if you're working on anything new. I told them you're *always* working on something new."

"Good homes?" Marianne Engel asked.

"Yes, they're good homes." Jack sighed. "I always find good homes, and your little beasties will be well looked after. Even though they're only bloody stone. You know that, don't you? Oh, and Princeton needs some repair work done."

Marianne Engel shook her head. "Not interested in travel right now."

"Right. Too busy looking after Crispy, here," Jack said. "Christ, Marianne, it's a great paycheck and you're going to let it pass you by. When art meets charity, it's bound to be a fuckup."

Marianne Engel gave Jack a big hug, saying a few words in my defense, but mostly she just giggled at Jack's bluster. This only made Jack angrier. "Remember when you brought Bougatsa home?" she said. "He was a stray, too."

• • •

In our supposed previous life, I'd given Marianne Engel a stone angel that I had carved—the one that sat on her bookshelf—while in this life she'd given me a stone grotesque that she had carved. The symmetry is much like the reversal of our jobs: back then, she had been the one who worked with books and I had been the one who worked with stone.

That observation is academic, I suppose, but my reaction to the idea of her carving me was entirely visceral. It's flattering when an artist wants to do you, of course, but it also made me feel awkward to contemplate that my hideousness would be so permanently captured. For the first time, I understood the fear savages have, that cameras will capture their souls along with their images.

"How would it work?" I asked. "What would I have to do?"

"You wouldn't have to do anything," she answered. "You would just have to sit there."

The reply made me think of our conversation after she forced me to apologize to Sayuri, when she had said that I would need to "do nothing" to prove my love to her. I didn't understand what she had meant, but if *this* was what she had been talking about, how could I turn her down? "Okay, I'll do it."

"It'll be nice to work from life for a change," she said. "I'll finally get to put the form *into* the stone, instead of pulling it out."

She started to remove her clothing and I asked what she was doing. She always carved nude, she said, and was not about to change now; did I have a problem with that? I answered that I didn't, but I really wasn't so sure. There was something about her unclothed body that affected me, the ex–porn actor and prodigious seducer of women, in a way I could not quite comprehend. There was something so raw and disarming about her nudity. . . .

But I could not tell her what to do in her own home. As soon as she was undressed, she pulled the pressure garments from my body and ran her fingers over the folds of my burned flesh, as though her fingers were memorizing a path. "I love that your scars are so red. Did you know that gargoyles used to be painted in bright colors to help their features to stand out?"

She walked over to one of her creatures and ran her fingers over it, just as she had been touching me moments earlier. As I watched her hands move, I imagined how a river runs perfectly over a stone for a thousand years. She pointed out the deeply carved lines under the eyes of one of her beasts. "See how the features are undercut to emphasize shadows, to create depth? The parishioners looking up at the gargoyle, they can't even see these details."

"So why do it?"

"We work also for the eyes of God."

Being carved made me feel more naked than any porno, and that first sitting was made bearable only by its shortness. I could take off my pressure garments for only fifteen minutes at a time, a limit that Marianne Engel always respected. It didn't matter that the work would progress slowly; I was confident that we would have years to complete me.

At the end of each session she would show me the progress she'd made and we would talk about whatever was on our minds. On one occasion she mentioned casually, while stubbing out a cigarette, "Don't forget that we've got a Halloween party coming up."

This was the first I had heard about it, I said.

"No, it isn't," she said. "Last year in the burn ward I promised we'd go, remember?"

"That was a long time ago."

"A year is not a long time, but I'll make you a deal. Would you agree to go if I told you another story?"

"About what?" I asked.

"I think you'll really like this one," she said. "It's about Sigurðr, my Viking friend."

XXI.

Of all the places in which a boy might find himself orphaned, ninth-century Iceland was among the worst. Sigurðr Sigurðsson's parents had arrived with the first wave of Norse immigrants and decided the land had a strange beauty that would be suitable for raising a family. But when Sigurðr was only nine, his father disappeared on an ice floe and, not long after, his mother went to sleep never to wake up. The boy took over the family land and resolved to make his way in life, but he failed: he was just too young, and soon found himself scavenging a living from the dead whales that washed up on the shores.

In truth, it was not a bad skill to possess: the flesh was used for food, the blubber for lamps, and the bones for any number of household items. All these things, Sigurðr could trade to support himself. Still, he felt there was something missing from his existence; even as a child, he knew it was not enough to carve a life out of the carcasses of the dead, and he longed to be strong and valiant.

So, when not cutting apart beached whales, Sigurðr dove. On the edge of a fjord, with the entire ocean stretched in front of him, he would take a moment as the world around him seemed to disappear. Then his legs would push him up into the air and there would

be a moment of brief weightlessness when the battle between sky
and sea was deadlocked, and Sigurðr would—just for this one beautiful moment—imagine himself floating near Valhalla.

But the sea always won, and the boy would cut the air like a
dropped knife. The water rushed up to meet him, and when he
sliced through the transparent surface he felt as if he'd come home.
Down he would go, searching for the bottom, before emerging from
the ocean with the feeling that he'd been cleansed. But the feeling
never lasted.

When he played with the other boys, because there was still a
little time for this, he always felt one step removed from them. He
liked to wrestle and run just as they did, and he even enjoyed drawing a little blood in a sporting contest, but there came a time when
all the other young men found young women with whom to wrestle. Sigurðr, poor Sigurðr, remained content to wrestle only with the
boys, and soon people started to wonder why he didn't seem to have
the slightest interest in taking a wife.

Sigurðr took to spending his evenings in the local tavern in an
attempt to display his manliness, but try as he might to keep his
eyes fixed on the breasts of the waitress, his gaze would invariably
wander to the hairy knuckles of the bartender. From there, his eyes
would go to the strong curve of Höðbroddr's buttocks and then, always, they would settle upon one man, a little older, named Einarr
Einarsson.

Einarr was a block of granite disguised as flesh, with a massive chest and thick forearms that could tame a man—or so Sigurðr
liked to imagine. Einarr's eyes reminded Sigurðr of the icy water
into which he dove, and his flaming hair was like the passion in the
younger man's heart. Einarr was by trade a carpenter, but he was
also a Viking.

The two men had a passing acquaintance, inevitable given the
sparse population, but little contact until the evening that Sigurðr
summoned his courage and headed over to talk. He stuck out his

chest farther than usual, lowered the timber of his voice, and laughed only his most masculine laugh. Still, it did not take long for Einarr to see that it was not a man who sat before him, but a lost boy.

There was something about Sigurðr, so pitiful and yet so hopeful, that touched Einarr's better impulses. He knew the boy had lost his parents, and he had seen him wandering the shores with bags of dead whale. Rather than dismiss the boy, he listened, and when Sigurðr said embarrassing things—and there were plenty—Einarr simply nodded. He saw no need to insult someone whose life was already difficult enough.

That evening in the bar was the first of many. Their relationship was a strange fit, but somehow a good one, because Einarr appreciated that aspect of Sigurðr's character which his Viking companions lacked. The young man, though not particularly intelligent, had moments in which he longed for something better. Sigurðr did not want to destroy, he wanted to create—but he didn't know how. He often spoke about how wonderful it must be for Einarr to build things from wood. While Einarr only grunted, inside he agreed—it *was* a good thing that he did for a living—and he also thought that perhaps this boy could do better for himself, if only he had a little guidance.

Soon Einarr proposed that Sigurðr assist him in the carpentry shop, and the offer was accepted with excitement. It would not be an apprenticeship, per se, because there was never any suggestion that Sigurðr would eventually set out on his own, but it would be a fine way to fill out his days. Sigurðr's heart was beating more quickly than usual the first time he arrived at Einarr's longhouse.

The dwelling was typical of the Icelandic style, constructed from the materials at hand. Rough stones had been laid in as foundation around upright posts of timber, and the walls were turf-sod with birch branches for infilling. Einarr proudly displayed one feature that was not common: in a corner of the longhouse, he had dug a trench that ran under the wall from a nearby stream. It was not even necessary to go outside to get clean water, because all one needed to do was lift the floorboards and dip in a bucket.

Every inch of the place was piled high with wood: some native to Iceland, some imported from Norway, and some that had washed up on the coast. All had to be kept inside so it was dry enough to work. On the walls hung dozens of irons, files, rasps, knives and chisels, and there were shelves to house the oils used to finish the woodwork.

Nearly all the benches, shelves, and even farming implements were carved with intricate designs. Sigurðr ran his finger gently along the twisting grooves of one such object, a cradle sitting near a wall. From the four corners of its body, posts extended upwards; each was a dragon's neck with a head that fit perfectly into the parent's hand so the child could be rocked to sleep.

"It is for my boy, Bragi."

Sigurðr knew that Einarr was a father and that he was married. He didn't need to be reminded of these facts. "It's good," he replied, then pointed to a barrel overflowing with thin wooden cylinders. "What are those?"

Einarr pulled one out and held it in front of his face, looking down its length, before handing it over.

"I have no particular skill with a bow, but tooling a shaft straight and true is another matter altogether."

"Einarr is showing off, is he?"

A woman, cradling an infant sucking at her tit, had come into the house unheard. Her eyes were an even brighter blue than Einarr's and her hair, swept back with a colorful headband, had streaks of bright blond where she had bleached it with lye.

"You must be Sigurðr. It is good to meet you finally."

"This is Svanhildr," said Einarr. "My anchor."

"Ah, your steadying influence, then?" asked the wife.

"No," answered the husband, "that which is dragging me down."

Svanhildr slapped him hard across the shoulder, and Einarr reached out his own hand—not to strike in return, but to cup the baby so its balance was not lost.

"The lucky little one," said Einarr, "is Bragi."

Svanhildr handed the child over to her husband, adjusted the treasure necklace around her throat, and closed her apron-dress. A chain of keys around her waist rattled in time with the many ornaments of her necklace and, as a result, her every movement was musical. She slapped her husband once more, tunefully, before taking the child back into her arms. From the look on her face, this was a woman pleased with her life.

The man and boy worked through the afternoon—mostly, Einarr demonstrated the uses of the tools—before Sigurðr returned home after declining Svanhildr's invitation to dinner.

The following day, when Svanhildr answered the longhouse door, Sigurðr handed a sack to her. "I brought shark," he said.

"How very kind," she said, politely exaggerating the bag's weight. "I will ferment it, and you will eat it with us when it is ready."

In the pause that followed, Sigurðr blurted, "It's good to find dead whales, but sharks are also useful."

"Yes. Come in." She kicked aside a stray piece of lumber. "That is, if you can find room among these logs. Sometimes I feel like I'm living in a forest."

Again the men spent the day together; this time it was the maintenance of the tools that was explained. When Svanhildr extended another dinner invitation, Sigurðr accepted. She served chicken stew with seaweed and, as the men ate, she rocked the dragon cradle until Bragi fell asleep.

They sat around the longfire until late in the night, smoke drifting through the vent in the ceiling. Svanhildr heated a small cauldron of ale and when the men's frost-cups neared their dregs, she would dip the ale-goose into the cauldron to refill them. When Sigurðr commented on the brew's excellent taste, Svanhildr explained her secret lay in the combination of juniper and bog myrtle. "It is often said that a man's happiness depends on the quality of his food," she explained, "but in Einarr's case it's more the quality of his alcohol."

Einarr grunted appreciatively and took another gulp.

That night, as Sigurðr walked back to his own house, he absentmindedly rubbed his fingers with the patch of sharkskin he had not given to Einarr. He had sliced it from the top fin because he knew it would make fine sandpaper, but somehow he had not found a good moment to hand it over. By the time he arrived at his own shabby dwelling, his fingers were so numb he didn't notice they were covered in blood.

In the afternoons that followed, Sigurðr discovered that while he had no real feel for woodwork, he did have a talent for paints. He ground the pigments—blacks from charcoal, whites from bone, reds from ocher—and applied them to the finished work. Sigurðr was thrice pleased: by the new skill he was developing; by the colors themselves; and by the smile on Einarr's face.

Einarr, too, was content. Not only did Sigurðr's painting improve his work, but also the young man was a good companion—not quite a friend yet, but certainly not only a workmate. To recognize this fact, one day Einarr handed over a long package, wrapped in worsted fabric and tied with a leather string. Inside was a sword with an intricately carved dragon handle. "It would be good for you to have a proper blade," Einarr said, "not that fish-cutter you have now."

Sigurðr nodded, because he didn't know what else to do. Since his parents had died, this was the first gift anyone had given him.

"Now," asked Einarr, "would you like to learn to use that?"

Einarr set about correcting the weaknesses in Sigurðr's technique, and the pupil was quick to incorporate the suggestions. Einarr was impressed. "Your body naturally knows which way to move, and this is good. There are many things that can be taught, but a feel for the attack is not one of them."

Sigurðr looked at his feet. He didn't want Einarr to see the blush the compliment had brought to his face.

"You will need a name for that," Einarr said. "I suggest Sigurðrsnautr. Because if you ever need to put your blade into a man, it will not be a gift that he soon forgets."

When Sigurðr returned home that evening, he turned the sword over and over in his hands. He liked the name—"Sigurðr's Gift." He

carefully tied together the ends of the leather strap that had wrapped
the package, and hung it around his neck. From that day forward, he
was never without it, but he always made sure the strap was carefully
tucked into his tunic. There was no need to display it; it was enough
to know what had once been in Einarr's fingers now constantly
touched his skin. To think of the fact sometimes raised small bumps
on Sigurðr's flesh, the way a blast of the northern wind might.

When the inevitable day came that Einarr left for a series of Viking raids, Sigurðr expected this would mark a return to his lonely
ways. But Svanhildr invited him for pancakes and ale each morning and—to his own surprise—Sigurðr kept showing up. Bragi was
growing bigger and soon added a new phrase to his growing vocabulary. He knew *mother* and *father* and *wood,* but one day he looked at
the man who had the mouthful of pancakes and said: "Sig Sig."

Though Einarr may have built the supply chests in the home, it
was Svanhildr who controlled them with her chain of keys. Not without careful planning could a Viking household make it through the
brutal winters, and Sigurðr grew to appreciate her work. She knew
all the methods for preserving meat—smoking, salting, pickling, and
more—so her husband did not grow tired of the same meals. After a
while, Sigurðr found himself helping her after breakfast, slicing the
meat into strips while she prepared the brines in which they would
soak.

Not once during her husband's absence did Svanhildr mention a
fear that he might not come home—but when word came that the
ship had returned, Svanhildr rushed to the shore and jumped into
Einarr's waiting arms. She kissed him passionately, then punched
him twice in the face, and then gently kissed the blood off his lips.
Sigurðr wasn't quite sure, but it almost seemed that when Svanhildr
pulled back her fist, Einarr offered up his chin to receive the coming
blows.

Sigurðr helped to carry the plunder back to the longhouse and
was amazed by the volume of goods: precious metals and bags
of coins, jewelry, tools snatched from foreign workshops, and the

bottles of wine that had not broken on the return voyage. But for all this, it was clear that Svanhildr was waiting for something more. Then Einarr drew out a jeweled book mount he had ripped from the cover of an edition of Gospels at one of the English monasteries, and pressed it into Svanhildr's hand. She admired it for a few moments before adding the bauble to her treasure necklace, and finally Sigurðr understood from where the great variety of her charms had come. Everywhere.

They drank ale and wine late into the night until Sigurðr, too drunk to stumble home, passed out on one of the benches that lined the walls. Here he lay, until awakened by the sounds of a fight—or so he thought, in the disoriented moments before he realized he was overhearing the coupling of his hosts.

Einarr thrust brutally into his wife from behind, his hands pulling back her hips. It appeared that Svanhildr was desperately trying to escape, and she was, but not really: it was part of their game. When she finally managed to break free, Einarr grabbed her kicking legs and flipped her over. When he entered her from on top, she dragged her fingernails across his back, carving streaks of blood into his flesh. She bit his neck so hard that he had to pull her head away by a fistful of hair. She barked in pain, then smiled wickedly and told her husband that he smelled like old fish and fucked like a girl. Einarr growled that she wasn't going to be able to walk straight come the morning.

It took a long time for Sigurðr to fall back asleep.

When he woke again, it was clear that Einarr—teeth marks ringing his throat—had already washed the stench from his body in the nearest hot spring. Bragi was running around, reacquainting himself with his father, while Svanhildr—bruises running down her arms—implored the boy to keep his voice down as she patiently untangled Einarr's hair with a whalebone comb. Every once in a while, she threw her arms around him from behind to whisper, *"Ég elska þig. Ég elska þig. Ég elska þig."* I love you. I love you. I love you.

When Sigurðr exaggerated a yawn to signal that he was awake,

Svanhildr jumped up from her husband and went to get a bucket of
fresh water so their guest could wash himself. Even before she had
brought it over, Bragi had launched himself into Sigurðr's arms. By
now, his vocabulary had improved and he squealed with joy: "Uncle
Sig!"

It was not long after that Einarr, for the second time, extended
an offer that would change Sigurðr's life: this time, to join the Viking crew. As Einarr explained, the long voyages were boring and he
missed his life back home; perhaps the company of a friend would
help ease that.

The offer was not without appeal, because Sigurðr often feared
he was not enough of a man. In the mornings, he jumped into water
and scavenged for dead animals; in the afternoons, he worked as an
assistant; when he felt lonely, he helped another man's wife with do-
mestic chores. Sigurðr only promised to think about it but he already
knew that he would accept the offer, and not least of all because
Einarr had called him friend.

Sigurðr soon found himself being considered by the Vikings.
There was some dissent—whispered rumors that Sigurðr was *fuð-
flogi*, a man who flees in horror when faced with the prospect of
sexually servicing a woman—but no one wanted to offend Einarr.
When one's existence depends upon the longboat, it is inadvisable to
upset the master carpenter. Besides, the Vikings believed there was
nothing inherently wrong with queer feelings in any case, so long
as one was the aggressor. The man who would submit himself to
another in sex might also do so in other matters, like battle, but there
was no evidence that Sigurðr had ever surrendered to another man,
only the suggestion that he might not mind doing so. After a few
tests of Sigurðr's strength and skill with weapons, he was accepted
on a trial expedition down the English coast.

The ship was an imposing thing, with cowhide shields and woolen
sails, at its head a fierce carved serpent. They steered by the sun and
the stars, the Vikings sitting on empty chests that would be full by
the time they came home. It was clear that there were members of

the Viking crew who relished the fight to come. They would prepare
for the siege with chants, by slapping each other across the face, by
cutting their own skin to whet their blades' thirst for blood. Some
would even imagine themselves as possessed by animal spirits, and
aided the process by taking large mouthfuls of *berserkjasveppur*—
berserker mushrooms—before hitting the English shore.

Einarr advised Sigurðr not to bother. He had used the mushrooms on his first raid, but they only disoriented him. However, he
did confess he sometimes used them back in his workshop when he
lacked inspiration for his carving. After a few mushrooms, he said,
it was easy to envision the flowing designs that elude a man while
sober.

Sigurðr soon discovered that the fighting came easily to him and
that it was a simple task to overpower the English; they would mostly
just hand over the loot in an effort to have done with it, especially
the monks. The raids were a great success and Sigurðr, with Einarr's
help, acquitted himself well. He was invited for a second run, then
a third, and after that he became a regular crew member. For the
first time in his life, Sigurðr felt that he belonged. He'd moved from
having no family to having two—Einarr's, and a fraternity of broth-
ers—and he believed that his newly earned manliness would, at the
end of his days, allow him to enter Valhalla.

So it went for years. In the intervals between the raids, Sigurðr
and Einarr practiced their weapons and improved their woodwork-
ing partnership. Einarr's carving became ever more imaginative,
perhaps because of the ale he sipped with increasing regularity or
the mushrooms he took when in particular need of inspiration. Sigurðr's skill with paint likewise progressed. The men spent most
days together and, usually, on each new day they liked each other
better than they had on the previous one.

It was inevitable, of course, that Sigurðr fell in love with Einarr.
It was no longer simply lust's first bloom, but something deeper and
truer and better. It was equally inevitable that Einarr knew, but he
had become an expert at pretending not to notice Sigurðr's occasion-

ally lingering looks. This is how they dealt with it: by acting as if it didn't exist. Nothing good could come from talking about it, so they didn't, and it hung between them like a long night with a dawn that never came.

As for Svanhildr, her love for Einarr also grew with each year; however, the excitement of his Viking way of life gave way to the harsh reality of his absences, and she became moody in the weeks leading up to each raiding expedition. Then came one time that was worse than any that had come before. She snapped whenever Einarr asked for a refilled frost-cup, berated the gods for no apparent reason, and even broke down into tears when Bragi scraped his knee while playing with a toy sword.

When Einarr could no longer stand it, he grabbed her shoulders and shook her until she gave up her silence.

"The problem is *you*," she said. "And your trips, when I'm with child."

A smile spread across Einarr's face.

"Stop that! I'm not supposed to be pregnant again," she lamented. "I'm old."

"But not *too* old," said Einarr. "Apparently."

On the night before the men were to leave, Svanhildr served them smoked pork and her latest ale but barely spoke. The following morning, she did not accompany Einarr to the shore. She just slapped him once across the mouth at their front door to say goodbye.

The raids went as they always did. The reputation of the Vikings was almost enough to win any fight before a sword was lifted and by the time they approached their final target, their ship was loaded heavily. Perhaps they had grown complacent, because they were less prepared than usual. The English village had been attacked many times without difficulty, but recently the townspeople had learned some methods to defend themselves in an attempt to restore their pride. They didn't expect to defeat the Vikings, but they desperately wanted to take a few of the intruders down.

As the Vikings poured out of their boat and across the sand, there came an unexpected exclamation of arrows across the sky. Sigurðr had a good eye; he spotted one arrow that posed a particular threat. He readied himself to move out of its path but then realized that if he did so, the arrow would hit the man behind him.

Einarr.

And so he did not move.

The arrow cut through the pelts across Sigurðr's chest and he fell to the ground with a sharp yell, his fingers wrapped around the shaft.

After their initial surprise, the Vikings quickly regained control and the village fell to the attackers, as it always did. But the battle no longer involved Einarr Einarsson or Sigurðr Sigurðsson, who were back on the shore. The arrow was lodged deep in Sigurðr's chest, embedded past the barb, and could not be pulled out without ripping the wound open.

Sigurðr knew this. He was afraid but gathered his courage even as he felt his eyes glazing over like ice forming on idle oars. "Einarr?"

"Yes."

"I am dying."

"You are not."

"Remember me."

"How could I forget a man," Einarr replied, "so stupid that he believes he's dying from a flesh wound?"

"Einarr?"

"What?"

"There is something I need to tell you."

"You're talkative for a dying man."

"No," Sigurðr insisted. *"Ég elska—"*

Einarr cut him off. "All this prattling makes you sound like a woman. Save your strength."

The look on Einarr's face let Sigurðr know that the discussion was finished, so he closed his eyes and let his friend carry him back onto the longboat. There Einarr cut away the flesh around the arrow's shaft, and Sigurðr howled in agony with each slice. When the trench had been dug wide enough, Einarr used tongs to pull out the arrowhead and then held it up so Sigurðr, barely conscious, could see the meaty fibers that clung to it.

"Svan must have fed you well," Einarr said. "There is fat near your heart."

Through the return trip, Einarr washed the bandages and checked Sigurðr's wound for infection but it seemed to be, if not healing, at least not getting worse. Almost before Sigurðr knew it, he awoke to the sight of Svanhildr holding out a bowl of leek and onion soup.

"The warmth will be good for you," she said.

"I can leave. It is not wise for a sick man to be in the home of a pregnant woman."

She seemed amused. "You are family, and we will hear of no such thing."

"But the baby . . ."

"Drink up. If I can smell the onions through your wounds, I'll know your insides have been damaged."

Over the following days Einarr and Bragi prayed to the goddess of healing, and Svanhildr continued to tend Sigurðr's wounds. The local healer blessed a number of whalebone runes in exchange for one of Einarr's best chests, and scattered them around the bench on which Sigurðr slept.

It seemed to work; Sigurðr's wound remained onion free. The first thing he did, when it was obvious he would live, was head into the workshop to bore a hole through one of the healing runes. This, he handed over to Svanhildr.

"I would be honored," he said, "if you added this to your treasure necklace. You don't have to, but—"

She cut his sentence short by throwing her arms around him, and nodding vigorously.

The recovery was not easy. Sigurðr had difficulty lifting his arms and occasionally there were shooting pains when he least expected them, but he soon grew tired of being looked after. He joined Einarr on his latest project, a boat intended to take Bragi into the coves for fishing. He was determined to paint every inch of it; such decoration was not necessary, by any means, but it felt good to have a brush in his hand again. The job dragged on for far too long, but Einarr never once complained about his friend's slowness.

Svanhildr's pregnancy progressed without difficulty, despite her advanced years for such an adventure. When she went into labor, young Bragi ran to fetch the midwife while the men stayed behind to comfort her. Another boy, healthy and beautiful and named Friðleifr, soon joined the family.

When it appeared certain that the child would survive, the men decided to drink to their good fortune. Even Bragi was allowed to stay up late and down a number of frost-cups filled with strong ale; since he now had a younger brother to watch over, his father contended that it was time for him to start drinking like a man.

The room was aglow from the longfire and the blubber lamps, and Einarr laughed as his boy—now, he noted proudly, his *older* boy—stumbled to his sleeping bench on wobbly legs. "No, not quite a man yet," he teased, while Sigurðr called out that the ale would put hair on Bragi's chest. Or, at least, hair on his tongue the following morning.

Within minutes the boy was snoring and Einarr, satisfied that his wife and new baby were also safely asleep, retreated to his workshop. He returned with a small bag that he tossed to Sigurðr; inside were a number of dried mushrooms. "Now we should truly celebrate. The gods smile upon us."

Each man ate a couple of the *berserkjasveppur*—Sigurðr didn't like the texture, but was never one to refuse his friend—before Einarr dumped the remainder into the ale bowl on the longfire. "We will boil the rest. It doesn't taste good, but the effect . . ."

As they sipped late into the night, Einarr tried to describe the beauty of the free-flowing lines that floated all around him, and Sigurðr found himself laughing at Einarr's every attempt. A few times Svanhildr lifted her head confusedly at one of Sigurðr's exclamations, but settled back into sleep without a word. The men drank until the mushroom bowl was empty, and then ate the soggy remains at its bottom.

"It was good when you gave Svan the rune for her necklace," Einarr said with a slur. "I wish I'd thought of it."

"She looked after me," said Sigurðr. "As did you."

"It was time for her to have something of you around her neck."

"I love," said Sigurðr, "her."

"I know."

"Bragi," added Sigurðr. "Bragi, I love, too."

"I have something for you." Einarr once again retreated to his workshop, and this time he returned with the arrowhead that had entered Sigurðr's body. He sat down heavily, closer to Sigurðr than before. "Give me your necklace."

"I didn't know . . ." Sigurðr murmured. "I didn't think you'd ever noticed it."

"I knew of it from the first, but was reminded when I cut this"— he held up the arrowhead—"from your chest."

Sigurðr handed over the leather strap, and when it was in his fingers, Einarr twisted it around and said, "It looks just like the day I wrapped Sigurðrsnautr with it."

Sigurðr stared intently into the fire, unable to meet his friend's eyes, as Einarr slipped the arrowhead onto the necklace. Then he held it out for Sigurðr to take.

Sigurðr started to reach for it, but then changed his mind and bowed slightly instead. Einarr hesitated momentarily, and then slipped the necklace over Sigurðr's head. Sigurðr could feel the hand brushing up against his hair, perhaps even grazing the nape of his neck. After all his years of imagining Einarr's fingers there, they finally were.

They paused a moment, eyes on each other.

Sigurðr leaned in a bit, and Einarr did not pull back. They were so close. Sigurðr cleared his throat, which felt clogged with boiled ale and fungus, and his voice cracked when he released the words he had waited so many years to say. *"Ég elska þig."*

Einarr narrowed his eyes a little, but otherwise his expression did not change.

Sigurðr leaned in a little further, and still Einarr did not pull away. So Sigurðr closed the remainder of the distance, settled his mouth to Einarr's, and kissed him.

Einarr did not react. Sigurðr read this as acceptance, and kissed harder.

Then Sigurðr felt Einarr pull back, followed by an excruciating thud at the side of his head. The blow sent him toppling off the bench and he looked up just in time to see Einarr jumping forward, leg swinging. The kick caught Sigurðr full in the ribs and drove all the breath from his lungs. Using his sword arm, Einarr drove one punch to the center of Sigurðr's stomach, and followed that with more. The attack was uncoordinated, heavy on frenzy and short on strategy, and mostly the blows missed.

Sigurðr tried to retreat but Einarr drove his shoulder into his chest, sending Sigurðr sprawling into one of the lamps, knocking it over. He tried to use the momentum to roll away, but Einarr followed with more wild fists. So many blows, so fast, and everywhere—into Sigurðr's jaw, off his shoulder, to his throat, and at the most tender place on his chest where the arrow had entered. He could barely breathe, both from the violence of the attack and the fact it was happening at all.

The baby. Friðleifr was now howling in the dragon crib, aware that something was terribly wrong in the world he barely knew. Svanhildr had jumped up and was screaming at her husband to stop, and Bragi stumbled off his sleeping bench, confused both by the fight and by the ale that still ran through his veins. He could not quite control his legs, and the floor seemed to lurch like a boat deck during a storm.

Einarr was beyond any understanding of the yelling voices.

Whatever demons the *berserkjasveppur* were making him see, he was fighting them as if they were the only real things in the room.

Sigurðr did not fight back with the conviction that one would have expected. His injuries limited his physical ability, true, but it was more than that: when he saw the stumbling boy Bragi and heard Svanhildr's screams, he simply lost the will. He became aware, not consciously but nonetheless completely, that his moment of weakness was a betrayal of those closest to him, the family that had taken in a confused boy and given him the life of a man. In one lustful moment, Sigurðr had crossed the unspoken line he and Einarr had spent more than a decade constructing.

So Sigurðr allowed his body to go limp; he would let Einarr punch that line back into existence.

When Svanhildr saw Sigurðr give up, she was afraid for his life, and turned away from her path to the baby's dragon cradle. She grabbed at Einarr's right arm when it was drawn back for another blow, and her husband automatically spun around with his left fist. It connected heavily, sending Svanhildr sprawling headfirst into a pile of lumber.

Bragi knew better than to engage his father directly; a boy who still played with toy swords was no match for a Viking. The beating of his uncle Sig terrified him, but Bragi could also see a greater danger: whale blubber had spilled out of the knocked-over lamp and ignited a pile of wood shavings, and the flames were spreading.

Bragi began yelling that the room was on fire, but even this was not enough to bring his father back. Einarr's fists, still inaccurate but unfailing in endurance, continued to rain down upon Sigurðr's body and there was nothing in the attacker's face but fearful rage.

The benches along the walls caught fire and those flames reached up to grab at the birch twigs that stuck out of the walls. There would be no stopping the blaze and—worst, Bragi saw—it was headed towards his mother, who lay motionless where she had fallen. There was blood leaking from her forehead, into eyes that were no longer open.

Bragi shook his mother, but without response. When he realized she could not be woken, he hooked his hands into her armpits and tensed his legs. He pulled with all his strength, but he was still too drunk and too small and he could only jerk her haltingly, a few feet at a time. Still, he would get her out. He had to.

As Bragi dragged Svanhildr towards the door, Einarr continued his merciless attack. Sigurðr could no longer have fought back even if he had wanted: his face was bloody pulp, many of his ribs had snapped, and his legs twitched with each connecting blow. Still, he was able to spit a few words through his broken teeth.

"Fire, Einarr," he sputtered. "Wife! Bragi!"

He kept repeating the words until they finally made it through. Einarr stopped his fists and looked around confusedly, like a man who did not know where he has woken up. He saw that Bragi was at the longhouse's entrance with Svanhildr but could go no further, stopped by a barrier of flames.

He bolted to them and kicked open the burning door. He grabbed Bragi and threw him out, but he could not do the same with Svanhildr—her unconscious deadweight made that impossible—so he lifted her over his shoulder and put his head down. The only way out was through; they might get burned, but they would live.

Sigurðr, lying shattered on the floor, saw Einarr and Svanhildr disappear through the curtain of flames and knew that he would never be able to follow. He could not imagine moving a few feet, much less the distance needed to escape, and thought: *So this is how it ends. In flames.*

The fire crackled around him like laughter, and he expected this would be the last sound that he ever heard. Then he heard the baby crying.

The edges of Sigurðr's tunic were ablaze and his skin felt as if it was starting to bubble. With a handful of broken fingers, he put out those flames; he might have burned his hands while doing so, but he couldn't feel them and it didn't matter anyway. Blood seeped out of the corners of his eyes and into his beard, but he wiped it away and began to crawl towards Friðleifr's cries.

Outside, in the glow of the longhouse, Svanhildr had regained consciousness and grabbed hysterically at Bragi. When she realized that Friðleifr was not with them, she threw her arms out and broke into screams. She began lurching towards the longhouse, and then it was Bragi who held her; he would not allow his mother to enter an inferno it was obvious she could not escape.

Einarr, his wits regained, also heaved his body towards the burning building. His heart urged him to burst inside, but his most basic instincts would not allow it. Unable to do anything else, incapable of moving towards the fire or away from it, he fell to his knees and buried his face in his hands. Svanhildr continued screaming at the burning house and Bragi continued to hold her back, until it was apparent that her rage was no longer directed at the building. The boy released his mother and she ran to Einarr, punching and kicking him until she dropped exhausted at his side.

Einarr never once lifted a hand to Svanhildr until she collapsed, and then he raised it only to reach out to her. The moment his open palm touched her, she jerked away, and he knew not to try again.

The following morning, the longhouse was little more than a blight of glowing embers strewn among the foundation stones. Others had arrived—farmers, Vikings, tradespeople—and had begun to comb the ruins. Einarr wanted to do anything but this, but knew he must.

He headed to the spot where the dragon cradle had last sat, but it was no more: there was only a pile of burnt sticks, and one smoldering dragonhead post that had not been incinerated with the rest.

A cry went up from one of the searchers: Sigurðr's body had been found. It was not where the beating had occurred, but perhaps a dozen body lengths away. The corpse was so badly charred that Einarr could not even recognize it as his friend; it was the shape of a human body, but melted to the bones.

The sight sickened Einarr, but the location puzzled him. Rather than heading for the door, Sigurðr had pulled himself into the corner of the house where the water trench ran. This might have made sense if the opening was large enough to escape through—but it was far too small. Sigurðr hadn't even opened the floorboards; he lay on top of them.

There was a noise.

Einarr and the men standing around the scorched body looked from face to face, as if to confirm that they were not mad, that there was indeed sound coming from a dead man.

Soft. A whimpering.

Underneath. The noise was coming from below the floorboards.

Two men pulled Sigurðr's remains to one side, the skull puffing out a breath of ashes, and Einarr began ripping up the planks. They were scorched but not burned through; it was clear that Sigurðr's body had acted as a buffer against the flames. When the boards were removed, Einarr saw that there in the flowing water, wrapped in his swaddling blanket and tied securely with Sigurðr's arrowhead necklace, was the newborn. The child Friðleifr was shivering and half submerged, but alive.

Einarr scooped his son out and held him tighter than he ever had before.

In the days that followed, Einarr and Bragi spent all their time at Sigurðr's favorite fjord, digging a massive hole. When it was large enough, they enlisted the help of the Viking crew to carry Bragi's boat—the one that Sigurðr had painted so brilliantly—to the gravesite. While it was being lowered, some of the Vikings grumbled that Sigurðr was not so important a warrior as to deserve such a fine boat grave, but no one dared speak such a thought aloud. They simply left Einarr and his family to bid farewell to the man who had saved their child.

Beside Sigurðr's body in the boat, they laid a number of items: his favorite frost-cup and the household's ale-goose, both pulled from the ashes; his paintbrushes and pigments; Sigurðrsnautr; and the single unburned dragonhead from Friðleifr's cradle. Then Svanhildr removed her treasure necklace and placed it gently across Sigurðr's withered chest, keeping only the healing rune that he had given her.

Svanhildr and Einarr also considered placing the arrowhead necklace into the grave, but ultimately decided against it. It would go to Friðleifr, a talisman to protect the child as he grew into a man.

Einarr filled in the grave by himself. Bragi and Svanhildr, the baby clutched tightly to her bosom, stayed with him as he worked through the night. Just as the sun was rising, the last shovelful was put into place and Einarr slumped exhausted, to look out over the ocean at the sun rising like the condemning eye of Óðinn. The boy Bragi had fallen asleep and Einarr, unable to keep the awful truth to himself any longer, confessed to Svanhildr how the fight had started.

When he was finished, Svanhildr touched her husband for the first time since the longhouse was burning. She couldn't offer any words of forgiveness, but she took his hand into her own.

"I don't know why I did it," said Einarr, tears running down his face. "I loved him."

They sat not speaking for a long time, Einarr weeping, until finally Svanhildr spoke. "Friðleifr is a good name," she said, "but perhaps not so good as Sigurðr."

Einarr squeezed her fingers and nodded, and then broke into new sobs.

"It is proper that we never forget," said Svanhildr, looking down on the sleeping face of the rescued baby at her breast. "From this day forward, this child will carry our friend's name."

XXII.

Keeping a low profile is not easy for a burn survivor at the best of times, but it becomes exponentially harder when he is in a fabric store with a wild-haired woman holding up swaths of white cloth against his chest, measuring out the proper amount for his angel's robes.

When it came time to pay, I stepped between Marianne Engel and the cashier, thrusting forward my credit card. Funny the sense of independence it inspired, given that payment would ultimately come from one of her accounts anyway. Still, I could live with the illusion.

After we had procured all our costume-making supplies, we ran a rather strange errand to a local bank. Marianne Engel wanted to add my name to the access list for her safety deposit box, and the bank needed a signature sample to complete the request. When I asked her why she wanted it done, she answered simply that it was good to be prepared, for God only knew what the future might bring. I asked whether she was going to give me a key for the safety deposit box. No, she answered, not yet. Who else was on the list? No one.

We went to a coffee shop to drink lattes with no foam, sitting on an outside deck while Marianne Engel educated me on the Icelandic version of *Hel*. Apparently it is a place not of fire but of ice: while

English speakers say that it's "hot as Hell," Icelanders say *helkuldi*, "cold as Hell." This makes sense: having spent their entire lives hammered down by the frigid climate, how could they fear anything more than an eternal version of the same thing? For the burnt man, might I add, it is particularly attractive that the notion subverts the Judeo-Christian idea that the means of eternal torment must be fire.

That Hell is tailored to the individual is hardly a new idea. It is, in fact, one of the greatest artistic triumphs in Dante's *Inferno*: the punishment for every sinner fits his sin. The Souls of the Carnal, who in life were swept away by the gusting fits of their passion, are in death doomed to be carried on the winds of a never-ending tempest. The Souls of the Simoniacs, who in life offended God by abusing the privileges of their holy offices, are doomed to burn upside down in fiery baptismal fonts. The Souls of the Flatterers spend eternity buried in excrement, a reminder of the shit they spoke on Earth.

It made me wonder what my version of Hell—if I believed in such a thing, that is—would be like. Would I be doomed to burn forever, trapped inside my car? Or would Hell be a never-ending stint on the débridement table? Or would it be the discovery that when I was finally able to love, it was already too late?

As I contemplated this, I spotted one of my secret fraternity coming down the street. It was a strange feeling, the first time that I'd seen another burn survivor in public, and one whom I knew, no less: Lance Whitmore, the man who'd given the inspirational talk at the hospital. He came directly to us and asked whether we'd met before. I couldn't blame him for not recognizing me, because not only had the contours of my face changed while healing, they were also hidden behind my plastic mask.

"It's nice to see one of us out in the daylight," he said. "It's not that we're ghosts, exactly, but we do a pretty good job of not being seen."

We made small talk for perhaps ten minutes and it never seemed to bother Lance that we drew curious stares from nearly everyone who walked past us. I don't doubt that he noticed, but I admired the way he could pretend he didn't.

. . .

I was in a white robe and my wings were made of stockings stretched over coat hangers, trimmed with silver tinsel. Marianne Engel adjusted my halo (pipe cleaners, painted gold) before rolling up my angelic sleeve to administer a shot of morphine, which flowed through me like the slightly curdled milk of human kindness. Bougatsa ran around nipping at our heels, and I wondered how the brain of a dog might process such a scene.

She was also dressed in a robe—or, more accurately, a dress that hung and bunched so loosely that it looked like a robe. Her hair was somehow even wilder than usual, despite being tied with a band that encircled her temples and came together in a knot on her forehead. A wide tail of fabric escaped her curls and cascaded down her back. She gathered this excess material into the crook of her elbow, letting it drape over her forearm as a waiter might hold a napkin. In her other hand she held an old-fashioned lantern, without oil, and around her left ankle—the one with the rosary tattoo—was a circle of leaves. She explained that it was to represent the laurel crown that should be on the ground at her feet, because a real one would impede her movement around the dance floor. I asked her who she was.

"One of the Foolish Virgins," she answered.

The party was at the oldest, most expensive hotel in town. A doorman with top hat opened the taxi door and took Marianne Engel by the hand. He bowed deeply, before looking at me quizzically as if trying to understand how my burn makeup could be so convincing. "Are you to be Lucifer, sir?"

"Excuse me?"

"The only fallen angel I know, sir." He bowed curtly. "Well done. Might I add the voice is an excellent touch?"

As we entered the lobby, Marianne Engel took my arm. The lights were low, and dark streamers fell from the ceiling. Spider webs clung to the room corners and dozens of black cats patrolled the place. (I wondered where they got so many; did they raid an animal shelter?) Guests were gathering in the main ballroom. There were half a dozen skeletons moving about, jangling their painted white bones on black leotards. Marie Antoinette, with powdered wig and plunging décolleté, was talking to Lady Godiva, whose long blond hair fell over a flesh bodysuit. A Canadian Mountie was having a whiskey with Al Capone. A woman dressed as a giant queen carrot, waving a vegetable scepter, stood beside her boyfriend the rabbit. A drunken Albert Einstein was arguing with a sober Jim Morrison and, in a far corner, two devils were comparing tails. A waiter glided by with a silver tray and Marianne Engel deftly plucked a martini glass, taking a gulp before kissing me on my maskcheek.

We found a table covered with a bloodred tablecloth, on which a candle stuck out of a collection of glass eyeballs. We sat together: on Marianne Engel's outer side was a man dressed as a rubber duck and on my outer side was a sexy policewoman.

It did not take long before I understood that Halloween would now be my favorite holiday. When the policewoman complimented my costume, I made up a story about how "in real life" I was an English teacher at a local high school. After Marianne Engel downed her third martini—interesting, in that she rarely drank alcohol—she dragged me onto the floor. She knew that I was secretly dying to dance with her; I wasn't exercising so diligently with Sayuri so I could spend my life as a wallflower.

The band struck up a waltz, and Marianne Engel drew herself to her full height and gathered me in her stonecutter's arms. She looked intently into my eyes and, for just a moment, I felt as if the sea were rushing up to meet me. I don't know how long we stood motionless before she launched us into the lilt of the music. I needed only to follow; she seemed to have an intuitive sense about the strength of my body. Never once did I worry about pushing my weaker knee beyond its limits as we spun in wonderful circles among the Romeos and the Juliets, near the Esmeraldas and Quasimodi, past the Umas and Travoltas. Marianne Engel's eyes were directly upon mine, at all times, and the other dancers in the room faded into a spin of unimportant background colors.

This went on, I don't know how long, and it would have continued longer if my gaze had not caught, out of the corner of my eye, a most interesting couple. At first, I thought my mind was playing tricks and I told myself that they could not really be there. They disappeared when Marianne Engel spun me in a half circle, and I fully expected they would be gone on the next turn. But they weren't.

I couldn't deny it this time: there was a Japanese woman in religious robes whose shaved head contrasted sharply with the red hair of the Viking with whom she was dancing. She was so graceful and he was so lumbering that it was like watching a sparrow ride on a bull's horns. Her mouth was held resolutely shut as his scabbard clanged awkwardly against her hip and when she readjusted her arm for a better position on his waist, some dirt fell from the folds of her sleeve.

Marianne Engel swung me around again and by the time we swiveled back to our original position, the couple was gone. "Did you see them?"

"See who?" she asked.

Just then, I saw a different couple. This time the woman was wearing Victorian clothing but it was practical, like something that would be worn not for dancing but for farming. It was not an outfit that would normally rate a second look at a costume party—except that it was drenched: water dripped from it onto the floor, pooling beneath her. The man looked jovial despite the wetness of this woman in his arms, not seeming to mind in the least. He wore a leather smock and had big arms and a bigger gut. She was smiling politely as he talked, but kept glancing over his shoulder as if looking for someone else. We were just close enough that I could tell that he was speaking in Italian and that she was answering in English. "Tom? I don't know. . . ."

Marianne Engel tried to spin me again, but I pulled free. My eyes left the couple for only a moment but that was long enough for them to disappear. I looked wildly around the crowd for any trace of them, but there was nothing.

I returned to the area where the Victorian woman's dress had been dripping. But the floor was dry. I searched the floor for the dirt that had fallen from the Japanese woman's sleeve. But the floor was clean. I was on my knees, sweeping my hands over the floor, and the other dancers parted around me as if I were mad. I crawled around, searching for anything but finding nothing. Marianne Engel leaned down to whisper in my ear. "What are you looking for?"

"You saw them. Didn't you?"

"I don't know what you're talking about."

"The ghosts!"

"Oh. Ghosts." She giggled. "You can't fixate on them, you know. It's like trying to catch slippery eels by the tail. Just when you think you've got them, they get away from you."

We stayed for another few hours, but I spent all my time looking for phantoms. I knew that I had seen an impossible thing: it was not a trick of my mind. I *had* seen them. YOU'RE AS CRAZY AS SHE IS. Fuck you, snake. I'm going to douse you with so much morphine it'll make you want to shed your skin early.

When we arrived home, Marianne Engel served tea in an effort to calm me. When that didn't work, she decided to continue telling me our story. Perhaps knowing whether or not we got married, she said, would make me feel better.

XXIII.

Before you said that you might someday ask me to marry you, I never seriously considered that it might happen. I admit I'd had some fleeting fantasies about it, but I'd already broken one set of lifetime vows and I wasn't sure that I wanted another. Part of me was afraid that I'd betray you just as I'd betrayed Mother Christina, so when you didn't mention marriage again I assumed that you had been talking idly, the way men do when they're feeling romantic. In truth, it didn't even bother me, because my life was already so much more than I had ever dreamed it could be. I was doing work for the Beguines, making improvements in every aspect of their bookmaking, and it was not long before the fact that I'd trained in the Engelthal scriptorium leaked out to certain prosperous citizens.

One thing never changes. The rich want to show off what they have and other people don't. In those days, what could have been better than books? One could exhibit not only wealth, but also uncommon intelligence and taste. Still, I was caught completely unawares when a noblewoman approached me with an offer of a commission, if I would produce a manuscript of Rudolf's *Der gute Gerhard* for her husband's birthday. I turned her down, thinking it would insult you if I appeared to feel it necessary to contribute to the household income. But there is another thing that never changes about the rich:

they think the poor always have a price. As it turns out, they're right. The noblewoman named a figure that exceeded what you were making in a year. I started to refuse again, but . . . well, we needed that money, so I asked for some time to think about it.

I didn't know how to broach the subject. We'd both agreed that your apprenticeship was for the best in the long term, but your salary was so small that you weren't even bringing home enough to cover our basic expenses. The couple who rented to us were aware of our situation and, even though they weren't rich themselves, kindly offered to defer a portion of the rent. This was the only thing that allowed us to keep going, but it made you feel that you were failing them as well as me.

For days I walked around our lodgings, starting to speak sentences that I never finished. You kept asking what was wrong, and I kept saying "Nothing." Finally, when you couldn't stand it anymore, you made me tell you what was on my mind. This was really just a trick on my part—buffering my own responsibility by making you force the confession out of me. I said that I wanted to start working with books again and told you about the noblewoman's offer. I made it sound like you'd be doing me a favor if you allowed me to take the commission.

You took it better than I'd expected, agreeing that if it made me happy then I should do it. Your way of making peace with it, although this was never spoken aloud, was that I could take the job as long as we both pretended that it was mostly a hobby. But it was not lost on either of us the way your eyelids peeled open in amazement when I told you how much money I'd been offered.

The noblewoman immediately provided a small advance. Small for her, huge for us. It took a few days before I could work up the courage to spend any of it, knowing that as soon as I did, I'd be well and truly committed. When I passed that first coin to a parchment seller, it was almost a feeling of relief, and I set to work.

I completed that first book and the noblewoman seemed pleased with it. I'm not sure if she recommended me to her friends or if they sought me out through other channels, but it didn't really matter. They found me, somehow.

There was a serious lack of qualified bookmakers in Mainz and because I came from Engelthal, I had a certain cachet. No one believes that his own town can produce true artists, but most people accept it as fact that in other places they fall off the trees like ripe fruit. More important, though, everyone acknowledged that the most desirable manuscripts came from religious scriptoria, so if a noblewoman couldn't get her book produced in an actual monastery, I was the next best thing. She could take special pleasure in proclaiming that she owned a manuscript created by an Engelthal nun—never quite mentioning, of course, that the nun was no longer actually *in* the order.

It wasn't long before I had more offers than time, and that's when the bribery started. When I mentioned in passing how much I liked to cook, a noblewoman immediately said that she would give me a selection of choice meats if I pushed her commission to the top of my pile. I accepted and soon discovered how quickly gossip travels through the upper circles. Straightaway I was offered all manner of delicacies and, before I knew it, oats and barley had replaced millet in our diet. We were given whichever fruits were in season—cherries, plums, apples, pears, and sloes—and luxury items like cloves and ginger, mustard and fennel, sugar and almonds. You have no idea what these things meant. Whenever I was not translating or copying I was trying out new recipes; I felt I was making up for all the food we'd never eaten. The landlady helped me because it was a rare treat for her to use spices as well, and I had to laugh about the fact that I was becoming a culinary sinner. After all, had not Dante placed a Sienese nobleman into Hell for discovering the "costly uses of the clove"?

Before long we were living like God in France. I kept the door open with a pot of stew constantly bubbling and soon we were the

most popular couple in the neighborhood. Even my Beguine friends
dropped in, although they always feigned disdain for the elaborate-
ness of the food. I would remind them that they'd pledged themselves to charity and it wasn't very charitable to hurt my feelings.
They'd pretend they were doing me a favor by eating, and I came to
learn that even Beguines were gossips over a full plate.

The Jewish women also dropped in and I was amazed to learn
how many of them were involved in business affairs, especially if
the husband had died and the wife took over the family trade. To be
quite honest, it inspired me. When I became too busy to accept new
manuscript commissions, it was one of these women who first suggested that I should hire workers and go into business.

By this point, your bruised pride had been soothed by the money.
You told me I could do as I pleased, so I decided to expand my activities. Why not? In the scriptorium, I had learned how several people
worked together to produce a book, so I had experience in dealing
with tradesmen and an understanding of every aspect of production.
The more I thought about it, the more convinced I became that I
could do it.

First, I found a parchmenter I liked. I gained his respect when
I showed him how he could improve the lime solution he used for
soaking his animal skins. After he got over the shock that a woman
could teach him anything, our relationship flourished. We entered
into a contract: he'd produce paper for me each month, at discount
if I ordered in bulk. Each delivery day we'd sit down to a bowl of
stew and discuss how much parchment I'd need the next month. We
became good friends, actually, and he grew to like my cooking almost as much as he did the business I gave him.

Next, I discovered an illustrator whose sensibilities matched
my own. Negotiations with him were quite easy, because he was
young and down on his luck. Each month I'd provide him with
several folio pages to illuminate with miniatures. He also acted as
rubricator, which meant there was one less person for me to man-

age. The arrangement worked out nicely for both of us; for the first time in his life, he could make a living from his artwork. He was so grateful that he kept his prices reasonable for me even when he had made his reputation and other bookmakers were clamoring to employ him.

There were other workers, mostly freelance scribes, but I won't bore you with the details. The best thing about the business was something that I hadn't really considered at all: suddenly, I could get my hands on books. When I was hired to produce editions of Virgil's *Æneid* and Cicero's *Dream of Scipio,* the patron provided borrowed texts from which I could work. Later, I had romances—Wolfram's *Parzival,* Hartmann's *Iwein,* and Gottfried's *Tristan.* In the evenings, I'd bring them to our bed and read to you. These were some of the happiest hours of our lives, because there was nothing I loved more than to have a book in my lap and your head nestled into the crook of my shoulder. I tried to teach you to read but you never had the patience for it. Besides, you said that you liked it better when I read to you anyway.

As time passed I spent more time managing the other scribes and less time copying myself, until I found that I had enough energy left in the evenings to concentrate on my translation of Dante. I had been forced to abandon it when we first came to Mainz because I didn't have writing materials, and when I first got writing materials I didn't have time. Now I had both, and I finally understood how Gertrud had felt about her Bible. I would fret over every single word to ensure that the translation was my masterpiece, and why should I rush? You and I had our entire lives in front of us.

Eventually your apprenticeship came to an end and you received your journeyman's papers. Normally this would have been followed by the *Wanderjahre,* during which you'd travel from city to city and study under different masters, but you had no intention of going anywhere. You'd find work in Mainz, where most of the stoneworkers already knew you and were fully aware why you would choose not to travel. No one would hold it against the man who had been the oldest apprentice the city had ever known.

We had so much good fortune in our lives that we barely spoke about the one thing that wasn't working out. Maybe we felt we had no right to complain, or maybe we just didn't want to jinx ourselves, but we had been trying to conceive and I had not yet become pregnant. In the back of my mind, I was always worried that you might decide I was an unsuitable partner after all, so you have no idea how relieved I was when, as soon as you had your papers in your hand, you announced that you wanted to marry me.

We decided the ceremony would be small but as soon as word leaked out, everyone we knew wanted an invitation. I'd like to think it was because of our popularity, but more likely it was because everyone anticipated an extravagant wedding feast. I supplied the food, the largesse of many bribes, and soon there was a legion of helpers in our kitchen. When our place proved too tiny, preparation spilled over into neighboring houses. Our landlady supervised everything and even the Beguines offered to help, though they were terrible cooks.

My only regret was that I couldn't invite Mother Christina, Father Sunder, and Brother Heinrich. I considered sending word to Engelthal, but I knew that they'd be compelled to decline, and I didn't want to put them in that position. I consoled myself with the thought that they'd have been there, if it were at all possible. And your only regret was that you were unable to invite Brandeis.

You didn't even know whether your friend was still alive. Worst of all, you could never go looking for him without betraying the fact that you had survived your burns and thus escaped the condotta, whose only rule was that no one escaped. You'd never been able to forgive yourself for the fact that Brandeis had enabled your escape, while he had to go back to the condotta. There were still times when you awoke from nightmares about the old battles.

We got lucky on the day of the wedding and the weather was just right. Stoneworkers mingled with bookmakers, Jews with Christians, and everyone, even the Beguines, ate until their stomachs were full. Almost all the guests stumbled home on drunken legs, and then there was only you and me, to spend our first night as man and wife.

When we awoke the next morning, you presented me with a small stone angel that you'd carved. This was my *Morgengabe*—my morning gift, a sign of the legitimacy of our marriage. The legitimacy of us. I'd always thought that it would be unimportant to me, any ritual acknowledgment of the love that I already knew to be true, but I could not stop crying tears of happiness.

You soon found steady work and the physical aspect agreed with you. Your health was consistently good and you loved working with stone. I was producing books, managing my staff, and continuing my work on *Inferno*. We kept talking about moving into that larger house but somehow never quite got around to it. We liked where we were, we liked our friends, and maybe something about being in the Jewish area of town suited us because we were outsiders, too. Maybe a bigger house was just a dream that we created when we needed one to keep us going. There was only one thing that could have made us happier—and then, we got that as well.

After years without success, I finally became pregnant. The single happiest moment I have ever lived is when I first told you and saw the look on your face. There was not a second of fear or doubt, there was only wonderful anticipation. You rushed out to tell all your stoneworking friends and when you returned you held me tightly, talking about the various advantages of a girl over a boy, or a boy over a girl.

It was shortly afterwards that we were in the market one day, buying vegetables, when a pack of young men started arguing with a vendor over some perceived slight. They were clad in dirty clothes and had the cocksure swagger that only youth can possess. Off to one side, an older man was watching the proceedings with the look of someone who'd seen this a hundred times, had grown tired of it, but knew nothing could be done except let the stupid scene play itself out.

I thought that I'd seen him before, but I couldn't put a name to the face. I took you by the arm and pointed him out, asking if you recognized him. You dropped the bag of vegetables, and the blood drained from your face. When you finally spoke, you could barely get his name out.

XXIV.

On the first of November, despite waking with a hangover from the Halloween party, Marianne Engel headed immediately for the basement. Over the next two days, her last remaining half-finished statue—the terrified lion/monkey—was given legs on which it could stand. When it was completed, she lay down upon a new slab and slept for a dozen hours before throwing herself headlong into a new grotesque. All the while, I was alone upstairs with my memories of the dancing ghosts that I couldn't have seen.

Her new goblin (a human face on the misshapen body of a bird) took seventy-four hours to complete, before she came upstairs to wash the grime off her body and gorge herself on whatever she could find in the fridge. I expected that she would, as usual, retreat to her bedroom to sleep off her fatigue, but no, she went right back downstairs to stretch herself over another block. After absorbing its stony dreams, she spent another seventy-something hours in the thrall of her fresh suitor. When she was finished, a warty toad with the screaming beak of an eagle had been uncovered.

She returned to her bed for a proper sleep, but after ten hours Marianne Engel was back in the kitchen drinking a pot of coffee and eating a pound of bacon. (When not actively carving, she was allowed meat.) As soon as her plate was clean, she took a few steps towards the basement stairs. "Another one is calling." When I asked how she would be able to sleep on the stone after so much coffee, she answered that it wouldn't be necessary. "This one was already talking to me while I was working on the toad."

Although it was only the second week of November, Marianne Engel was already starting the month's third new grotesque. The increase in production was unsettling enough, but there was also a change in intensity: she was throwing herself into a frenzy that outdid even the most torrid of the sessions I'd already witnessed. Sweat ran down her body, leaving trails in the stone dust, and she had to open up the massive oak doors to let in the cool autumn air. She never extinguished the hundred red candles that surrounded her, and their crowns of fire responded to the wind like wheat waltzing in the field. With her tools flying around, I could not help but think of a farmer wielding his harvest scythe in a desperate effort to out-race the coming winter.

* * *

When this third statue was finished, Marianne Engel immediately embarked on the next.

The hammering had become so insistent that the air of the house seemed empty whenever she put down her tools. Sometimes it—the noise, not the rare silences—even drove me out of the house. I never went far, usually hiding behind the corner of the fortress to watch the parishioners visit St. Romanus. Father Shanahan would stand on the front steps, glad-handing them on their way out, imploring them to come back the following week. They all promised that they would, and most even did.

Shanahan seemed a sincere enough fellow, as far as priests go, although I must admit that I'm hardly an impartial observer. I've always felt a strange kind of fascination/revulsion towards men of the cloth: because I despise the institutions for which they stand, I want to despise them as people as well. But all too often I find that I cannot hate the man, only the robe.

I imagine the reader's natural impulse is to assume my atheism has been cultivated from rough experience: the childhood loss of relatives, a career in pornography, my drug addiction, an accident in which I was burned to a crisp. The assumption would be incorrect.

There is no logical reason to believe in God. There are emotional reasons, certainly, but I cannot have faith that nothing is something simply because it would be reassuring. I can no more believe in God than I can believe an invisible monkey lives in my ass; however, I would believe in both if they could be scientifically proven. This is the crux of the problem for atheists: it is impossible to prove the nonexistence of a thing, and yet theists tend to put the onus on us to prove just that. "An absence of proof is not proof of absence," they say smugly. Well, true enough. But all it would take is one giant flaming crucifix in the sky, NO MONKEY IN YOUR ASS? seen by everyone in the world at the same time, WHAT ABOUT A SNAKE IN YOUR SPINE? to convince me that God does exist.

• • •

Marianne Engel emerged to ask me to pick up some instant coffee. I thought this a strange request, given that the basement had a coffee-maker that used regular grounds, but since it was her money that kept the household running, I could hardly refuse.

As soon as I returned, she yanked the jar out of my hands, grabbed a spoon, and headed back down into her workshop. I thought about it for a few moments, telling myself that she couldn't possibly . . . and then peered down from the top step to see that indeed she was.

Between drags on her cigarette she was thrusting the instant coffee into her mouth, chomping at the crystals like a baseball player working over a wad of chewing tobacco, and washing it all down with the brewed coffee in her oversized mug.

* * *

The doorbell rang.

If you are like most people, a doorbell rings and you answer it; but for me, it's more complicated. For me, it is a test of will. What if the visitor is a Girl Scout selling cookies? What if she takes one look at me, wets her pants, and faints? How could I explain an unconscious, urine-soaked Girl Scout on my front porch? For someone who looks the way I do, that's pretty much an invitation for the good townspeople to light their torches and chase you to the old windmill.

I decided to take my chances and face the challenge, even if it was a Girl Scout. When I opened the door, I saw a middle-aged man and woman, probably husband and wife, in good clothing. The woman pulled back as if she were Nosferatu and I the sun. (Occasionally, I find it enjoyable to cast someone else in the role of monster.) The man instinctively stepped in front of his vampiric wife and shielded her with his arm. Her lips drew up over her teeth.

"Yes?"

"I, ah—we," the heroic man stuttered, not quite sure of what to make of me, while the woman shrank back farther and smaller. The man, steeling his nerves, blurted, "We wanted to visit the church! That's all!" Just in case I was as stupid as I was burned, he hitched his thumb in the direction of St. Romanus. "We saw that it's—ah, ah—closed, and then we saw this place with, you know, all the gargoyles and stuff, like that, like a church has, and—so, you know, we naturally thought that maybe this place is like, ah, ah, ah, affiliated with the church. Or something." He paused. "Is it?"

"No."

* * *

Marianne Engel was doing something new with her stonework: adorning each emerging statue with a number. The first was **27**, the next was **26**, the third was **25**; she was currently working on number **24**.

When I asked her about it, she said, "My Three Masters recently told me that I had only twenty-seven hearts remaining. This is the countdown."

• • •

I waited until I saw the participants in Father Shanahan's Thursday night Bible study class start to shuffle out. It was time to head over to St. Romanus and complain about the parishioners who mistook the fortress for some sort of Christian outreach program.

I walked up the church's front steps, looked left and right, and went through the front door. My steps echoed, but Shanahan—standing in the middle of the pews, looking up at the windows—didn't seem to notice. He was in deep contemplation of a stained-glass representation of Christ on the crucifix. It was strange to see someone observing such a thing at night, because there was no light to stream in and make Jesus look all shiny and superior.

He was unaware of my presence until I spoke, offering him the proverbial penny for his thoughts. My wretched voice startled him, as did my plasticked face when he turned, but he regained his composure promptly. With a quick laugh he suggested that, for once, he might even be able to offer full value on that penny.

"Strange how one can look at this every day"—he said, indicating the Christ—"and still find something new. The four arms of the cross represent the four elements of the Earth, of course, but see how Christ is pinned to it, with His arms outstretched and His feet together? It forms a triangle, and three is the number of God. The Holy Trinity. Three days of the resurrection. Heaven, Hell, and Purgatory. You get the idea. So four meets three, Earth meets Heaven. Which is perfect, of course, for is not Jesus the Son of both God and Man?"

He adjusted his glasses, and chuckled a bit. "You caught me in a bit of a fancy, I'm afraid. Can I help you?"

"I live next door."

"Yes, I've seen you."

"I'm an atheist."

"Well, God believes in you," he said. "May I offer you a cup of tea?"

He indicated his room tucked away behind the pulpit and, for some reason, I decided to follow him. Two chairs sat in front of his desk, obviously for couples who thought that a bit of the good word might help their troubled marriages. On his desk, beside a Bible, was a picture of him with his arm slung across the shoulder of another man. Next to them was a woman, quite pretty, and what appeared to be her teenaged son. The woman's head was tilted towards her husband but her gaze was steadfastly focused upon Father Shanahan, who looked somewhat uncomfortable in his white collar. When I asked whether these were his brother and his sister-in-law, Shanahan seemed surprised that I could place them so quickly. "Do we look that much alike, my brother and I?"

"His wife is an attractive woman," I said.

Father Shanahan cleared his throat as he poured some water into his electric kettle. "Yes. But then again, so's Marianne."

"You've met her."

"She knows her Bible, even better than I do, but she always de-clines my invitations to attend Mass. Says the problem with most Christians is that they show up at church once a week to pray that God's will be done—and when it is, they complain." He placed two cups on the desk, as well as a small pitcher of milk. "Can't say that I entirely disagree with her."

He sat down in front of me and adjusted his glasses once again, even though they were already sitting correctly. I expected he would make some small talk, so it was surprising when he said, "Is it pos-sible to take off your mask during our conversation?"

The way he asked made it clear that he was not intimidated by the mask, but simply curious about my appearance. I explained that my rehabilitation required it to remain on at all times. He nodded understandingly, but I could see just a hint of disappointment across his features. I suggested that I could take it off for a moment, if he really wanted to see what was beneath. He nodded that he would like that, yes.

When I removed the mask, he leaned forward to take a closer look. He scratched behind his ears and moved side to side so that he could inspect me from all angles. When he was finished, I asked, "Do I look like you hoped?"

"I had no expectations. I considered studying medicine before I entered the seminary. I still have subscriptions to some journals."

The moment of his career decision came, he explained while pouring the tea, when he learned that emergency room doctors were taught to consider incoming heart attack victims as already dead. It's a method to cope: if the patient lives the doctor can believe that he has brought someone back but if the patient "remains" dead, the doctor knows that it wasn't anything he did wrong.

"But only God has the power over life and death," Father Shanahan said. "While a doctor can extend a man's physical life, a priest might help him achieve life everlasting."

"Do you really believe that?"

"It's a job requirement."

"Let me ask you a question. Is it possible to believe in souls without believing in God?"

"For some, perhaps." Shanahan took a sip from his cup. "But not for me."

◆ ◆ ◆

Number **24** was finished. Number **23** was finished. Number **22** was finished. It was the last week of November, and Marianne Engel finally returned upstairs. She seemed to have reached the limits of how long a body could go without a proper meal or the comfort of a real bed.

I'm not much of a cook, but I forced a meal on her and made

damn sure that it was thick with calories. Even though she was obviously done in, all the caffeine and nicotine left her in a state of
manic exhaustion. She bounced on her seat, her eyes unfocused, and
dropped her utensils often. When the meal was finished, she tried to
stand but found herself physically unable. "Can you help?"

I put my stair-climbing practice to good use and did my best to
steady her from behind, half pushing her up the steps. When we
reached the washroom, I opened the faucets and she sat down heavily in the tub. There was no point in putting the plug into the drain
until we rinsed away the top layer of filth, so I helped her scoop water over her body. When she was finally clean enough to be properly
bathed, we filled the tub.

I sat beside the tub, working her skin. Large black bags had taken
residence under her eyes. I washed the stone chips from the thick
tangle of her hair, which now hung like vines that someone had forgotten to water. The worst change was simply the weight she had
lost: certainly ten pounds, maybe twenty. It did not look good on her
because it had come off too fast, in exactly the worst way. I vowed
that I would make her start eating better, more. Daily.

The cleaning reinvigorated her enough that she could walk unaided to her bedroom. As soon as she was in the sheets I turned to
leave, thinking she would drop immediately into sleep. She surprised
me when she called me back.

"Mainz. The marketplace. Don't you want to know who?"

XXV.

U ntil that moment, we weren't even sure that he was still alive. You spoke his name as if trying to convince yourself that you were really seeing him again, after so many years.

"Brandeis."

He had some new scars and a lot more gray in his hair, and he favored one leg that hadn't been stiff when I first met him at Engelthal. But mostly he just looked weary. The young mercenaries continued to harass the vendor and Brandeis' face betrayed a look that combined disgust with a complete lack of surprise.

You pulled me into the shadows behind a stall. Most of the soldiers were new and wouldn't know you, but you could never be entirely safe, not with these men. You had concluded years before that the only reason your disappearance had never been investigated was that everyone, Brandeis included, believed your burns had killed you.

That you desperately wanted to speak with him goes without saying. You could not—you *would* not—let this opportunity pass, but the problem lay in how to approach Brandeis without being seen. When the young men started to push the shopkeep, you thought you might be able to sneak into the middle of the scrum. I was completely against the idea, although I knew that wouldn't stop you. But just as you took a step forward, a new man entered the scene, and its entire nature changed. Immediately the young soldiers backed away from the vendor, as if they were too scared to do anything more without permission.

The first thing I noticed about this man was the cruel intelligence of his eyes. They seemed to shine with a lust for violence, as if he thought that chaos existed only so that he might take advantage of it.

"Who is that?" I asked.

You answered with an icy voice. "Kuonrat the Ambitious."

The way the others deferred to him made clear that Kuonrat was now the leader of the troop. With only a few words and the tip of his sword at the shopkeep's neck, a solution was brokered. The mercenaries took what they pleased, and the vendor was allowed to keep his life.

Kuonrat was the very last person before whom you could dare to reveal yourself, but I was bound by no such constraint. Before you could stop me, I stepped out of the shadows and headed towards the group. I knew that you couldn't follow: showing yourself would have put me in greater danger than letting me proceed. I pulled my neckline open and headed directly for Brandeis.

It was a calculated risk. Kuonrat had never seen me and Brandeis was unlikely to recognize me, so many years later and not wearing my nun's habit. I did my best imitation of a prostitute, making it perfectly clear that I was offering myself to Brandeis. It was really quite an act considering that, even though I wasn't showing yet, I was carrying your child inside me. A few of the other soldiers hooted as I leaned forward to whisper into Brandeis' ear—naming a price, they thought. I whispered two things: your name, and that I was the nun who'd cared for you at Engelthal.

Brandeis pulled back and his eyes narrowed upon my face as he sorted through his memories from the monastery. After he regained his composure, he informed the others that he would meet them later, and implied that an afternoon of fornication lay ahead. Even

Kuonrat nodded his approval and said, "Perhaps when you're finished with him, you can come back for the rest of us."

The idea turned my stomach but I laughed a "maybe" as I dragged Brandeis away. It would have been too risky for you to reunite with him in public so I took him back to our home, where I knew you'd be waiting. Brandeis could hardly believe his eyes that you were still alive. "I thought—I was so sure—I went back to Engelthal once, but they told me nothing. . . ."

I served our best ale and set about making a meal. I wanted to make a good impression, I wanted Brandeis to see how well I looked after you. You told him everything that had happened over the years, and he was amazed that you'd made such a life for yourself.

When it was his turn to speak, Brandeis told about how things had changed in the condotta. How they had become worse. Herwald had been mortally injured in battle and it was Kuonrat who brought down the final sword on the old man's neck. This was no act of mercy; Kuonrat was staking his claim. When he challenged anyone who would dare oppose him for leadership, no one stepped forward.

Kuonrat took to admitting only the most bloodthirsty recruits. Their fighting instincts were sound, but the new soldiers were stupid and dishonorable. It was true that they killed more, but also they *were* killed more. They attacked with passion, not with intelligence, and Kuonrat goaded them like a master with a pack of wild dogs. Should they die, the countryside was ripe with an endless supply of boys looking to prove their manhood. It was a waste of Kuonrat's time to worry about protecting a renewable resource. And besides, he knew from personal experience that those who remained in the troop for years sometimes developed a greed for power.

Despite his methods, there could be no arguing with Kuonrat's results. The condotta had become known for its peculiar ruthlessness and its ability to defeat even much larger forces by sheer brutality. Success emboldened him and he'd started to question the entire practice of hiring out the troop. Why, he asked himself, should the nobility be in possession of the land if his condotta was the means by which the land was defended? Money was no longer enough. Kuonrat wanted more power. He was preparing to start taking territories for himself.

The years under Kuonrat had strengthened Brandeis' desire to leave the condotta, but escaping had become even less conceivable. The rule remained that once you were in the troop, you were in for life, but now there was something more. Kuonrat had never forgotten how Brandeis had stood up to him when you were injured on the battlefield; he was always looking for an excuse to exact retribution. If Brandeis were ever to bolt, Kuonrat would send the most talented trackers after him, men whose determination was matched only by their viciousness.

For all his despicable traits, Kuonrat was not stupid. He knew that he could not attack Brandeis without provocation, as the troop still included a number of old soldiers who respected Brandeis both as an archer and a man. And so, for the most part, Brandeis was left alone. But the unspoken threat was always there.

It was so strange to see you in the company of an old friend, one with whom you'd faced death on the battlefield many times. Brandeis had shared a part of your life that I could never understand. There was a strange closeness in the way you both tried to play at toughness but could not quite suppress the tenderness in your voices. I could tell that you missed the old days—not the battles but the camaraderie. It's funny, the things one remembers; from that night, a single moment stands out in my memory. During the meal, Brandeis raised his hand in an almost imperceptible gesture, but you knew to pass him the water. It was an action that you must have repeated over a thousand campfire meals and it had not been forgotten in the years that you had been apart. Neither of you even seemed to notice.

At the end of the evening, a heavy silence fell. The two of you just stared at each other, maybe a full minute, until Brandeis said it aloud. "I cannot continue to live as I am living."

"I will help in any way I can," you said.

But no escape could occur that night. If Brandeis disappeared, the mercenaries would know to track down the "prostitute" with whom he'd last been seen. It was agreed that he would return to the condotta and play it out as if he'd had his pleasures with me. The troop would spend a few more days in the city and then head off for its next assignment. After a month had passed and the days in Mainz were a distant memory, only then would he make his escape.

If all went well, no one would be the wiser. Brandeis had no family in Mainz, no ties to the city whatsoever. Who would even remember his afternoon of sex a month previous? The plan was set.

At our door, the two of you stood in manly poses with your chests thrown out. He slapped your shoulder and you punched his arm. I hugged him and promised to pray for his safety. Brandeis said this was a good idea, and congratulated me once more on my pregnancy. When he took my hands in his, I could feel the scar tissue on his palms, and only then did I remember that he'd been burned while pulling the flaming arrow from your chest. As he headed out into the night, I was intensely aware of exactly how much we owed him.

The next month crawled by. We talked about Brandeis but never more than a few words at a time, almost as we had previously avoided speaking about our desire for a child, as if we were afraid to curse it. Five weeks. "Do you think . . . ?" I asked. "He'll get here when he gets here," you answered.

Six weeks, no Brandeis. I couldn't help but worry, and I was vomiting in the mornings because of my pregnancy. "He'll get here when he gets here," you kept saying. I went through wild swings of worrying about his safety—and ours, as well, after he arrived. You kept assuring me that everything would be fine, and I tried hard to believe you.

Seven weeks. I was at home working on a manuscript, sitting near the window, when a heavily cloaked figure came shuffling sideways through the street. I recognized the stiffness of the leg and immediately knew it was Brandeis even though his face was hidden. His robe was covered in the snow that'd been falling since early morning, and it was a good day to be entirely bundled up. No one would think twice about a man simply trying to remain warm. I let him in when no one was passing on the street.

He gulped down hot soup and explained how he'd been traveling for eight days, backtracking and circling, avoiding cities. Rather than buy food, he'd killed small animals so that there'd be no merchants to remember him. He was certain that he hadn't been followed. Still, we didn't send word to your worksite but let you come home at the regular time. It was important to make everything look as normal as possible.

The first few days would be the most dangerous. Kuonrat would have dispatched a group of his best trackers as soon as Brandeis was found to be missing. The two of you always kept an eye out the window, a crossbow never out of reach. Brandeis had brought two with him, his own and another that he'd stolen for you.

You took turns not sleeping, and Brandeis didn't dare even to unpack his bag. You packed one for yourself and instructed me to do the same. All this was very upsetting, of course, more than I could have imagined. Should something go wrong—not that it would, of course—I was responsible not only for myself but for our unborn child. I said that I didn't understand how it was possible that Brandeis might have been successfully tracked in so large a country. When I voiced this opinion, the two of you looked at each other and said nothing. Which said everything.

But nothing happened. Weeks passed, and no one came looking. You both started sleeping through the nights, though only after you strung a line of bells across the top of the door. Eventually you decided that it might be safe for Brandeis to venture outside the house. With his hood still pulled over his head, of course.

No lurking figures pounced out of the shadows, so after another week Brandeis began to accompany you to construction sites. Your recommendation was enough to find him some manual labor. He worked hard and took his lunches with you but otherwise kept to himself. Nobody asked too many questions; to your colleagues he was just another unskilled worker. Before long, we decided that he should get a room of his own because I was waking in the night with leg cramps. A little privacy would be good for everyone.

We had so many friends that finding lodgings was easy, just a few streets outside the Jewish area. I insisted on paying the deposit with money from my business and, this done, we finally decided to allow ourselves a proper celebration. Not that the two of you were fully convinced that his escape *was* a success, but you were willing to acknowledge that it *seemed* to be a success. It was a great feast, and you were so happy because you finally felt as though you'd repaid your debt to him.

I was healthy and beginning to outgrow my clothes, the pregnancy seemingly well on schedule. There was even a point during the meal that the baby kicked and you insisted that Brandeis place his hand on my belly. He was hesitant but when I assured him that it would please me if he did, he tentatively pressed his palm there. When he felt the movement, he jerked back his hand and looked at me in wide-eyed amazement.

"This is because of you," you said to Brandeis. "This life is because you saved mine."

With that, we lifted our cups to the fact that we had all escaped our previous lives into better ones.

But one should never divide the bear skin before the bear is killed. The very next day, while Brandeis was gathering the last of his possessions from our place, one of the Beguines came running to our door. I knew this couldn't be a good sign, as I'd never seen one run before. She placed her hands on her knees and panted for a few moments before she was able to gasp out that a small group of men—"savages, by the looks of them"—had been asking around the marketplace for a man matching Brandeis' description.

Apparently, Mainz was not as big as I'd thought. Despite all the care we'd put into keeping our visitor hidden, even the Beguines knew that he had been staying with us. To their credit, they recognized that giving out this information to strangers was inadvisable, but it was only a matter of time before someone spoke without considering the consequences. Brandeis asked a few questions about the "savages," and the Beguine's answers took away all doubt. These men were definitely trackers dispatched from the condotta. To this day, I have no idea how they managed to find him, but how doesn't really matter. The only thing that mattered was that Mainz was no longer safe.

Brandeis offered to flee alone, leaving a trail so obvious the trackers couldn't help but be drawn away from us. "They're only looking for me. You have a good life here, so don't—"

You wouldn't even allow him to finish his sentence. Your honor wouldn't have it. You said that the trackers would find our place no matter what we did, and that when—not if, but when—they did, there was a good chance one of them would recognize you. What a coup that would be for them, dispatched to find one deserter but able to bring back two. It would earn great favor with Kuonrat, and the message would be clear: even a soldier who'd managed to escape for years and was presumed dead would eventually be hunted down.

You and Brandeis both argued that I should not come—because I was too far along in my pregnancy, because I would slow you down, because travel would endanger the child. I countered that the greatest danger of all was for me to remain in Mainz, where the trackers would find me and do whatever was necessary to extract information. Ultimately, I said, it didn't matter what arguments were made. I would not be left behind, and if you wouldn't take me, I'd follow anyway. Yes, I was pregnant, but I was still able to travel and I owed as much of my good fortune to Brandeis as you did. Finally, if you and I lost each other, where could we meet again? Our life in Mainz had been found out and we could not return. I argued that it was in fact *because* I was pregnant that I had to stay with you, rather than chance a permanent separation.

I took away all your options and I had the advantage that there was no time for arguments. So we gathered a few things, only the most valuable, and prepared to leave as soon as possible.

I packed the *Inferno* and Paolo's prayer book, and when you weren't looking I slipped the *Morgengabe* angel into my bag. You wouldn't have allowed such dead weight, but it was too dear to me to leave behind. I also packed my nun's habit, as I'd already learned that it could make a useful disguise. We took all the money we'd put away for the house that we'd never actually bought, and you and Brandeis went to buy three horses. I sold off my spices and books to whoever would buy them, although on such short notice I got almost nothing. Within a few hours of the Beguine's arrival, we were heading out of Mainz. I had my bag, while the two of you took only your crossbows and the clothing on your backs. The life we'd spent years building was gone, just like that.

I wasn't a skilled rider at the best of times and my pregnancy didn't help. Even as we rode out of town, you didn't stop trying to persuade me to head in a different direction. Three sets of horse tracks going in the same direction were easier to follow than two sets going in opposite directions, you argued. I refused to hear it and countered that the best thing we could do was put as much distance behind us as possible.

We rode until the horses were too exhausted to continue. My back ached, pain coursed my spine with every clop of the hooves, and there was agony in my lower stomach. But I refused to complain, because I was with you.

We found a small inn and I was sent to deal with the innkeep, because the less the two of you were seen, the better. Before we went to sleep that first night, I asked where we were headed. Brandeis answered, "It's better not to have a destination. If we know where we're going, the trackers will know too." I didn't understand how this could be true, but I was too tired to argue.

Over the next days, we would ride for as long as I could manage and then take a room, none of us venturing out except when I went in search of food. It did not take long before the traveling started exacting a toll on me. My breasts were aching and my leg cramps were growing worse, and the muscles at my ribs felt stretched and torn. I knew I was slowing us down, it was apparent to all of us, and this gave fuel to our constant arguments. You pointed out that my frequent stops to urinate not only slowed us, but made the trail easier to follow. You even threatened to leave me behind but, of course, you couldn't bring yourself to do it.

In towns we cut through back alleys and in the wilderness we forced the horses through icy streams and over rocky outcrops. They hated it, but no more than I did. The horses could not keep up the pace we needed, too much running and not enough rest. When they wore out, we traded them for new ones. The trackers would be forced to do the same or be left behind.

Despite constantly looking over my shoulder, I never saw the trackers. I wanted to believe we'd lost them. Honestly, I couldn't see how they could possibly remain on our trail, with all the tricks that we were employing while riding. But then again, they'd found Brandeis in Mainz. I had no real idea of their capabilities but the two of you had lived with these sorts of men, so I had to trust your fear. You kept pushing us forward at a relentless pace.

Each day increased my worry about what the riding might be doing to our child—could it cause an unnatural birth? I had to keep convincing myself, hour after hour, that escaping the trackers was worth any risk. In the rare moments when I was not worrying about the baby, I strengthened my resolve by remembering how, when we first left Engelthal, you bought us a spot on a pig wagon. I tried to convince myself that our current situation was just one more test in our lives to be overcome, and at least there wasn't the smell of pigs.

But after about a week, I simply could not go farther. You and Brandeis were still holding up, but I pleaded for rest. We'd traveled so many miles that surely we would be safe for a day. You agreed. Not because it was safe, but because it was time to make a plan. I didn't care why. I would take the break for whatever reason.

We'd been riding in circles to confuse our followers and, as an unintentional result, we had not traveled that far from where we'd started. We found ourselves close to Nürnberg, which was an advantage because even if the trackers had managed to stay behind us, the city itself was large enough to hide us for a few extra hours.

We found an inn and the two of you sat around a table discussing the next move. Maybe we'd go north, to Hamburg, or maybe it would be safer to go east, into Bohemia or Carinthia. There was even talk about heading to Italy. You knew a few rudimentary phrases from the Italian archers, and I could act as translator for the rest. After a year or two, we could return to Germany. It was unlikely that our pursuers would guess this destination and even if they did, Kuonrat would have to devote significant long-term resources to continue the hunt in another country.

Our stay in Nürnberg was supposed to last only a day, but my body didn't cooperate. For three days, I was in too much pain to continue. My heart raced constantly and I was short of breath. I craved food, but could not keep it down. I longed for sleep, but my mind outraced the closing of my eyes. My pregnancy was rebelling and finally, grudgingly, I accepted that you were correct: I was too weak to continue. It was decided that I'd be placed in the care of the Church. You'd hand me over with a fistful of coins, enough to pay for my care through the pregnancy, and when you were confident that you'd escaped, you'd come back for me. The plan was set; you'd allow me only one more night of sleep before it was put into action. I asked where you would go after leaving me, but you would not tell me even this. "It's better not to have a destination. . . ." I cried myself to sleep that night, with you stroking my hair and assuring me that everything would be all right.

Fate, however, had a different view. In the middle of the night there came a series of heavy thuds against our door, shaking the pile of furniture that you'd pushed up against it, and it was instantly clear that we'd been discovered. The only way out was through the window, even though we were on the second story, some fifteen feet up.

I struggled to lift myself out of bed but was unable, and you had to pull me out by the arms. While I recovered my breath, Brandeis gathered the bags; you craned your neck around the window frame to check whether anyone was outside, and threw up your hand in warning to stay back. "Crossbow," you commanded.

Brandeis grabbed a crossbow and inserted an arrow into the channel. As soon as the string was set, he put the weapon into your hands and you pushed the front end through the window. There was the whiz of the arrow through the air and a thud as it hit something solid. You gave another hand signal indicating the way was now clear and went out the window first. It wasn't that you were lacking manners, but someone had to catch me on the way down. Behind us, I heard the door splintering under an ax.

Despite the immediate threat of the attack, I froze at the window. The drop was too much, too risky for the baby. Brandeis stood between me and the door, yelling at me to jump. But I remained immobilized, looking down at your open arms, until I heard Brandeis' voice behind me—"Marianne, I'm sorry"—as he pushed me through the open window.

I went out with my arms wrapped around my belly and you took the full force of my fall by rolling backwards into the snow as you caught me. I heard shouting from above; a few moments later, Brandeis came tumbling out the window.

There was something strange about the way he fell, but most of my attention was focused on the dead tracker across the street. His face was pushed into a puddle of dirty snow, his neck twisted at an awkward angle because of the arrow sticking through it. Then I realized that the snow was not dirty, but red from the little geysers of blood still pulsing from his neck.

You jerked me in the direction of the horses and the next thing I knew, we were hurtling through the streets of Nürnberg. You and Brandeis were on either side of me, directing my horse and determining my path. Between my fatigue and the shock of the attack, I was pretty much useless.

I watched my horse snort out its steamy breath as it ran, all the while thinking about the man in the street who had no more breath. It was the way that he died that I found so unnerving, the way you'd killed him without a thought, without uncertainty. I'd watched your face as you sent that arrow flying, and it didn't even cross my mind that the target might be a person. Your mouth had been clenched, your eyes had narrowed, and your finger did not hesitate. You took a quick breath before pulling the trigger but it was not to steady your soul, only your hands. It had all happened in—what? A second? Less? Could this really be all the time it took to kill a man?

We were just outside the city limits when I saw Brandeis' steed rear. The horse didn't exactly throw him off; rather, Brandeis just slumped to the side. The animal gave out a confused whinny and twisted around, as if it had lost its bearings without its rider. There was blood everywhere, in the snow, on the horse's flank, all down Brandeis' leg. The cloth of his pants was ripped open and there was a huge gash in the upper part of his thigh where the skin was peeled back like a demon's smile, spitting mouthfuls of blood. His face was pale, his lips quivering. "One of them threw an ax. It caught me on the way out of the window. I'm sorry."

I pressed my hand to his forehead and it was so cold, so clammy. I didn't know how he'd managed to stay on the horse as long as he had. You washed out the wound with a handful of snow, and a pink puddle collected around the steaming wound. You asked for fabric, so I pulled out the first thing I could find in my saddlebag. My nun's habit. I should have found something different but I was in shock, I think, and it was on top. You shredded it into a makeshift binding and tied it above the wound.

You sent Brandeis' horse in the opposite direction with a slap, hoping it might act as a decoy, and scooped Brandeis out of the snow. You reminded me that the trackers were still behind us, but now they were bound to be angry, and you pulled Brandeis up onto your horse and steadied him against your back. You looped his arms around you and tied his hands together in front of your waist.

"We're not far from Engelthal. Even mercenaries will respect a house of God."

My stomach knotted because, of all the places in the entire world, Engelthal was the very last I wanted to visit. But I understood how dire the situation was and I swallowed any protest I might have had. Brandeis needed immediate attention, so we fled in the direction of the monastery.

He hung off your back like an overstuffed scarecrow being delivered to the field. Your horse struggled under the strain and we couldn't travel quickly, but you pushed as hard as you could. We abandoned back paths and took the most direct route, because the time for stealth was past. We couldn't stop to check Brandeis' wounds and I had to fight my own racing heart. As we rode, I asked the question of you that I could no longer contain. "How could you shoot that man? Through his throat?"

"I was aiming for his chest." It was so detached, the way you said it, and it was clear by your tone that the discussion was ended.

When I started to recognize the landscape, I pointed out the best paths. At the gates of Engelthal, I dismounted awkwardly and pounded on the door. It made more sense for me to make our plea and, besides, it would have been too time-consuming to unstrap Brandeis from your body.

Sister Constantia was the one to open the gate, and a look of confusion immediately crossed her face. "Sister Marianne?"

I explained our situation and I could see that she kept looking over to you, taking in the fact that you were the burned soldier she'd helped to tend years before. When Sister Constantia finally found her voice again, she said, "Normally . . . normally, I would let you in . . . but this is not normal." Her eyes went down, almost with embarrassment, to my swollen stomach.

I couldn't understand the hesitation. No matter what had been gossiped about my disappearance, we needed protection or Brandeis would die. I gestured towards him for emphasis. I saw Sister Constantia's face register the fact that the bloody rags wrapped around his legs were the shredded remains of my nun's habit.

"If you cannot invite us in," I pleaded, "get Mother Christina. She will not allow this man to die."

"The prioress is in Nürnberg and will not be back soon. Sister Agletrudis is acting in her absence. I will get her." Before heading into the monastery, Sister Constantia added just one more thing. "But she has never forgiven your desecration of the scriptorium."

I had no idea what Sister Constantia meant, but I could be certain that I'd find out when Agletrudis arrived.

XXVI.

November ended with the completion of statue **21,** bringing the month's total to seven.

Statues **20** and **19** were completed in the first week of December. Statue **18** arrived in the second week. Marianne Engel's preparation periods on the stone were becoming longer, but her bed had remained unvisited since the night she told me about Brandeis. Our lives now consisted of only three actions. She carved and forgot, and I watched.

I watched her ignore Bougatsa; she forgot to help me bathe. I watched her push aside every plate of food I prepared; she forgot to put a gift into my St. Nick's shoes on the windowsill. I watched her smoke a hundred cigarettes a day; she forgot to change whatever album was on the stereo. I watched her eat jars of instant coffee; she forgot to clean the blood from her fingers. I watched the flesh of her body waste away, I watched her cheeks becoming shrunken, I watched her eyes becoming ever darker; she forgot how to string words into a coherent sentence.

YOU'RE *I am not* USELESS.

I pleaded with her to take a break, but she insisted that she was running out of time. It was now not only the statues but also her Three Masters who were urging her to work faster.

I called Gregor and Sayuri because I didn't know what else to do. They tried to talk some sense into her, but they might as well have been talking to the walls. I'm not even sure that Marianne Engel registered that they were in the room with her. When I tried to enlist Jack's help, she turned the conversation to how the situation was affecting her. "I've got no more room at the gallery and she keeps sending over all these statues. It's not like they're big Christmas sellers, you know." I slammed down the phone and headed directly to my morphine kit for comfort.

I had to hire workers to move the extra statues out of the base-ment and into the backyard. I was against this, hoping the crammed workshop would force Marianne Engel to stop, but she insisted. When I protested she started screaming at me in a language I didn't recognize, and I crumbled. It was obvious that something terrible was going to happen.

"You can't keep working like this."

"Monsters are divine portents."

"You're covered in blood. Let me give you a bath."

"The blood of life."

"Why don't you eat something?" I coaxed. "You're wasting away."

"I'm becoming pure nothingness. It's glorious."

"If you get sick, you won't be able to help the grotesques."

"If I get sick, I will rejoice because God has remembered me."

She refused to come upstairs, to bathe, or to sleep, so when she was stretched out over the stone in preparation, I would bring down a bucket with warm water and soap. If she would not go to the clean-ing, I would bring the cleaning to her.

The sponge over her ribs was like a car over speed bumps. Gray liquid dripped off her body, falling to the workshop floor to create patterns in the dust. Bougatsa yelped in the corner. When I turned her onto her side so that I could clean her back, her angel wing tat-toos seemed to sag with the loose skin.

• • •

Jack was doing nothing to help me, but she could hardly have been unaware of the frantic carving, given her overflowing gallery. The longer Jack did not offer the help for which I refused to ask, the more my resentment grew. When I could no longer contain it, I stormed her shop and demanded, without so much as a hello, that she do something.

"What do you expect *me* to do?" Jack said. "She cares more about you than she ever did about me, and you can't get her to stop. So just try to make her eat and drink water, and wait until she collapses."

"That's it?" I said. "You're making your fat commission, and that's all you've got to say?"

"Christ, you're a prick." Jack jabbed me in the shoulder with the pen she was holding. "Is she taking her medicine?"

I explained that I had tried to mix it into her coffee crystals but she had figured out the deceit. She had marched up to the belfry and launched the jar past my head, shattering it against the wall. "Do you know how hard it is to get coffee crystals out of a bookshelf?"

Jack nodded. "The one time I tried to sneak her medicine into her, she wouldn't speak to me for three months. Thought I was part of the plot against her."   •

It calmed me somewhat to hear that Jack had tried the same trick that I had. We ended our conversation with moderate civility, and Jack promised to come by the fortress that evening.

She brought food that Marianne Engel would be able to see was not stuffed with drugs—bread, fruit, cheese, and so on—and tried to engage her in conversation. It didn't work. Marianne Engel was angry at us for interrupting her; she stood breaking the bread into little pieces that she dropped among the rock chips on the floor, then turned up the stereo until it drove us away. Climbing the stairs, we could hear her talking to herself excitedly in Latin.

Though we'd accomplished absolutely nothing, the effort had drained us. Jack and I sat silently in the living room for a quarter hour, barely looking up from the floor. I finally realized it was not that Jack didn't care, but simply that she—having been through this before—really did know that there was nothing either of us could do. Still, as she left, Jack said, "I'll be back tomorrow."

In the morning, I found Marianne Engel sprawled over newly completed statue 17. I hooked an arm around her and she didn't have the strength to pull away from me despite her best efforts. "No, I have to prepare for the next one." She meant it but she simply couldn't resist me, and I helped her up the stairs.

Once again I rinsed the dust, sweat, and blood from her body, while her head lolled around the tub's porcelain rim as if she were a marionette whose puppet master was on a break. She kept telling me, all through the washing and even as I was putting her into bed, that she needed to return to her workshop. But within seconds of hitting the sheets, she fell asleep.

• • •

Marianne Engel was still unconscious when Jack arrived that evening. Finding myself alone with Ms. Meredith again, I spun the cap off a new bottle of bourbon.

Jack told me about the customers who purchased gargoyles. The names were impressive: prominent businessmen, heads of state, noted patrons of the arts, as well as a Who's Who of the entertainment business. I recognized a number of chart-topping musicians and A-list Hollywood actors, as well as one writer who is almost universally recognized as the king of the horror genre. One director, known for his highly poetic films about outcasts, had purchased at least half a dozen works. (With his mop of wild dark hair and gaunt face, he could easily have been mistaken for Marianne Engel's anemic half brother.) While I was not surprised to discover that a number of churches bought her gargoyles, I was caught unawares at how many universities were also major clients.

Jack ate most of the Chinese food that we ordered in, washing it down with glass after glass of bourbon. She wiped the sauce from around her mouth with the back of her sleeve and asked whether my penis was really gone. When I confirmed it was, she apologized for joking about the fact earlier. I accepted her apology with as much grace as I could muster and she got a little weepy at this point; I was discovering that alcohol—as it often does with even the manliest of drinkers—tended to make her sentimental. When I asked Jack whether she was planning anything for Christmas, she basically answered by reciting her life's story.

She had become pregnant while still in her teens and had given birth to a boy, Ted, who was now in his thirties. Jack married Ted's father, who proved violent and constantly drunken, and she stayed with him only because there didn't seem to be any other option. She'd managed to finish high school, but college was out of the question. When Jack got pregnant a second time, her husband blamed her for trying to wreck his life: "You go get knocked up again, even though we got no money. Bitch!" Ted, six at the time, watched his father beat his child-heavy mother at least once a week throughout the pregnancy.

On an evening in Jack's seventh month, her husband administered a particularly heavy beating. When he passed out from the alcohol, Jack packed a few small bags of clothing and bundled up young Ted. She placed the boy by the front door and then returned to the bedroom with a frying pan, which she used to bash her sleeping husband in the head. Jack claimed that she did this to ensure he didn't wake up and give chase, but I suspect it was mostly because it felt good. For days, she said, she scanned the local paper to see if she'd killed him. When no obituary turned up, she was mostly relieved but also slightly disappointed.

"After I left my husband, I was sometimes worried that he'd be waiting at my mother's hospital. She had schizophrenia," Jack said. "But I never saw the bastard again. Wasn't motivated enough to be a stalker, I guess."

It was a revelation that Jack's mother had been schizophrenic. Was there a connection, then, to Marianne Engel? Indeed there was.

"I loved my mother and I had to visit her, especially since no one else did. My father was long gone. I suppose he couldn't stand watching the woman he loved go crazy."

I made some small comment that her life sounded as though it had been difficult.

"Damn straight. All the men in my life have been such shits that while Ted was growing up," Jack confided, "I secretly wished that he'd turn out gay."

"And?"

"No such luck," she grumbled, refilling her bourbon.

"Well, don't give up hope," I said, trying to be helpful.

"Yeah, whatever." She took another large sip. "Anyway, things were pretty difficult but we got by. Gave birth to Tammie, that's the kid I had inside me when I left my husband. Got a job as a waitress. Moved up to cook, then assistant manager. Crappy little greasy spoon, but what can you do? Some lawyer tracked me down after my father died, and he'd left me a bit of money. So I guess the bastard was good for something, after all." She held up her glass towards heaven. "I knew I couldn't raise two kids with what I was making in that restaurant, so I used some of that money to enroll in a night course, accounting. Got decent grades, and was able to get a bad position with a good company."

"That's still a long way away from being a gallery owner," I noted, "and Marianne's agent."

"Not as far as you might think. I kept visiting my mom in the hospital and one day I noticed a new patient, a young girl. Attractive, you know, sitting alone at a table. Drawing. She was different from the others. Maybe it was the hair and eyes."

"Marianne," I said.

"Bingo," Jack said. "Except she didn't have that name back then. She was a Jane Doe who the police had found on the streets. Marianne Engel is just what she asked the doctors to start calling her one day."

Marianne Engel was not her real name. My surprise at the fact brought a smug look to Jack's face. It pleased her that there were still things about our mutual friend that she knew and I did not.

"The nurse told me she had been found with no identification, and fingerprints turned up nothing. She wouldn't, or couldn't, tell them anything about her past. Maybe her parents were dead or maybe they just abandoned her, who knows? Anyway, after a few visits, I decided to say hello. She was shy, then. When I asked her to show me her drawings, she wouldn't. But I kept asking and, after a few more visits, she finally did. I was blown away. I'd expected incoherent doodles and all that, but here were fantastic beasts, monsters, and they were so ugly, but they all had something so fragile about them. Something that gave them life in their eyes."

Jack paused. I looked out through the slots in my plexiglass facemask and, for a moment, I was worried that she was going to add that there was something sympathetic in my eyes, too. But she only took another slug of bourbon and continued speaking. "She said that she wasn't really a sketch artist. Said she was a sculptor and that these creatures were waiting to be released from the stone."

"So," I said, "even as a teenager . . ."

"Yeah, even as a teenager," Jack confirmed. "I guess I was kind of fascinated by the idea, but I didn't know shit about art. Most of the time, I think I still don't. But I do know this—there's something unique about her vision. I liked it, and it turns out that so do a lot of other people. But in those days, I just nodded my head, because what the hell was I going to be able to do about it? As the months passed, I kept coming to visit my mom, and Marianne kept showing me drawings, and I don't know . . . she just grew on me. I suppose I felt sorry for her. She was so young, and maybe I understood about being trapped someplace that's no good for you. The asylum was the right place for my mom, no question, but it was the wrong place for Marianne."

"So what happened?"

"The doctors played around with her meds forever until they found a combination that worked and her condition leveled out. Marianne can function, you know, when she takes her medicine. But she's always thought that it's poison against her hearts." Jack paused.

"Yeah, that fantasy is nothing new, either. One time I even got them to take chest X rays to show her that she had only a single heart and she still wouldn't believe me."

"But how did—?"

"I'm getting to that, if you'd just shut up." Jack jabbed her chopsticks at me, a piece of kung pao chicken wedged between them. "After the docs got her all straightened out, they put her in a group home and she ended up getting a job in a cafeteria. Washing dishes, can you believe it? When I heard about it, I paid her a visit and found her elbow deep in dirty water, and all I could think about were those amazing sketches. In the meantime, she'd gotten her first tattoo, one of those Latin sayings on her arm. When I asked why, she said that since she couldn't afford stone, she might as well use her body as a canvas. All those tattoos she's got, she got them when she couldn't carve for some reason. Anyway, I said, Fuck this. If she wants to carve so bad, I'll help her. So I paid for a course in the evenings, even though all I had was a little money left from my father's death, and all this when I had a couple of kids at home. Completely stupid, right?"

It was stupid, but I also thought (although I certainly didn't say it aloud) that it was wonderful. Jack took another of Marianne Engel's cigarettes—because Jack didn't smoke, as she'd told me more than once—and continued with her story. Whenever she got to a dramatic part, she poked the cigarette around in the air as if trying to pop invisible balloons.

"The instructor said Marianne was the most gifted student he'd ever had, that she just took to the chisel. When I couldn't afford to shell out any more cash for lessons, he told Marianne to keep coming anyway. Said that someday he'd be bragging that he was once her teacher. So I made another stupid decision and suggested to Marianne that I should be her agent. She accepted, even after I pointed out that I knew squat about selling artwork. But I knew enough to get her a half-decent set of tools, which I found at an estate sale, just dumb luck, and then some stone. This first block was this horrible, cheap stone that practically crumbled away under her chisel, right, but she gets the gargoyle out anyway and it looks pretty good. So now I have this statue and I have to sell it before we can afford a second block of stone, so I borrow this beat-up old truck to drive around to different galleries with this big statue in the back. Finally I find someone willing to display it but only if they get a bloody outrageous commission, but by this point, we're totally out of options, and so I say yes. When it finally sells, can you fucking believe this, I actually lose money on it. The whole process takes months and Marianne Engel is getting tattoos the whole time, going crazy without any stone. But eventually we sell another, and another, and then suddenly we have some cash flow and it all works out."

I was fascinated to hear a history on Marianne Engel that did not include medieval monasteries. It made me realize how completely I had been engrossed in her fairy tales.

"When she really got rolling, the statues just didn't stop coming. That was the first time I saw how she could get like this, you know? The first time she worked herself into collapse." Jack cast her eyes up towards Marianne Engel's room. "She was younger and stronger, and I thought it was just the flame of youth. The passion of first creation. I had no idea it would be like this for—how long now? Going on twenty-something years."

"She must be doing all right," I said, "I mean, the house and everything . . ."

"Yeah, moneywise, sure. Marianne is the best in the world at what she does, and I'm not just saying that. Five years in, we set up the gallery. Ten years, we got her this place. Cash down, not even a mortgage."

"How did you become her conservator?"

"Just sort of happened along the way," Jack answered. "No, fuck that, it took a lot of paperwork and endless visits to the courts. But you gotta remember that she doesn't have a family, at least none that I know of. She never told me anything about her life before we met and, honestly, I don't know if even she knows."

"Jacqueline," I said, "you never did answer my original question."

"Don't call me that, fuck, and I can't even remember your stupid question."

"If you were doing anything this Christmas."

"No, my mother died about ten years back and my kids don't talk to me anymore." She grabbed her coat and said it was time for her to leave. At the door, she added, "Don't think we're all buddy-buddy now. If it was my decision, you still wouldn't have a credit card."

"Understood," I confirmed. "I hope this doesn't sound bad, but I'm actually pretty glad that Marianne collapsed. At least she'll have to take some time off."

Jack snorted. "She's not finished yet."

. . .

When Marianne Engel woke, she proved Jack correct. She ate a huge breakfast, then descended into the basement, where she spent the next four days. All her movements were sluggish, as if someone had taken a film of her working and was running it at half speed. She simply lacked the energy to work faster.

IF YOU SLIPPED HER A LITTLE MORPHINE *What?* SHE WOULD FALL ASLEEP.

On the twentieth of December, Sayuri came for my final exercise session before the holidays. We tried our best to ignore the slow tap-tap-tapping of Marianne Engel's lethargic tools.

"Gregor tells me that you're going to meet his parents," I said. "Big step."

"He's never done this before," Sayuri said, "taking a girl to meet them."

"How do you feel about it?"

"No drama for me, but I'm a bit nervous for him. I think he feels like he's never good enough for his folks."

"Does he think you're going to disappoint them?" I asked incredulously.

"He's more worried that they'll think *he's* not good enough for me." Sayuri increased the resistance settings on my exercise bike and implored me to fight, fight, *fight!* "It's ridiculous."

"So, do you think he's planning on . . . ?" I tapped at her wedding finger, which was completely ring-free.

"No," Sayuri responded quickly. She drew back her hand, but I could see on her face that she didn't mind the idea of it. "He just wants me to see his hometown."

There had been a change in the sound coming from the basement—the slow metronome of the hammer was missing. By this point in our living together, I knew Marianne Engel's carving schedule well enough to realize she couldn't possibly be finished with her current statue. "I should check on her."

`MORPHINE IS GOOD.` *Not for her.*

I couldn't see her when I started down the basement stairs. I called out, but there was no answer. Half a cigarette was smoldering in the ashtray. Then I saw her behind a mostly completed gargoyle, her arms splayed at awkward angles. Her fingers were still half closed around her hammer; her chisel had bounced a few feet away.

When I came around the rock, I saw that she was unconscious, with a large gash on her forehead. I presumed this was from falling headfirst into the stone as she passed out.

⋅ ⋅ ⋅

The hospital held Marianne Engel for four nights. Her head was stitched closed, and an IV pumped her arm with electrolyte solution to combat the dehydration. Luckily, she was too exhausted to work up much anger over the fact that I had put her under the care of the enemy doctors. I left her side only to go home to get some sleep. I let Bougatsa share my bed, even though Nan would have had a fit about the irritation that dog hair can cause burned skin. `YOU CAN'T EVEN LOOK AFTER YOURSELF.` In the mornings, I immediately returned to the hospital. `HOW CAN YOU LOOK AFTER HER?`

Marianne Engel was released on Christmas Eve. Honestly, the doctors should have held her longer, but they discharged her in consideration of the date. When we got home, she wanted to eat marzipan and nothing else, but I persuaded her to eat some mandarin oranges as well. I hauled my television and video player from the belfry into her bedroom and we watched *It's a Wonderful Life*, because that's what normal people do on Christmas Eve. After it ended, she insisted that I stay in her bed, because she wanted to wake into Christmas Day with me at her side.

I lay in that bed with my thick pressure suit pressed up against her thin nakedness, aware that I should have been enjoying our closeness. But I wasn't; I was contemplating why her body affected me as powerfully as it did. I had spent much of my adult life in the company of naked women—it had been my job during the day, and my hobby at night—but with Marianne Engel it had always seemed different. It *was* different.

There are many possible explanations for my discomfort. Perhaps her body had a greater effect than that of other women because I actually cared for her. Perhaps it was because for the first time in my life, as a result of my penectomy, I could not dismiss the woman's body by conquering it. Perhaps my feeling was simply pheromonal. All these theories are plausible, and to some extent perhaps all are valid, but on that Christmas Eve, lying beside her unable to sleep, I worked it through. The principal reason, I believe, that her body so thrilled mine was this: her body affected me as if it were not only human, but also as something that approached memory and ghost.

The first time that I had seen her body, fully, was in the burn ward when she had undressed to show her tattoos. The sight made me aroused and bashful, and when I ran my fingertips over the plumage of her angel wings her body trembled and, in return, trembled my heart. At the time, I did not understand why I felt the way I did, but in the many months that had passed, I had grown into the realization that it was because my fingers felt not as if they were visiting her body for the first time but as if they were returning to a familiar location. I did not understand this until I saw how, when Marianne Engel gave me my first bath in the fortress, she had reached out to touch my body as if it was hers to touch. She moved her arm just as I had reached towards her winged back that first time. It was as if the other's flesh was already owned, and the reaching hand belonged to a master who had been long absent and was now returned. When I had touched her that first time, it did not feel like the first time I had touched her.

Now, in the bed next to her on this Christmas Eve, her body retained that effect upon me. When I lay beside her, it was as if I were meant to be there, as if my body had rested against hers thousands of times before. So it felt as if I were lying not next to a person, but next to the memory of a person, while at the same time that memory was undergoing a transformation into something even less material. Her body was all too human in its ravagedness, but it also struck me as an entity becoming ghost, as if in her thinness she were slipping into something less than solid. I ran my fingers across her bumpy ribs and traced the gaunt hill of the pelvic bone that overlooked her stomach. Her body, whose flesh and memory had always confused and excited, still felt as if it belonged to me but also as if it were disappearing. It was not only that she was losing substance as she worked, it was as if she were working to lose substance; as if it were not only the gargoyles that were backwards art, but also the artist herself, progressing to a state in which they were both less and more than the material from which they started.

So this is how her body—flesh, memory, and ghost—disarmed me.

I woke, after I finally fell into a short and fitful sleep, before she did. I brought her eggs on a tray, and worked up the courage to give her that year's gift. Again it was writing, as I apparently had not learned my lesson from the previous year's poems. I had written from memory the stories she'd told me about her four ghostly friends—"The Good Ironworker," "The Woman on the Cliff," "The Glassblower's Apprentice," and "Sigurðr's Gift"—and bound them between covers. On the front was the title *The Lovers' Tales, as told by Marianne Engel.*

"It's the perfect gift. Not only for me, but also for Sigurðr. For a Viking, the worst Hell is to be forgotten." She took my hand in hers and apologized. Her intense carving over the previous weeks had taken her over completely and, as a result, she had neglected to get me a proper gift.

"But," she suggested, "how about I explain what Sister Constantia meant when she said I had desecrated the scriptorium?"

XXVII.

awn was breaking when Agletrudis appeared at Engelthal's gate, wearing a smile so thick with Schadenfreude that it seemed impossible it could fit on a nun's face. She nodded in your direction, where you were still propped up on the horse with Brandeis' bloodied body, and said, "I see you've brought your lover."

I couldn't betray my anger if we were to have any chance of being taken in. I needed to appeal to her better instincts; she was, after all, dedicated to a life in God. "We require sanctuary. Without your help we will die."

"Ah," Agletrudis said, nodding and clasping her hands behind her back. "So your adventurous spirit has found what it was looking for. Perhaps even more." Like Sister Constantia before her, Agletrudis surveyed the bulge of my stomach.

I steadied my voice. "You can imagine that it was not easy for us—for me—to come here." My hands were also behind my back, but because I didn't want Agletrudis to see that they were curled into fists. "There's nowhere else for us to go."

Agletrudis tried to produce a sympathetic look, but her smile only grew more ugly. "This puts us in a most interesting situation. Our mission is one of mercy, and we are taught to find forgiveness for every sinner. And yet, the difficulty lies in the fact that most of the sisters place you in a category beyond the merely sinful."

This struck me as a vast overreaction to the fact that I'd left Engelthal. "When I left, it was never my intention to disrespect the monastery or the Lord."

"Or Mother Christina, I'm certain." Agletrudis had not lost her ability to strike in the tenderest spot. "Had you simply disappeared, it's unlikely anyone would object to extending help now. But because of your actions on that night, poor Sister Gertrud died of a broken heart."

Gertrud would not have cared one bit about my leaving, except for the fact that my absence would have slowed down work on her Bible. "What are you talking about?"

"There is no use denying it, Sis— Oh, excuse me. *Marianne.* Do you not remember that I saw you that night exiting the scriptorium? I remember it, and I also remember how the next morning, poor Sister Gertrud found her work all in ashes. Every chapter, every verse." Agletrudis paused with a dramatic sigh. "How could you torch her Bible?"

It was the sigh that explained everything. *She* had burned *Die Gertrud Bibel* the night I left, and she had blamed it on me. And so, I'd become known as the sister who destroyed Gertrud's life's work, the nun who reduced the Word of God to dust and ran off to live as a killer's mistress.

Agletrudis' eyes positively glowed. "Mother Christina has ordered that your name be expunged from all the chronicles, and now that Father Sunder has passed—I trust you know that he, too, has died?—we are removing your name from his writings as well."

I'd always considered Agletrudis to be little more than a lackey to Gertrud, an inferior in the ways of treachery. How quickly one's perceptions can turn. It was a revelation to understand, in an instant, the wickedness of which Agletrudis was capable. With my disappearance, she would have reassumed her position as heir to the scriptorium. But this was not enough for her. She had to ruin my name forever, and to achieve this she was willing to sacrifice the life's dream of her mentor.

I'm not proud that I couldn't stop my fists. My right hand connected with Agletrudis' shoulder, the first punch I'd ever thrown. I was aiming for her head but I guess my anger affected my aim. The second and third punches were better, despite my pregnant clumsiness, and landed on her jaw and her chest. She fell backwards, though I'm not sure how much from the force of the blows and how much from surprise. When she got up, she smiled a red mess of teeth ringed with blood.

"I will not lower myself to strike a pregnant whore," Agletrudis said, "but I'll be sure to pass your regards to Mother Christina."

There was no point in staying, as we'd never be allowed in the monastery now, and there was still the matter of the trackers hot on our trail. I forced myself to remount and you let me gallop away some of my rage before asking where we were going. I said I didn't know. You suggested Father Sunder's cottage. I said he was dead. You asked whether Brother Heinrich were also dead. I didn't know. You said that we were out of options, and their house was our new destination.

Brother Heinrich was shocked to find us at his entrance after so many years, but he didn't even hesitate. He only threw the door open as wide as it would go, and I will always remember him for that. You carried Brandeis directly to the small bed that had been yours during your recovery.

Brother Heinrich looked as though life had sucked most of the wind out of his lungs. He was no longer steady on his feet, and he hobbled around to gather water and fresh bedding. He helped us to treat Brandeis, doing his best to hold him down as you rinsed out the wound. When Brandeis stopped struggling, worn through, it was Brother Heinrich—not you or me—who stroked his hair lovingly, though he had never met Brandeis before. When Brandeis finally slipped into uneasy sleep, Brother Heinrich said he would prepare some food. "I have so few visitors, let me invite you . . ."

I insisted on helping and it amused Brother Heinrich that I could now cook. When he complimented me on my new skill, I finally found the courage to express my condolences on Father Sunder's death. Brother Heinrich nodded his head as he chopped the vegetables. "He lived a good life and died in his sleep, so there's nothing to be sorry about. There was a lovely remembrance and all the nuns said that the Devil rejoiced at his death. Not because the Enemy had won a new soul, but because Friedrich would no longer be able to harm Him with his prayers."

There was a telling quiver to his voice. *Friedrich,* he had said. Not *Brother Sunder,* as he had always called him in life. In front of me, at least. He tried to smile but could not quite manage it, and I understood why he looked so old. Brother Heinrich was waiting his turn.

"Did you know that Sister Gertrud also died? Her heart just seemed to give up after . . ." Heinrich's voice trailed away. He meant, of course, the burning of her Bible. "Marianne, when the burnt remains were found, Sister Gertrud realized that her Bible would never be completed in her lifetime. It was no secret, the bad blood between you two, but you should know that I never believed you burned it. And neither did Friedrich. He died certain of your innocence."

At that moment a cramp seized my stomach, and my hands instinctively went to the child. I could not look upon Brother Heinrich's face, wondering whether he would blame my sin of leaving Engelthal for the situation in which I now found myself. But this is what he said: "Friedrich would have been so pleased that you are with child. He always knew that your love was true."

Right there in the middle of the kitchen, all the previous weeks caught up with me. Losing the life that you and I had built together in Mainz, discovering that I'd been accused of a horrible crime, and learning of Father Sunder's death. Agletrudis smiling at the gate, as acting prioress. My pregnancy, which I worried about every moment of every day. I had been running on willpower and nervous energy since we had left Nürnberg, but in that instant all my remaining strength drained out. I broke down completely into the tears that I'd not been allowing myself. I collapsed, my body folding into the old man's arms.

It was so good to be held again, simply held, and spoken to with kindness. You'd been so busy fighting for our lives, driving the horses forward and planning our next move, that you had no time to spend on calming my emotions. I didn't blame you, but I missed your kinder attentions. Brother Heinrich stroked my hair, just as he'd done with Brandeis, and he put me into his own bed. He covered me with blankets and told me exactly what I needed to hear: that everything was going to be all right.

A few days passed and we had no choice but to stay right where we were. I hoped that we might have somehow thrown the trackers off, but you assured me that we most definitely had not. You said with absolute certainty that, with one of the trackers now dead, the others were regrouping and trying to figure out what resources we had at our disposal.

We had been cleaning Brandeis' wound diligently and hoping it would heal, but we were hoping for too much. It became infected and he fell into a terrible fever, becoming delirious. You had seen this before, on the battlefield, and you knew what you had to do. Brother Heinrich held Brandeis' shoulders and I held his legs, while you used a hunting knife to carve away part of your friend's thigh. When we finished, our clothes were covered in blood and there was a chunk of flesh in a bucket. When I looked at the damage to Brandeis' thigh, I primarily felt two emotions: shame at my fear that the wound might somehow infect me and harm the baby, and guilt because the injury existed at all. If I had not hesitated at the inn's window, Brandeis would have been able to escape ahead of the ax.

It was Brother Heinrich who first noticed the two men on horses. They remained a safe distance from the house, past the ridge that I used to play on as a child, but there was no doubt that they were watching us. They were trackers, of course. When I asked why they didn't come for us, you said, "They know that we have crossbows and that we can use them, so they've sent for reinforcements."

It was unlikely that they'd figured out your identity yet, as they hadn't caught a good look at you. Even if they had, they might not have recognized you—not only had you been burned, but also they might not have joined the condotta until after you left it. They couldn't have known who I was, no matter how long they had been in the troop, but they must have guessed there was a reason we'd stopped running. Did they know about Brandeis' wounds? Most likely, as they would have seen the bloody snow at the side of the Nürnberg road. Had they guessed at the pregnancy under my winter cloak? Probably not. But for all the questions they must have had about us, I had a bigger question about them: what would happen when the other mercenaries arrived?

We had huge arguments. Brother Heinrich thought he should go out as a man of God in an effort to reason with them. You laughed at this suggestion. Brandeis, in a moment of lucidity, argued that he should face his fate like a man, as this was the only chance they might spare the rest of us. We should flee to reclaim our lives, he argued, while he distracted them by riding in the opposite direction. But of course we couldn't allow him to commit suicide like that. You wanted to stand and fight, right then and there, but who could fight beside you? Not the pregnant ex-nun. Not Brandeis, in his delirium. Not Heinrich, an old man. So what you really meant was that *you* should take them on alone. Your reasoning was that if you were able to slay these two soldiers, at least Heinrich and I could escape before the rest arrived. You'd take Brandeis in the opposite direction, whether he was ready or not. This, you stated, was by far the best option. We couldn't stay and wait for certain death to come to us.

In the end, none of the arguments mattered. When the rest of us were asleep and you were supposed to be keeping watch, you took your crossbow and crept out into the night. We didn't even know that you had gone until you returned and awoke us.

"They're dead," you said. "Dawn is coming and others will arrive soon, so we must be quick."

I could not contain my shock that you'd killed, any more than I'd been able to when we were fleeing Nürnberg. This time, however, my naivety angered you. "Don't you understand what will happen if they catch us? They'll kill Brandeis and me, but they'll use you as a plaything until you wish that you were dead. Your pregnancy won't make any difference. They'll rape you, and if you're lucky, your life will bleed out before your spirit does. So don't stand there judging me, thinking I have no regard for life. I'm doing everything I can to preserve ours."

Finally I accepted that I could no longer both stay with you and protect our child. Our parting was inevitable. I would return to Mainz and hide myself in a beguinage until you returned. You'd take Brandeis in the opposite direction; with the best trackers already dead, perhaps the two of you had a chance.

Brother Heinrich would go to Engelthal, for it was certain that the monastery would accept him if he came without me. I thanked him with all my heart, kissed him on the forehead, and said that I would pray the mercenaries did not destroy his home when they arrived.

"Do not waste your prayers on such a silly thing, Sister Marianne," he said. "It's only a building. I live in the House of the Lord."

"Our child," I said, "will owe its life to you. If it is a boy, we will name him Heinrich."

"You would honor me more," the old priest said, "if you named him Friedrich."

I promised that I would. The weather was changing, so maybe luck was finally turning in our favor: ever since we'd left Mainz, we'd been praying for a storm to erase our tracks. Brother Heinrich pulled tight his winter coat and slipped Father Sunder's pluviale over it, as an extra layer to protect against the storm. He sank into the snow as he walked away from us, his step unsteady, and in a few minutes he was gone. The last I saw of him was the image on the back of Father

Sunder's pluviale, of Michael and the angels fighting the dragon in Revelation, being swallowed up into the white.

Brandeis' crossbow was useless to him, so you thrust it into my hands even though I protested that I didn't want it. You told me that I didn't have to fire it but I *had* to take it, just in case, and you wouldn't allow me to leave without it. I agreed only because you were so adamant.

You gave me a quick lesson in loading the bolt and setting the catch. "You brace the instrument against your shoulder, like this, and here's how you sight the target. You steady the weapon by slowing your breathing. In, out, in, out. Steady. Aim. Trust the arrow. Breathe. Release."

You placed the crossbow into the holster across my horse's flank and opened my winter coat to let one hand rest upon my bulging stomach. You used the other hand to slip your arrowhead necklace over my head. "It is for protection, and you need it more than I. You can return it when we meet again, because I promise that our love will not end like this."

Then you slapped my horse into action. I looked over my shoulder once, at you watching me ride away, before addressing all my attention to the trail that would take me and our unborn child away from danger.

The snow swirled in front of me. I tried to imagine what would happen to you next. How many mercenaries would come? A dozen? Two dozen? I supposed it depended upon whether they were currently fighting on behalf of some lord, somewhere. Or would Kuonrat bring all his soldiers, so they would see what happened to deserters? I wondered what chance you really had of escaping with your life. I had seen your skill with the crossbow, but the sheer numbers . . . How could you escape a past that was so determined to make you pay? The wind picked up, and the whiteness of the storm was blinding. The cold cut through my clothing and into my bones.

I couldn't do it. I couldn't go on without you. I'd been a fool to think that I could leave you, just when you needed me most. I'd been traveling for about half an hour when I turned the horse around and drove it back hard in the direction that I'd come. I only prayed that I was not too late.

It was already difficult to retrace my tracks, but I knew all the paths that led to Heinrich's house. Still, even when I was less than a hundred feet away, I couldn't see it in the swirl of snow. But then I heard the voices of many men, carried to me on the wind, and I knew that in the hour I had been away, the condotta had arrived. The only question was whether you and Brandeis had managed to get away first.

I drove my horse up onto the ridge that overlooked the house, into the brush that I'd hidden in when I was a child. I didn't even consider that there might be soldiers up there; it was only by luck that I found myself alone. I maneuvered into a thicket where I could tether the horse to a low-hanging branch, and took a position where I could make out the action below. I knew that with the blizzard, there was no chance I'd be spotted.

Almost immediately I saw what I feared most: you had not managed to escape, and soldiers were pulling you from the house. A clear voice cut through the flurry. It was Kuonrat the Ambitious, laughing at his own good fortune. "Not one deserter, but two! Two!"

Soldiers held your arms behind your back and pushed you down onto your knees. Kuonrat took a step forward and placed his hand under your chin, twisting your head up so that your eyes met his. Still laughing, he looked as if he were trying to convince himself that his luck really *was* that good. A ghost delivered from the very recesses of his memory. A ghost that he could use to teach a lesson to the living.

What could I do? I considered that I might take out the crossbow and begin shooting. In the blizzard, the soldiers would never see the arrows coming until it was too late, and they might not even be able to tell where they came from. But what good would that do? There were at least two dozen of them, paid killers, and I'd never used a crossbow in my life. I'd be lucky to take down even one. But, I thought, if I could manage one good shot, what would happen if I hit Kuonrat? Would the troop scatter if they saw their leader fall?

Of course not. They were professionals and I knew that I didn't have it in me to kill anyone, not even Kuonrat.

It took a number of soldiers to hold you down, but Brandeis was so weak it took two soldiers to hold him up. When they released him, he slumped onto his knees while Kuonrat demanded, "What do you have to say?"

The harsh storm winds blew directly towards me, past them, and carried their words to my vantage place. Whether it was good luck or ill fortune that I was able to hear every word, I am unsure, but in the moment I was thankful that I did not have to sneak closer.

Brandeis assumed the posture of a miserable sinner asking for forgiveness and the wind carried his words to me. "I deserve any death you choose. Make it as horrible as you desire, as horrible as you can. Use me as the example that I should be. I renounce my decision to run away from the condotta. I was like a frightened child. I request only that you punish me, and me alone."

"It is always interesting to listen to the bargains of those who have nothing to offer," Kuonrat said to many laughs.

Brandeis refused to let this laughter interfere with his final actions on this earth. His executioner was standing in front of him but never once did Brandeis beg for his own life. No, he used his final moments to plead, passionately, that the life of his best friend be spared.

Brandeis pointed out that when he left the condotta, it was entirely his own misguided decision—but when *you* left, it was not your decision at all. It was the Lord's will that you were struck down in combat, but not killed. It was the Lord's will that the battle had occurred so close to Engelthal and that you were delivered there. It was the Lord's will that you were able to heal from injuries that should have taken your life. There could be no greater proof that God wanted you alive, Brandeis argued, than the fact that you still were.

Brandeis gestured in your direction. "This life is the Lord's will, so forgo his punishment and double mine. I know that you are a wise and just leader, Kuonrat, and I know that you would not want to defy God."

It was a smart tactic to keep repeating that your survival was the Lord's will. If anything could stay your execution, it would be Kuonrat's belief that killing you would violate God's intentions. It was clear that he had no regard for man, but perhaps God was a different story.

The storm hurled a great burst of snow across the landscape. Brandeis instinctively turned his head to shield his eyes and I saw a swift bolt of silver, as if an extension of Kuonrat's arm. A red surge sprayed across the ground and Brandeis' head flew for a few feet before gravity brought it down.

Kuonrat wiped his sword clean, the steel still steaming with the heat of the blood. "The Lord's will does not matter. Only mine does."

He turned and said, with a laugh into your shocked face, that he had something much better for you. Something not nearly so painless or so mercifully quick. After all, your disappearance had continued for much longer than that of Brandeis.

Kuonrat gathered his mercenaries and gave out their tasks. One third of the men were to scour the woods for deadwood and twigs. Another third was sent into Heinrich's house to secure any items of value—food, money, clothing—that the troop could use or barter. The remaining soldiers were ordered to prepare you.

The soldiers pulled you past Brandeis' body. The blood leaked from his neck, still, adding to the large red blot in the snow. The mercenaries pushed you up against Heinrich's cottage, your back to the wall. They kicked at your ankles until your legs were spread wide, and pulled out your arms until they were stretched across the face of the building. When you showed resistance, they beat you and spat in your face and laughed as if this were some great joke.

A soldier, bigger than the others, walked towards you carrying an ax. My heart caught in my throat, because I was certain that he was coming to dismember you. But this was not the case. The other soldiers, the ones holding out your arms, unpeeled your fingers from your clenched fists until your palms were open and exposed. One of the soldiers held something against your right hand. The larger soldier turned the ax backwards, and I realized that the object was a nail. He used the blunt side of the ax like a hammer to drive the nail through the flesh of your palm. Even as far away as I was, I could hear the bones in your hand cracking like the neck of a chicken being broken. You howled and you jerked at your hand, trying to pry it away from the wall, but it was held fast. They did your left hand next, another nail through the open palm, another splatter of blood across the wall. Your shoulders wrenched futilely and all the veins in your neck looked as though they were about to explode.

Next the soldiers tried taking hold of your legs, but you were kicking wildly because you were in such pain. So the axman brought the sharp side of the ax head forward and swung it hard right above your knee where the ligaments meet the bone. Your thigh contracted but your shin hung useless, dangling as if connected to your body by half-cut twine. The soldiers laughed more at this, another great joke, and your hands continued to leak blood down the wall.

They grabbed you by the ankles, and it was ridiculously easy now, driving nails through your feet so that you were skewered to the wall about ten inches above the snow line. The sound of the bones breaking in your feet, so thin those bones, was so awful and the blood, there was so much blood everywhere. You looked like you were levitating, hanging from your hands; you looked like a ghost already, floating against the backdrop of the house. They wanted your weight to hang, because that would be all the more painful. They loved the way that the nails in your hands couldn't really support you, and they loved driving new nails into your forearms so you wouldn't fall right off the wall. The blood was draining out of your body and Brandeis lay headless on red snow, the stain now larger, now redder, and steam, steam rising. I got the crossbow from my horse, and I took a step towards the horror, wanting to run down the hill to you, and then pulled back by the umbilical cord of our unborn child, I realized there was nothing I could do. The crossbow hung in my hand, so useless at my side, my heart beating so loudly that I was certain the mercenaries would be able to hear it above the storm. There were also cries coming from me that I couldn't control but a part of me didn't care and a part of me even wanted to be caught, to die, because what good was my life now? But they didn't hear me, the wind still carrying my sounds away, and they were too busy laughing, laughing in time with the dripping of your blood, and I couldn't do anything about it without ending the life of our child.

Now the mercenaries who'd been sent for wood were returning and Kuonrat pointed to the space under your feet. They piled the wood halfway up your legs. And I knew what was coming next. The wind and the whipping of the snow made it difficult to light the fire, but the mercenaries were used to living in the wild, so they knew how to hunch their bodies into windbreaks. Soon enough, a spark caught and the twigs started to smolder and there was smoke and I could hear the popping sap as the fire caught, and it reminded me of your breaking hands and feet. Little flames were approaching your toes but you couldn't lift them out of the way, and they were nailed to the wall anyway. And then Kuonrat instructed his archers to take up their bows and to light their arrows in the flames and the archers did it, and when the tips were on fire, they lined up in a semicircle and they angled in on you. Kuonrat told them they were not to kill you but they were to shoot the arrows as close to your body as possible, that was the game, the goal was to light the wall on fire and slowly burn you from all sides rather than just from the bottom up. But then Kuonrat had a better idea and changed his instructions and told the archers that they could hit your body, just not in any spot that would be fatal—piercing your arms and legs was fine, but piercing your head or chest was not—and he had such glee in his voice, such utter pride in his brilliance, and the archers lifted their bows and started calling out body parts—"Left hand!" "Right foot!" "Upper thigh!"—and they were good shots, they usually got the places they called. When an arrow hit its mark, everyone cheered, and if an arrow missed everyone jeered, like it was a carnival game, and the flames under you were growing larger, new flames were bursting out all around your body, igniting with every arrow.

Over the laughs and happy shouts of the mercenaries, Kuonrat called out his final goodbye to you, "Everything burns if the flame is hot enough. The world is nothing but a crucible."

And then I knew what I had to do.

I reached into my coat and found my necklace. I clenched my hand around the arrowhead that Father Sunder had blessed, and I prayed for strength.

I lifted the crossbow. I tried to remember the lesson that you'd given. *It's all in the breathing,* you had said, *you steady the instrument by slowing your breathing. In, out, steady, in, out, aim.* I checked once more that the arrow was properly loaded. I knew I would have only one shot, the first shot of my life and the last. *It's all about the breathing. Trust the arrow. Calm.*

I asked the Lord to deliver the arrow straight and true, directly to your heart, through the snowstorm and the condotta.

XXVIII.

etween Christmas and Valentine's Day, Marianne Engel stopped
carving. There was only one afternoon in late January when she
went into the basement to complete the gargoyle that had been
left unfinished when she passed out and was admitted to the hospital.
When this little task was put away, quickly and without any drama,
she returned to focusing on her recovery—and back to preparing
meals.

Since I had been released from the hospital, only once had she
brought forth an extravagant feast: Japanese food, on the night of
Sei's story. But every third or fourth day during this period, she
would go shopping before disappearing into her kitchen for hours.
Each time she emerged, she came with a spread of delicacies from
another region of the world.

Among the more notable meals was Senegalese, a rare culinary
step outside Asia or Europe. For appetizers we had black-eyed pea
fritters and fried plantains, followed by a sweet milk-rice soup called
sombi. The main dishes: Yassa poulet, chicken marinated overnight
and then simmered with onions in lemony garlic-mustard sauce;
ceebu jen, fish in tomato sauce with vegetables on rice, the national
dish of Senegal; mafé, a meat dish in peanut sauce that can be made

with chicken, lamb, or beef—so, of course, she made all three versions; and a seafood stew with shrimp, perch, and unripe bananas. For dessert, she served Cinq Centimes, the "five-cent" peanut cookies popular in marketplaces, and ngalax, sweetened porridge made from millet couscous. Throughout the meal we sipped on mango, bissap, and monkey bread fruit juices, before ending with tea. And as much as I enjoyed the feasts Marianne Engel was preparing, the greatest benefit was that her tattooed angel wings were starting to plump out again because of the calories.

Things appeared to be good for everyone, in this century at least: there was Marianne Engel's returning health; Sayuri talked about the great success of her trip to meet Gregor's parents; and Gregor confided over coffee that he was more or less certain that Sayuri liked him. Even Bougatsa was pleased, as he was able to go for daily walks with his mistress again.

Often at midnight, Marianne Engel and I would take trips to the ocean. Despite the hour and the biting cold there were usually a few teenagers on the shore, drinking beer and making out. She would light bonfires, tending them as they sent ashes into the sky, and feed me from the picnic baskets that she always prepared, often with leftovers from the previous day's international buffet. She lit the fires in an effort to lessen my fear of them; she said I needed to come to some sort of understanding with the elemental forces of the universe. They weren't going away, after all.

I could not look at the fires without emotion, but surprisingly I thought less about my own fate in the car than I did about my fourteenth-century counterpart in the flames, nailed to the wall. I begged Marianne Engel to continue the story but she urged patience, citing more nonsense about single days in the vastness of eternity. Instead, she told me other stories that I knew were not true, creation and Armageddon myths, but I didn't care. If she believed them, that was enough.

Then she would look out over the ocean, stretch her legs in its direction, and lament the fact that it was not yet warm enough to go swimming. "Oh, well," she'd say, "I suppose the spring is coming soon enough. . . ."

· · ·

My pressure garments came off in early February and it was like emerging from a slough in which I had been swimming for nearly a year. My mask and dental retractor were also removed and my face was finally returned to me, albeit unrecognizable as the one I had before.

I experienced the panicked exhilaration that comes with starting anew. It's not easy to look the way I do: in popular culture, one only sees a face like mine on the Phantom of the Opera, on Freddie Krueger from Elm Street, or on Leatherface from deep in the heart of Texas. Sure, a burn victim may "get the girl"—but usually only with a pickax.

I hesitated to claim possession of my face, but this was also why I had to: if I didn't, it seemed inevitable that my face would take possession of me. The cliché goes that at twenty a person has the face that God gave him, but at forty he has the face he has earned. But if the face and the soul are intertwined so that the face can reflect the soul, surely it follows that the soul can also reflect the face. As Nietzsche wrote: "The criminologists tell us that the typical criminal is ugly: *monstrum in fronte, monstrum in animo* (a monster in face, and a monster in soul)."

But Nietzsche was wrong. I was born beautiful and lived beautiful for thirty-plus years, and during all that time I never once allowed my soul to know love. My unblemished skin was numb armor used to attract women with its shininess, while repelling any true emotion and protecting the wearer. The most erotic of actions were merely technical: sex was mechanics; conquest a hobby; my body constantly used, but rarely enjoyed. In short, I was born with all the advantages that a monster never had, and I chose to disregard them all.

Now my armor had melted away and been replaced with a raw wound. The line of beauty that I had used to separate myself from people was gone, replaced by a new barrier—ugliness—that kept people away from me, whether I liked it or not. One might expect the result to be the same, but that was not entirely true. While I was now surrounded by far fewer people than before, they were far better people. When my former acquaintances took a quick glance at me in the burn ward before turning around to walk out, they left the door open for Marianne Engel, Nan Edwards, Gregor Hnatiuk, and Sayuri Mizumoto.

What an unexpected reversal of fate: only after my skin was burned away did I finally become able to feel. Only after I was born into physical repulsiveness did I come to glimpse the possibilities of the heart: I accepted this atrocious face and abominable body because they were forcing me to overcome the limitations of who I am, while my previous body allowed me to hide them.

I am not a hero in soul and never will be, but I am better than I was. Or so I tell myself; and for now, that is enough.

• • •

Marianne Engel entered my room on February 13, midnight, and took me by the hand. She led me down the stairs and out the back door. Snow was falling, making it look as if the stony monsters littering the backyard were wearing white hoods.

She pulled open a gate that allowed us to enter the cemetery behind St. Romanus. Gravestones popped out of the snowdrifts like gray tongues and we tiptoed past them to the center of the cemetery, where she had already laid out a horsehide blanket. Above us, the moon was a magnificent blister in the midst of a gooseflesh of stars. Marianne Engel tried lighting candles but the wind kept blowing her matches out, and she laughed at this. She pulled her coat tighter around her body. I hated the cold but I liked being near her.

"I've brought you here to tell you something," she said.

"What?"

"I'm going to die soon."

No, you're not. "Why would you say that?"

"I've only got sixteen hearts left."

"You're going to live until you're an old woman," I assured her.
With me.

"I'm already old." She smiled, wearily. "I hope this time, death
takes."

"Don't talk like that. You're not going to die." *You're not going to die.*

She put her hand on my cheek. "My last heart has always been
for you, so I need you to prepare."

I was going to tell her that she was talking nonsense, but she
moved her finger over my lips. When I tried to speak anyway, she
kissed me on my thin lips and all my words were pushed back into
my mouth.

"I don't want to die," she whispered, "but I need to lose the shackles of this multitude of hearts."

"It's just—you have this medical condition." I wondered to what
degree I felt such tenderness towards her because of her schizophrenia, and to what degree despite it. "I know you don't want to believe
it, but it's true. . . ."

"How little you believe, and how very much it takes to make you
believe," she said. "But you will. Now let's go inside."

The way she stated that we should go inside with such finality,
such certainty, made me fear the worst. "Why?"

"Because it's freezing out here," she said, and my relief must have
been visible. "Don't worry, I'm not ready to die tonight. We still have
things to do."

"Like what?"

"Like getting you off the drugs." NOT LIKELY. She said, "Do
you really think I don't know you've been buying extra morphine?"

◆ ◆ ◆

That morning, Valentine's Day, when I woke, I looked into the small wooden box that held my morphine stash to find it empty. I staggered into Marianne Engel's bedroom, where her body lay unmoving. I shook her by the shoulders and when she opened her eyes a little, I asked where my kit was.

"Get into bed with me. You'll be okay."

"You don't understand. There's a snake in my spine—"

"Silly boy," she said. "You should know better than to listen to snakes. They lie."

"You didn't give me enough time to adjust to the idea," I pleaded. "Tomorrow, I'll quit, but give me a day—"

`I AM ALMOST HERE . . .`

"Suffering is good for the soul."

"No it isn't!"

"If you cannot love the pain"—she tried to put a positive spin on it—"you can at least love the lessons it teaches."

`. . . AND THERE IS NOTHING . . .`

I preferred to remain uneducated. "I can get my prescription refilled and—"

"I flushed it down the toilet," she replied, "and Dr. Edwards won't refill it again. And I've put your credit card on hold, so unless you're going to rob me to buy street drugs, get into bed."

`. . . YOU CAN DO ABOUT IT.`

"Sleep," Marianne Engel said. "Just sleep."

◆ ◆ ◆

Morphine comes from the opium poppy, *Papaver somniferum,* and was first isolated in the early 1800s by the German pharmacist F.W.A. Sertürner. It is named for Morpheus, the Greek god of dreams, and I can testify that that is most appropriate. Morphine has a nocturnal, delusional quality that had colored every aspect of my life since it first swam upstream in my veins.

Though the primary use of morphine is to alleviate pain, it can also relieve fear and anxiety, decrease hunger, and produce euphoria. Whenever I injected, it flooded my body with a divine sweetness that made life bearable. Morphine also decreased my sexual drive, which, while perhaps not a desirable side effect for most, was a godsend for a man who lacks a penis but retains the ability to produce testosterone. As a negative, however, I was constantly constipated.

But what the morphine really did for me—its absolutely most vital function—was keep the snake silent, at least for a while.

When I first came to live with Marianne Engel, I was taking about one thousand milligrams a day. Over time my dosage had crept up with my tolerance and towards the end, I was taking that amount, times four.

XXIX.

YOU KNOW WHERE YOU ARE, DON'T YOU?

The blackness and my awareness arrived together. I was instantly awake, my eyes peeled wide, but I could see nothing. I could feel by the quality of the air (moist, massive) that I was in a constricted place. The atmosphere was almost too heavy for breathing, with the scent of rotting wood, and I was on my back. A feeling of smothered panic lay on top of me.

I AM HERE.

I could hear—no, *feel*—the glee in the snake's voice; she was happier in my spine than she had ever been. The morphine had been keeping her in check but now, in this place, that protection had been lifted. The snake thrashed in celebration.

THERE IS NOTHING YOU CAN DO ABOUT IT.

I tried to extend my arms but my hands met a barrier on all sides, only inches away. Flat, smooth wood. A few feet across; a few feet deep; the length of my body. *For a human, there is only one box of this size.*

YOU ARE IN A COFFIN.

This was not real. I tried to remember everything I'd learned about morphine withdrawal, because that was the reality of my situation, not this imagined tomb. I had studied, like the student who

prays the test will be canceled, about the weaning from the addiction. Cold-turkeying off morphine is not life-threatening, as it is with
some other drugs, but it can result in strange visions. Clearly, this
was one of them.

There were so many reasons that this could not be real. How
could I have been taken from the bedroom and buried without waking? If the wood of the coffin was already rotting, how could I have
been underground that long? How could there still be oxygen? All
this was impossible; therefore, I was hallucinating.

But are people who hallucinate rational enough to realize it?
Aren't hallucinations supposed to be, by definition, irrational? I didn't
feel as if I'd lost touch with reality; in fact, this felt too much like reality. Do hallucinating people note air quality? Do they think about
how long it takes before the wood of a coffin gives out, or how long
before the worms find their way in? If I was really in withdrawal,
why was I not craving my drug? So although I *knew* this experience
couldn't be real, I had to wonder why I was asking such logical questions.

It was not long before I discovered that withdrawing addicts lose
their composure in exactly the same manner that careless million-
aires lose their money: gradually, then suddenly. After careful consideration, I instantly lost all control in what can best be called the
opposite of an epiphany: instead of my thoughts coming together
in a moment of clarity, they bolted from the center of my mind like
victims trying to escape the epicenter of a disaster.

Although there was clearly no room for leverage, I threw my fists
around frantically, pounding at the wood weighted down with six
feet of dirt. I clawed until my fingernails peeled back and screamed
until my throat was emptied of all hope. I had believed, in the hospital, waiting for the next débridement session, that I knew fear. But
that was bullshit; I'd known nothing. To wake alive in a coffin and
know you're waiting for the end? *That's* fear.

My hysterical little rebellion proved useless, of course. So I
stopped. Even if I somehow managed to break through the wood, it

would not change the fact of my death, only the means: rather than be killed by lack of oxygen, I'd be suffocated by the dirt that stormed the coffin. As hungry as I was for air, the earth is always more ravenous. And so, a hush fell on my box like a cadaver's blanket. With nothing to do but wait, I made the decision to be dignified.

My breath echoed, as if the coffin were a shabby little concert hall. I decided I would listen until I could listen no more, and then the very last, soft note of my final breath would trail out into the dark. I'd go gently, I promised myself, because I'd already—given the severity of my accident—managed to live much longer than I should have.

Then I realized how incredibly foolish this was, all this thinking about dying in a hallucination. No problem. Steady. What had I taught Marianne Engel in Germany? *It's all about the breathing. You steady the weapon by slowing your breathing. In, out, in, out. Steady. Calm.* I am the weapon, I told myself; a weapon of living, forged in fire, and unstoppable.

And then. I felt. Something. And this something can only be described by a word I don't want to use: a new-age, stupid word that I must bring into play because, unfortunately, it is the only correct word. I felt a *presence*. And it was right beside me. A woman. I don't know how I knew it was a woman, but it was. It was not Marianne Engel, because the breathing was wrong. I hadn't realized until that moment that I could identify her by the cadence of her breathing, but I could, and this wasn't her. It occurred to me that perhaps the breath was coming from the snake. Perhaps the bitch had finally exited my spine for a direct confrontation. After all, you can only talk behind someone's back for so long.

But no, it was a human body calmly lying beside me. Which was ridiculous, because there was no room in the coffin—the imaginary coffin—for anyone else. Still, just in case, I snuggled against the wall on my side. Her breathing was relaxed, which somehow made it even more frightening.

A hand touched mine. I jerked away. I was surprised that I could feel her flesh; I had assumed this entity was immaterial. Her fingers were tiny but she was still able to force her hand into mine.

I tried to sound courageous while demanding to know who she was, but my voice broke. No answer. There was only the continuation of her breathing. Again: "Who are you?"

Her fingers gripped a bit tighter, intertwining with mine. I asked another question. "What are you doing here?"

There was still only the sound of her soft, relaxed breath. With every question she did not answer, I became a little less afraid. The way she clutched my hand was no longer menacing, but comforting, and soon I could feel myself lifting, almost—no, not almost: *definitely*—floating. My back began to lift away from the wood on which I lay.

I felt like a levitating assistant whose hand was being held by the magician. I felt us moving through the lid of the coffin, and then we were traveling up through the soil. An orange glow spread across the insides of my eyelids as we got closer to the surface, and I was not even sure whether I was still breathing.

I felt the tug of earth as I broke into the sunlight, and the color exploded. I was lifted upwards, a few inches above the surface of the ground. Soil trailed off my chest and I could feel it trickle down my ribs, falling from my sides. I was floating in the air unsupported; the woman did not break the grave's surface with me. Only her hand came through, connecting me to the earth like a balloon on a string. Her hand held mine for perhaps a few seconds before it let go and was pulled back into the grave. It was then that I realized that she could not leave: she had not been a visitor to my coffin, I had been a visitor to hers.

My body settled onto the mound of dirt. My eyes adjusted to the light. I was on a mountain and I could hear a river nearby. It was peaceful, just for a moment, until the ground beneath me started to move once more. For a panicked instant, I was worried that the silent woman had decided to pull me back down, but this was not what was happening. On all sides of me a hundred little eruptions began, like burrowing animals clawing their way out of the soil.

There were, at first, only glints in the light. But then shapes began to emerge: flowers, with colorless petals. When I looked closer, I could see that they were made of glass. Lilies. Blooming everywhere were a thousand glass lilies, glowing with pulses of light that seemed to come from within.

I reached out to pluck one. As soon as I touched it, it froze under my finger. Turning from glass into ice, all the thousands of flowers—as if they were connected by one soul—began to shatter in tiny explosions. With each came the release of a single word, in a woman's whisper, and together they fashioned a symphony that sounded like pure love. *Aishiteru, aishiteru, aishiteru.*

The bursting lilies raced down the mountain like dominoes detonating their way to the horizon. Underneath the joyous blanket of *Aishiteru* in the sky, the mountain itself shook and trembled and fell, flattening itself into tundra that unfolded everywhere. Just moments after it began, all around me the frozen shards of flower had become a field of ice that extended as far as my eyes could see.

I stared into this vast icy wilderness and it stared mercilessly right back at me. The arctic wind whipped hard against my shaking body. I was now completely aware that I was naked, save for the angel coin necklace that never left my neck.

The grave was gone—naturally, now that the entire mountain had disappeared—but there was a simple robe lying where it had been. When I picked up the garment to measure it against my body, flecks of dirt fell from it and were carried away by the powdery ballet of the blowing wind. The robe was much too small but because it was all I had, I put it on. I looked as ridiculous as you might imagine a burnt man in a tiny woman's garment would look, but when you're freezing there's little profit in worrying about fashion sense.

The robe was the same one that I had seen on the Japanese

woman at the Halloween party. Without a doubt it, and the grave it had come out of, had belonged to Sei.

• • •

The gleaming bleakness of this new world engulfed me. How complete was my change of venue: from the smallest and blackest space I could imagine, to the widest and whitest. For miles around I was the tallest object, enormous simply by virtue of possessing legs upon which to stand, and yet I felt dwarfed by the immensity of the sky. To stand on tundra is to feel concurrently grand and inconsequential.

The thin robe was little protection against the cold, and the wind cut to my marrow. Something moved at the edge of my vision. I was already developing snow blindness, but I squinted to confirm the sight: a trudging bulk outlined against the vicious blankness. The figure seemed to be coming towards me, but it was hard to tell on such a flat surface. I headed towards it. Whatever it was, it couldn't be any worse than standing still, awaiting hypothermia.

After some time I realized that the object moving towards me was a man. He must help me, I thought, for to not help me would be to kill me. The first detail I could make out was his thick red locks, which stood out against the snow like bloodstains on a bedsheet. Next I could see that he was wrapped in heavy furs and wore thick boots. His pants were thickly strapped leather and his coat was an animal thing. Over his shoulder, he seemed to be carrying a parcel of pelts. Puffs of steam exited his mouth. Ice frosted his beard. He was close now. Deep creases lined the corners of his eyes and he looked older than I believe he actually was.

When he arrived in front of me, he held out the package he'd been carrying on his shoulder and said, *"Farðu í þetta."* I understood what this meant: *You will put these on.*

I unwrapped the package to find a full set of clothing, thick skins with fur that would protect me. I pulled them on as quickly as I could, and soon I felt the air between my body and the material starting to warm. *"Hvað heitir þú?"* *What is your name?* I was shocked to hear Icelandic out of my mouth as well.

"I am Sigurðr Sigurðsson, and you will come with me." His answer confirmed the identity that I had guessed; but only hesitantly, because here—wherever *here* was—Sigurðr was unburned despite the way his life had ended. Which made me wonder why my body was still damaged.

"Where are we going?" I asked.

"I don't know."

"When will we get there?"

"I don't know." He squinted against the horizon. "I've been traveling a long time. I must be getting close."

Around his waist Sigurðr wore a scabbard, the same one that had been clanging against Sei's hips when they were dancing. He extracted Sigurðrsnautr by its serpent handle, and handed over his belt and sheath. "Put this on. You'll need it."

I asked why. He answered that he didn't know.

I threw away Sei's robe, thinking it useless now that I had the skins. Sigurðr picked it up and handed it back to me. "In Hel, you must use everything that you have."

I twisted the robe around my waist, as a second belt above the one that Sigurðr had just given me. I asked him how he could tell in which direction we should head.

"I don't know," he answered. Sigurðr was quite a conversationalist. He used his sword as a walking stick, the blade cutting into the snow with each step. For a man who didn't know where he was going, he took very resolute strides.

"Is this a hallucination?" It struck me as supremely odd to be in a hallucination, asking whether it was a hallucination, in a language that I didn't understand. (In fact, how many people in the entire world know the Icelandic word for "hallucination" is *ofskynjun?*)

Sigurðr answered that he didn't think it was an *ofskynjun,* but couldn't be positive.

We walked. And walked. And walked. For days, but the sun never set. Perhaps you think this an exaggeration, that I really mean we walked for hours, which seemed like days. But no, I mean days. We traveled in constant fatigue but we never came to the point of needing sleep, and despite my bad knee, I felt I could continue indefinitely. I thought of the places in the farthest northern reaches of the world where the sun remains in the sky for six months at a time. Would we have to march that long?

Sigurðr remained a man of few, and confused, words; for the most part, the only sound that came from his body was a slightly musical clacking from under his pelts, around his neck. After a while I stopped talking to him, except to try to make him laugh. I never succeeded. Sometimes I stopped walking simply to break the monotony. I would beg Sigurðr to wait for just a minute but he would always state that there was no time for rest. When I asked why, he would answer, "Because we need to get there."

When I asked Sigurðr where "there" was, he didn't know. So I told him that, given the fact he didn't know, I could see no reason to continue to follow him. He would snort, say that I was allowed to make this stupid decision, and continue walking without me. Just when he was about to disappear from view, I'd take off after him in a hobbling run. Because of course I needed him—what would I do in this place alone? And so we plodded ever onwards, heading to the place that he couldn't define and I couldn't imagine.

Hallucinations should be better than this, I thought. Walking the tundra for days is boring and I was surprised I could hallucinate anything that mundane, for that long. The cold was too piercing; the patterns of snow were too perfectly random in their swirls; and my tiredness ached too honestly to be imagined. The only thing that didn't seem realistic was my ability to continue with neither rest nor food.

Of course it was a delusion. A damn fine, cold, protracted hallucination. Withdrawal should not be like this. Unless . . .

"Sigurðr, did I die?"

He finally laughed. "You're just a visitor here."

If this place was Sigurðr's, as the coffin had been Sei's, I wanted to know more about it. About everything. I decided to abandon all subtlety. "That sound coming from around your neck—is it made by the treasure necklace that once belonged to Svanhildr?"

He stopped walking, perhaps deciding whether to confirm. He did: "Yes."

"Do you have the arrowhead necklace, too?"

"That went to Friðleifr."

"His name was changed to Sigurðr, you know."

He didn't say anything for a few moments, until he answered in the softest voice I had heard him use. "Yes, I am aware. It was a great honor."

"Will you tell me about Einarr?"

The question made him restart his stride. "That story is not for you."

"I've already heard it."

Sigurðr turned and leveled his eyes at me. "No. You've heard Marianne's version of my story, which is a different thing. How do you dare to think you know my heart, when you don't even understand your own?"

Leave it to a Viking to disarm you with eloquence when you least expect it. I shut up and started walking again.

I kept thinking that something was just ahead, but nothing ever was. I kept thinking that we'd encounter a ridge overlooking a valley, or moss sprouting out of granite crests, but each "ridge" was nothing more than the current horizon being replaced by a new horizon. I prayed for anything to break the monotony. A boulder. A moose's hoof print. A frozen sled dog. A man's name pissed into the snow with swooping yellow letters. But we encountered only more ice,

more snow. On the third day (I think it was the third), I just stopped.
Gave up.

"There's nothing out there. Whatever you think you'll find . . ."
My voice trailed away. "Sigurðr, you've been going 'there' for more
than a thousand years, and you don't even know where there is."

"You travel until you arrive," he said, "and you have now come
far enough."

This place was absolutely no different from any other place on
the tundra. I spun around in all directions, throwing my arms about
to emphasize this point. "What are you talking about?"

"Look into the sky."

My eyes went up. Despite the fact that no one was within miles,
a single flaming arrow was arching directly towards me.

I wanted to move but was frozen to the spot, my only reaction
to cover my head with my hands. (Although, after hearing all of
Marianne Engel's stories, a more logical decision would probably
have been to cover my heart.) The arrow missed me by a few inches,
striking the ground, and the earth broke open like an albino monster
unhinging its jaw. Huge segments of ice lifted and twisted, throwing
us wildly around. A large chunk hit my right shoulder, sending me
bouncing into another ragged block. There was a moment of clarity,
similar to that moment when I'd driven over the cliff, in which everything slowed as I watched it unfold. Water languidly erupted from
a crack in the ground, and I finally understood why there had been
nothing to distinguish the landscape in all the time that we'd been
walking. We had not been on land at all, but on a massive sheet of
ice. Frozen slabs pirouetted around me and soon I found that gravity
was pulling me into the newly uncovered sea.

An immediate chill cut through me completely. My pelts were
useless; worse than useless, actually, because they absorbed water
and started to pull me down. At first I was able to claw my way along
the bobbing ice at the surface, digging my fingers into any cracks I
could find. I felt the warmth of my body suck itself into the core of
my stomach, but soon the heat was not safe even there. I could feel

my movements slow, and my teeth were clattering so violently that they drowned out the cracking of the ice around me; I wondered whether even my keloid scars were turning blue.

Sigurðr was nowhere to be seen. He must have been swallowed amid the bobbing ice. A block brushed up against the left side of my body and another smacked at my back. They were circling around me, closing in and pushing me down. Any scientist will explain that broken ice redistributes evenly on the surface of the water, and this is what it was doing in an attempt to cover the hole that the arrow had opened. So even in a hallucinatory ocean the basic laws of physics still seemed to apply; this, no doubt, would have brought a smile to Galileo's face.

I could no longer hold my head above water, the ice tap-tap-tapping against my cauliflower ears, and I closed my eyes because this is what one does when going under. I felt my body shut down. *So this is how it ends. In water.* I slipped under, and actually felt some relief. *It'll be easier this way.*

I had no trouble holding my breath for many minutes, dropping the entire time, until I tired of waiting for my lungs to give out. I opened my eyes, expecting that I would not be able to see more than a few feet. Just as it had been difficult to gauge distance above the ice, so it was underneath: once again there was nothing to supply perspective. No fish, no other creatures, no weeds, only clear water. Bubbles escaped from the folds of my clothing and rolled up along my body until they caught at the corners of my eyelids. Funny. In the real world I couldn't produce tears of water, but in an underwater world I could produce tears made of air.

A glow emerged, above me, in the distance. It refracted through my bubble tears and I wondered, *Is this the corridor of light that leads a dead man to Heaven?* Not bloody likely. The way things were going, it was probably one of those saber-toothed fishes that uses dangling phosphorescent flaps of skin to lure in other animals to eat. As it turned out, however, the glow was neither the path to Heaven nor a Machiavellian fish. It was the fire of the burning arrow that had crashed into the ice, now clenched in one of Sigurðr's hands as he came plunging through the ocean towards me.

The light (a fire that doesn't extinguish in water: so much for natural physics still applying in a supernatural place) played across Sigurðr's beard and into the creases around his eyes. His long red hair stretched out around his head like a glowing kelp halo, and he was smiling serenely, as if something wonderful were happening. He held out the arrow like an Olympian passing the torch and, all the while, we continued our slow descent through the water. My fingers closed around the shaft, I felt glorious warmth spread through my body, and Sigurðr smiled like a man who had done his job. Like a man who would continue to be remembered. He nodded his approval and plunged far below, leaving me to continue falling liquidly alone.

I fell through the bottom of the ocean.

I dropped only a few feet before I hit the ground. When I looked up, the floor of the ocean—the water that should have been a ceiling above me—was gone. My feet were on solid matter and the light had changed from the ocean's crystal blue to a dead gray.

I was now in a dark wood of twisted trees.

• • •

I heard the scurrying patter of feet across the forest floor, coming from at least three sides. Twigs snapping, brush rustling. I held up the arrow to use as a torch. The flash of a four-footed animal sliding among the tree trunks, then a glimpse of another creature. How many were there? Two—no, there went another! Three, at least! What were they? My mind ran wild with bestial imaginings: a lion, a leopard, perhaps a wolf. If they came for me, how could I protect myself? I had the Viking's scabbard, but not the sword; I had the Buddhist's robe, but not the faith.

Directly ahead was a path that led through the forest, over a small hill, and I could hear the approach of another, bolder animal. There, a hint of it through the trees. It appeared bipedal, so perhaps some sort of fabulous forest ape? Apparently not. When it came around the corner, I could see that it was a man, dressed in simple clothing, with a large stomach and stubble on his cheeks. When he saw me, a broad smile spread across his face and he lifted his arms out as if preparing to embrace an old friend after years apart. "Ciao!"

"*Tu devi essere Francesco.*" *You must be Francesco.* With Sigurðr, I had known Icelandic; with this one, I understood Italian.

"*Sì,*" he confirmed, taking my hand. "*Il piacere è mio.*"

"No, the pleasure is mine. A mutual friend has shown me some of your work. It's good."

"Ah, Marianna!" Francesco beamed. "But I'm just a simple craftsman. I see you've brought the arrow. Good. You might need that."

"What do we do now? Please don't say that you don't know."

Francesco laughed until his bear's belly shook. "Sigurðr's always been a little confused, but I know exactly where we're going." He paused for effect. "Straight into Hell."

You have to appreciate a man who can say such a thing with a straight face, and I couldn't help but laugh. "Well, I think I'm getting used to that, anyways."

"This Hell will be more complex, so you'd be wise not to laugh too hard." But, to reassure me after his warning, he added, "I've been sent to lead you, at Marianna's request. She came with prayers for you."

"I guess that's a start." And so we set off on our infernal quest. I was armed with a flaming arrow, a Buddhist robe tied around my waist, a Viking snowsuit, and an empty scabbard, and I had a fourteenth-century metalworker as my guide. I couldn't have been more prepared.

• • •

We passed through a set of gates, and soon we were standing in front of a river that I recognized from Marianne Engel's bedside readings. "Acheron."

The river was a terrible thing, with ice bobbing amid garbage and misshapen beasts. There were rotting chunks of flesh, as if a thousand years of coffins had been emptied into congealing blood. The fetid perfume of decay permeated everything. There were almost-men, only somewhat human in shape, floundering in the horrible liquid. Shouts for mercy were thrown out of pleading mouths; I knew that these creatures would continue drowning, unaided, forever.

A mist rose from the river. Through it floated, so calmly as if to seem above the currents, a boat carrying the ferryman Charon. It/he was a dark man-creature, at least eight feet tall, in a ripped, molding robe. His beard was like knotted seaweed and his nose was only half there, with bite marks where the rest must have been ripped off in a battle. From his shriveled mouth jutted rotten teeth, jagged and broken. His skin was gray, wet, and leathery, like that of a diseased sea turtle, and his hands were arthritic claws that held a gnarled wooden pole. His eye sockets were empty but for the blaze within: each eye was a wheel of fire. As he steered towards the shore, he blasted out words more like thunder than speech. "THIS ONE IS NOT DEAD."

While no small man, Francesco looked feeble compared to Charon. Nonetheless, he refused to be bowed and drew up to his full height to reply, "This is a most special case."

Charon, now landed at the bank, swept his talons in a dismissive motion. "THIS ONE CANNOT CROSS."

"He has come far already, so please hear us. Allow us this courtesy, we who are so much less than you. How long has it been since you were visited by one of the living?"

"LABOR NOT TO TRICK ME. HE IS NOT TO CROSS HERE. ANOTHER CRAFT THAN MINE MUST GIVE PASSAGE."

"Charon, be not so quick with your dismissal," my guide said. "Forces greater than we have set this voyage into motion."

Charon's eyes upon me felt like a condemnation, as if he were looking into the most ignoble corners of my soul. I held the flaming arrow so close to my body that I feared my clothes might go up in flames, but I needed the warmth against his stare.

Charon turned his attention back to Francesco. "YOU MAY SPEAK MORE."

"We request that you allow us to cross. We've brought payment." Francesco bowed slightly and held out a gold coin.

"THIS IS PAYMENT FOR ONE."

"Of course, you are correct." When Francesco beckoned to me to step forward, I shook my head. *Who brings money to a hallucination?* And then Francesco tapped his chest, to remind me of what was hanging on mine.

I removed the angel coin from my necklace and passed it over into Charon's claw. He paid particular attention to the side that depicted the Archangel Michael killing the dragon. A strange expression crossed the boatman's face; I got the feeling it was as close to a smile as his ugly mouth could manage. He stepped to one side and swept an arm to indicate that we were invited to board. Francesco nodded. "We deeply appreciate your generosity."

The ferryman dipped his pole into the foul water and sent us into the middle of Acheron. The boat, adorned with skulls and ropes of human hair, was constructed of rotten wood, and yet no water entered the gaping breaches in the bow. Small whirlpools folded in upon themselves everywhere, dragging down the perpetually drowning bodies. Occasionally, Charon would use his oar to flail at one of the sinners.

Two figures in the distance, clawing their way ever closer to the ferry, looked strangely familiar. A man and a woman. But my attention was diverted by a screaming man, only feet from the boat. He gulped in a mouthful of the rancid river as others sinners pulled him under. He grabbed at anything in his reach and took a severed leg down with him.

Seeing the look of revulsion on my face, Francesco said, "None are here by accident. Hell is a choice because salvation is available to anyone who seeks it. The damned choose their fates, by deliberately hardening their hearts."

I couldn't agree. "No one would choose to be damned."

Francesco shook his head. "But it is so easy not to be."

The couple was now close enough that I was certain (as I could be, that is, given their bodies' decay) that they were Debi and Dwayne Michael Grace. They were pleading for my help, reaching their hands—full of broken fingers—towards me. But the horde of sinners grabbed relentlessly at them. Debi might have been able to reach the ferry, if Dwayne had not clutched at her frantically in an effort not to be yanked under. She responded in kind; each tried to use the other for leverage to push up and away from the multitude. Their battling against each other only ensured they went down to-gether.

It did not take long before Charon dropped us at the other side and steered his boat back into the fray. "I think I did quite well," I said, trying and failing to smile. "Didn't Dante faint when he met Charon?"

• • •

A mountain stood in front of us, rising from Acheron's shore, and Francesco took the lead.

The pitch was gradual at the beginning but soon cut sharply up. It became necessary to wedge our hands into cracks wherever we could find them. This was not easy with my missing fingers, and I had to pass the burning arrow from hand to hand each time I shifted my body. The higher we went, the harder the damp winds blew.

Francesco advised me to tuck the arrow into Sigurðr's scabbard.

I didn't see this as a very good plan; I was quite sure my animal pelts were not fire retardant. Nevertheless, I did as I was told. There was a slight tickling along my hip where the flames danced, but my clothes did not burn.

Human forms were carried in the gale around us, jerked about like struggling fish caught on lines. I knew who they were: the souls of the Carnal, swept up by their passion on Earth and so doomed in Hell. I considered my own career as a pornographer, which didn't bode well. I asked Francesco if this was where I would end up, someday.

"You never knew passion," Francesco yelled back, "until you met her."

He didn't need to say her name; we both knew about whom he was talking.

I tried to ignore the howling, both wind and human, and eventually we passed through the worst. When I was finally able to let go of the cliff's wall, my fingers remained curled like the pincers of a frightened lobster.

• • •

The path opened off the mountain and we entered into a place that was hotter. I cupped my hands around the arrow's flame and my fingers finally started to uncurl; as soon as I was able, I began to peel away the outer pelts of my Viking clothing. Remembering Sigurðr's advice, I did not discard them.

As I bundled up the furs to carry them, I noticed that my amputated fingers were slightly longer at their nubs and there was some hair growing out of my forearms where the follicles had been destroyed. I touched my skull and found that new stubble was emerging there as well. My scars were perhaps a little less thick, a little less red. I'd run my fingers over my body a million times, like a blind man memorizing a story in Braille, but now I was reading a different plot.

Try to imagine, if you can, the emotions of a burnt man discovering that his body is regenerating, or of the man growing hair after having resigned himself to a lifetime of beef-jerky baldness. I excitedly informed Francesco of my discoveries.

"Remember where you are," he warned, "and remember who you are."

We came to the edge of a forest where screaming trees grew out of burning sands. A shimmering heat rose, distorting everything, and the tree limbs looked as if they were moving. Birds flew around, snapping at the branches. "The Wood of Suicides," Francesco said.

I soon realized that the trees were not exactly trees. The branches were human limbs, gesticulating wildly, with blood running out like sap. Tormented human voices poured out from the holes that had been ripped by the birds—which were not birds, I could see now, but Harpies that resembled vultures with pale female faces and claws as sharp as razors. Their stench overwhelmed us every time one flew anywhere near.

"The voices from the trees," Francesco said, "can only come forth after the Harpies have ripped their flesh and their blood is flowing. Suicides can only express themselves through that which destroys them."

"*Quod me nutrit, me destruit,*" I muttered under my breath, too low for Francesco to hear.

I remembered then that he had deliberately inhaled his wife's plague before commanding his brother to shoot him through with an arrow. "Is this what Hell is like for you?"

"My choice to die came within hours of my inevitable death, and it was a decision made with love, not cowardice. An important distinction to remember." He paused for a moment, then added, "Although my afterlife is not this one, there is a reason that I am your guide here."

I thought he was going to say more, but he only told me that we still had a great distance to travel.

I was now stripped to the waist. My skin was definitely improving. We continued through the woods and I heard what seemed, at first, to be the murmur of a throbbing beehive. As we came closer, I realized that it was a waterfall at the wood's edge. The rushing wind swept back our hair, mine still growing.

This waterfall did not fall over the edge of any cliff; it just dropped straight down from the sky and cut through the desert floor in front of us. Francesco indicated that I needed to throw Sigurðr's scabbard into the waterfall, as it would make an appropriate gift. *Why? And for whom?*

After removing the flaming arrow, I did as instructed. I watched the leather loop of the belt tumble down, bouncing in the froth, before being finally swallowed into the angry mouth at the bottom of the waterfall.

Almost immediately, a dark figure emerged and started climbing towards us.

• • •

This creature was three united bodies working together from a single torso. It had six gangly arms, whose six hairy hands reached into the waterfall to secure handholds, and it moved like a spider climbing a web. At first I thought there must have been some rock behind the waterfall but as it came closer, I could see its hands were wrapping around the liquid itself, twisting the streams of water into something like ropes. The beast had a sharp tail that cut into the waterfall, and though it was still some distance away, its smell already reminded me of piles of decaying mayflies on a beach.

"Geryon," Francesco said, "who was once a king in Spain but is now the monster of fraud. It's the guardian of this waterfall, and is the one who must deliver us into the pit."

When Geryon reached ground level, its six legs pushed against the stream and it catapulted towards us, making a perfect six-point landing.

It was a large thing (as most things in Hell seemed to be), its torso littered with shiny scales. Its three heads were about six feet above my single one. Each face had similar features: all were lumpy with great welts, large lips that held rotting teeth, and eyes like black pearls housed in half-opened shells. Still, despite their ugliness, the faces seemed to be without deceit. All three heads began to speak at once.

"whAt do you . . ."

"why Are you . . ."

"how dAre you . . ."

". . . WANT?"

". . . here?"

". . . disturb me?"

"We wish to enter the next circle," Francesco answered.

"No, it cANNot . . ."

"we will Not . . ."

"this oNe . . ."

". . . be doNe!"

". . . help you!"

". . . is Not deAd!"

"It is true that we ask a great deal, and it is true that this one is not dead," Francesco admitted. "But he is a friend of Marianna Engel."

The name seemed to mean something to Geryon and the three heads muttered amongst themselves. Eventually, they took a vote— "yes. No. yes"—before deciding to take us. (Who would have guessed that the monster of fraud was a democracy?) It turned so that we might climb onto its broad back. Francesco ushered me up first, whispering, "I'll ride between you and the tail. It's poison-ous."

When we were settled, the beast took a robust leap from land's edge towards the waterfall. When we hit the water, I saw Geryon's hands plunge into the liquid and grasp the fluid that flowed through its fists like translucent snakes. While it was difficult to keep my grip,

I noticed that my arms were stronger than they had been since my accident. At one point Geryon's three heads said, "ΝΟΤ . . . SΟ . . . ΤΙGΗΤ."

As we neared the bottom, Francesco called out over the water's roar, warning me to prepare for the next level. It would be, he said with a tone that forced me to take note, particularly unpleasant.

. . .

We dismounted and Geryon disappeared back into the waterfall. I took stock of exactly how far my healing had progressed. Most of my skin was smooth, and the pancreatitis scar that had adorned my stomach was gone. Nearly all of my hair had regrown. My lips were once again full. I bounced on my shattered knee and found it strong. My lost fingers were more than half recovered and I used them to rub, at the juncture of my legs, the small nub of my emerging cock.

"We are now in Malebolge, home of the Seducers. In this Circle," Francesco advised, "I am useless to protect you."

I could hear what sounded like gunshots and crying voices, coming ever closer. Soon they were upon us: men and women in an endless line being driven by horned demons. What I'd thought were shots were actually the cracks of the demons' flaming whips, brought down repeatedly with merciless precision. The seducers were hunchbacked in fear, curling their bodies to stave off the thrashing for an extra half-second. Their arms hung limply, only jerking upwards in their sockets each time the whip connected. Perhaps the seducers had once been of great beauty, but they were no longer; now, they were little more than lumps of well-beaten flesh.

The woman closest to me was struck and blood jumped out of her mouth. When I gasped, she was alerted to our presence. She looked up and I saw that much of her face had been eaten away by maggots. Her right eye looked like a bulging egg and her left one dangled an inch out of the socket on the optical nerve. With her egg-eye, she winked at me lasciviously, and she licked her lips. For this she was whipped to the ground by a legion of demons that didn't let up even as she lay writhing in agony. Her skin opened in crisscrossing patterns until she was practically spilling out of herself. Dozens of snakes emerged from holes in the ground, twisting up her like chains upon an escape artist.

After she was tightly serpentbound, more snakes—different snakes, with oversized fangs dripping with venom—appeared from the holes and began to roll merrily over her. Eventually a cobra took a position above the seductress's face, pausing only a moment before it dove down to attack the mongoose of her neck. Spurts of blood cascaded into the air before showering down upon her body, each drop erupting into a tiny bead of fire. Flames quickly engulfed her, and her bulbous eye swelled until it burst like an overfilled balloon. She screamed until her vocal cords were incinerated; all the while, the serpents remained lashed around her body. Her flesh fell away, like tender meat, to expose the skeleton within. Her bones glowed yellow, then red, then black, before finally crumbling into the earth. She disappeared this way, into nothingness—except for what should have been her spine.

Her spine was not a spine; her spine was a snake that looked directly at me from its nest of ash. It flashed a dastardly, reptilian smile, and hissed: `AND THERE IS NOTHING YOU CAN DO ABOUT IT.`

The snake continued joyfully leering at me even as it began to tremble and new ribs burst forth from its sides like fingers breaking through tightly stretched plastic. Next, arm and leg bones emerged. The ashes of the incinerated sinner began to reconstruct into human tissue, first sifting into intestines, and then weaving into a new circulatory system. Red liquid flowed up out of the ground to enter the new vessels. Muscles twisted around the bones like ivy growing over a fence, and skin pulled up out of the soil like a blanket which tensed itself over the sinewy form. Hair sprouted and new eyeballs gelled in the sockets. The seductress was rebuilt, not into the beaten form I'd first seen, but as she must have looked upon the Earth. She was as physically beautiful as any woman I had ever seen.

She rose from the ground and took a step towards me, her arms held out for an embrace. How alluring she was, with her soft skin and pleasing hips. The demons, who had been tending the other seducers and only now noticed that her rebirth was complete, set upon her again with their whips before she could reach me. She was shepherded back into the procession of sinners and the cycle was made clear to me: she would once again be beaten into pulp, she would once again be bound by the snakes, and she would once again be disintegrated by the fire. It would be repeated over and over, for eternity, just as it would for all the others in this pageant of seducers.

I understood now why Francesco had warned me against this Circle, because it was during the rebirth of the seductress that the healing of my body finalized. The lava flow that was my skin had fully receded and there was no longer any indication that I'd ever been burned. My body was as perfect as it had been on my best day before the accident; the only mark that remained was the scar that I had been born with on my chest. I, like the seductress, had been restored as fully, beautifully human.

Though I didn't want to, I fell to my knees and started to cry. Once I started I could not stop.

To this day, I remain unsure of the true nature of my tears. Did I cry because the fate of the seductress so closely mirrored my own? Was it the cumulative effect of the horrors in the three Hells that I had experienced? Was it because I'd regained a human form that I had never dreamed would be mine again? Or was it because back in the real world, my body was deep within morphine withdrawal?

I don't know the answer. But eventually I continued to cry simply from joy that my tear ducts worked again.

• • •

Francesco clasped a gentle hand on my shoulder. "Styx lies ahead."

As disoriented as I was, I knew that something was amiss. After all, I'd heard the story of *Inferno* in two different lifetimes; I knew we were supposed to have encountered Styx earlier than this. Wiping dry my eyes, I told Francesco as much.

"But this is your journey," Francesco said, "not Dante's."

We moved towards the river's edge, where a boat was rapidly approaching, as if it knew we were coming. "The boatman is Phlegyas, son of Ares. When his daughter Coronis was raped by Apollo, Phlegyas set fire to the temple of the god. Apollo killed him with arrows and condemned him to this punishment."

The most striking thing about Phlegyas was the large, angular stone that floated above his fragile skull, looking as if it might drop at any moment. As a result, he constantly lifted his tormented eyes to appraise the situation. With every push of the pole in the water, the ship carried the boatman closer to us and the stone followed, never leaving its tenuous position. Phlegyas had become sallow from so long without sun; the veins of his face stood out like purple spiderwebs and his hair was falling out in stringy bunches. Spindly arms stuck out of his robes, which had long since been stained the color of sweat.

"Who is this, that dares bring an arrow to my shore?" Phlegyas' attempts to menace were nullified by his preoccupation with the stone above his head. Even as he attempted to glower, his eyes twitched upward with the rock's every little movement.

"You will have to forgive our foolish friend," Francesco said, "for he is young and still alive."

"That does explain much." Phlegyas nervously bobbed his head to the left, before allowing it to settle back to the center of his shoulders.

"Will you carry us across the water, so that he may finish his journey?"

"Why would I do that? This one is not dead."

Francesco began to speak. "He is a friend of—"

"Marianne Engel," Phlegyas cut him off. *"This matters not to me."*

The boatman pushed upon his pole to turn the boat around, but Francesco called out, "Much depends on your help, Phlegyas."

Intrigued, perhaps, Phlegyas turned his face back to us. *"And why is that?"*

"If you know Marianna, then you know this is a journey of love."

"What care I for love?"

"Was it not love for your daughter that brought you here? Would you doom another to likewise be trapped forever in Hell, where he does not belong?"

For the first time, Phlegyas seemed to pay more attention to me than to the rock. *"Tell me about your love for this woman."*

I answered as sincerely as I could. "I cannot."

Phlegyas furrowed his brow. *"Then why should I honor your request?"*

"Any man who believes he can describe love," I answered, "understands nothing about it."

This answer seemed to satisfy Phlegyas and he waved us aboard with no need of fare. As we crossed Styx, my eyes were fixed upon the three flaming red towers in the distance.

"Dis," Francesco said. "The capital of Hell."

We were let off at a set of enormous iron gates. These were guarded by the Rebellious Angels, whose dark and unsympathetic eyes looked as though they were judging everything. They were naked and sexless, and had glowing white skin beset by large boils; from their backs spanned molting wings and, instead of halos, they had flaming hair.

The leader of the Rebellious Angels stepped forward. "YOU CANNOT PASS. THIS ONE IS NOT DEAD."

"I get that a lot," I said.

Francesco shot me a dirty look before turning his attention back to the leader. "That he is living is not your concern. Those rules do not apply at this gate, because it is his fate to enter this door."

"AND WHO IS HE?"

"The one," Francesco answered, "who enters the Kingdom of Death in his life."

It did not matter, however, what he claimed as my identity. With great howling and activity, the Angels refused all that Francesco requested. It was clear that my guide had finally met a barrier through which he could not sweet-talk us.

We stepped away from the Angels to consult with each other. I asked what we could do now, and Francesco looked at me as though my question were exceedingly foolish.

"We will pray," he said.

When I answered that I did not pray, he sternly rebuked me. "You're in Hell. You'd better start."

Francesco took the burning arrow from my hand and plugged its tip into the ground, then laid out the Viking pelts for us to kneel on. Next, he took Sei's robe from around my waist and promptly began to rip it apart. He wrapped a long, thin strand of fabric around my head until my vision was completely obscured. When I heard the sounds of more wrapping, I assumed that he was covering his own face.

"There will soon be things at which we cannot look," he said. "Even under the mask, keep your eyes shut tightly."

It was the first time in my life that I had ever prayed and it felt unnatural, but after all that Francesco had done for me, the least I could do was honor his request. I could hear Francesco's words, whispered in Italian, as he praised God and asked for guidance. For my part, I prayed for my withdrawal to end. And for the safety of Marianne Engel, wherever she was.

I heard the approach of footsteps and a flickering of something in the air. It came closer, closer . . .

"Do not look," Francesco commanded. "They have called upon Medusa."

And then I realized the source of the flickering sounds: they were made by the tongues of the snakes of her hair. They were thrusting out to smell me, the first living meat to visit Hell in ages, and then a serpent's tongue tentatively licked my cheek. Then another, and another, and another. My skin, now healed, was fully capable of experiencing sensations again, and what a cruel joke that among them were the kisses of a hundred snakes. They tried to push their triangle heads underneath my blindfold, to lift it up, to make me look at the gorgon, but I held it in place.

Medusa, her face but a few inches in front of mine, began to hiss. Her rancid breath was upon me and I could imagine her own serpentine tongue. *"Look. Look at me. You know that you want to. Thiss iss but a fantassy. Will you leave without taking all your dream hass to offer? I will only ssssatisfy your curiosssity. . . ."*

I knew better. If ever I were to become a statue, it would be by the hand of Marianne Engel rather than the stare of the gorgon.

A quiver began underneath my feet, like a fledgling earthquake. I could feel the snakes of Medusa's hair pull away from my face. The shuddering of the earth continued to grow and soon the very air was trembling, as if splitting open to admit something new. The iron gates around Dis clattered as if a wild beast were rattling to get out, and the Rebellious Angels yelped a series of excited bleats. I felt Medusa pull away, and heard her footsteps in a hasty retreat. I thought it might be a trick and asked Francesco if she was really gone.

"I think so, but remain vigilant. It's best to keep your blindfold on."

I could hear the branches breaking from the dead trees, and the dust being stirred up from the ground caused me to cough. "What's happening?"

"I prayed that a Divine Messenger come," Francesco answered, "but I hesitate to believe that the appeals of one as unworthy as I would be answered."

Though Medusa might still be lurking, I could not help but remove my blindfold. After all, how often is one given the chance to see a Divine Messenger? The sky, which had been uniformly dark since our entry, now looked as though God had accidentally knocked over the palette of Heaven and every wondrous blush of Existence was plunging from above. On the forward cusp of the colors, with golden streaks trailing behind him, was the most beautiful Being that I've ever seen.

Apparently, and despite his own advice, neither could Francesco allow the opportunity to pass untaken. He had removed his mask and was trying not to look directly at the Messenger, as if he wanted to show respect, but found himself unable to not stare. In a voice filled with awe, he said, "Clearly you are blessed."

I was too bedazzled to do anything more than repeat the word. "Blessed."

"Michael," Francesco whispered. "The Archangel."

Michael was perhaps seven feet tall and his hair flowed behind him like a wild blond river. From his back reached two immaculate wings with a span of at least fifteen feet, and he glided as though the wind existed only to carry his perfect body. His skin was as radiant as the brightest sunlight and his eyes were huge, flaming orbs. Although he shared this trait with Charon, the effect was exactly the opposite: while the boatman's eyes gave him a sinister look, Michael's eyes made his face too brilliant to gaze upon directly.

The Archangel landed softly in front of the gates of Dis. The Rebellious Angels, knowing better than to stand in the way, split to either side. The air danced in splendor everywhere around Michael, shimmering as if even it were too awed to touch him. I would describe the colors but there are no names for them; they do not exist within the spectrum of human vision. For the first time I understood how the world must look to the colorblind, because those colors made me feel as if I always had seen, until that moment, with but the tiniest fraction of my potential.

The ground upon which Michael stood was no longer the ashen muck of Hell, but more green than green. The charred trees that had loomed over us with barren limbs now bloomed with fresh leaves. Michael lifted his arm with impossible grace and the gate's sickly rust was thrown off instantly. When his finger simply grazed the gate, it flew open.

The Archangel turned towards us. Francesco lowered his head and made the sign of the cross. I kept my head up, my eyes focused. Unlike Francesco, because I had never longed to see the divine, I was not burdened with the fear of what might happen if I did.

Michael smiled.

I realized then, for the first time, that I was not hallucinating. I was indeed in Hell, and I was indeed in the presence of the Divine. It was beyond all doubt: I am far too human to imagine anything like that smile. It was like a kiss upon all my worst secrets, absolving them straight away.

With a single sweep of his wings, Michael took flight again, twisting like an immediate tornado that sprang up from the ground. Behind him trailed the colors that he had brought, sucking upwards to disappear in his wake. The too-green of the grass was replaced once again with the dull gray of mud. The health of the trees was leached out. The gates rusted over instantly, but were left open. The colors disappeared like bathwater running to the drain, except that the drain was in the sky. Where Michael disappeared, the last of the colors followed him through a tiny hole in Hell's awning.

When Francesco finally found his voice, after several stunned minutes, he said, "You must walk through the gates alone."

I shook Francesco's hand. It felt such an insufficient gesture, and I told him that I didn't know how to thank him.

"It is I," Francesco answered, "who must thank you. It was not only for Marianna that I took this task; it was also repayment."

"For what?"

"My father was an archer named Niccolò, who was killed while serving in a German condotta. But his friend Benedetto escaped with the help of two German archers, and he brought my father's crossbow to Firenze." Francesco, at this point, clasped my hands in his. "That bow was all I ever knew of my father."

"My copy of *Inferno* belonged to your father?"

"Yes. He would want you to have it." Francesco bowed deeply. "*Grazie.*"

• • •

The Rebellious Angels dared not stop me as I walked through the gates. I knew what I was supposed to find next: the Sixth Circle, the home of the Heretics, littered with graves and tombs ringed with fire. But the moment I walked through the gates, I found myself no longer in Francesco's Inferno. Instead, I emerged on a cliff overlooking an ocean. When I spun around to look behind me, the gates of Dis had disappeared.

Gulls cut over the water with happy squawks. The grass was tinged with cool dew and I could feel every blade tickle the skin of my feet. I was now entirely naked, my skin fully healed; the clothing that I had been wearing was gone, and I no longer had my coin necklace. It was dawn, the breeze cooled me, and I felt wonderfully alive.

Perhaps two hundred feet away on the cliff, a solitary figure stood motionless, looking out over the ocean. Of course I knew who it was. As I drew closer, I saw that she appeared to be in her mid-forties but that there was something infinitely older in her expression, as she squinted over the miles of water. Her hair was pinned to the back of her head, and her shawl was draped over her shoulders, held tightly closed at her bosom. Her dress was worn at the hem and there was dirt on her boots. I spoke her name. "Vicky."

"Yes." Her eyes never wavered from their nautical discipline.

"Do you see him?"

"I see him everywhere."

I looked out towards the horizon. There were no boats on the ocean. There was only the long, lonely expanse of water.

I asked, gently, "Do you think Tom is coming back?"

"Do you think that's why I stand here?"

"I don't know."

A strand of hair unwound from the pin at the back of Vicky's head. She tucked it back into place. "Of course it is."

The breeze rustled her dress against her legs. Waves crashed over the rocks below us. For a long time, we did not say a word. I was thinking that I must be nearing the end of my Hellish journey. *This is the final ghost.* We stood there, commanding that lonely post at the edge of the world, each waiting for something over which we had no power.

"You don't have the burning arrow," Vicky said, finally. She was correct. I had left it behind at the gates of Dis, plugged into the ground as my makeshift altar. Perhaps it was burning still, a testament to the fact that I had been there. "It's no matter. You won't need it here."

"What do I do next?"

"Maybe it's your time to wait too." She dug the heels of her boots firmly into the ground and set her shoulders more stiffly against the sea breeze. "Love is an action you must repeat ceaselessly."

In this moment, I was allowed to glance into the grand nothingness of her existence: she really would stand forever, awaiting Tom's return. As far as I could tell, she hadn't even noticed my nakedness. I doubted that she noticed anything other than the promise of the water that stretched in front of her.

"This is not my place," I said.

"Are you sure?"

"I think I'll head inland."

She didn't take her eyes off the sea. "Good luck."

There was something about the way she wished me luck that I didn't understand—until I took my first steps. I felt the ground tremble as if something were happening behind me, under me, all around me. I momentarily wondered whether it was the return of Michael, until I saw that the edge of the cliff was shifting. Afraid that it would collapse beneath me, I bolted. There was the tremendous crack of rock breaking away and I churned my legs as quickly as I could. When I looked over my shoulder, I expected to see the cliff falling away behind me.

But the cliff had not fallen away. Its edge was following me, always the same distance behind despite the fact that I was now running. I felt the familiar swish in my spine. `I AM HERE.`

My first thought was that I might have been running in place, on a sort of soil treadmill, but this was not the case. When I say the edge of the cliff was following me, I mean that literally. The stone constantly changed its shape to stalk me, keeping pace so that I never moved any farther from the precipice. When I veered to one side, the cliff circled like a well-trained sheepdog. `THERE IS NOTH-ING YOU CAN DO ABOUT IT.`

I ran for as long as I could, darting this way and that, but the cliff was unrelenting. It doesn't matter how fast you move, I learned, if you never go anywhere. `YOU CANNOT LEAVE.` Soon I recognized that I was not in any immediate danger. If the cliff were going to swallow me, it would have done so already. I headed back to where Vicky was standing.

"I tried to leave once too," she said, "and the cliff followed me."

"That's why you stand here?"

"No."

I looked over the edge of the cliff, to see that at its bottom were rocks that could shred a person.

"If you jump," Vicky whispered, as if worried that the very stone under our feet would overhear, "you'll lose the skin that you have regrown and be put back in your burnt body."

"But this is only a hallucination. None of this is real."

She shrugged. "Is that what you learned from the Archangel's smile?"

`YOU SHOULD JUMP.`

Why would the snake tell me to jump? To cause me pain. That was in the interest of the snake, because the bitch thrived on my pain. I touched my skin where the nerve endings had once been incinerated.

If I jump, I thought, *I lose this. I lose my nerves and my hair and my health and my beauty. My fingers and penis will recede again. My face will become weathered granite. My lips will wither, and my voice will be ground back into sharp ugly bits. I'll become the gargoyle again, but this time by my own choice.*

`YOU HAVE ALWAYS BEEN A GARGOYLE, BRANDED IN HELL BEFORE YOU WERE EVEN BORN.`

I asked Vicky what would happen if I stayed on the cliff.

`I WAS NOT PUT IN YOUR SPINE AFTER YOUR ACCIDENT. I HAVE ALWAYS BEEN HERE.`

"I think," Vicky answered, "that Marianne Engel will come for you."

`SHE IS NOT COMING FOR YOU.`

"Why do you think that?"

Vicky answered, "Sometimes love outlasts even death."

`HOW COULD SHE LOVE ONE SUCH AS YOU?`

I looked into the thrashing tide below us, crashing over the rocks. `YOU SHOULD JUMP.` *Perhaps Vicky is right. Perhaps this is a test of my patience.* `YOU SHOULD END.` *Marianne Engel came to me in the hospital when I needed her most, and she will come for me now. Right?*

`BUT THIS IS NOT EVEN YOUR HELL. YOURS IS YET TO COME.`

Hell is a choice.

I THOUGHT YOU DIDN'T BELIEVE IN HELL.

"Vicky," I asked, "am I dead?"

"I don't know."

"Are you dead?"

"Not as long as I wait for Tom."

I AM THE ONLY ONE WHO REALLY KNOWS YOU.

Sunlight sparkled on the waves. The entire ocean stretched out in front of me.

YOU'VE ALWAYS WANTED TO BELIEVE WE ARE DIFFERENT . . .

I looked down and—though I can't explain why I felt it so strongly—I was certain about what I had to do next.

. . . BUT YOU CANNOT EXIST WITHOUT ME.

A calm entered my body. As my fear left me, it entered the snake. Because the serpent knew that I'd made a decision that was good for me, bad for it.

YOU ARE ME.

I turned to Vicky and asked, "Shall I give your regards to Marianne Engel?"

"Please do."

THIS IS A MISTAKE.

My legs pushed me up into the air. As I leapt towards the sun, I felt the snake rip backwards out of my body. As I moved forward, the snake could not. It left through my asshole, fittingly enough, yanked out like an anchor plunging from a boat.

There was a brief weightlessness; a balancing point between air and the water waiting below. *How strange,* I thought, *how like the moment between sleeping and falling when everything is beautifully surreal and nothing is corporeal. How like floating towards completion.* There was a moment of perfect suspended weightlessness at the top of the arc. Just for this one beautiful moment, I imagined myself moving into the sky forever.

But, as it always does, the battle of gravity won. I was sucked perfectly down and cut the air like a dropped knife, the rush of the water coming up to meet me. Even as I was falling, I knew I was doing the correct thing. I closed my eyes and thought about Marianne Engel.

Contact, and the calm sheen of water opened to envelop me. As I cut the surface, I felt as if I'd come home and I—

XXX.

—looked up into the eyes of Marianne Engel.

My body was wrapped in layers of wet cloth, to lower my fever. I was back in her bed, in our home, and her hand was resting on my cheek. She told me that it was over and I told her that I had been in Hell. She said that it sure looked that way, and handed me a cup of tea. I felt as if I hadn't had a drink in years. "How long was I . . . ?"

"Three days, but nothing is better than having suffered. It is a short hardship that ends in joy." Same old Marianne Engel.

"Let's agree to disagree."

She steadied my hand on the cup, as it was shaking badly. "How do you feel?"

"Like a brand plucked out of the fire."

She smiled. "Zechariah 3:2."

I checked my body: my skin had returned to its damaged state; my face had tightened; my lips had receded; fingers were missing; my knee was stiff; the hair on my forearms was gone and there were only wisps on my head.

My hand, just as it always had, went to my chest. Where I expected to find my angel coin, I found nothing, despite the fact that it had not been off my body since Marianne Engel had given it to me almost fourteen months earlier.

"Your coin served its purpose," she said.

I checked in the sheets, under the bed, all around, but my neck chain was nowhere to be found. Marianne Engel must have removed it during my withdrawal. I told myself it was only a strange coincidence that she had done so while I was hallucinating about handing it over to Charon.

"Don't worry," she said. "I'll replace your necklace with a better one."

...

I felt better than I had in years, even before the accident, by simple virtue of an undrugged mind and veins not sluggish with narcotic syrup. This is not to say that I never felt a twinge of desire rising for the old drug—I did; the habit had been with me too long—but it was different. I could do without morphine; I wanted to do without it. I looked forward to my sessions with Sayuri and progressed faster with my exercises.

But best of all, the bitchsnake really was gone.

I was better able to look after myself than at any time since my accident, and Marianne Engel returned to her carving. She took up exactly where she'd left off, resuming an immediately unhealthy velocity. All I could do was to clean her ashtrays and try to curb her intake of coffee on the spoon. I brought her bowls of fruit that became still lifes rather than meals, and when she finished a statue, only to collapse onto the next block of stone, I washed her body. I promised myself that if she approached physical collapse again, I would do anything and everything necessary to stop her. I promised myself.

From February nineteenth to the twenty-first, she pulled statue 16 out of the stone. On the twenty-second, she slept and absorbed; from the twenty-third to the twenty-fifth, she extracted number 15. She took a day of rest and then she worked until the first day of March, producing number 14. One does not need to be a mathematician to realize that this brought her past the halfway point of the final twenty-seven hearts: thirteen more hearts and she would be finished. Thirteen more hearts until she thought she would die.

Her return to carving seemed to affect even Bougatsa, who lacked his usual bounce. When we came back from our daily walks, he would eat a huge bowl of food before settling lethargically to drool on my orthopedic shoes.

• • •

In early March, I had a routine checkup with Dr. Edwards. We reviewed my charts and talked about a minor surgery that was scheduled for the end of the month. She seemed genuinely pleased. "You've been out of the hospital for over a year and things couldn't be going any better."

I kept my mouth shut about the fact that Marianne Engel was, at that very moment, stretched out on new stone, readying herself. Lucky **13** was calling.

"You know," Nan added, "it just goes to show how wrong a doctor can be. There was a point when I thought you had given up, and then you became one of our hardest-working patients. And when you left, I was certain that Marianne wouldn't be able to look after you."

• • •

Marianne Engel produced statues **13, 12,** and **11** (an old woman with donkey ears; a horned demon with its sloppy tongue hanging out; and a lion's head with elephant tusks), taking only a few hours off during the process. She had already lost the weight she'd gained after Christmas, and her speech was becoming confused again. Statue **10** came into existence around March twentieth.

I was scheduled to enter the hospital for surgery on the twenty-sixth. Before I went in, I needed to decide what to do with Bougatsa. Not only did I doubt Marianne Engel's ability to look after him when she could not even look after herself, but also the dog, perhaps in an example of animal empathy, was losing weight. I wondered whether I could use this to induce enough guilt to get her out of the basement, and decided to give it a try.

I made her stop carving long enough to explain that if she chose sculpting over Bougatsa's care, I would have to place him in a kennel. (This was not only a bargaining tactic, but also the truth.) Marianne Engel took a look at me, and a look at Bougatsa, and she shrugged. Then she returned to her work on statue **9**.

• • •

There was a large puddle of shit on the floor. It was not mine.

In all the time I'd lived in the fortress, Bougatsa had never once relieved himself inside. I am somewhat loath to write a detailed description of the stool, but two things need mentioning. First, the stool was more liquid than solid. Second, it contained leafy remains.

The only plant in the house was the one that Jack had brought. (Perhaps there had been others before my time, but they had become casualties of Marianne Engel's negligence while carving.) When I inspected it, it was quickly apparent that Bougatsa had been making a meal of its leaves. Most were gone, and the ones that remained all had jagged edges in the shape of teeth marks.

I tracked the dog down and found him stretched out in the study, breathing shallowly. When I swept my hand along his side to comfort him, fur came off in my fingers. His ribs were a story of starvation and I was shocked: not strictly at his thinness, but because I didn't understand how it could be possible. In recent weeks, Bougatsa had been eating much more than usual; in fact, he never seemed to stop eating.

I headed into the basement to inform Marianne Engel that her dog was seriously ill, because I wanted to shame her into coming with me to the veterinary clinic. But it didn't work out quite like that. She was hunched over a beast whose eyes seemed to be issuing a stern warning to keep away. I spoke anyway. "There's something wrong with Bougatsa. He's sick."

She looked up at me, as if she had heard some mysterious clatter coming from an area of the room that was supposed to be empty. Blood was flowing from one of her wrists where the chisel had gone wrong, and streaks of red were painted across her forehead where she'd wiped it. "What?"

"You're bleeding."

"I am a thorn prick on Christ's temple."

"No," I said, pointing. "Your wrist."

"Oh." She looked at it, and some blood flowed into her open palm. "It's like a rose."

"Did you hear me? Bougatsa is sick."

She tried to pull a strand of her hair away from her breast, where it was awkwardly pasted with sweat and stone dust, but her fingers couldn't quite gauge the distance. She missed, over and over. "Then go to the infirmary."

"You mean the vet?"

"Yes." Drops of her blood fell into the rock chips at her feet. "Vet."

"Let me look at that." I reached towards her wrist.

Marianne Engel, with a sudden look of terror in her eyes, raised the chisel in my direction. Only once before had she threatened me with violence, when she'd thrown the jar of coffee at me in the belfry. At that time I was certain she meant to miss me but I could tell that if she lunged at me now, with the chisel, she would mean it. She looked as though she didn't know where she was, or who I was; she looked as though she would do anything to defend her ability to keep working.

I took a step back, lifting my hands in the gesture people automatically make to show they mean no harm. "He's your dog, Marianne. Don't you want to come with us? With me and your dog, Bougatsa?"

The name seemed to stir her memory. The knots of her hunched shoulders released and she let out the breath she'd been holding. Most important, she lowered the chisel as the fear left her eyes.

"No."

There had been no anger in her voice, but also no regret. Her voice was simply dull and hollow, lacking any nuance of compassion, as if her words were not new sounds but echoes.

By the time I had my foot on the stairway's bottom step, all her attention was once again focused on the stone in front of her.

. . .

The veterinarian was a plump woman named Cheryl with red hair and bright eyes, probably of Irish heritage. One of the first things she asked was why I looked the way that I do, which was so much better than trying to pretend that there was nothing wrong with my appearance. "Car accident."

"I see. So when did you start noticing the problem with, ah"—she glanced at the chart that her receptionist had filled out—"Bougatsa? Greek pastry, right?"

"Yeah. Same color. I found diarrhea on the floor this morning, and I think he's been eating leaves."

"I see." Cheryl nodded. "His coat always like this? It seems to be lacking luster."

"You're right," I answered, "and it feels kind of greasier than usual. His problems started recently, but this morning it was like they just jumped up a level. He's definitely losing weight."

She asked whether he was lacking energy, and I confirmed he was. Then she performed a few little tests on him, shining a light into his mouth and eyes, with Bougatsa whimpering passively through-out the process. I asked what she thought the problem was.

"Does he seem tender in this region?" She asked this while press-ing at Bougatsa's stomach, and then answered her own question. "Actually, he doesn't seem to mind it too much. Were there any signs of undigested fat in his stool?"

Who—other than a veterinarian—knows what undigested fat looks like in dog shit? I answered that I'd forgotten to run a chemical analysis before arriving, so I couldn't say definitively. Cheryl gave me a scowl before lifting Boogie's tail to inspect his anus. "Has he been eating his own excrement?"

"Jesus Christ." Once again, Cheryl expected far more from my observational skills than I felt was reasonable. "I don't know. Maybe?"

"I can't be sure what the problem is," Cheryl said, "without running a few tests. Would you consent to leaving him here for a day or two?"

This wasn't the time to explain that Bougatsa was not actually *my* dog, so I just signed the release forms. When I asked whether the tests would be painful, the good vet looked offended. "Not if I can help it."

I told the dog to be good for Dr. Cheryl and he slopped his tongue out to lick my hand. Some people might view this as a sign of affection, but I'm fully aware that dogs do it only because it is an inborn instinct for grooming.

◆ ◆ ◆

When I called a few days later, Cheryl still hadn't found the cause of Bougatsa's problems but assured me she was getting close. She sounded apologetic but, truthfully, this was actually what I'd been hoping for.

The clinic would be convenient housing while I had my operation, so I explained my situation and asked whether Bougatsa could remain until I got out of the hospital. The vet was agreeable, saying it would provide time to do a thorough diagnostic workup.

Now I only had Marianne Engel to contend with. I didn't want to leave her alone at home, but she was an adult and I was only going to be in the hospital one night, two at the most. Should she follow her regular schedule, she would be carving the entire time. Had I been home, she would only have ignored me anyway.

As soon as I was settled in at the hospital, all the old faces filled my room. Both Connie (ending her shift) and Beth (starting) dropped in to say hello. Nan was there, and after a few minutes Sayuri and Gregor entered at a respectable distance from each other, touching hands only when they thought no one was looking. When I said the only person missing was Maddy, Beth informed me that she'd recently married and moved away. My first assumption was that her new husband must be some sort of bad boy—perhaps a Hell's Angel or a corporate lawyer—but, much to my surprise, he was a graduate student in archaeology and Maddy was accompanying him to a dig on the coast of Sumatra.

Everyone asked about Marianne Engel; and I lied, sort of. I said she had a pressing deadline for a statue, seeing no need to add that her Three Masters were the ones who now set her timetable. Everyone nodded but I could see that Sayuri, at least, was not buying my story. I couldn't look her in the eyes, and this alerted Gregor to my deception as well.

When only Nan and I remained in the room, I asked—since I still had a few hours before my surgery—if she wanted to go for a walk around the hospital grounds. She looked at her schedule, checked her pager and cell phone, and called the nurse's station before she finally agreed. Halfway through our stroll, she even slipped her arm into the crook of mine and pointed out some patterns in the clouds that she said reminded her of a school of sea horses. I treated her to a hot dog from a vendor and we sat on a bench as the people walked by. Nan got a mustard stain on her shirt and I thought it looked good on her.

◆ ◆ ◆

I counted backwards when the mask was placed over my mouth. By this point, I was an anesthesia expert and I knew I'd wake up in a few hours. Undoubtedly there would be residual soreness, but I was used to pain and had been through enough surgeries to know that I would be fine. At least, as fine as I ever was.

Except it didn't work out that way. My routine surgery had a complication: sepsis. Such infections are not uncommon in burn patients, even those as far along in their recovery as I was, but luckily the infection was not particularly severe and my body—so much stronger because of my exercise regimen—would be able to cope. Nevertheless, I needed to remain in the hospital until it passed.

Sayuri called Cheryl to extend Bougatsa's stay, while Gregor volunteered to inform Marianne Engel of my situation. He decided to drive to the fortress to tell her in person, since she was not answering her phone. I warned him that there was a good chance that she wouldn't answer the door and, as it turned out, I was correct. After ten minutes of pounding, Gregor gave up even though he could hear Bessie Smith wailing at full volume from the basement.

Jack had an extra set of keys, so I called her to request that she check in on, and feed, Marianne Engel. Jack assured me that she would do so, and even asked whether I needed anything brought to the hospital. There wasn't, because I'd made so many visits that I habitually packed a full bag (fresh pajamas, toiletries, books, etc.) for even the smallest of operations.

With these few things put in order, there was nothing left to do but lie in my bed (which, by the way, no longer felt like a skeleton's rib cage) and heal. Each evening, Gregor brought me new books, and once he even sneaked in a few beers. Because, as he explained with a glint in his eye, he was a bit of a rebel. I assured him that he most certainly was.

After a week I was released, and Gregor booked off an hour to drive me home. When we arrived at the fortress, all was silent. Normally this would mean nothing—maybe Marianne Engel was out for a walk, or preparing on a fresh slab of stone—but I had a bad feeling. I didn't even bother to check her bedroom; I headed directly for the basement, with Gregor following.

Even though I had lived with her for more than a year, I was not prepared for what I saw. First, there were three newly completed statues: numbers **8**, **7**, and **6**. Given that I'd been gone only a week and it usually took her more than seventy hours to complete a single piece, the arithmetic suggested that she'd been working not only without a break but also with greater fervor than usual. This I could hardly believe.

Marianne Engel was not working or asleep on new stone. She was sitting in the middle of her three new grotesques, covered entirely in stone dust that emphasized her every emaciated bone. She had been skinny when I'd left for the hospital, but she was much thinner now. She must have eaten nothing since I'd last seen her. Her chest heaved a wretched little victory with each breath, and her skin, which was so bright when she was healthy, looked as though it had been rubbed over with old paraffin. Her face was a skeletal mirror of what it once had been, with such large dark circles under her eyes that they gave the impression of gaping sockets.

A crimson gloss of blood coated the medieval cross tattooed on her stomach, oozing from a series of deep gashes on her chest. Her right hand lay open on the floor, cradling a gory chisel in fingers that looked like an old lady's, ready to snap under even the slightest pressure.

Across the flaming heart on her left breast, Marianne Engel had carved my name deeply into her flesh.

I have no doubt that Gregor Hnatiuk is a good doctor but his practice mostly involves speaking to people, trying to figure out their problems, maybe prescribing a few pills. He was not prepared to see what Marianne Engel had done. He didn't seem to be able to accept the scene as real, perhaps in part because she had long since stopped being a patient and had grown into a fond acquaintance. He was unable to distance himself and kept blinking as if trying to reset the wayward gyroscope of his mind, surprised each time he opened his eyes to find that nothing had changed.

Marianne Engel turned her euphoric face towards me, her eyes filled with tears not of pain but of joy. Her face was filled with vacant wonder, as if she had seen something far too marvelous for mere words to describe.

"God sent an immense fire into my soul." Her voice quivered with delight, as the blood continued to flow out of my name on her breast. "My heart was utterly inflamed with love, and I hardly noticed the pain."

Despite his initial shock, Gregor recovered first and ran upstairs to phone emergency services. Meanwhile, I tried to convince Marianne Engel to rest calmly, but she just kept talking. "That which abides the fire shall become clean." She stared at me wildly, as if waiting for agreement. "The water of separation shall purify."

Gregor returned, bringing with him a blanket to cover her shaking body. As we draped it over her, he tried to reassure her. "The paramedics are coming, and everything will be okay. You just need to relax."

Marianne Engel paid no attention to the words. "The Lord is a consuming fire." Ten minutes later, when the EMS team arrived and Gregor led them into the basement, she was still going on. "That which can't abide the fire shall go through water."

The female paramedic asked whether there was a history of substance abuse and I assured her there was not; she nodded, but I'm not sure she believed me.

"The skies sent out a sound," Marianne Engel was saying, as they knelt beside her and checked her vitals, and it was as though she were trying to convince them. "The arrows went abroad."

The paramedics strapped Marianne Engel to a board and carried her out. I was allowed to ride in the ambulance with her, while Gregor followed in his car. I held her hand as they slipped an IV tube into her arm. "When the rock was opened," she slurred, "the waters gushed out."

In a few moments, the drugs put her to sleep. As soon as she was under, I gave a more detailed medical history—as much as I knew, in any case—so the paramedics could radio ahead to the hospital. When we arrived at the emergency entrance, two doctors and the on-duty psychiatrist met us and Gregor took over the task of admitting her. I continued to hold her unconscious hand and talk soothingly, saying all the things I wanted to tell her, but still couldn't, when she was conscious.

• • •

When I finally returned to the veterinary clinic, Cheryl sat me down. "Do you know what pancreatic insufficiency is?"

I said I did, if it was anything like pancreatitis in humans.

"Dogs can get pancreatitis as well, but that's not quite what Bougatsa has. Pancreatic insufficiency is common in large breeds like German Shepherds, and symptoms come on quickly, which sounds like what happened here. To put it simply, he can't break down his food into smaller molecules because he lacks the proper enzymes. As a result, he's not absorbing any nutrients, and that's why he's hungry all the time. He's been eating as much as he can, even plants, to make up for the lack, but no matter how much he eats, he isn't getting the nutritional benefits. It's kind of like he's been starving to death."

"But that's the bad news," she said. "The good news is you caught it quickly and it's completely treatable, controllable with diet. He'll be his old self in no time."

She took me to the kennel and I would almost swear there was a sparkle in Bougatsa's eyes when he saw me coming. But it was probably only because Cheryl had given him some food he could finally digest.

• • •

The doctors told Marianne Engel they were only treating her for exhaustion, but the truth was that they were also monitoring her mental state closely. Gregor came by her hospital room often, but

his visits were driven by friendship rather than professional interest. Because of his personal involvement, a different psychiatrist was
handling the case.

I came every day and the doctors even let me bring Bougatsa
by the hospital once. Canine therapy, they called it. Marianne Engel
came out to sit on a bench in the sunlight and pet him a bit. She
seemed shocked by his thinness, as if she didn't remember that his
condition had developed in front of her eyes. The dog, for his part,
forgave her completely for deserting him when he needed her most.
Dogs are stupid like that.

When she was released at the end of the week, it was against the
strongest recommendations of her doctor. I was hesitant, as well:
of all the damage she'd inflicted on herself, most had come through
simple disregard for her own body. Carving my name into her chest
was a willful and horrifying act, which made me feel I was no longer
simply neglectful of her but also a cause of her pain. As she was
physically recovered, the hospital couldn't keep her without a court
order, however, and no matter what I said I couldn't talk her into a
few more days. When we returned home, Bougatsa ran all around
the house, knocking over the plant that a few weeks earlier he'd
been eating.

◆ ◆ ◆

Marianne Engel had been home only two days before she started
peeling off her clothing to prepare for her next stone. When she
came to the bandages wrapped around her chest, she removed those
as well. "I can't communicate with these on."

I was not going to let her do this again. I had already watched her
collapse twice. I would not fail her a third time; I would not allow
my name to become infected on her flesh.

What followed could not properly be called an argument, because arguments involve an exchange of opposing ideas. This was

all me. I spoke softly; I yelled; I cajoled; I threatened; I pleaded; I demanded; I spoke with logic; I spoke with emotion; I spoke word after word after word after word that she completely ignored. She gave the same answer repeatedly: "Only five statues left. I'll rest when they're finished."

As I could not talk her out of it—logic is useless in the face of obsession—I would have to find another way to protect her. I decided to visit Jack, even though she had broken her promise to care for Marianne Engel while I was in the hospital.

When I walked into the gallery I saw a trio of familiar grotesques and, on the wall behind them, a picture of a healthy Marianne Engel. Chisel in hand, her mutant hair artfully tousled, she was leaning against one of her early creations. The short caption under the photo mentioned nothing about her mental illness: "Unlike most modern sculptors, this local artist with an international reputation refuses to use any pneumatic tools, preferring to carve in the medieval tradition. . . ."

A young couple walked around one of the larger works, running their fingers over the edges. They were discussing its "wonderfully tactile sense"—but where could they put it? Nothing turns the stomach quite like moneyed thirtysomethings discussing art. Jack, seeing a prospective sale, attempted to walk right past me with a dismissive hand lifted in my direction and said, "I'll be with you in a minute."

"Why did you abandon her?" I asked. For once, I was pleased with the rasping quality of my voice—it made my proclamation of her failure sound all the worse.

Jack immediately aborted her approach to the customers and pulled me into an alcove to launch into a vigorous defense against my accusation. The way she spoke reminded me of a train derailing: all her words were boxcars, hurtling frantically forward, threatening to fly off the tracks and burst through the end of each sentence in a devastating mess. She claimed that she had gone to the fortress every night I was in the hospital, forcing her way in past the furniture piled up against the front door. Once inside, she had stood between Marianne Engel and her statues, refusing to move until she at least ate some fruit.

"You found her in the middle of the afternoon, right?" Jack was referring to the time of day when Gregor and I arrived at the fortress. "I work, you know. I'm not like you—I pay my own bills. I can't shut down the gallery to fritter away the day with her. And if you'd bothered to call, I would have rushed right down to the hospital. But *no* . . ."

We debated who was responsible for what, until the young couple couldn't help but stare in our direction. I shot them my most monstrous look, the one that would let them know to mind their own goddamn business.

Jack viewed this as an excellent opportunity to point out that her customers funded my life. I countered that they paid for her life as well, while she piggybacked on Marianne Engel's talent. "You're probably overjoyed that she's already carving again."

In that instant, all the anger on Jack's face was replaced by genuine surprise. "She's what?"

It became impossible for me to continue my attack: there could be no denying Jack's concern. "She's never had manic sessions so close together before. Once a year, maybe. Twice, in a bad year."

In that moment, I hated Jack for the fact that she'd shared twenty years of her life with Marianne Engel. It was the very worst kind of hate, built upon envy, but it was also hate that I had to put aside. Jack's experience would be invaluable, so I leveled my voice as well as I could. "What do I do now?"

"I don't know." She flipped the sign from "Open" to "Closed," shooing out the remaining customers, and I followed her out of the shop. "But we have to do something."

◆ ◆ ◆

Jack knew a lawyer who specialized in matters of involuntary hospitalization. I suppose this was only natural, after all her years of dealing with psychiatric patients—first her mother, then Marianne Engel.

Clancy McRand was an old man who sat behind a big wooden desk that sported a computer covered with small yellow Post-it notes. He kept pulling down on the lapels of his coat, as if doing so would allow him to close his jacket over a stomach that he refused to admit was as large as it really was. McRand cleared his throat a lot, even though I was doing most of the talking. He jotted down the facts on his big yellow legal pad, and Jack offered a few comments when he asked questions to which I didn't know the answers. He seemed to know a fair amount about Marianne Engel already, from the thick file he had pulled out of the cabinet when we first arrived. It was clear that Jack had engaged McRand's services in the past, perhaps in setting up the conservatorship.

When we had told him everything that might be relevant, he said we might have a case but that it wouldn't be easy. *Things never are,* I thought, *if lawyers can drag it out for a fat payday.* However, as he explained the process, I came to understand that it was not his greed that would delay things. It really was the system.

Usually, a relative of the patient filed the petition for emergency commitment. While it was legally possible for anyone to file, McRand explained, the process was slowed if the petitioner was not a close family member. Because Marianne Engel had no family, she would need to be examined by two physicians before the petition could even be filed. If she refused to be examined—as I knew she would—I'd be forced to submit a sworn statement that she was "gravely disabled." McRand looked at me inquisitively to ensure that I'd be willing to do so and I assured him that I would, but I'm certain he caught the hesitation in my voice as I said it.

"Umm hmm," McRand harrumphed, before he continued. Once my petition was properly filed, Marianne Engel would be required to appear before an examining physician at a hospital. If she refused—as, again, I knew she would—law officers would compel her to attend. In my imagination, I saw two beefy cops placing her into a straitjacket and dragging her by the elbows into court.

If the examining physician agreed with my assessment that she was gravely disabled, an emergency commitment of seventy-two hours would be imposed. At the end of this time, the hospital director could file another petition for a longer-term commitment. This was essential because—once again, as we were not relatives—neither Jack nor I could do it ourselves. Without the cooperation of the director, we would have no legal right to proceed with the petition.

Assuming that the hospital director did agree, a hearing would come next. Here Marianne Engel would be compelled to testify, as would I, and Jack in her role as conservator. It was possible that others would be called as well, people who had observed Marianne Engel's recent behavior. Perhaps Gregor Hnatiuk and Sayuri Mizumoto, for example. The mental health commission would preside over the hearing, although Marianne Engel would have the legal right to a jury trial. And, if it came to that, she could hire her own lawyer.

In court, Mr. McRand warned, there was little doubt that *my* character would be brought up. Given my career in pornography, my admitted drug addictions, and the fact that Marianne Engel was paying all my medical bills, any judge would be reluctant to suspend her legal rights just because I thought it was a good idea. Viewed objectively, she was the upstanding citizen, not I. The court might even find it amusing that I wanted her declared incompetent when she appeared to run her life so much better than I did mine. And— McRand seemed hesitant to bring this up but knew he'd be negligent if he didn't—Marianne Engel could present an attractive face to a jury. "You, on the other hand . . ." It was not a sentence that needed finishing.

I pointed out that she had carved her chest with a chisel. What stronger proof could possibly be needed to prove that she was a danger to herself? McRand conceded with a sigh that the incident could possibly be "a good start for a case," but that there was no evidence she posed a threat to anyone else. "If harming oneself were reason for commitment, psychiatric hospitals would be filled with smokers and fast food customers."

How could I ask everyone we knew to testify against Marianne Engel in a case that we would almost certainly lose? More to the point, how could *I* testify against her? Given her conspiracy theories, the last thing she needed to believe was that her closest friends were actually enemy agents trying to prevent her from giving away her hearts.

"So . . ." Mr. McRand sighed in conclusion, pulling on his lapels one more time before resting his hands on his round stomach.

I thanked him for his time and Jack told him to send the bill to her gallery. As we walked out of the office, Jack reached up to put her arm around my shoulders. She told me that she was sorry, and I believed that she was.

Our sole consolation was that Marianne Engel had only five statues left in her countdown. Though it would be painful to watch her finish them, at least it wouldn't take long. All I could do was look after her as well as I could. When she completed the final stroke on her final statue, she would discover that the effort hadn't killed her after all.

• • •

Bougatsa's new diet included a steady intake of raw cow pancreases, which allowed him to digest other food by replacing the pancreatic enzymes that his body lacked. While there are powdered dietary supplements that contain the necessary enzymes, Cheryl and I decided to use actual meat. I became well acquainted with the local butchers, who were puzzled by my order until I explained why I needed them, and then they were all pleased to know they were helping the dog on the end of my leash, because it's not often that a butcher gets to feel like a doctor. Every day Bougatsa looked a little better and every day Marianne Engel looked a little worse.

She was pale from lack of sunlight, although she would occasionally wander up from the basement to grab more cigarettes or another jar of instant coffee. She was becoming a framework of bones etched permanently in dust, her flesh falling away under the force of her physical exertion. She was disappearing, ounce by ounce, like the rock chips that she chiseled off her grotesques. She finished statue 5 before the middle of April and immediately began preparing for 4.

The anniversary of my accident—my second Good Friday "birthday"—passed without her noticing. I visited the accident site alone, climbing down the embankment to find that the greenness of the grass had now completely overtaken the blackness of the burns. The candlestick from my previous birthday was still standing where we'd left it, grimy from a year's weather, a testament that the site had remained unvisited since then.

I put down a second candlestick, another of Francesco's alleged creations, and slipped a candle into its expectant iron mouth. I said a few words after lighting it—not a prayer, because I only pray when in Hell—as a remembrance of things past. If nothing else, living with Marianne Engel had instilled in me a certain fondness for ritual.

She kept working through the remainder of the month, but her pace was slowing considerably. This was inevitable. When she finished 4, she had to take two days off before starting 3. The revolt of her body could not be ignored. Even though she took extra time to prepare, statue 3 still took almost five full days to finish.

Statue 2 took her until the end of the month, and it was only a formidable display of willpower that kept her moving at all. After finishing, she crawled into the bathtub for a proper cleansing before (finally) climbing into bed to sleep for two straight days.

When she woke up, only the final statue would remain. I wasn't sure whether I should fear this or be overjoyed; then again, Marianne Engel often made me feel that way.

◆ ◆ ◆

She emerged from her bed on the first day of May and I was greatly relieved to see how much better she looked. I became doubly pleased when, rather than head directly into the basement to commence her final statue, she joined me for a meal. When we spoke, all her words were in the correct order and afterwards we went on a walk with Bougatsa, who was giddy with the long-anticipated return of her attention. We took turns throwing a tennis ball for him to chase down and return in a mouthful of slobber.

It was Marianne Engel who first broached the subject. "I have only one statue left."

"Yes."

"Do you know which one it is?"

"Another grotesque, I suppose."

"No," she said. "It's you."

During the previous months my statue had stood, covered in a white sheet like the caricature of a ghost, in the corner of her workshop. At first I had been disappointed that she'd lost interest in it, but as she grew thinner I was thankful that I didn't have to sit for her while she wasted away.

I only had to think for a moment before I volunteered to sit for her again. While I wished that she would give up this idea of a final statue altogether, at least I could keep an eye on her while she worked. There was also the advantage that, if my earlier sittings were any indication, she would proceed with my statue at a much more relaxed pace. I was not a frantic beast screaming to be pulled out from under an avalanche of time and stone; I would allow her all the time at my disposal, never rushing.

Curiosity compelled me to ask Marianne Engel whether, when we'd started the statue so many months previous, she'd already known that it would be her final work. Yes, she answered, she had known. So I asked further, why did she bother starting it at all, knowing that she would need to put it aside?

"It was part of *your* preparation," she answered. "If it was already under way, I thought there would be less chance you'd refuse now. It looks like I was right."

We started that very day. Being naked in front of her always made me feel awkward, but I felt less self-conscious now that she, too, was physically imperfect. While her unhealthy thinness was not yet a match for my injuries, it did at least bring us somewhat closer in misshapenness.

• • •

Work on my statue continued for about ten days, with about half of that time spent on the fine details. Often Marianne Engel would come to my chair to run her fingers over my body, as if trying to memorize my burnt topography so she could map it on the stone as accurately as possible. Her attention to every nuance was so intense that I had to comment on it; she replied that it was vitally important that the finished statue be found perfect, with nothing lacking.

Things went more or less as I hoped that they would. She never approached the intensity of her other carving sessions, usually working for less than an hour at a time despite the fact that I could sit as long as was necessary now that my pressure suit was gone. She seemed to be savoring this, her final work. She smoked less, and the lids on the jars of coffee crystals remained shut. She leaned close while working the stone, whispering into it with a voice too low for me to hear. I leaned forward, trying to catch what she was saying but I never quite could; it didn't help that my hearing had been so damaged in the accident. I tried to draw out the truth with a casual comment. "I thought the rock talked to you, not the other way around."

Marianne Engel looked up at me. "You're funny."

And so it went, until she stepped back after the inevitable last stroke of her chisel. For what seemed an eternity, she inspected my stony doppelgänger before deciding that there was no longer any difference between him and me. Satisfied, she said, "I want to add the inscription in private."

She worked until late in the night and, although my curiosity was almost overwhelming, I respected her request for privacy. When the final word was engraved, Marianne Engel came upstairs. Naturally, I asked if I could read what she'd carved.

"There'll be plenty of time for that later," she answered. "Right now, we're going to go to the beach to celebrate."

I liked the idea. The oceanside always relaxed her and it would be a good way to mark the occasion. So she packed me into the car and we soon found ourselves among the driftwood.

The waves beat rhythmically against the shore and her body was pressed wonderfully up against mine. Bougatsa bounded around happily, kicking up sand everywhere. Down the way, teenage boys drank their beers and tried to impress girls by acting like jerks.

"So," I said. "What now?"

"The last part of our story. Which, in case you've forgotten, begins with you being burned by the condotta."

XXXI.

Out. In. I concentrated on my breathing. Steady. Be simple. Aim. Be calm. I called my target. "Heart."

I don't know what I expected the arrow to look like as it flew away from me. I was surprised to find that my eye actually focused on the target at the end of the line, rather than on the arrow itself.

Despite the storm, my arrow flew as if guided by wire, never wavering. Everyone knows the story of the master archer who could split an arrow already lodged in the bull's-eye. That was how my arrow entered your chest, in the same spot where you'd previously been pierced. The first time you'd been shot, the volume of Dante slowed the arrow enough to save your life and you were brought to me. This second arrow met no opposition, and you were taken from me.

Your head kicked back with the impact and your mouth popped open to push out a surprised final breath. Your chin bounced twice off your chest, before your head came to rest on your deflated body. You drooped from your pinned hands, and the wall of Brother Heinrich's house continued to burn all around you. My arrow had spared you any further pain and, for this, through my tears, I thanked the Lord.

The mercenaries roared in confusion, and Kuonrat demanded to know who had been careless enough, or stupid enough, to fire a lethal shot against his strict orders. He was livid that one of his soldiers might have shown mercy.

I should have spent less time thanking God and more time escaping. An inspection of my arrow quickly revealed that it did not come from any of the soldiers' bows, and the angle of the shaft showed that it had come from the top of the ridge. An arm went up, and the soldiers immediately began to advance in my direction. They couldn't see me yet, but they knew where I was.

I dropped the crossbow, as I knew I'd never fire another shot. My horse was close, the ridge was slick, and the branches were thick enough to slow a man. As the soldiers slipped their way up the slope, I was able to unhook my horse and take off just ahead of their outstretched hands. I didn't have much of a head start, but it would take them a few minutes to scramble back down the slope and mount their own horses. I had another advantage, as well. I knew the area from my youth, and the mercenaries did not. With the snowstorm raging, I thought I might even have a chance.

I should have known better. The horsemanship of every soldier was superior to my own, and their animals were better rested and better fed. I hadn't been on the trail for more than a few minutes before they were hard upon me. I knew that if I stayed my course, they would catch me in moments. The path was coming to a fork, with one side leading to a safe trail and the other side to a sharp precipice overlooking the River Pegnitz. As a child I'd occasionally walked its edge, but only when I was feeling particularly reckless or wanted to test the idea that the Lord did have a purpose for me.

Desperate times call for desperate measures so, although I knew that it was too narrow for my horse by half, I chose the dangerous trail. The animal sensed the peril and I had to drive my heels into his flanks to coerce every step, chanting the same prayers that I'd always said as a girl. When the horse began to rear, I switched back to my harshest words to try to get a few more steps out of him. It wasn't long before his hoof hit an icy root and we lurched awkwardly to the side.

As we skidded down the cliff, the horse tried to right himself on scrambling hooves, but could find no purchase. He tipped to his side, confused and frightened, throwing me off. As I surrendered to the inevitability of the fall, there was a brief moment in which I felt almost weightless. It was surreal, as though I were floating in perfect balance between the snow and heaven, and I found myself looking directly into the face of my horse. A horse's eyes are usually so dark and calm—when I was growing up the nuns joked that a horse could see all of God's secrets, even if the prioress could not—but his eyes were peeled wide with terror. The moment was over as quickly as it started, and was replaced with the spin of brush and snow as we continued to plunge downwards.

When we finally rolled to a stop, it took a moment before my head cleared enough to assess the path we'd just gouged in the snow and I began to panic at the thought of what the tumble might have done to our child. When the baby kicked at me almost immediately, perhaps angry at all the activity, I took it as a sign of health and had never been happier for the discomfort.

The soldiers had not followed me out onto the precipice, wisely choosing to remain back where the trail was still safe. At least one of them had his bow out, before deciding that the distance and the storm made any shot impossible. He obviously lacked the same faith that I had in God.

The mercenaries would find another way to the bottom, but I knew it would take them at least fifteen minutes. Perhaps, I thought, my tumble might actually be the stroke of luck that would make my escape possible. My momentary excitement disappeared when I tried to right the horse and discovered that one of his legs was twisted at an impossible angle. It was obvious that he would be going no farther with me. I didn't even have the option of putting him out of his misery, as I no longer had the crossbow. But I wouldn't have been able to do it anyway. One killing that day was already one too many.

What good was it to be fifteen minutes ahead of the soldiers, when they had horses and I did not? To one side of me was the cliff I'd just come down, and to the other side was the Pegnitz. It usually didn't freeze over completely, but even when it did it was not safe for a person's weight. Making it across was out of the question, and there was no advantage to climbing back up the cliff. All I could do was choose one direction along the riverside to run and hope for the best. But this was ridiculous, too, because the only possible outcome was that the mercenaries would chase me down from behind. My capture was only a matter of time.

Kuonrat had cut Brandeis' head from his body without a thought, and had ordered your death with a laugh. I knew that when I was caught, as you had explained, I'd be killed quickly only if I was lucky. Rape seemed far more likely.

The thin sheet of ice on the river started to look much better. The odds were against a safe crossing, but I had to attempt it. If I did make it somehow, the soldiers couldn't follow. They would be forced to let me go, because even the smallest man in the troop would certainly break through. Why should they risk it? The mercenaries didn't know who I was, other than some tramp who'd been living with an ex-soldier, and what difference would it make to them whether I lived or died? Kuonrat had proved his point, and two dead deserters were already one more than he'd anticipated. This had to have made him happy.

The bag containing my *Morgengabe* and books would be unnecessary weight to carry across the river, but I could not stand to lose such precious items. So I hid my bag in the crevice of a nearby pile of rocks, determined that if I lived I would return to retrieve it.

I took my first steps onto the ice and it seemed relatively solid, but ice is always thickest close to shore. Just downriver, I could see exposed areas of water that looked like black blankets laid out on the white surface. A few more steps, and I heard a slight creak. Blowing snow swept wildly in front of me, and I was now maybe fifteen feet from shore. If the ice broke, would my feet still be able to touch bottom?

I continued with tiny steps, sliding one foot in front of the other. I moved as quickly as I dared, but it was not fast enough. I heard the mercenaries riding ever closer, so I forced myself to shuffle faster towards the center. Distance from the shore was safety, I told myself, and the single most important thing was to get out of range of their arrows.

I felt the ice give, a little bit, more than before, and my arms instinctively circled my belly. I looked back to see the soldiers approaching the shore, where they'd found my lame horse. When they saw me, they lifted their bows in my direction and I knew that I hadn't gone far enough yet. A few arrows were let go but the wind was strong and they flew wide. I knew the soldiers would learn from this first volley and adjust their aim for the second round. There was little doubt that I would be hit.

The second volley never came. Kuonrat gave a signal and the archers lowered their bows. It struck me as unlikely that he was worried about wasting ammunition; while it might have been that he thought I would deserve to live if I made it across, I doubted that as well. Most probably, he just enjoyed the sport of watching a woman on thin ice.

The way the soldiers stood made it clear that they'd wait me out for as long as it took. Knowing that I couldn't return the way I'd come, I took another step towards the far shore. The ice underneath me buckled and I went down on my knees, throwing my hands out so that I landed on all fours. I told myself that if I could just make it past the middle of the river, I'd survive, because that should be the thinnest point of the ice. I told myself that if I could only make it over that imaginary line, my unborn child would live.

The question was the best way to proceed. Should I spread myself out on my belly and slide slowly? This idea, distributing my weight as evenly as possible, made sense. But then I wondered if this would simply increase the possibility that I'd find a thin spot which would collapse the ice in a chain reaction that would swallow my entire body—and, of course, I feared putting any weight on my stomach regardless. So should I sprint, hoping speed would carry me over the ice? My body said no, but my faith argued that I should. After all, it was the breath of God that had carried my arrow with perfect precision to your heart. Wasn't it possible that the same breath would be at my back, lifting me past the danger? If there was ever a moment to surrender to the protection of God, this was it.

I looked across the river, to the other side, imagining myself as an arrow and the path in front of me as my trajectory. I lifted myself slightly and felt the ice swell. I tensed my legs, and jabbed my rear foot into the ice to gain as much traction as I could. I lifted one knee and curled my shoulders forward. I said a quick prayer and looked to the freedom on the far shore, concentrating on it as my target. And then I pushed off, surrendering to the Lord's protection.

I only made it a few steps before the ice gave out and I fell forward as if breaking through a window. The watery chill cut through me completely and the weight of my soaked clothing began pulling me down. My first thought was of the baby and my arms went out frantically, to grab at anything. If I could latch on to the edge of the hole, I thought, I would be able to pull myself out. But the ice I grabbed at only broke away, and the hole grew larger with my every attempt to escape it. I could feel my heat being drained from me. From my baby. After a few minutes my mind was still racing, but my body stopped reacting.

The river's current pulled me down and away. Although I knew that it was I who was moving, the hole seemed to be slipping away from me overhead until there was no opening, only a hard tile of ice above me. It couldn't have been very thick, but when I pushed my palms against it, nothing happened. There was nothing below me to brace my feet against, only water. My only hope was to hold my breath and pray for the current to sweep me to another opening.

It's a strange feeling when one's body shuts down completely.

This vessel that has carried you, that has served you faithfully for an entire life, stops reacting to the commands of your soul. It's almost as if someone has flicked a switch to cut the electricity. I soon understood that even if the river's current did bring me to an opening, it would be too late. My hands would not be able to hook onto its edge and, even if they did, I would lack the strength to pull myself out of the freezing water.

The most damning realization was that I could no longer expect our baby to be unharmed. With this, my spirit surrendered. I closed my eyes, because this is what one does when underwater and dying. My body dropped, and all my fear just left. There was a moment of startlingly beautiful acceptance. *It'll be easier this way,* I thought with some relief, in the final moments before everything went black.

What happened next—I can tell you about it, but I can't explain it. Not properly, not in a way that you could understand. At birth, I was given the gift of languages and I've been perfecting that gift for seven hundred years, but the words to describe what happened on that day do not exist. Not in English, nor in any other language I know.

When I woke, it wasn't really like waking, because I hadn't been asleep. It was more that I'd been in a state without any consciousness, and now I was returned into awareness. But not awareness in the way that we perceive the world around us: it was something greater, something sidelessly wide and endlessly deep. I was still under the ice, still being swept by the Pegnitz, but at the same time I was not in the water of a specific river. I was in the water of the entire world, the entire universe, but I wasn't even "in" the water so much as I was a part of it. I was indistinguishable from the water itself; I had become fluid.

When people die and somehow come back, they always talk about a tunnel of light. This was not my experience. There was light but it was not a tunnel, it was all around me. Luminous air supported me, keeping me aloft even though there was no ground that I needed to be kept aloft from. It was in me and it was through me;

I was the water and I was the light. I felt as though I were floating liquid radiance, a steady glow without warmth or cold. I no longer had any sense of my body.

Time does not exist when one's body no longer exists, because there is only the body's perception of time. We rarely notice our innate feeling for time until it's removed. This is why amnesiacs are so confused when they become first aware of their condition. It's not because they've lost memories—we all lose memories; it's because they've lost time.

I became aware of presences. You couldn't call them ghosts or spirits, because they possessed not even that much form. They existed only because I could sense them. But *sense* is again the wrong word, because how could I sense something with no substance? Like the light and the water, they were inside me. I felt them so completely that I knew that not only were they inside me, but they always had been. I had been ignoring them, all my life, in a kind of self-defense. It's like listening to a conversation—you can't concentrate on the words if you're also listening to the clock across the room and the cars outside and the footsteps down the hall and the breathing of the man sitting beside the woman sipping tea. You cannot process all this, so you concentrate only on the words of the speaker. So it is with the infinite voices of the human body. You listen to your own thoughts, and you shut out the rest.

But now I could embrace every voice within me. I could hear all those presences, and they sounded like golden circles. I could taste them, and they tasted like comfort. They touched me, and it felt like music.

See? I wish I could explain it, but I cannot. It is impossible. Anyone who believes that she can explain the Eternal Godhead has never truly experienced it.

Three presences separated themselves from the host and came forward. Although they did not assume physical shapes, I recognized them nevertheless as the humans that they had been, even though in my physical life I'd only ever met one of them, Father Sunder.

The second was Meister Eckhart and the third was Mechthild von
Magdeburg.

I knew this was not a trick, but a gift to be embraced. It was
natural, even comforting, when Father Sunder indicated that he was
pleased to be in my presence once more. Words were not used; it
was more like I could feel his thoughts brushing up against mine. It
was the same with Meister Eckhart and Sister Mechthild when they
communicated. Our "conversation" was a kaleidoscope of brilliant
vibrations.

They were not there to take me away, they explained, because
I was not ready. I had not died properly and I was unfinished. They
would help me achieve a state in which I was ready to die and, to this
end, they had been assigned as my Masters.

Why am I not being sent to Hell? I communicated. *I have killed the
man I love.*

**That's not the way it works. Eve's sin was to eat fruit, and for
this she was punished with the Fall of Mankind. For the transgressions of your life, what atonement is necessary?**

This is not for me to decide.

**But it is. Your path has taken you from the Life of God and
made you the hand behind a death. Do you repent?**

No. Even in the Eternal Godhead, I could remember my life with
you. *I may have betrayed my monastic vows and I may have betrayed my
prioress and the Lord God in doing so, but I have never betrayed myself. I
have remained true to my heart, and I will never repent my love. It is the one
great thing I have ever done.*

My Three Masters understood that I would hold to my love for
you, even in my life's end. Surely they had seen it before, and surely
they would see it again.

**Your heart has always been independent, your supreme and
most damning gift. Therefore it is through the processes of the
heart that your penance will occur.**

So be it.

You learned to give your heart over completely to the one, but

you have not yet learned to share the heart beyond the self and the other.

I confess this as true.

You shall be returned to the world, and your chest shall be filled anew with thousands of hearts. You must give each away, until all are gone but one.

How shall I achieve this?

These hearts must be given out of your chest and die for you, while finding life in others. This is so you can overcome your earthly nature and be made ready for Christ.

I do not understand the method of releasing these hearts.

You will learn the method.

And when only my final heart remains?

That one you cannot give away yourself. Your last heart must be passed over to your lover. He must accept it, but he cannot hold it. He must release it, to release you. Only in this manner may you finally be delivered to the Lord.

I do not understand the purpose of my lover's involvement.

Your lover will know the purpose.

This is where it was left. I was pulled from the Godhead, the light and water stopped flowing through me, and I was violently plunged back into the cold dark currents of the Pegnitz.

When I awoke, I was lying on my back and could not open my eyes. They were fused shut with ice and it must have taken five minutes of effort before I could blink them unglued. It was early morning and the storm had stopped. I tried to speak but was unable to produce any sound, because all my body was paralyzed. I was so much colder than I had ever been.

I began by wiggling my toes and fingers, until I managed to force entire limbs into action. I compelled myself to stand, tottering unsteadily. I was behind a shed of some sort, and a farmhouse was a hundred feet away. I stumbled towards it, hampered not only by frozen limbs but also by the fact that my clothing was stiff with ice. Smoke was rising from the chimney and I don't know if I could have made it without that promise of heat. I thumped on the door a few times until a farmwoman answered and her eyes peeled back in horror at the sight of me. To her, apparently, I was the dead coming to call.

When she realized that I was not quite dead yet, she called out to her husband and began stripping me of my frozen garments. The old man fed me soup, while the woman wrapped me in blankets and massaged my limbs to get the blood circulating. When I was sufficiently recovered, we tried to piece together what had happened. I'd been washed some miles down the river and had come to rest in an open spot that was not frozen over. It was only by chance that the old farmer had come across my body and dragged me out. My eyes were staring straight ahead, my hair was frozen into stiff fingers, and my body showed not a trace of life.

The farmer believed that everyone deserved a proper burial, and that was why he had pulled me from the river. The ground was frozen too hard to be opened for a grave so, with little choice, he decided to leave me behind their shed and bury me come spring. He couldn't bring a dead body into their home, of course, but for practical reasons rather than superstitious. It would simply thaw and start to smell. We supposed, together, that the water had been so cold that it made me appear dead. Such things had been known to happen; there were many stories of people immersed in cold water and revived long after they should have died.

I stayed with them a few days, but never told them how I came to fall into the river. I just said that I was out for a walk when the ice gave out underneath me. There was no need to recount the story of Engelthal, or of the mercenaries, or my Three Masters. My survival alone was difficult enough for them to accept.

When I was well enough to travel, I returned to the shore of the Pegnitz to retrieve my hidden bag, and then proceeded to Mainz. Where else would I go? I moved into a beguinage and adopted the life of contemplation and prayer. It was a partial return to the life I had before I met you, but I was changed so fundamentally by your love that I could not return fully to what I had once been. I did not continue in bookmaking, although in time I did finish my translation of *Inferno*. My reason for doing so was selfish—not that I thought I was creating a masterpiece to outlive me, but that working on the translation made me feel closer to you.

The rest of my story is unimportant. My years have been spent giving out hearts but I could never imagine an end to my penance until recently, because I always knew that I could never give away my final heart until we met again.

XXXII.

Vast and black, the ocean stretched away from the shore until its horizon disappeared into the night. I spoke with as much gentleness as I could manage. "I know you believe that story is true, Marianne. But it's not."

She looked down into the sand. Her breath caught in her throat, then came rushing out in a confession. "Our baby didn't survive."

She looked up, out over the ocean, and then back down at the sand again.

"When I woke up the child was . . ."

She covered her face with her hands; it was clear she could not look at me.

"Just gone," she said. "As if I had never been pregnant, as if God's hand had reached into my womb and pulled out my child as punishment."

"You can't believe that."

"I try not to. I try—I *want* to believe that it was a mercy. That the baby . . ." Her voice was so soft that I could barely make out the words. "That the baby died because of the freezing water, and God removed the child from me so I wouldn't have to confront the truth in the living world."

"If you believe in God," I said, restraining my natural inclination to add that I didn't, "you should also believe in His kindness."

"I've always wanted to believe it was a mercy," she went on, weeping. "If it was a punishment, that would be too much."

"Marianne, there was no—"

"Our child did not survive," she insisted. "This is not a thing that one forgets, no matter how old one lives to be."

I knew better than to keep trying to convince her it was only her imagination. This was another argument that I simply could not win.

It was clear that she was not speaking to me, but for herself, when she added, "It was a mercy, it had to be. It *had* to be."

Since I could not persuade her this medieval child had never existed, I decided to concentrate on our current lives.

"You're not going to die, Marianne. There are no Three Masters."

"All my hearts are gone."

"Feel this." I took her hand in my own, and I pressed it to her chest. "Your heart is still beating."

"For now. What comes next depends on you." She looked out over the ocean for a few moments before finally whispering, even though the nearest people were dozens of yards down the beach, "Do you remember what you said when I was leaving Brother Heinrich's house before the mercenaries arrived? You promised that our love would not end."

I remained silent, not wanting to encourage her, as she pulled her arrowhead necklace up over her head. "This has always been yours, and someday you'll know what to do with it."

"I don't want it," I said.

She pressed it into my hand anyway. "I've kept it all this time so that I could return it to you. It will protect you."

I could tell she would not let me refuse it, so I took it. But so she would not think that I was endorsing her story, I said, "Marianne, I don't believe this was ever blessed by Father Sunder."

She leaned her head into the crook of my shoulder and said, "You're a wonderful liar."

And then she asked a question she had never asked before.

"Do you love me?"

Our bodies were pressed into each other, our chests touching. I'm certain she could feel my heart racing. My birth-scar was against the place where, under her sweater, she had carved my name into her breast.

Do you love me?

I had never admitted aloud to anything more than "caring" for her. I had rationalized that she knew the truth without my speaking it. But really, I was just a coward.

"Yes."

For so long, I had wanted to confess myself.

"Yes. I love you."

It was time to stop failing her, so I brushed back the wild cords of her hair and poured out the words that had been in the crucible of my heart, becoming pure, since the first moment I had met her.

"I spent my entire life waiting for you, Marianne, and I didn't even know it until you arrived. Being burned was the best thing that ever happened to me because it brought you. I wanted to die but you filled me with so much love that it overflowed and I couldn't help but love you back. It happened before I even knew it and now I can't imagine not loving you. You have said that it takes so much for me to believe anything, but I *do* believe. I believe in your love for me. I believe in my love for you. I believe that every remaining beat of my heart belongs to you, and I believe that when I finally leave this world, my last breath will carry your name. I believe that my final word—*Marianne*—will be all I need to know that my life was good and full and worthy, and I believe that our love will last forever."

There was a moment in which we just held each other, and then she stood up and began walking towards the ocean. She peeled off her clothing as she went and the moonlight made her skin seem all the whiter. By the time she reached the water she was entirely nude, ghostly in her pale brilliance. There she turned and faced me for a moment, under stars that sparkled like frost through the bitter cold; she stood as if trying to memorize what I looked like, looking back at her.

"See?" Marianne said. "You do have God."

She turned away from me and waded calmly into the ocean. The water climbed up her legs and back, and soon it shrouded the tattooed wings inked into the alabaster of her skin. She leaned forward and began to stroke out into the vastness of the ocean, her black mess of hair trailing behind.

I didn't do anything but watch her move away from me until, at last, the waves swallowed the whiteness of her shoulders.

After a quarter hour Bougatsa began to howl terribly and turned in agitated circles, imploring me to do something. But I just sat there. So he ran into the tide, ready to swim, until I called him back. I knew the water was too cold and it was already too late. He trusted me enough to do as I said, but he whimpered as he lay at my feet. Still, his eyes remained hopeful. It was as though he believed that if only he waited long enough, eventually you would come wading back to us, out of the ocean.

XXXIII.

Everyone agreed that Sayuri was exceptionally beautiful in her gown. Her mother, Ayako, cried happily in the front row and her father, Toshiaki, kept raising his hand to cover his happily trembling upper lip. When Gregor slipped the ring onto her finger, Sayuri's smile had never been more radiant.

It was an August wedding, in a garden under a cloudless blue sky. Luckily there was a gentle breeze; my tuxedo didn't allow my skin to breathe properly. Special arrangements had been made to ensure that the groomsmen, of whom I was one, would stand under a large elm tree during the ceremony; it was one of the many kindnesses shown to me by the bridal couple. I was surprised that they had invited me into the wedding party at all, despite the closeness we'd grown into, but neither Gregor nor Sayuri seemed to mind that there would be a monster in their wedding pictures.

Technically, my date was the bridesmaid opposite me, but really, my escort was Jack Meredith. She managed mostly not to embarrass me, despite the massive amount of Scotch she consumed later during the reception. Clearly there was nothing romantic about her accompanying me, but we'd been spending a fair amount of time together in the preceding months. At some point, she had discovered that she could actually stand me. Our new understanding was almost a friendship, although I won't go quite that far.

For their wedding gift, I gave Sayuri and Gregor the *Morgengabe* angel. They looked at it strangely, not knowing what to make of this strange little statue, and asked if Marianne Engel had carved it. I didn't try to explain that, apparently, I had; nor did I attempt to explain that, despite its age and weathering, it was the finest gift I could give them.

At the reception Sayuri would not allow herself any champagne, because her pregnancy was just starting to show. There had been some debate about whether the wedding should occur before or after the birth, but Gregor is an old-fashioned sort of man. He wanted the child to be "legitimate," so he and Sayuri flew to Japan, where he hired a translator to convey his honorable intentions to Toshiaki. Sayuri could have done this herself but Gregor did not want her to translate, to her own father, his request to marry her. When Toshiaki granted permission, Ayako cried and bowed many times while apologizing—although for what, Gregor was not quite sure. After Ayako wiped dry her eyes, they all drank tea in the garden behind the house.

Sayuri's parents did not seem bothered in the least that she was living abroad or marrying a foreigner, nor that she was well past the age of fresh Christmas cake. (In fact, Ayako pointed out that, as greater numbers of Japanese women were getting married later in life, the cutoff age for spinsterhood was no longer twenty-five. Single women who reached the age of thirty-one were now being called New Year's Eve noodles.) The only thing about the marriage that troubled Sayuri's parents, just slightly, was that she had decided to take her husband's family name. They privately lamented that "Sayuri Hnatiuk" lacked any sense of poetry and, despite their best efforts, they could not learn how to pronounce it correctly.

Towards the end of the day I had the opportunity to chat with Mrs. Mizumoto for a few minutes, with Sayuri acting as translator.

Sayuri had already told her mother about Marianne Engel's passing in the spring, and Ayako offered her most sincere condolences.
When I thanked her for this, I could see that she found the growl of
my voice shocking but was too polite to mention it. Instead she only
increased the width of her smile and, in an instant, I understood
where Sayuri had learned her mannerisms. We spoke pleasantly for
a few minutes and I assured Ayako that I thought her daughter was
destined for a happy married life despite the fact that Gregor, even in
a tuxedo, looked an awful lot like a chipmunk. Sayuri hit me on the
arm for saying this but apparently translated it accurately anyway.
Her mother nodded her head enthusiastically, agreeing: *"So, so, so, so,
so, so, so!"* All the while she held her hand in front of her mouth, as
if trying to prevent her laughs from escaping.

As our conversation was coming to a close, Mrs. Mizumoto offered a final deep bow of condolence. When she came back up, she
gave me a hopeful smile, put her hand upon Sayuri's stomach, and
said, *"Rinne tenshō."*

The translation was not easy for Sayuri, who suggested the closest approximation was either "Everything comes back" or "Life is
repeated." Sayuri added that this was the type of thing old Japanese
ladies sometimes say when they think that they're more Buddhist
than they really are. It appeared to me, from the dirty look she shot
her daughter, that Ayako understood more English than she let on.

But as they walked away, they hugged each other tightly. Ayako
seemed to be quick to forget her daughter's comment about old Japanese ladies, and Sayuri was just as quick to forgive her mother for
laughing at the image of Gregor as a chipmunk.

• • •

After Marianne Engel disappeared the authorities searched along the
shoreline for three days but did not find a body. Nothing was found
but long, lonely expanses of water. The problem with the ocean is
that you cannot drag the entire thing, and it was as if the water had

removed all evidence of her life but refused to offer any confirmation of her de-th.

Marianne Engel had no life insurance, but suspicion was directed towards me nevertheless. Rightfully so: less than six months before her disappearance, she had changed her will to name me as the primary beneficiary. This situation did not sit well with the police, especially since I was with her when she went missing. They questioned me at length but the investigation showed that I had no knowledge of the will, and the teenagers who drank beer on the beach testified that it was not uncommon for "the burnt guy" and "the tattooed chick with weird hair" to come late at night. She often went swimming, they confirmed, regardless of the weather. On that particular night, I had done nothing but sit on the beach while the dog ran around in circles.

Jack also spoke on my behalf. Her words carried special weight because she was not only Marianne Engel's conservator but also the person whom I had replaced in the will. Despite this, Jack spoke highly of my character and told the police that she had no doubt of the love between Marianne Engel and me. While she did confirm that I didn't know about the changes to the will, she also added, "I thought I would have plenty of time to talk Marianne out of it later. I didn't expect her de-th to come so soon."

Jack Meredith can speak words that I cannot write. Words like *de-th*. Words like *suic-de*. These words make a coward of me. Writing them would bring them that much closer to being real.

The legal proceedings accounted for most of my time during the summer, but in truth I barely paid attention. I didn't care what the police decided about my responsibility in the disappearance and I didn't care what the lawyers said about the will. In the end, Jack had to retain an independent lawyer on my behalf, because, without counsel, I would have signed any document put in front of me, just as I had in the hospital when my production company was put into bankruptcy.

Marianne Engel had bequeathed almost everything to me, in-

cluding the house and all its contents. Even Bougatsa. Jack, despite
the years of service she had given in managing Marianne Engel's
business affairs, received only the statues that were already in her
gallery.

In a collection of shoeboxes at the back of a closet, I found bank-
books from a dozen accounts holding hundreds of thousands of dollars, now mine. Marianne Engel had been entirely debt-free, perhaps
because no financial institution considered her an acceptable credit
risk. I also discovered a series of receipts that revealed the truth of
my private hospital room. It was not, as Nan had said at the time, a
"happy accident" that the room was available so she could research
recovery rates for patients in private, versus shared, rooms. Nor, as
I guessed at the time, had I been put in a private room primarily so
Nan could keep Marianne Engel away from the other patients. The
truth was that Marianne Engel had paid for the private room so she
could tell me her stories without being disturbed. She just had never
told me.

Nothing that I inherited will become mine for a number of years
yet, because there was no body. Only after sufficient time has passed
will a "presumptive de-th certificate" be issued for Marianne Engel,
and until then her assets will remain in escrow. Luckily, the courts
determined that I could continue living in the fortress as it was already my primary residence when she went missing.

The local newspapers, and even a few international ones, carried
short articles about the disappearance of a mentally ill but highly talented sculptress. "Presumed de-d," they all said. Because nothing improves an artist's reputation more than a tragic end, Jack was able to
sell the gallery's remaining statues in record time. Although I had to
violate the terms of the will to do so, I gave Jack most of those that
still remained at the fortress. (I kept only the statue of myself, and a
few other favorite grotesques.) My lawyer advised against this, but it
wasn't as if the police were monitoring my actions. It was common
for trucks to come and go, so no one in the neighborhood paid any
attention when a few more statues were hauled away. When Jack

brought over a check for their sale, less her commissions, I pressed the payment back into her hand.

She deserved it more than I did. And even though the bank accounts were frozen, I had ample money on which to live.

Marianne Engel, despite her generally scattered thinking, had foreseen the possibility that she might not always be around to pay my bills. After her disappearance, I found an envelope addressed to me, containing a key to the safety deposit box that she'd arranged would be accessible to me. When I opened the box, I discovered that it contained more than enough cash to provide for all my needs until the will came into force.

There were two other things in the box, as well.

◆ ◆ ◆

Ultimately the police determined that I was without culpability in the disappearance of Marianne Engel. But they were wrong.

I killed Marianne Engel. I killed her as surely as if I had lifted a gun or tilted a bottle of poison.

As she walked towards the ocean, I knew that she was not going swimming. I *knew* that she would not return, and I will not pretend otherwise. And yet, I did nothing.

I did nothing, just as she had once requested that I do, as a way of proving my love.

I could have saved her with nothing more than a few words. If I had told her not to enter the water, she wouldn't have carried out her plan. I know this. She would have returned to me, because her Three Masters had told her that I needed to accept her final heart but then release it, to release her. Any effort that I made to stop her would have constituted a refusal to release her, so all I had to say was *"Marianne, come back."*

I didn't, and now I'm doomed to live with the knowledge that I didn't say three simple words that would have saved her life. I'm doomed to know that I didn't take her to court in an attempt to have her committed, that I didn't try hard enough to sneak medicine into her food, that I didn't handcuff her to the bed whenever her carving got out of control. There are literally dozens of actions that could have prevented her from dy-ng, all things that I did not do.

Marianne Engel believed that she had killed me seven hundred years ago, in an act of kindness, but that story was fiction. The reality is that I killed her in this lifetime: not with kindness, but through inaction. While she believed that she was freeing herself from the shackles of her penitent hearts, I knew better. I am not schizophrenic. And still, I remained quiet. Ineffective. Murderous.

I face this fact for a few moments each day, but that's all I can stand. Sometimes I even try to write it down before it slips away, but usually my hand begins to shake before I can get the words out. It never takes me long to start lying again, trying to convince myself that Marianne Engel's imaginary past was legitimate simply because she believed it so deeply. Everyone's past, I try to rationalize, is nothing more than the collection of memories they choose to remember. But in my heart, I know this is just a defense mechanism that I manufacture simply so I can go on living with myself.

All I had to say was *"Marianne, come back."*

◆ ◆ ◆

The word *paleography* comes from the Greek *palais* (old) and *graphia* (script), so it is not surprising that paleographers study ancient writings. They classify manuscripts by examining the lettering (size, slant, pen movement) as well as the writing materials (papyrus or parchment, scroll or codex, type of ink). Good paleographers can determine the number of writers who worked on a manuscript, can assess their skill, and often can even assign the manuscript to a specific region. With religious writings, they can sometimes identify not only a specific scriptorium but even a particular scribe.

Not long ago I engaged the services of two of the world's foremost paleographers: one an expert in medieval German documents and the other an expert in medieval Italian documents. I hired them to look at the items that I had found, in addition to the cash, in the safety deposit box.

Two copies of *Inferno,* both handwritten but by different hands: the first in Italian and the other in German. Both appeared, to my untrained eye, to be hundreds of years old.

Before I would tell either paleographer what I wanted examined, I made them sign strict nondisclosure agreements. Both men found my request unusual, almost humorous, but consented. Professional curiosity, one supposes. But when I presented the manuscripts, both men realized in an instant that they'd been handed something exceptional. The Italian blurted an excited profanity, while the German's mouth twitched at the corners. I assumed a pose of complete ignorance regarding the origins of the books, saying nothing about where I'd acquired them.

Because *Inferno* was immediately popular with readers, it is one of the most common works to survive in copies from the fourteenth century. The Italian paleographer had little doubt that my copy was among the very earliest, perhaps made within a decade of the first publication. He begged that I allow him to confirm his findings with other experts, but I declined his request.

The German was not as quick to assign an age to the translation, partially because his initial examinations provided some bewildering contradictions. First, he wondered how a manuscript so remarkably well-preserved had gone unnoticed for so long. Second, it appeared that a single hand had penned the entire work, which was highly unusual for such a long document. Third, whoever had produced the book was exceptionally skilled. Not only was the script beautifully formed, but the translation itself was better than most, if not all, modern ones. But it was the fourth point that was most puzzling: the physical attributes of the manuscript—parchment, ink, lettering—suggested that it had been produced in the Rhine area of Germany, perhaps as early as the first half of the 1300s. If this was true—though it hardly could be—then my manuscript predated

any known German translation of *Inferno* by several centuries. "So
you see, I simply must be mistaken." He trembled. "I must be! Unless . . . unless . . ."

The German requested permission to perform radiocarbon dat-
ing on both the parchment and the ink. When I granted it, he had
such a look of orgasmic joy on his face that I was afraid he might
pass out. *"Danke, danke schön, ich danke Ihnen vielmals!"*

When the tests were completed and the parchment was dated
to 1335, plus or minus twenty years, the German's mood stepped a
notch higher. "This is a discovery that is so far beyond anything that
I . . . that I . . ." He couldn't even find the words for his flabbergasted
delight; the translation had been made within decades of Dante's
original Italian. I decided that it would not hurt to allow further research, and I even gave the German a push in a certain direction: I
suggested that he might want to focus his investigation on the scriptorium at Engelthal. The German's mouth twitched again, and he
went back to his work.

When he contacted me some weeks later, he seemed to have
finally accepted that he was investigating an impossible document.
Yes, he confirmed, the work gave many indications of having been
done at Engelthal. And yes, the copying was highly indicative of a
particular scribe whose work was well known in the years circa 1310
to 1325. In fact, this scribe had always posed a minor mystery to
scholars of German mysticism: her literary fingerprints were on a
huge number of documents, her talent exceeding that of any of her
peers, and yet her name could not be found anywhere. Such a secret
could only have been kept by a coordinated effort between the prioress and the armarius of the time but, as Engelthal was otherwise
proud of its literary reputation, the great question was: what was it
about this particular nun that required such secrecy?

The German's mustache was positively dancing as he spoke of
all this but, he admitted, some points contradicted the Engelthal hypothesis. The parchment was of a different quality than that found
in the monastery's other documents, and the inks seemed to be of

a different chemical composition. So while the workmanship suggested that it came from Engelthal, the German explained, the physical materials did not. And—need he even add this?—Engelthal would almost certainly have had nothing to do with Dante's great poem. "It was not their particular milieu, if you understand what I mean. Not only was it in Italian, but entirely blasphemous for its time."

The German asked, somewhat sheepishly, whether I had any more "hints" for him. As it turned out, I did. I suggested that he might now want to divert his attention from Engelthal to the city of Mainz, paying attention to privately produced books from the mid-1320s. The scribe, I said, might have written under the name of Marianne. The German's bushy eyebrows furrowed under the weight of this new information and he begged to know how I could offer such specific suggestions. I said it was just a hunch.

He spent the better part of a month seeking out manuscripts that matched my parameters. He called often, sometimes to update me on progress but usually to complain that the confidentiality agreement was holding him back. "Do you have any idea how difficult it is to request such documents when I can't explain why I need them? Do you think I can just go to the library and check out books from the fourteenth century?"

I could tell he was about to start talking to his colleagues, with or without my permission, so I declared his research concluded. I thought he was going to smack me in the face, but instead he launched into a series of impassioned pleas: "This is one of the major discoveries in the history of the field . . . far-reaching implications . . . radically alter what we think about German translation . . ." When I continued to refuse, he changed his tack. He begged for a few more days of study and I swear that he actually batted his eyes at me. I refused this request as well, certain that he'd use the time to make a high-quality copy of the original. When I demanded my manuscript back that very minute, he threatened to go public with what he knew. "A contract of law is nothing compared with such a great gift to the world of literature!" I told him that his sentiment was highly admirable; nevertheless, I would sue him into bankruptcy if he spoke a single word. At this, he suggested that Dante should have added another Circle to Hell for "book-haters" like me.

In an effort to offer some small consolation to the man's ego, I assured him that should I ever bring forth the German translation of *Inferno,* I would publicly acknowledge all the research that he had done. In fact, I would invite him to publish his findings concurrently, so that he was in no way deprived of academic acclaim. And then the German greatly surprised me. "I couldn't care less if you include anything about who I am. This discovery is simply too important to keep hidden away."

As of this day, I still haven't decided what I'll do with the copies of *Inferno* that Marianne Engel left me. When I'm feeling particularly fanciful, I tell myself that I'll take the Italian copy into the grave with me, just in case I run into Francesco Corsellini one more time and I can return his father's book to him.

· · ·

I'm keeping my fake toes but I've declined fake fingers; the toes help with my balance, while the fingers are only vanity. Besides, with a body like mine, fake fingers are the equivalent of replacing the headlights on a crashed car.

There are still things I could do to improve my appearance, small surgeries or corrective cosmetics that might soften my roughest edges. A plastic surgeon offered to rebuild my ears using cartilage from my ribs, or to provide prosthetic ears that look like real ones. But, like fake fingers, pseudo-ears lack a functional use: neither cartilage nor plastic will allow me to hear again. The theory is that they would make me feel more human by making me look more "normal," but when I slipped on the prosthetics, they made me feel like Mr. Potato Head. As for a phalloplasty—the surgical construction of a new penis—I just haven't gotten around to it. Maybe one day I will, but I've had enough surgeries for now. I'm tired. So recently I told Dr. Edwards, simply: "Enough."

"I understand," she said. And then the look crossed Nan's face, the one I knew so well, the look she wore when weighing the benefits of telling the truth against lying or keeping quiet. As always, she decided on the truth. "You once asked why I chose to work in the burn unit. I'm going to show you something that I've never shown another patient."

She pulled her white coat aside and rolled up her shirt, to reveal a large hypertrophic scar that covered the entire right side of her torso. "It happened when I was only four years old. I pulled a pot of boiling water off the stove. It's our scars that make us who we are." And then she left the office.

So I'm left with a Depression-era dustbowl of a skull. The top of my head is like infertile fields after a windstorm, bunched up in drifts of bullied dirt. There are subtle shifts in color, shades of red and brown. All is dry and wasted, as if the skin has been waiting years for the rain to come. A few wisps of tenacious hair sway across the furrowed landscape of my skull, like survivor weeds that don't know they're supposed to be dead.

My face is the field after the stubble has been burned. My lips, once so full, are thin like dehydrated worms. Knowing the medical term *microstomia* does not make my lips less ugly. Still, I prefer this mouth to the one I had before I told Marianne Engel that I loved her.

Pre-fire, my spine was strong; post-fire, it was replaced with a snake. Now the snake is gone and I'm rediscovering my backbone, which is a good start. My right leg is filled with metal pins and I could view them as shackles forged from the remains of my crashed vehicle. I could decide to drag my accident everywhere. I won't.

I'm exercising harder than ever before. A few times each week Sayuri takes me to the local pool, where she leads me through a series of workouts. The water itself adds buoyancy, reducing stress on my joints. On the days when I'm not in the pool, Sayuri is teaching me to skip in the backyard. I suppose it must puzzle anyone who looks over from St. Romanus. What do they think about the monster bouncing around the yard, driven by a tiny Japanese woman? Occasionally Father Shanahan sees me and waves, and I always wave back. I've decided not to dislike him, despite the fact that he's a priest.

After my workouts, Gregor comes over to pick Sayuri up and the three of us have tea. At our most recent gathering, I shared the news that this book was going to be published. They had no idea I had been writing this story; I'd been keeping it a secret, because I didn't know what I would do with it when it was finished. But though I'm keeping back the *Infernos*, I have made my decision to release this book into the world. I am still unsure whether it is the correct thing to do so—my emotions on the matter change often—but silence is too painful.

My friends were excited by my news, although Sayuri confessed that she still could not read English nearly as quickly as she would like. Then she excitedly grabbed her husband's arm as if she'd just had the greatest idea of her life. "Wait! Will you read to me before we go to sleep each night? That way we'll get the story at the same time!"

Gregor looked a little sheepish about Sayuri's display of affection but I assured him that it sounded like a wonderful idea, adding, "And you might even learn something about the history of your wedding present."

I am more than my scars.

* * *

When I returned home after her disappearance, after my initial statements to the police, I went down into the workshop to read what Marianne Engel had carved into the pedestal of my statue.

Dû bist mîn, ich bin dîn:
des solt dû gewis sîn;

dû bist beslozzen in mînem herzen,
verlorn ist daz slüzzelîn:
dû muost och immer darinne sîn.

"You are mine, I am yours; you may be sure of this. You've been locked inside my heart, the key has been thrown away; within it, you must always stay."

• • •

Lebrecht Bachenschwanz produced the first known German version of *The Divine Comedy* (*Die göttliche Komödie*) in the years 1767 to 1769, and the translation of *Inferno* in my possession is at least four hundred years older than that. While amazing, this hardly proves that Marianne Engel translated the book in the first half of the fourteenth century; it only means that *someone* did. But if Marianne Engel was not the translator, how did the book come to rest in her safety deposit box? How did it exist for almost seven centuries with absolutely no record of its existence? As with so many things, I don't know.

I've written so much about the German translation that you might assume there's nothing exceptional about the Italian original, save its age. I assure you that nothing could be further from the truth. There are a few defects in the manuscript's condition that, while lowering the book's monetary value, are of considerable interest to me.

It is obvious that the book was in a fire at one point. The pages are singed at the edges, but the flames did not creep far enough inwards to burn away any of the words. Somehow, the book was spared extensive fire damage; in fact, it is the other flaw that is more obvious.

There is a wide cut through the book's front cover, produced by a sharp instrument. A knife or an arrow, perhaps. The cut penetrates into the book's body so that when the cover is opened, there is a slit

of almost equal size on the first page. This slit, situated in the middle
of each page, becomes smaller the deeper one turns into the book.
The back cover of the book bears only a small exit wound; it's apparent that the sharp instrument was almost, but not quite, stopped by
the thickness of the manuscript.

It took me a long time to work up the courage to remove my
neck chain and insert the arrowhead into the wound of the manuscript's cover. It slid in perfectly, like a key finding the correct lock. I
pushed further until the arrowhead was engulfed by the book and its
tip just barely peeked through the slit in the back cover.

These days, I like to imagine that if a man were to enter through
that slash on the book's cover, as if it were a door, he could walk
right into the very heart of *Inferno*.

• • •

There were a number of reasons that Jack and I decided not to get a
grave for Marianne Engel, but two stood above all others. First, it felt
strange with no actual body to place into it. And second, who would
visit this grave, anyway, except the two of us?

I don't want to visit a grave.

• • •

Every day I wake up with Bougatsa sleeping at my feet. I feed him
raw pancreas, and then we load ourselves into the car to head to the
ocean.

I look out over the ocean as the sun rises. It's my vigil, an hour
of the day devoted to remembering Marianne Engel, and it's also the
only time that I allow myself in the direct sunlight. Too much expo-
sure is not good for my skin, but I like the warmth on my face.

Bougatsa usually runs around, picking up little pieces of driftwood in his mouth and then dropping them at my feet. He begs

me to throw them for him, and I do, and then he goes bounding out into the tide. But there are some mornings when he doesn't feel like running and just lies at my feet staring at the ocean. It's just like the night she walked in; it's as if he still expects that she will come wading back out to us. I guess he doesn't know any better. He's just a stupid dog.

All the while, I'm composing in my mind. These pages that you have now read, most of them originated at my lonely command post at the edge of the world where the earth falls into the sea. I have spent much time there, in this grand empty space between memory and desire, creating this cracked empire of sentences in which I now live.

I wanted to write this book to honor her but I have failed, just like all the times that I failed her in life. I know my words are nothing more than pale ghosts, but I need Marianne Engel to exist somewhere.

• • •

Every Good Friday, this anchored yet ever-changing anniversary of my accident, I go to the little creek that saved my life and light one more candle. I offer thanks for two facts: that I am one year older, and that I am one year closer to death.

When Marianne Engel gave me the arrowhead, she said that I would know what to do with it when the time comes. But I already know. I shall wear it always and proudly, and when I am an old man and my living is done, I will slip the arrowhead from my necklace. I'll place it on a shaft, straight and true, and I will ask a dear friend to shoot that arrow through my heart. Perhaps that friend will be Gregor, or Sayuri; perhaps it will be someone I haven't met yet. The arrow will fly to my chest and split open my birth-scar like a seal that has been waiting to be opened.

This will mark the third time that an arrow has entered my chest.

The first time brought me to Marianne Engel. The second time separated us.

The third time will reunite us.

◆ ◆ ◆

Ah, but don't let me sound too serious. I still have a lifetime of work
ahead of me.

After Marianne Engel's disappearance, I took it upon myself to
learn about carving. I suppose my motivation is selfish, because carving helps me feel closer to her. I love the movement of steel against
stone. One usually misinterprets rock as unmoving, unforgiving, but
it is not: stone is like flowing water, it's like dancing fire. My chisel
moves as if it knows the secret wishes of the stone, as if the statue is
guiding the tool. But the strangest thing I've discovered is how natural carving seems, as if I have done it before.

My skills are not nearly as developed as Marianne Engel's were,
and when I create a little statue it rarely looks as I imagined. But
that's okay. In fact, it's not often that I even produce original stonework. More often, I use her tools to chip away at the statue of me
that she left behind.

Standing in front of my likeness still embarrasses me a little, but
I remind myself that it is not vanity. I am not looking at myself; I
am looking at a part of Marianne Engel that remains. And then I lift
the chisel and target a small area—the corner of my elbow, a fold
in my burned skin—and strike with the hammer. With each stroke,
another piece of me falls away. I can only stand to shave off a tiny
splinter at a time because each time a stone fragment hits the floor, I
am slightly closer to becoming nothing.

The Three Masters stated that Marianne Engel's lover would
know the reason he had to release her final heart, to release her. And
I do: the end of her penance was the beginning of mine. Allowing
her to walk unhindered into the ocean was only the starting point of

my task, because releasing her did not occur in an instant. It is an ongoing process that will last my lifetime, and I will not allow myself to die until I have carved away the last trace of my statue.

With every fragment of rock that falls from me, I can hear the voice of Marianne Engel. *I love you. Aishiteru. Ego amo te. Ti amo. Ég elska þig. Ich liebe dich.* It is moving across time, coming to me in every language of the world, and it sounds like pure love.

ACKNOWLEDGMENTS

My sincerest thanks to Angela Aki, dear friend and the first person ever to read this book; Bette Alexander and Jolanta Benal, perfectionists; Liuba Apostolova, who is made of starlight; Marty Asher, Jamie Byng, Anne Collins, Gerry Howard, Anya Serota, and Bill Thomas, the early believers; the Brattis, my second family; all the staff at Canongate, Doubleday, Janklow & Nesbit, and Random House Canada; Dr. Linda Dietrick and Dr. Ann-Catherine Geuder, advisors on all matters Germanic; the editors (Anne, Gerry, and Anya) who, with elegant scalpels, helped debride the dead parts; Dr. Kathy J. Edwards, who patiently answered all my burning questions; John Fontana, who makes me look good; Helen Hayward, killer teacher; my international proofreaders Kyoko Aoyama, Yoichi Takagi, and Miko Yamanouchi (Japanese), Úa Matthíasdóttir (Icelandic), and Giuseppe Strazzeri (Italian); Eric Simonoff, the novel's greatest champion; Dorothy Vincent, who took the book around the world; the publishing assistants essential to getting things done, particularly Katie Halleron, Eadie Klemm, and Alexa Von Hirschberg; Joe Burgess, Kirby Drynan, Liz Ericksson, Kevin and Alex Hnatiuk, Alison and Helen Ritchie, and Paige Wilson, friends with feedback; my family, nuclear and extended, for their support and love; and Harley and Fjola, for everything.

To the following resources, I am particularly indebted: *Medieval Germany: An Encyclopedia*, edited by John M. Jeep; *The Mystics of Engelthal: Writings from a Medieval Monastery*, by Leonard P. Hindsley; *Henry Suso: The Exemplar, with Two Sermons*, translated, edited, and introduced by Frank Tobin; *Light, Life and Love: Selections from the German Mystics of the Middle Ages*, edited by W. R. Inge; *The Inferno*, by Dante Alighieri, translated by Robert Hollander and Jean Hollander; *The Divine Comedy: The Inferno, The Purgatorio*, and *The Paradiso*, by Dante Alighieri, translated by John Ciardi; *Surviving Schizophrenia: A Manual for Families, Consumers, and Providers* (fourth edition), by E. Fuller Torrey, M.D.; *Rising from the Flames: The Experience of the Severely Burned*, by Albert Howard Carter III, Ph.D., and Jane Arbuckle Petro, M.D.; *Severe Burns: A Family Guide to Medical and Emotional Recovery*, by Andrew M. Munster, M.D., and the Staff of the Baltimore Regional Burn Center; *Holy Terrors: Gargoyles on Medieval Buildings*, by Janetta Rebold Benton (in which is printed a version of the legend of the dragon La Gargouille); the website Viking Answer Lady; and the King James Version of the Holy Bible.

ANDREW DAVIDSON was born in Pinawa, Manitoba, and graduated in 1995 from the University of British Columbia with a B.A. in English literature. He has worked as a teacher in Japan, where he has lived on and off, and as a writer of English lessons for Japanese websites. *The Gargoyle*, the product of seven years' worth of research and composition, is his first book. Davidson lives in Winnipeg, Manitoba.

burnedbylove.com

THE GARGOYLE

SPECIAL FEATURES

THE STORY BEHIND *The Gargoyle*
By Andrew Davidson

The Gargoyle has been in release for seven months as I write this, and it seems every day I'm telling another reader or reporter how the book escaped my desk and crawled out into the world. The story has been retold a number of times, in the press and on the internet—but in fragments, and often with inaccuracies. This is inevitable, of course, so when Vintage Canada approached me for an essay to append the Canadian paperback edition, I saw an opportunity to set the account down in one place, completely and truthfully.

Well, at least as I understand it.

The story begins in Pinawa, Manitoba, where I was born in the spring of 1969. The town was founded less than a decade earlier to support a government nuclear research facility about a hundred kilometers east of Winnipeg. This is right in the middle of nowhere—which is, I suppose, exactly where you'd want a nuclear research facility. But this location created an interesting problem: how could you entice respected scientific minds, capable of working almost anywhere in the world, to live there?

A good start would be to build on the banks of the Winnipeg River; it's a beautiful natural setting, and offers plenty in the way of outdoor activities that don't involve mountains. Then you'd build a curling rink, tennis courts, baseball diamonds, shopping facilities, a bar, a beach, a pool, a golf course, an indoor skating rink, and an outdoor skating rink. You'd lay in snowmobile and skiing trails, set up competitive sports leagues for the children and recreational ones for the adults, and ensure there were a local theater group and a public library. You'd erect schools and fill them with (mostly) excellent teachers, and you'd build a hospital. You'd pay the workers handsomely and keep living costs quite reasonable. And so on.

It sounds like I'm writing a travel brochure for the town, but I actually have a point—which is that during the years until my high school graduation in 1987, Pinawa was an exceptional place to live. The population hovered around two thousand, with little turnover, so I knew almost everyone in town and always felt safe. I took part in all the recreational activities, got a solid education, and—most important, in regards to *The Gargoyle*—took hundreds of books out of the library each year. I even read many of them. As far as subject matter, everything was of interest: biographies to science texts to myths to serious fiction. I never thought I was preparing for anything; all I knew was that I enjoyed books and the price was right.

So it went until I entered grade ten, when I was confronted with an English teacher who would abide nothing less than the best efforts of her students. This teacher had the nickname of "Killer," which I suspect she regarded secretly with pride. After my first step into her classroom, my marks plummeted in my other subjects. How could they not, given that all my homework time was devoted to *Macbeth* and *Tess of the D'Urbervilles*? My greatest achievement in high school was that I received the top mark in English each year; I damn near gave up sleep in an effort to please the Killer. She taught me the basic skills of composition and, even better, she instilled in me the desire to learn how writing really *worked*. Inevitably, I began writing truly horrible teenage poetry that was based far too heavily on song lyrics by The Doors.

My writing didn't stop after high school, it just expanded into new forms. I spent the first half of my twenties writing mediocre stage plays and the second half writing slightly less mediocre screenplays. There were short stories along the way, too, and other works that didn't even deserve to be categorized as any particular form. It was not that I was blazing bold new paths in literature; no, I was simply not skilled enough to stay on the paths that already existed. Despite my obvious difficulties with words, somehow I managed to pick up a university degree in English Literature and a diploma in the then-new discipline of creating digital media content—webpages, CD-Roms, digital video and audio editing, and the like.

As I approached the age of thirty, writing in coffee shops overnight while trying to avoid a real job, I had a bit of a crisis. You see, I suspected there were countries outside of Canada but I'd never lived in any of them.

A number of my acquaintances had taught in Japan and were constantly telling me about the great time they'd had there. It seemed relatively easy, which was a big draw for me: the English conversation schools regularly had recruiters looking for prospective teachers in Vancouver, where I lived at the time, and the only real requirements were a university degree and the ability to speak. I had a few interviews and, almost before I knew it, was on a plane to Japan.

I went without preconceived notions: if I didn't like the country, I would honor my one-year contract and it would be an interesting life experience; if I did like it, I'd stay a while longer. As it turned out, I renewed my contract over and over. During my first two years I traveled as a substitute teacher covering short stints while the school was waiting for their permanent teacher to arrive. I worked in about fifteen cities during that time, from Sapporo on the northern island of Hokkaido to Naha on the southern island of Okinawa. My final three years were in a Tokyo office, creating internet lessons for Japanese learners. This was the perfect job for me, bringing together my degree in English and my diploma in digital media creation. And in the evenings, as always, I kept writing.

Here's the truth about the writing I did before *The Gargoyle*: it was not good. In my early twenties I ignored this fact, and somehow managed to publish three poems in such obscure publications that even I can't remember their names. By my early thirties, however, I was well past dreaming that someday I would make a living from storytelling. I was writing because I enjoyed doing it; I was writing because it was my way to entertain and educate myself; and I was writing because I felt grouchy and incomplete when I didn't.

But when I started *The Gargoyle*, something changed. Skills that I had barely been aware I was acquiring started to come together, and the writing I had done since I was sixteen revealed itself as the practice it needed to be. Poetry was about the beauty of the line and the concentrated idea; stage plays were an education in dialogue; and screenplays forced me to work with action and visuals. Without doing that preliminary work, I wouldn't have been prepared to start the novel that I was not yet aware was going to be a novel. I thought I was simply starting the next project that would pass my time for a while. Perhaps it's a good thing I didn't know, because I wonder if I would have even begun if I'd known that eight years later I would be in New York, still red-lining in the final edits.

At the time, the only thing I knew for certain was that I had to get the woman in my head to shut up.

When I was writing anything, even personal letters, this woman would take over my pen and make me write down the stories she wanted to tell. I tried, at first, to remain in control of my work—no one was going to tell me what to write, dammit—but she insisted she had something to say and I was going to take it down, and that was that. I lost my will to resist her on May 1, 2000, and started *The Gargoyle* because I could no longer not start it.

She arrived with her name fully intact—Marianne Engel—and she also came with her look: impossibly wild hair and eyes that shifted between blue and green. Invariably she was standing in front of a church, ranting about things that sounded insane but, for some reason, I knew were not. My job was to figure out *why* her stories weren't crazy.

The first real decision Marianne Engel allowed me to make by myself was that, though she demanded I set down these stories on her behalf, I could not write in her voice. The reason was her unreliable nature—already I was wondering whether she was a liar, a schizophrenic, or someone who had actually lived what she claimed. And yet, I also knew that I could not write in the third person omniscient: there could be no author hovering above the action who saw and understood and could explain everything. With Marianne Engel, explaining everything was never an option. So, I needed a narrator who was not her, but who could say:

"This is what I saw, and this is what I think of it—but what do you think?"

Well, Marianne Engel had already informed me that there was a man, that he was in a hospital, and that she needed to speak to him. I thought that would be a good place to start looking for my narrator.

That this man is a burn survivor is related to an idea I'd long been carrying as the starting point of a story. Everyone has had a relationship end and experienced the feeling of having "been burned." It is a clichéd image, to be sure, but it is a cliché because it is apt and true. I was intrigued by the idea of a relationship that did not end with the feeling of being burned, but one that began with such a feeling—taken to the literal level.

It happened that at the time, even before Marianne Engel came to me, I was reading about survivors of severe burns. This might seem somewhat specialized and peculiar, but it's the kind of reading I often do. I can't even remember why—perhaps I had come across an article in the newspaper, or maybe it was that vague idea floating around in my head—but the more I learned about the treatment of burns, the more I wanted to know. It was fascinating, grotesque, and more amazing than anything I could imagine in the darkest corners of my imagination: in other words, from a dramatic standpoint, it was perfect. So I challenged myself to write a character who had been badly burned, in part so I'd have to do more research—because this relates to one of my strongest beliefs about writing.

During university, I'd taken many courses on writing and was often told that it's best to write about what one knows. Over the years, I've found this to be the worst possible advice. I would suggest that one should write about what one wants to know. There will be months, even years, of research, so it's essential to find something that can hold your interest. Furthermore, I believe there is an "energy of discovery" that you can capture in your writing: if you learn something so compelling you have to include it, chances are that at least a few readers will be glad you did.

The Gargoyle was not written and then supplemented with research as needed. I read widely and sometimes a single bit of new information twisted my novel in another direction. To give an example: I had no idea that burn survivors often recover on beds that use air floatation technology to reduce friction and facilitate healing—but when I did learn this, how could I not include it? And with the narrator in this bed it became my duty, as steward of the character, to imagine how it might feel. I thought he might liken the sensation to skydiving, which led him to remember a youthful episode in which he attended an air show. While I was writing this scene, an Asian woman (bald and wearing a robe) wandered into the action. I didn't know what to make of her but I knew I needed her. I wish I could give a scholarly answer as to why—quote a theory of story construction, or cite classical references—but the truth is that she just felt like she belonged. Eventually this woman led me to the story of the Japanese glassblower Sei, and that led me to write the other love stories Marianne Engel tells in the novel. So, from this discovery of air floatation beds, I came to incorporate a vivid detail of the narrator's rehabilitation, reflect upon a childhood memory, introduce a new character, and include four love stories.

Another example of the influence of wandering research

can be found in the sections regarding medieval Germany. I had no intention to take the story to this place and time when I started writing; in fact, I had been working on the novel for a year before I came across a reference to a monastery called Engelthal. While I knew Marianne Engel's last name meant "angel" in German, I'd never heard of the monastery. But the translated meaning—"Valley of the Angels"—is quite charming, and it seemed a possible solution for a problem that I had been unable to solve. You see, the first time Marianne Engel visited the narrator in the burn ward, she claimed she'd known him for centuries. Very dramatic. However, it was also problematic, because she was unwilling to share with me exactly what she meant.

As soon as I learned about the monastery, however, Marianne Engel opened up about her days there. It was as if she had been waiting for me to find this one key to her past before she would be willing to tell the whole thing. It was only then, in Engelthal, that I truly began to understand the journey upon which she wanted to take me. Now that I had earned her trust, she kept talking and I kept writing it down.

When I moved from Japan back to Canada in 2004, pushed out of the country by the crush of people in Tokyo, I had a somewhat finished manuscript—and I liked it. It was far better than anything that I'd written previously; it was even, I dared to think, publishable.

Emboldened, I decided to do everything necessary to find an agent. In some ways, this process would prove to be as challenging as writing the novel itself—but having already spent thousands of hours on the writing, I felt that it was too late to back out, or back down.

I decided I would start by approaching the most distinguished agents I could imagine. If I had to query one hundred agents before I got a reply, so be it. Two hundred? Fine. Five hundred? If necessary. In fact, if I had to, I'd approach every agent on the planet.

Fate, however, was kind.

I learned early of an agent named Eric Simonoff, who represents an incredible list of clients. In fact, the first time I looked over those names, I knew without a doubt that Eric was far too good for me. Nevertheless, I was philosophically committed to being rejected by him before I could move on.

I wanted to follow the guidelines for respectful submissions, sure, but I also reasoned that my query letter needed to set me apart. Its opening lines were: "It would be an egregious lapse of judgment for you to represent me. Allow me to outline ten reasons why." Then I did, indeed, list ten reasons; sneaky me, with my reverse psychology.

This approach intrigued Eric enough that he asked to see the manuscript, which I promptly sent. I already knew *The Gargoyle* was not at its optimal (read: shorter) length; the problem was that I'd been working on it for so long that I could only see the trees, and not which parts of the forest needed the axe. I hoped that Eric would like my writing enough to take me on and set me up with a professional editor who'd have the ability to thin the book in ways that I could not.

It didn't happen that way. After a few weeks, Eric wrote back that he had been "defeated by the (book's) girth." I didn't blame him; I could hardly expect him to read it when I could barely lift the damn thing. A consummate gentleman, he took the time to write some very positive comments and the general tone was encouraging, but the message was: "Thanks for submitting, but no."

But still. He hadn't called me names, so I promptly emailed him to point out that nowhere in his correspondence did he specifically request that I *not* resubmit the novel to him. I proposed to take the book off the literary agent market while I carved away the bloat, and send it back to him in a year or so. He answered "yes"—perhaps thinking he'd never hear from me again, or perhaps because he was wondering what I could do. Reinvigorated by his tiny bit of interest, I went back to work on the book in January 2006.

All I had to do was the editing I didn't know how to do.

I made a simple decision that would guide me through this next stage: I would remove every word that didn't move the plot forward. It didn't matter how much I liked a section. It didn't matter if I had spent a hundred hours working a paragraph until it was "just right." It didn't matter if I thought the writing was the best in the book, as far as placing one word after the other. If it didn't move the story forward, it was gone. Eventually I was able to reduce the book by about thirty-five percent of its previous length. And it was better. Much better.

In October 2006, I printed *The Gargoyle* as a one-of-a-kind, properly produced book with blurbs on the back cover—blurbs taken directly from my previous email exchanges with Eric. I used everything he said that was good about my writing to sell myself back to him. The next-to-final blurb was Eric's statement that he liked my writing, but the story was too long. I followed this by blurbing myself, stating that he'd been completely correct but now that the book was much shorter, he should give it another look.

Eric received this version on a Thursday, and the following week he called to offer his representation. I thought long and hard about his proposal during the five seconds I was unable to speak. Then I accepted, and I believe my exact words were: "Gah. Offer? For me? Uh . . . yes? Really?" (Pause.) "Gah."

In December, the book was passed from Eric's hands into those of Anne Collins, a vice president of Random House Canada. She liked it enough to spearhead its acquisition, and enough to offer the professional editing I had so long craved. Anne did not disappoint: how very much she seemed to know about my book that I did not, and how very considerate she was in sharing that information. Under her guidance, I worked on the book for another few months.

In the spring of 2007, the book was offered to the rest of the world. Doubleday and Canongate took it into America and the U.K., respectively; these companies also provided two more fantastic editors—Gerry Howard and Anya Serota—with whom I would work. I spent much of that summer collecting pages of notes from my three editors, collating them into a bulging master manuscript. All the while I was cursing the fact that every new comment meant another ten hours of work for me—because damn their talented hearts, they were rarely wrong and I often was.

In the meantime, *The Gargoyle* had become entrusted to the able hands of foreign rights agent Dorothy Vincent and so far, she's arranged for twenty-six translations. I don't know exactly what kind of voodoo she's using but I'm all in favor of it. Because of those publications, I've been privileged to meet readers from Japan to Germany to Croatia, and I expect that the book will keep me traveling a while longer. It makes me wish that I had some of Marianne Engel's linguistic abilities, because it's a strange feeling to talk to people who have read your book in languages you'll never understand.

Then again, I should be used to things I don't understand. For example, how a guy born in the middle of nowhere is now traveling everywhere, and all because he was trying to shut up the weird woman living in his head.

Even when I explain it to myself, it remains a mystery.

Andrew Davidson
February 12, 2009